Praise for
SEDUCING THE HEIRESS

"This book has it all: a fabulous hero, a wonderful heroine, and sizzling passion. Read it and watch the sparks fly!"
—Christina Dodd

"Guaranteed to seduce readers everywhere. This book is something truly special, an unforgettable story filled with passion, intrigue, and sweep-you-away romance."
—Susan Wiggs

"This decadent Regency romance is carried along by a spunky heroine and sumptuous descriptions of upper-class life...there's enough glitz to keep readers coming back."
—*Publishers Weekly*

"Drake entices readers [and] twists the traditional with an unconventional heroine and a bad-boy hero that readers will adore."
—*Romantic Times BOOKreviews*

"I absolutely adored this story! Witty, hilarious...[like] reading a Julia Quinn novel. I'm definitely looking forward to the next book in this series!"
—The Season Blog

"Olivia Drake's *Seducing the Heiress* will land on your keeper shelf. The author takes what could be a been-there, read-that story of a scheming scoundrel and a headstrong hoyden and weaves a tale of wit, seduction, secrets, and sensuality that's as vibrant as it is refreshing."
—*Michelle Buonfiglio's Romance: B(u)y the Book®*

"Drake weaves a sensual tale, full of intrigue and true romance...guaranteed to seduce and leave the reader breathless."
—*South Bend Romance Novel Examiner*

Never Trust a Rogue

OLIVIA DRAKE

St. Martin's Paperbacks

This is a work of fiction. All of the characters, organizations, and events portrayed in this novel are either products of the author's imagination or are used fictitiously.

NEVER TRUST A ROGUE

Copyright © 2010 by Barbara Dawson Smith.

All rights reserved.

For information address St. Martin's Press, 175 Fifth Avenue, New York, NY 10010.

ISBN: 978-0-312-94346-2

Printed in the United States of America

St. Martin's Paperbacks edition / September 2010

St. Martin's Paperbacks are published by St. Martin's Press, 175 Fifth Avenue, New York, NY 10010.

10 9 8 7 6 5 4 3 2 1

Never Trust
a Rogue

Chapter 1

Females were nothing but trouble.

Handing the reins of his mount to a groom, Thane Pallister, the Earl of Mansfield, braced himself for the inevitable scene to come. He'd had plenty of time on the long ride from London to Oxfordshire to contrive an explanation for his uncle about his current predicament with the fairer sex.

Twelve years had passed since Thane had returned to the manor house where he had spent his youth. When he'd left here for good at the age of eighteen, he had come to despise this old pile with every fiber of his being. It had been more a prison than a home to him.

Yet, as he peeled off his riding gloves, he was surprised by a pang of nostalgia. On this unseasonably sunny March day, the place looked so . . . ordinary.

Neatly manicured boxwoods framed the front of the Elizabethan house. The tall edifice was fashioned of brick and timbers with mullioned windows that reflected the blue sky. As his gaze traveled upward, the steep roof with its myriad chimneys sparked a flash of memory.

A long time ago, he had clambered over those slate tiles while his cousin Edward had cowered by the stairs leading down to the servants' attic. On a whim, Thane had lowered himself feet-first into one of the chimneys. He must have had some vague notion of bracing himself on the sides and then popping back out to frighten his cousin. Instead, Thane had lost his traction, plunged down the dark shaft, and landed in the library, covered from head to toe in soot.

Luckily, it had been summer and no fire had blazed in the grate. But he had startled Uncle Hugo at his reading, and the prank had earned Thane a thrashing with the dreaded willow switch.

Back then, he'd had a knack for getting into trouble. He had been too fidgety to focus on his schoolwork, too keen on escaping the confines of four walls, too ready to commit any act of willfulness in order to break the boredom of routine. Thank God, maturity and military discipline had granted him the ability to control his impulses.

At least most of the time.

Stuffing his leather gloves into the pockets of his greatcoat, he headed up the granite steps. The double oak doors, carved with matching crosses, had once graced the chapel of a monastery. It felt odd to approach the house as a visitor when, as a lad, he had been forbidden use of the front entrance.

A footman in dark green livery answered Thane's knock. He didn't recognize the smooth, impassive features beneath the formal white wig and wondered what had happened to Sewell, the old butler with the hatchet face, who had borne Thane's tomfoolery with stoic fortitude.

The footman took in his fine garb at a glance and stepped back to allow him entry. "Welcome to Waverly Park."

"Is my uncle at home?" Thane asked, stepping into the dim-lit great hall. "Tell him Mansfield has come to call."

The footman's blue eyes bugged slightly in recognition, for he would have heard of the master's renegade nephew. "Yes, my lord. If you'll be so good as to wait in the antechamber."

The servant indicated a room to the right, then hastened down the long corridor that led to the back of the house. Apparently, Uncle Hugo still spent his days ensconced in the library. Old habits died hard.

Thane stripped off his greatcoat and tossed it over a chair. After being confined to the saddle since the crack of dawn, he had no intention of sitting like a stodgy squire in a room that had last been decorated during the reign of Queen Anne. He had too much on his mind, and a pressing need to return to London as soon as he was done here.

A feeling of restiveness crept over him. He had sworn never to return to this house. Only a sense of obligation and a summons from his uncle had lured him back. Whatever their differences in the past, he owed Uncle Hugo the courtesy of an explanation. It would have been the act of a coward to do so by letter.

Thane took a measured stroll around the entrance hall. Little had changed here. The oak-paneled walls still displayed medieval shields and paintings so darkened with soot and age, it was difficult to discern the subject matter. A suit of armor stood on a dais beneath the curve of the staircase.

He walked closer to the display. There was a dent in the breastplate exactly where he remembered it. A long time ago, he had stood on a stool, plucked off the helmet and stuck it on his head, and then chased Edward around the hall. Unfortunately, the narrow eye slits had impaired Thane's vision, and he'd crashed into the suit of armor, knocking it down. The deafening clatter had brought the entire household at a run.

A flicker of humor quirked Thane's mouth. How well he recalled tearing around here like a demon on the rare occasions when his uncle was away from home. It had been sheer joy to slide in his stockinged feet on the marble floor. He had thrived on the danger of being caught. To sit placidly reading had never held any interest to him.

At last the servant returned with the news that the master would see him in the library. Thane headed down the long passageway, his footsteps sharp and decisive. He wanted this interview over with and done, like a dose of bitter medicine that must be swallowed.

Reaching the end of the corridor, he turned left and entered a spacious chamber with orderly rows of leather-bound books filling the floor-to-ceiling shelves. A fire hissed on the hearth. Beside it, his uncle sat in a nut-brown wing chair, his feet propped on a fringed stool and crossed at the ankles.

The shrunken quality to him caught Thane by surprise. The years had not been kind to the Honorable Hugo Pallister, younger twin brother of Thane's late father. The familiar gray wig sat on Hugo's head, for he held stubbornly to the fashion of his youth. Deep grooves flanked his down-turned mouth, giving him a perpetual sour frown.

He looked up from the book in his lap as Thane approached. No smile of greeting graced his uncle's thin lips, nor had Thane expected one. Those pale blue eyes, underscored by baggy skin, had a sunken look, although they were as sharply observant as ever.

If Hugo noticed the disfiguring scar from the saber cut on Thane's cheek, he gave no indication. Thane didn't doubt his uncle still harbored resentment at being foisted with the care of his young nephew upon the death of Thane's parents all those years ago.

Some things never changed.

Thane inclined his head in a slight bow. "Hello, Uncle. It's been quite a long while since last we met."

"Indeed." Hugo clapped the book shut and set it aside. "And whose fault is that? I should not have been obliged to summon you here. You have been back in England for a month now, yet you did not deign to call upon me at once."

"Five weeks," Thane corrected. "I returned from Belgium in the middle of February." And a bitterly cold and uncomfortable journey it had been, burdened as he was with a petulant female in tow.

His uncle waved a gnarled hand. "All the more reason to chastise you. Now, fetch me a whiskey. And I suppose you'll want refreshment yourself."

Clenching his jaw, Thane went to the side table and poured two glasses from the decanter. There was a grudging tone to his uncle's voice, but that was only to be expected. Hugo was a pinchpenny who didn't part easily with his favorite Scotch malt.

Thane delivered the drink, then took up a stance by the fire, resting his forearm on the oak mantelpiece. He had no wish to turn this into a social visit, yet the politeness drilled into him by a long-ago governess induced him to say, "You're looking well, Uncle. How have you been?"

"I suffer from gout and rheumatism, as you'd know if ever you'd bothered to send me a note of inquiry. All these years, and nary a word from you. Why, I never had even a notion of where you were garrisoned."

Surely, Hugo hadn't expected him to write as if they were loving relatives. The thought startled Thane for a moment before he rejected it as ludicrous.

He took a sip, letting the whiskey burn down his throat. His uncle still wielded complaints like a broadsword. He'd had no real interest in hearing from the nephew who had been a thorn in his side. If Hugo truly had wanted to keep in touch, he could have tracked Thane down through the Home Office.

He'd certainly had no trouble nosing out the news of Thane's return—and the circumstances surrounding it.

"Do forgive me," Thane said with a touch of irony. "But I was busy serving the king."

"It is not the role of a peer to fight wars. You shirked your duties by running off to follow the drum. The proper place for a man of your rank is here in this country, watching over your estates and taking your rightful seat in Parliament."

The military had been a hard life, surviving cold and mud and limited supplies, enduring the fall of comrades on the battlefield, yet Thane had no regrets. To have chosen the safe, boring existence would have been anathema to his temperament. "I didn't come today to quarrel about the past. Rather, I felt you deserved an explanation in regard to my ward."

"Indeed I do. Your behavior has been a disgrace." Hugo slapped his palm on the arm of the chair. "As head of this family, I must chastise you for harboring an innocent young lady in your household. Have you no sense of decency at all?"

In spite of his resolve to stay calm, Thane felt a hot jab of anger. Since reaching his majority, *he* was now the head of the family, not his uncle. And after years abroad as the commander of a cavalry brigade, Thane didn't appreciate being dressed down like a lowly recruit. "I can assure you, there's been no hint of impropriety. Miss Jocelyn Nevingford does not reside in my town house, but rather, in the one beside mine."

"But there *is* a connecting door." Malice in his rheumy gaze, Hugo shook a knobby finger at Thane. "You needn't try to pull the wool over my eyes. I wrote to Fisk, and she has sent me a full report."

Mrs. Fisk had once been a nursemaid in this house. When Thane had come here as an orphaned boy of five, the widow had taken him under her wing, crooning him to sleep at bedtime and providing comfort in times of distress. She was one of the few people he trusted, which was why he'd asked her to come out of retirement and take on the role of companion to Jocelyn.

Thane couldn't blame Fisk for supplying information; she was a kindly old soul who saw only the best in people. And she could scarcely have written of anything indecorous when nothing had occurred. The nasty details had been supplied solely by his uncle's caustic imagination.

Gripping his glass, Thane stared down at Hugo. "A full report, do you say?" he said coolly. "Then I'm sure you'll know Jocelyn is fifteen years of age. That her parents died last autumn when their carriage overturned during a rainstorm near Brussels. That she was riding with them and only by a miracle of God survived the accident herself. I hardly think those facts are the fodder of scandal."

"It most certainly *is* a scandal for a bachelor to adopt a girl not of his own family," his uncle stated. "There must be someone else who can take her in. It's more fitting she go to a blood relative."

Jocelyn had one elderly great-aunt in Lancashire who had exhibited such horror at the prospect of taking in a crippled girl that Thane had invented another relative so he wouldn't be forced to abandon Jocelyn with the inhospitable old woman. Besides, there was the vow he'd made to her father, James, Thane's best friend. Before the battle of Waterloo, James had wrested Thane's promise to watch over Jocelyn in the event of his death. Ironically, James had survived a hail of bullets that day, only to lose his life a few months later in a carriage mishap.

His throat thick, Thane finished off his whiskey and set down the glass on a table. "There's no one," he said flatly. "Believe me, I've searched."

"Then send her away to a cottage in the country. You've the means to hire all manner of servants to watch over the chit. That's what any decent gentleman would have done."

Hugo's suspicious gaze raked him up and down. "But since your return, you've no doubt become one of the fast crowd, the gamblers and the rakes. It would not surprise me to learn you have wicked designs on her person."

Thane's irritation took a sharp upward spike. "For God's sake, she's suffered a traumatic injury. Do you think so little of me that I would force myself on a mere girl, let alone a crippled one?"

Uncle Hugo looked unmoved. He nursed his whiskey and glowered over the rim of the glass. "I do indeed. You were always the wild one, a ne'er-do-well devil just like your father."

Thane could see the tentacles of envy that had squeezed any benevolence out his uncle's nature. Nevertheless, those words stirred an echo of the inadequacy Thane had fought against as a youth.

Abandoning his cool, he snapped, "So you still resent my father for being born three minutes ahead of you. If not for a quirk of fate, *you* would be the Earl of Mansfield."

An angry flush darkened Hugo's face. His fingers tightened around the glass in his hand. "By gad, you're as disrespectful as ever. I don't know why you can't be more like Edward. He's been married these past eight years. And *he* has sired two sons."

Thane hadn't known. But the news came as no great revelation. His cousin had always been a dull dog who followed convention. "Then you should rejoice," Thane said. "If I die without issue, the title will go to you and then to Edward and his eldest. In truth, it wouldn't surprise me to learn that you'd prayed for my demise on the battlefield."

Something flickered in Uncle Hugo's eyes, something like shock. One of the logs popped, then fell in a shower of sparks. Thane had the discomfitting sense that he'd stepped over a line.

Hugo gave a disgusted shake of his head. "Think what you will. I summoned you here to warn you not to ruin that girl's reputation. If you insist upon this foolish course, at least find yourself a wife, someone of suitably high birth who will lend you respectability. For once in your life, boy, do your duty."

The disappointment in his uncle's tone stung Thane worse than the blow of a willow switch. It was ridiculous to care what the man thought of him. This conversation had gone on long enough.

He made a stiff bow. "I'll take your advice under consideration. Good day, Uncle."

Pivoting, he strode out of the library. Find a wife? He'd sooner roast in Hell than conform to his uncle's demands. He had far more important tasks to accomplish than to make idle chitchat with giggly debutantes in the ballrooms of London. Most pressing of all was his appointment with the chief magistrate at Bow Street.

Thane turned his mind to his secret mission. If all went as expected, in the coming weeks he would be very busy indeed.

Chapter 2

Most genteel young ladies counted sewing or singing among their greatest accomplishments. But not Miss Lindsey Crompton. If there was one skill at which she excelled, it was spying.

After a quick glance up and down the deserted corridor, she closed the door of the study. Luckily, no other guests from the ball had wandered into this wing of the house. She held up a candle to view a rather shabby room with a threadbare Persian rug on the floor and a pair of wingback chairs by the unlit hearth. Shadows flickered over shelves of musty volumes that looked as if they hadn't been cracked open in years.

Her pale green gown rustling, Lindsey hastened toward the mahogany desk that dominated the room. The distant sound of musicians tuning their instruments warned her there was little time to waste. If she failed to return to the ballroom for the next dance, Mama would be livid. Mrs. Edith Crompton had arranged for a string of eligible noblemen to partner her middle daughter in every set.

Her mother didn't know it, but Lindsey was equally determined to remain a spinster. She had no interest in marrying any of the toadying gentlemen who coveted her enormous dowry. Having an aristocratic husband would hinder her plans for her life. For that reason, she intended to find a means to rebuff each and every one of the fools.

Placing the silver candlestick on the desk, she wrinkled her nose at the stench of stale smoke from an ashtray where Lord Wrayford had stubbed out a cheroot. Beside it, an empty crystal glass rested in the sticky residue of spilled brandy. Men and their nasty habits! How did women put up with such nonsense?

Muttering under her breath, she opened the top drawer and examined the contents. Inside lay a clutter of quill pens, a silver box of fine sand for blotting ink, assorted bits of string and sealing wax, and a stack of cream stationery embossed with a gold *W*.

Nothing of interest.

She turned her attention to the next drawer. Here a jumbled heap of papers piqued her curiosity. Perching on the edge of the chair, Lindsey proceeded to sort through the mess. It was a task she relished, for there was nothing more fascinating to her than the guilty pleasure of poking through someone else's private belongings.

The dire straits of Lord Wrayford's finances soon became apparent. There were numerous bills from tailors, from boot makers, from jewelers and tobacconists and wine merchants. Most of the accounts were overdue, judging by the many dun notices from creditors demanding immediate payment.

No wonder Lord Wrayford was her most persistent suitor.

Or perhaps *ardent* would be a more fitting term for the way he always stared at her fashionably low-cut bodice. The thought made her skin crawl. The previous day, he had taken her on a drive through Hyde Park, turned the carriage onto a deserted path, and attempted to plant a slobbery kiss on her lips. A hard jab to the ribs had set him straight, but it hadn't proved sufficient to discourage him for good. This evening, he had secured more than one dance with her—as if she belonged to him already.

No matter. This ball at his house was the perfect opportunity for her to thwart him for good. It gave her the chance to find a damning piece of information that would put an end to his courtship once and for all.

Unfortunately, overdue bills would hardly be sufficient to quash her parents' matchmaking plans. Lord Wrayford was heir to the Duke of Sylvester—a creaky old man with one foot in the grave. The mere thought of Lindsey as a duchess transported Mama into a state of rapture.

And it filled Lindsey with an equal measure of revulsion. Imagine, having to spend the rest of her life making dreary calls to gossipy old biddies, shopping for the latest fashions, and attending endless parties. Nothing could be further from her own secret ambitions.

Lud, it was such a nuisance being society's premier heiress!

As she started to close the drawer, something caused the wood to stick. She bent down for a closer look and spied a crumpled piece of foolscap stuck in a crack. She worked it free, placed the paper on the desk, and smoothed out the wrinkles beneath the pale light of the candle.

A short message was penned in black ink, the script distinctly masculine.

This note is a certified duplicate IOU for the sum of one thousand gold guineas, duly won from Wrayford on the 25th day of March 1816, and payable to me in full by 30 June 1816.
    Mansfield

The name struck Lindsey with an unpleasant jolt. Mansfield . . . the Earl of Mansfield. He was that celebrated war hero, the one who was always surrounded by fawning ladies. As the stories went, he had led a reckless charge at Waterloo that had routed the French and turned the tide of the battle from near defeat to victory.

Although Lindsey had seen Mansfield from afar a few times since her debut a fortnight ago, they had never been introduced. The earl's considerable wealth elevated him to that echelon of blue bloods who didn't need to marry money and therefore saw no reason to welcome commoners like her into the ton. Although the Cromptons were richer than everyone but the royal family, they were considered outsiders since Papa had earned his vast assets from trade in India.

Judging by the IOU she held in her hand, Mansfield was far from an admirable man. He was a typical upper-class rogue who frittered away his life at dice and card playing. He preferred the company of wastrels like Wrayford over that of honest, working folk. Even after nearly two years in London, Lindsey found such elitism a distasteful contrast to the relaxed standards of India. At least there she'd had the freedom to pursue her own interests, so long as she took care to do so behind Mama's back.

Lindsey took a deep breath. She mustn't let personal judgments overshadow her purpose here. Emotions only served to cloud the sharp intellect required by the art of detection. All that mattered was the information she held in her hand.

Lord Wrayford owed Mansfield a considerable sum.

She allowed herself a smile of triumph. Although her parents had no objection to her marrying a penniless nobleman, they surely would be appalled to learn that Lord Wrayford had accrued such a large gambling debt. Papa would object to his hard-earned wealth being placed into the hands of a wastrel. Only look at how he had opposed her sister Portia's now-husband, Colin, when everyone had believed *him* to be a worthless reprobate.

Yes, this piece of evidence would come in handy indeed.

Mindful of the softly ticking clock on the mantel, Lindsey bent down to close the drawer. It was nearly midnight and time for the supper dance. She must make haste back to the ballroom before Mama became suspicious.

Rising from the chair, Lindsey picked up the silver candlestick and hurried across the room. But as she opened the door a crack, the sound of voices echoed out in the corridor.

Lindsey cocked her head, her senses alert. There were two distinct sets of footsteps, one heavy, the other light. A man and a woman.

They were heading this way.

It wouldn't do for any guests to find her snooping in Wrayford's study. Or worse, what if Wrayford himself came in? He might seize the opportunity to put her in a compromising situation and then coerce her into marriage.

She glanced around for somewhere to hide. Crouching behind the desk or a chaise would only make her look extremely guilty. It might be best to brazen it out.

Her nerves thrumming with tension, Lindsey flattened herself to the wall by the door. The paneling smelled of dusty oak that had seldom known a coating of beeswax polish. Cocking her head, she strained to make out the hum of conversation.

Unfortunately, the partially closed door muffled their words.

She felt a trifle silly, skulking here like a dastardly villain in one of the adventure novels she liked to read. The footsteps likely belonged to servants going about their duties. No one else had any reason to venture into this room during a party. Portia and Blythe were forever teasing Lindsey about her suspicious nature and maybe her sisters were right—

The door handle rattled.

Lindsey realized in alarm that she still clutched the purloined IOU in her hand. She had but an instant to conceal it. Since the slim-fitting ball gown lacked pockets, she stuffed the folded paper down into the bodice of her dress.

Just in time.

The door swung open. A man and a woman appeared silhouetted against the dimness of the passageway. His hand on her upper back, he steered her ahead of him into the study. His dark head was tilted down as he spoke to his companion.

It was a gentleman and a lady.

No, not a lady. A maidservant. An uncommonly pretty one at that, slim and young, in a gray serge gown with a white mobcap perched atop her fair hair.

Lindsey blinked at the incongruous couple. Before she could fathom their purpose here, her gaze fastened on the tall, broad-shouldered gentleman behind the maid. The world tilted on its axis.

Mansfield?

He was the very gentleman whose signature was scrawled across the IOU tucked inside her corset. What stroke of ill fate had brought him into this room?

The maid spied her and uttered a squawk of surprise. She shrank back against the earl. He lifted his head and stared straight at Lindsey, the dark slash of his brows lowering in a scowl.

Clearly, he had expected to find Lord Wrayford's study deserted.

Mansfield's eyes were so dark a brown they were almost black. They seemed to penetrate her very soul. Fighting the impulse to shrink back, Lindsey had the uneasy sense that he could see into her mind and guess her illicit purpose here.

Ridiculous.

Lifting her chin, she returned his stare. She had trained herself to assess a person's character at a glance. He stood a good six inches taller than her, and the boldness of his gaze gave a clue to his success in the military. He would be the sort of daredevil leader who inspired his men to follow him into wild deeds of bravery.

And considering his excess of masculine allure, it was little wonder that Mansfield enjoyed great success with the ladies. He cut a dashing figure in his coffee brown coat and white cravat, the formal white breeches encasing long, muscled legs. A thin scar ran at an angle across his left cheek, likely a legacy of the battlefield. Those chiseled features held a coolness that bespoke confidence and hinted at secrets.

Her heart fluttered of its own volition. She would be lying to herself if she denied he was quite the handsomest man she had ever seen. But that was all the more reason to be wary of him. Men of his ilk were always conceited. They viewed themselves as king cobras when by moral standards they were lower than a common garden snake.

The maidservant cast a wide, imploring glance up at the earl. He glanced down and gave her an almost imperceptible nod. Without saying a word, she ducked under his arm and fled the study.

As the *tap-tap* of departing footsteps faded into the distance, Lindsey's mind raced. Why would the Earl of Mansfield bring a maidservant to a deserted area of the house during a party? Why had the girl looked so alarmed? What could he possibly want with someone so far beneath his lofty stature?

Struck by nasty speculation, Lindsey tightened her fingers around the candlestick. *What indeed!*

"Pray excuse me," she said coldly, stepping toward him. "I was just departing."

She was forced to halt when he blocked her exit by remaining in the doorway. Something about his speculative perusal unsettled her. He didn't know her, she was just another anonymous debutante, so would he detain her?

His gaze flicked to the bosom of her gown and lingered there a moment. Lindsey was keenly aware of the purloined paper nestled between the corset and her bare skin. Was a corner of the IOU poking out of her bodice?

Surely not.

She resisted the urge to pique his interest by glancing down to check. Mansfield was gawking because he was a man. A wicked rogue who thought nothing of ogling a young woman's figure.

He inclined his head in a bow, affording her a glimpse of his thick black hair. "Miss Crompton. What an unexpected pleasure."

She could not have been more startled—or suspicious. "How do you know my name?"

"Heiresses are always the talk of the ton. Especially the beautiful ones."

His compliment stirred a peculiar warmth in the pit of her stomach. Thank goodness she wasn't one to fall prey to a man's oily charm. "War heroes are also the subject of gossip," she countered. "You are Lord Mansfield."

"Thane Pallister to my friends."

Thane. How very unusual. But he must be mad to think she would address him by his first name when they had just met. "How good of you to introduce yourself, Lord Mansfield. If you will please step aside now."

The earl again ignored her request. He settled his shoulder against the door frame and folded his arms across his chest. His bland expression revealed nothing of his thoughts. "First, I'd like to know why you're trespassing in Wrayford's study."

"I wished a few moments of quiet from the crush in the ballroom. Have you an objection to that?"

"This room seems an odd choice, considering its distance from the party."

"Then why are *you* here? Or perhaps I should pretend not to have noticed the little tryst you had planned with the housemaid."

He surprised her by laughing. "You're quite right. Some topics should never be broached in polite company. Especially by innocent young ladies."

The candle flame played over the smirk on his too-handsome face. Lindsey blamed him for the blush that heated her cheeks. It caught her notice that the cad hadn't denied his plan for an indiscretion. "I'm well aware of the conventions, my lord. But I find it silly to pretend ignorance of what is right in front of one's nose."

"A no-nonsense girl. You remind me of someone." He frowned and then snapped his fingers. "Ah, yes. It was a governess I had when I was perhaps six or seven years of age."

"A governess."

"Miss Pinchgill was her name. She was a stickler for the rules. Whenever I was naughty, she rapped my knuckles and then made me sit in the corner for hours." His mouth twisted wryly. "I invariably deserved it."

Lindsey wavered between being insulted by the comparison and smiling at the image of him as a mischievous lad. One thing was certain: she must not encourage further conversation.

"How fascinating," she said in a tone that implied it was anything but. "Now, pray stand aside. It is highly improper for us to linger here unchaperoned."

"As you wish, Miss Crompton. Far be it from me to ignore the proprieties."

Mansfield stepped back into the dimly lit corridor,

affording her enough space to slip past him. Gripping the candlestick, she glided through the doorway. She was keenly aware of his tall, muscular form looming in the shadows. A peculiar tension assailed her insides, and she cursed the effect he had on her.

High-and-mighty noblemen had always irritated her. She scorned them as snobs who judged a person by his bloodline. There could be no other reason why she suddenly was anxious to escape the scrutiny of those disturbing dark eyes.

As Lindsey started to turn away, his hand flashed out. It happened so fast that she had time only to gasp. His fingers brushed the top of her bare breasts and dipped into the valley. Her nipples contracted in instant reaction. Goose bumps skittered over her skin as he deftly plucked out the IOU.

"What have we here?" Glancing at the paper, he cocked an eyebrow. "Ah, just as I suspected. You've been rifling through Wrayford's desk. The next time you play at thievery, I would advise you to make certain the loot is tucked deeper into your bodice."

Every fiber of her body quivered with emotion. Shock at Mansfield's ungentlemanly assault on her. Rage at his audacity in touching her bosom. Alarm that he now possessed the proof she needed to reject Wrayford's suit.

Heedless of the candle in her hand, Lindsey made a wild grab for the paper. "Blackguard! Give that back to me."

She collided with him as he whipped the IOU up out of her reach. His arm clamped around her waist, catching her hard against his chest so that Lindsey found herself locked in an unintentional embrace. Surprise held her immobile. She could feel the strong beating of his heart, smell his aroma of exotic spice, see the faint black shadow along his jaw where he had shaved. Her fingers itched to trace the thin curve of the scar that bisected his cheek.

In one dizzying instant, she noticed that his eyes were quite beautiful from close up. The irises were not a flat dark brown as she'd first thought, but scattered with gold flecks that glinted in the pale light of her candle. His ebony lashes were lowered slightly to guard his thoughts. The mysteries she sensed in him held a powerful allure. If she stared long enough, surely she might discern the depths of his soul. . . .

He flinched, abruptly releasing her. "Blast it!"

Lindsey took an involuntary step backward and saw him sucking his forefinger. Only then did she realize what must have happened. Hot wax from her candle had dripped on his hand.

It served the knave right.

Her body still quivered from their close contact. Aside from her father's affectionate hugs, she had never known a man's embrace. That must be why her skin felt scorched.

"Cad," she snapped. "You merit far worse than that."

He quit babying his finger and scowled at her. "It was you who came flying at me in a rage."

"Because *you* stole the paper from me in a most improper manner. I want it returned at once."

Chuckling darkly, Mansfield placed his hand—and the IOU—atop the door frame, well above her head. The action parted the flaps of his coat and stretched his white shirt and the dark waistcoat over his broad chest.

His gaze scrutinized her from head to toe, as if measuring her worth. "Now what could you want with a private receipt between me and Wrayford? You must be intending to blackmail one or the other of us. Since we've only just met, I must presume your target is Wrayford."

"Blackmail? How absurd. I've no need for money."

"Not all blackmail involves currency. Perhaps you intend to use this document to secure Wrayford's hand in marriage. You'll threaten to expose his debts to the world if he fails to make you an offer."

"I beg your pardon?"

"He's the heir to a dukedom. Any woman of your station would be keen to claim the title of duchess."

Of your station?

Lindsey released a furious huff. She was as incensed by his presumption as by the phantom feel of his fingers on her bosom. "Odious man! It is Wrayford who pursues *me*. I want no part of him."

"Indeed?" Skepticism weighing his tone, Mansfield raked her with his gaze. "Then you intend to use this IOU to turn your parents against him?"

"My purpose is no concern of yours."

"Now there you are wrong. My name is on this paper, and I believe that all debts between gentlemen should be kept private. You will not be showing it to anyone." He tucked the document into an inner pocket of his coat. "Good evening, Miss Crompton."

With that, he sauntered down the passageway in the opposite direction from the ballroom.

Glaring at his departing figure, Lindsey fumed over a host of wild scenarios. She could dash after him and wrestle him again for the paper. She could knee him in a man's most sensitive place, as her old nursemaid Kasi had instructed her to do in a moment of peril.

But the ball gown was too slim fitting for her to inflict any real damage. And she had no wish to venture within an arm's length of Lord Mansfield ever again. He was too arrogant, too masterful, too full of his own vain self-worth.

Yet perhaps all was not lost, after all.

A sense of resolve lifted her spirits. If Mansfield would not surrender the IOU, then by the heavens, she would find a way to steal it back from him.

Chapter 3

A violent movement jolted Lindsey out of a deep, blissful sleep. Opening bleary eyes, she squinted against the watery sunlight. For a moment, she couldn't identify her surroundings. Where was the netting that protected her from insect bites while she slept? What had happened to her bamboo dressing table and the lazily circling overhead fan operated by a *punka-walla* boy who sat outside her bedchamber all night?

Then she blinked in recognition. She was no longer in India. This bedchamber with its delicate green wallpaper and cherrywood furniture had been her home for two years now, ever since her family had moved to London.

The mattress shook again. She rolled over to see her younger sister scrambling onto the canopied bed. Blythe scooted into a sitting position, her curly auburn hair caught back loosely with a white ribbon. She arranged the skirt of her yellow muslin gown over her crossed legs and fixed Lindsey with a dazzling smile.

"Wake up," Blythe chirped. "I've come to hear your report about the ball."

Groaning, Lindsey drew the coverlet up over her head. She wanted her dream back. It had left her with a sense of fervent anticipation and the misty memory of a looming dark figure. She had been walking toward him, straining to make out his features. If only she could slip back into slumber and recapture that image . . .

"Go away," she mumbled into the feather pillow. "I've told you never to wake me up for such nonsense."

Blythe tugged off the blankets. "Come, Linds. Don't be a slugabed. It's past noon and I've been waiting *hours* for you to awaken."

"Noon?" Lindsey pushed onto one elbow and rubbed her gritty eyes. She seldom slept so late. Now awareness brought the nagging impression of something important that had to be done today, but her groggy mind couldn't quite grasp what it was.

"Didn't you hear the mantel clock chime? It was loud enough to wake the dead." Her hazel eyes bright with eagerness, Blythe rushed on, "Do tell me all the gossip. Who did you see last night? Did you dance every set? Is there any truth to the rumor that Miss Beardsley was caught kissing one of the footmen?"

"Miss *Frances* Beardsley?" Lindsey smothered a yawn as she tried to picture the vapid blond debutante doing something so risqué. "If it's true, no one breathed a word about it to me. Where did you hear such tittle-tattle, anyway?"

"From my maid, of course. Servants always know the best gossip."

"Then mayhap you should have badgered *them* for news about last night's ball, rather than awakening me."

"Oh, pooh. It isn't fair you're allowed to attend parties when you don't even appreciate them." Looking decidedly glum, Blythe released a pitiful sigh. "Meanwhile, I shall *die* of boredom cooped up in this house. One morning, Underhill will find me expired in my bedchamber and then you'll be sorry!"

Lindsey's heart softened. Poor, exuberant Blythe. It wasn't her fault that at sixteen years of age she was still under the strict guardianship of Miss Agnes Underhill, the impoverished gentlewoman who had been employed to teach the Crompton girls the ins and outs of English society. Lindsey could sympathize, and yet when it came to the social scene she would have gladly switched places with Blythe.

Lindsey swung her feet over the edge of the bed, her toes curling against the coolness of the rug. "Well. If you're so anxious to hear my report, you should at least have the courtesy to order my tea."

"Oh, certainly!" Her face brightening again, Blythe bounded off the bed, trotted to the brocaded bell rope by the fireplace, and gave it a quick tug. Then she hastened back, clasped her hands to her bosom, and fixed Lindsey with a starry-eyed gaze. "There, *now* will you tell me all about the ball? Lots of gentlemen must have courted you. Was there anyone special? Someone who tried to steal a kiss, perhaps? Someone who swept you into his arms and made you feel tingly all over?"

Mansfield.

The earl's image sprang into her mind, all arrogant nobleman and swaggering masculinity. To steady herself, Lindsey curled her fingers around the carved cherrywood bedpost. *That* was the memory she had been resisting, the discomforting thought of scuffling with him in the corridor at Lord Wrayford's house.

Mansfield was also the misty figure in her dream. The realization struck her with dismaying certainty. Had she been able to see his face, doubtless the dream would have turned into a nightmare.

Little did her sister know, the Earl of Mansfield had done far worse than try to steal a kiss. He had thrust his hand into Lindsey's bodice to steal the IOU. The recollection was so vivid it made her breasts tighten beneath the embroidered white cotton of her nightdress. A flushed awareness swept her body as if he were standing right here, his fingers burning into her flesh.

"What's wrong?" Blythe asked. "Your face is all pink." Her eyes as round as saucers, she peered avidly at her sister. "Something *did* happen last night. Something romantic. Oh, you must tell me all about it!"

Lindsey concealed a jab of dismay. The last thing she needed was for anyone to guess about her encounter with Mansfield. Blythe would take the offensive incident and transform it into a spun-sugar confection with hearts and flowers on top. She would have them madly in love by evening and betrothed by the morrow.

For her sister's benefit, Lindsey contrived a scornful laugh. "Don't be ridiculous. You know I've no interest in these hoity-toity gentlemen. And I do hope when you make your own debut you don't encourage them to steal kisses at every turn. Now kindly allow me a moment of privacy."

As she stepped toward the adjoining dressing room, Blythe called out, "Do hurry. I have a secret to tell you. It's something you'll find truly hair-raising—"

Shutting the door, Lindsey cut off her sister. Quite likely, Blythe had exchanged a glance on the street with a handsome gentleman and had read more into it than she ought. Such juvenile nonsense was the usual subject of her confidences.

Heading to the china washbasin, Lindsey splashed cold water on her hot cheeks. The intensity of that fantasy about Lord Mansfield had rattled her composure. It wasn't like her to have such a strong reaction to any man.

Any woman of your station must be keen to claim the title of duchess.

She clenched her teeth. What a vile, arrogant rogue! One would have hoped that the discipline of military life would have developed in him a high standard of moral decency. The officers she had met in India had been, for the most part, men of honor. But despite the façade of a famous war hero, Mansfield was a scoundrel, a reckless gamester like so many other gentlemen of privilege. He was the lowest of the low, the sort who appealed to tarts and naïve debutantes, not to a rational woman with a firm plan for her life.

A plan that had nothing to do with the distractions of men.

Once she spurned all of her suitors, she intended to live independently, set up her own discreet agency, and solve mysteries for highborn clients. It would be difficult to convince her parents—Mama in particular—but the final result would be worth the effort.

Going to the dressing table, Lindsey loosened her braid and gave her long dark hair a vigorous brushing. The soothing action sufficed to restore her equilibrium. How silly to let herself be distracted by nonessentials. Mansfield was no more to her than a means to an end. He possessed the IOU that she needed to discredit Lord Wrayford. Sleuthing was a particular talent of hers, and she welcomed the challenge of contriving a scheme to retrieve the document.

She would have to find out where Mansfield lived, what his daily schedule entailed, and when there might be an opportune time to search his home unobserved. It was a tricky situation since decent young ladies were forbidden from paying an unchaperoned call on a bachelor household.

Lost in planning, Lindsey headed back into the bed-chamber, only to discover it was no longer necessary to fob off her sister with a few choice tidbits of gossip.

In the middle of the fine Aubusson rug, Blythe stood facing Miss Underhill. The governess was a tall, spare woman dressed in a gray gown that might best be termed her uniform since she wore it every day. The white maiden's cap on her dull brown hair enhanced the sallowness of her complexion.

Blythe's lower lip protruded in a pout. "I can't leave now; I *won't*. Linds was about to tell me everything that happened at the ball. And anyway, there's no purpose to these lessons. It isn't as if I plan to travel to the Continent anytime soon."

"Every refined young lady must learn to speak French. It is expected of you."

"Oh, pooh. English is good enough for me. Besides, I haven't the knack for foreign tongues."

"Hmph. I've heard you speak fluent Hindi to Kasi. Now, come with me at once, or I shall be forced to report your disobedient behavior to Mrs. Crompton."

"I don't care if Mama scolds me," Blythe countered with a toss of her curly auburn mane. "I'm sixteen and it's about time I had a say in my own education."

Lindsey recognized the opportunity to avoid a discussion of the previous night. She stepped forward, took her sister's arm, and steered her toward the open door. "Miss Underhill is right. Portia and I both had to endure our lessons. What must be done is best done cheerfully."

"But—"

"And furthermore, I won't be held to blame for keeping you from your schooling. Run along now and we'll talk later."

Trudging through the doorway, Blythe looked back over her shoulder to drill her sister with a petulant frown. "All right, but you had better not renege or I'll—*oh*!"

She collided with a sturdy young maid who was entering the bedchamber, toting a large silver tray of food. Her face was tucked down and a voluminous white mobcap covered all but a fringe of dark hair.

The maid yelped as dishes and cutlery clattered in a jarring cacophony. A piece of toast went sailing backward into the corridor. A porcelain cup flew in the other direction, landing on carpet and rolling beneath a green-striped chair by the hearth.

The girl jerked up her head to reveal a startled expression on her broad, pale features. In one instant, Lindsey recognized her personal maid, Flora. In the next, she saw the tray tilting, the dishes sliding, steamy liquid sloshing from the spout of the blue teapot.

She sprang past her sister to grab the tray. Flora clung tenaciously and they engaged in a little tug-of-war until Lindsey snapped out, "Let go!"

The maid relaxed her grip. Clutching the silver handles, Lindsey carried the heavy tray to a table and set it down.

When she turned around, Blythe was making a fuss over checking the yellow gauze of her skirts. "Lud, that was close! This is a new gown. The dressmaker delivered it only yesterday."

"I trust there was no damage done," Miss Underhill said, before turning a critical eye on the maid. "How very careless. You must learn to watch where you are going."

Flora stood frozen, her blue eyes wide with horror. Then abruptly she burst into tears and buried her face in her hands.

The display startled Lindsey. Flora was usually an unflappable, efficient worker who performed her duties well. With her skill at hairdressing, no one could ask for a more adept maidservant. Something must be terribly amiss for her to exhibit such an uncustomary outpouring of emotion.

Placing an arm around the young woman's waist, Lindsey guided her to a striped footstool by the fireplace. Flora was shaking with the force of her sobs, and the sight of her distress touched Lindsey's heart.

"There was no harm done," she said soothingly. "It was

an accident. I'm sorry if my sister and Miss Underhill upset you."

"It's really *my* fault for bumping into you," Blythe chimed in, looking rather subdued, for in spite of her self-centeredness, she possessed a generous spirit. "I didn't mean to sound so critical."

"Nor did I," Miss Underhill said. She whipped out a crisply folded handkerchief from a pocket of her skirt and pressed it to the maid's hand. "Now, you may cease your caterwauling. I have no intention of reporting such a minor mishap to the butler."

Flora used the handkerchief to scrub at her wet cheeks. "Th-thank you, m-miss. But-but 'tisn't me post wot's worryin' me. 'Tis—'tis the Serpentine Strangler!"

Baffled, Lindsey sank down onto the chair in front of the maid. What was she babbling about? Judging by the utter fright in those watery blue eyes, something dreadful had happened. Flora was shivering, tears still flowing, lips quivering.

"There, there." Lindsey took one of the girl's chapped hands and rubbed it. "Calm down so you can tell me what this is all about."

"There'll be no telling of any sort," Miss Underhill said sternly. "Perhaps in India you were allowed to gossip with the servants about criminal activities, but we are not so relaxed in our standards here."

"Oh, don't be stuffy; you want to hear about it, too," Blythe said. "And I know what happened. A maidservant was found murdered over a fortnight ago. She was strangled in Hyde Park, and her body was left along the banks of the Serpentine!"

Glancing up, Lindsey stared at her sister in horrified amazement. "A maidservant was *murdered*? You can't mean . . . one of ours?"

"Of course not. She was employed by Lady Entwhistle."

"But . . . how do you come by your information?" Lindsey felt a little nonplussed by the news. "And why did *I* never hear of this?"

"My maid confided in me only this morning. You see, no one took notice until there was a second murder a few days ago. The circumstances were nearly identical to the first one. That means the same man must have done it." Blythe drew up another stool and sat down, leaning forward as if they were engaging in a cozy gossip. "The news has spread below stairs in every house in Mayfair. *That's* the secret I was going to tell you, Linds, before you so rudely tossed me out of here."

Lindsey had no patience for games. "Kindly share all the details. Who were these two girls? Do you know their names?"

Blythe shrugged. "Me? I haven't the slightest notion—"

"Maria Wilkes was the first," Flora broke in, her eyes red and damp. "'Tis wot I 'eard the 'ousekeeper say. I don't know the other. Oh! I—I fear there's a killer on the loose. An' wot's worse is that—"

"Enough." Silencing the maid with a sweep of her hand, Miss Underhill tut-tutted in disapproval. "I hardly think this is an appropriate discussion for the ears of young ladies."

"It's too late now," Blythe declared, her small chin jutted at a stubborn angle. "You know how Linds loves a good mystery. If I don't tell her the rest, she'll pester me to no end." Returning her gaze to Lindsey, she went on, "Apparently the housemaid, Maria Wilkes, had a gentleman lover, and she crept out of Lady Entwhistle's house after dark to meet him—"

"Blythe Crompton!" the governess chided. "You shouldn't know of such things, let alone speak of them."

"Pish-posh. I'm practically an adult. There's no need

to sweep indiscretions under the rug and pretend they don't exist."

"Nevertheless, this conversation has gone on too long. You must proceed to the schoolroom posthaste. Such an unfortunate tragedy has nothing whatsoever to do with any of us here."

The governess was bending down to reach for Blythe's arm when Flora let out a loud sob. Burying her face in her hands, the maid launched into another torrent of weeping.

Everyone froze in place.

Lindsey was the first to move, getting up to kneel beside Flora and give her a comforting hug. "You needn't be frightened. You're quite safe here in this house. I'm sure the authorities will apprehend the murderer very soon."

Flora lifted her head to gaze teary eyed at Lindsey. "Oh, 'tisn't fer meself that I fear. 'Tis fer me cousin, Nelda. Oh, sweet Jaysus. She's gone!"

"Gone? Gone where?"

"I—I dunno!" Flora took a deep, shuddering breath. "She was in service, miss, at a fine house on Curzon Street. I went to visit her yesterday evenin', on me 'alf day off. But she weren't there. Cook told me Nelda left with nary a word of warnin'. Nobody knows where she went."

"Perhaps she found a better position in another house."

Flora gave a vigorous shake of her mobcapped head. "Nay, miss, she wouldn't! Ye see, she was undermaid to Lord Mansfield and thankful to 'ave such a fine post—"

"Wait," Lindsey interrupted. "Did you say . . . 'Mansfield'?"

"The Earl of Mansfield," Miss Underhill said, her thinned lips conveying disapproval. "A fine, respected old family from Oxfordshire. The current earl is regarded as a dashing war hero."

Blythe perked up. "Have you met him, Linds?"

Lindsey felt exposed as everyone stared at her. She was forced to admit, "Yes, but only briefly."

"Well!" Miss Underhill said. "I must advise you to avoid him in the future. Since selling his commission, he has fallen in with the rogues and bounders of society. And there's talk of a scandal in regard to his ward, a young lady who occupies the town house adjacent to his."

The news startled Lindsey. In spite of her resolve to appear uninterested in him, she was overwhelmed by morbid curiosity. "A young lady? Who is she?"

"Miss Jocelyn Nevingford, age fifteen." The governess thoughtfully tapped her chin with a bony finger. "I believe there's a tenuous connection between her family and yours. I seem to recall my father speaking of a Squire Nevingford who hailed from the same area of Lancashire as the Cromptons."

"But why would Mansfield be appointed her guardian?" Lindsey persisted.

"I'm hardly privy to the particulars of His Lordship's private life. Now, that's quite enough gossip for one day. Blythe, come with me at once and not another word out of you. This time, I will brook no more of your nonsense."

Apparently heeding the severity in Miss Underhill's tone, Lindsey's sister rose reluctantly from the stool. She flounced after the governess, grumbling all the way out the door.

Lindsey breathed a sigh of relief. At last, she could focus on helping Flora, who was still dejectedly sniffling into the borrowed handkerchief. *Poor dear.* How terrifying it must be to imagine her missing cousin falling into the hands of a killer.

Lindsey patted the girl's hand again. "Don't despair, darling. Somehow, I'll find Nelda. I promise I will."

Lindsey meant every word. Now she had an even more pressing reason to find a way into Lord Mansfield's house.

Chapter 4

"With all due respect, sir," said Cyrus Bott, "it was a surprise to return from Brighton and hear that Lord Mansfield has been brought in on this case. I had no notion you were displeased with my handling of the investigation."

Three men occupied the second-floor office at Number Four Bow Street. Cyrus Bott and Thane sat in straight-backed chairs across from the magistrate, who was ensconced behind his desk.

Bott was a dapper young man whose dark blue coat and brass buttons marked him as a member of the famed Bow Street Runners. His thatch of wavy brown hair and limpid blue eyes brought to mind a dreamy poet rather than an officer of the law who served writs and tracked down criminals.

Josiah Smithers, the chief magistrate, wore the black robes and tightly curled wig of his profession. His dour face betraying a hint of impatience, he peered at Bott over the gold-rimmed spectacles perched on the end of his bulbous nose.

"Your work on the case has been more than adequate," Smithers said, glancing down and shuffling the papers in front of him. "However, this second murder has attracted a nibble of interest from the newspapers. If there's a third death, it will be splashed all over the front pages, and that is precisely the situation we wish to avoid."

"I assure you, sir, I'm following every lead—"

"There is only so much you can do on your own. We've ample reason to believe our culprit to be a man of high stature. You yourself concluded as much. His Lordship heard about the murders and volunteered his services, for which I'm thankful. He has entry to circles where you cannot venture."

Bott opened his mouth as if to disagree again. Then he slid a cryptic look at Thane and lowered his eyes in acquiescence. "As you say, sir. I will, of course, bow to your superior judgment."

Thane understood the ambition behind the man's objections. The Bow Street Runner had a vested interest in solving the case himself. He didn't want anyone else poaching on his turf, let alone someone who outranked him.

Thane decided to throw him a bone. "Smithers has given me quite a bit of information about the murders. I've done some poking around on my own, but it would help if you told me everything you know. I'm sure your perspective will be most invaluable."

Bott hesitated, then launched into a detailed account. "As you know, the first victim was Maria Wilkes. A night watchman stumbled upon her corpse at dawn while taking a shortcut through Hyde Park. She had been strangled to death some hours earlier. Since her garb clearly identified her as a maidservant, I made extensive inquiries around Mayfair and found that she'd been employed as a housemaid by a Lady Entwhistle."

Smithers looked at Thane. "What do you know of Her Ladyship, m'lord?"

"I've been checking into her associations," Thane hedged. "Until I find out more, it would be remiss of me to sully her name without due cause."

Little did they know, the merry widow's reputation was already tarnished in the best circles. Lady Entwhistle was renowned for her many affairs, including frequent romps with a select group of gentlemen. For the purpose of the investigation, Thane had cultivated an acquaintance with them. He wondered what Miss Lindsey Crompton would say if she knew that her suitor, Lord Wrayford, was one of those scoundrels.

That fact would make a far more damaging scandal than the IOU she'd stumbled upon while rummaging through Wrayford's desk. The same paper Thane had plucked from her bodice the previous evening.

His fingers still burned from brushing against the silken warmth of her breasts. The memory was so vivid, so consuming, he had been in a perpetual state of physical discomfort ever since. She was lovely, to be sure. Yet it was her saucy character and sparkling blue eyes that lifted her above this season's crop of insipid debutantes.

That and her blatant scorn for men of his ilk.

Shifting position on the chair, Thane realized to his chagrin that Bott was still talking. The Runner had moved on to discuss the second victim.

". . . Dorothy Huddleston's body was discovered in another area of the park, farther down the Serpentine. The circumstances were much the same, only this time a gentleman's cravat was found lying on the ground beside her, as if the culprit had dropped it in haste. Through my inquiries, I was able to discover she was employed by an elderly couple, a Lord and Lady Farthingale."

Who, interestingly enough, lived on Bruton Street, two doors down from Wrayford. It might be a meaningless coincidence, but Thane intended to keep a close watch on Wrayford as a possible suspect. He had already questioned a maidservant in Wrayford's house—the same girl

Thane had been with when he had first encountered the cheeky beauty Lindsey Crompton.

"May I add," Bott said in a conspiratorial tone, "news of the second murder has spread like wildfire throughout the servant class. They've dubbed the culprit the Serpentine Strangler."

"Good God," Smithers muttered darkly. "If the news sheets hear of that moniker, it will be emblazoned in headlines everywhere. And it is bound to spark an outcry from the upper classes as well. They'll be demanding my head on a pike if I don't capture this villain."

"You'll be pleased to know," Bott went on, "I was able to track down the family of the second victim in Brighton. It seems Dorothy Huddleston was literate enough to send letters to them. She wrote about a new man in her life, a gentleman who was paying his addresses to her."

"Who?" Thane asked.

Bott shrugged. "Alas, the fellow was not identified. But the story corroborates that of Maria Wilkes. Several of the servants in the Entwhistle house verified that Wilkes, too, was being courted by an unnamed gentleman."

Courted? Thane privately took issue with the term. These girls would have to have been incredibly naïve not to have realized that a man high above their station could have only one purpose in flirting with a comely servant girl.

Unless, of course, he also had murder on his mind.

"Where is this cravat?" Thane asked. "The one that was dropped near Miss Huddleston."

"I have it right here with me, as I've been taking it to various tailors and haberdasheries around town. Regrettably, it has no distinguishing characteristics." Reaching inside his coat, Bott withdrew a folded length of wrinkled cloth and laid it on the desk. "As you can see, it is made of the finest linen, a quality only a well-to-do gentleman could afford to purchase."

Thane took the cravat and unfolded it across his lap. He had dozens like it in his own clothespress. On this one, a few dirt smears marred the snowy white fabric.

"I would surmise, then, that this was the murder weapon."

Bott inclined his head in a nod. "That was my thought, as well."

A dark picture sprang into Thane's mind, of a young woman struggling against her attacker while being choked to death with this very cloth. Grimly he said, "May I have this?"

Bott sat up straight. "With all due respect, m'lord, I cannot see that it would be of any great use to you. As I said, I've already taken it around to every shop in Town."

"Nevertheless, I would like to show it to my valet. He may have some thought as to its origin."

"An excellent notion," the magistrate said, rising to his feet and picking up a hefty legal tome. "Now, this meeting must come to a close as I am due in court shortly. I will, of course, order extra patrols in the vicinity of Hyde Park, in case the villain attempts to strike again. Bott, carry on with your investigation. Your Lordship, once again, I greatly appreciate your help. Without you, we would not have access to the great houses of the city."

Bott still looked disgruntled, but Thane ignored him. The fellow would get over his snit soon enough when he realized that Thane had no interest in milking any glory from solving the case.

He had seen enough needless death on the battlefield. His sole interest was achieving justice for the two women who had died—and preventing any others from suffering the same fate.

He tucked the cravat into an inner pocket of his coat. As he strode downstairs, Thane passed the crowded antechamber where throngs of unwashed masses sat on benches, awaiting their turn with one of the magistrates or to visit prisoners in one of the holding cells. He proceeded outside into the dull gray afternoon and headed to the iron post where his horse was tethered. While bending down to untie the reins, Thane glimpsed her slim figure out of the corner of his eye.

Miss Lindsey Crompton.

He jerked upright and spun toward her. Only to realize his mistake as she reached out to open the door to Bow Street Court.

Instead of a finely etched profile, this woman had a crooked nose and a coarseness to her features.

Instead of an upswept mass of rich brown hair, this woman wore a dark bonnet adorned by a broken peacock feather.

Instead of a willowy form with generous breasts, this woman was painfully thin, almost sickly.

Irked with himself, Thane swung onto his horse and negotiated a path through the congestion of drays and carriages on the cobbled street. How very foolish of him. His imagination was conjuring ghosts.

It was the image of Lindsey Crompton that haunted him. He had committed an act of supreme idiocy by reaching into her bodice the previous night. He had succeeded only in branding himself with the unforgettable memory of her luscious curves.

When she had flown at him in a rage, intent on retrieving the IOU, she had knocked him off balance. Not in a physical sense, but in his mind. She was magnificent in her anger, all fiery woman. For a brief moment while he'd clasped her close, sexual awareness had entered those big blue eyes. Her lips had parted as if hungering for his kiss.

A visceral thrill gripped him. He had wanted to do more than kiss her—still wanted. He'd burned to carry her upstairs to the nearest bedchamber and coax sweetness from her tart tongue. God help him! She was a vixen who would make a man's life a misery.

But his body ignored logic. The fire of attraction still smoldered in his gut.

Charged with the critical task of tracking down a killer, Thane had no time for the games of courtship. Nor had he any interest in marrying at the moment, as his uncle had commanded him. Thane would not allow himself to deviate from his purpose. Miss Lindsey Crompton was a distraction to be ignored.

Nothing more.

Chapter 5

Some distance away, in the posh area of Mayfair, the object of Thane's dark musings was approaching his residence on Curzon Street.

Slowing her steps, Lindsey tilted her head back to gaze past the frame of her straw bonnet at the long row of town houses. Unlike the freestanding Crompton mansion in Berkeley Square, some three blocks distant, these homes adjoined one another in a continuous line down to the far corner.

Number Ten belonged to the Earl of Mansfield. Identical to the other fine brick houses, it rose four stories tall. White marble columns flanked the front door, while a triangular pediment carved with two fierce griffins crowned the top of the entryway.

She strained to see into the tall windows, but they were set too high off the street and she could catch only a tantalizing glimpse of shadowy rooms inside the swags of blue draperies.

Was Lord Mansfield at home? What if he appeared suddenly at a window, looked out, and caught her spying on him? The prospect caused an undue fluttering of her heart. How awkward it would be if he discovered her right here in front of his house. He was just arrogant enough to surmise that she was sweet on him and was acting like a love-struck schoolgirl.

Lindsey bristled at the notion. Nothing could be further from the truth. She was here for a dual purpose—to discover what had happened to Flora's missing cousin, Nelda, and also to find the IOU.

Lindsey's errant mind traveled back to that close encounter in Lord Wrayford's study, when Mansfield had reached into her bodice. His audacity proved him to be no gentleman. He was a rogue and a gambler, and if she never saw him again, it would be too soon—

"Not wise, missy. Not wise."

The muttering voice snapped her out of the reverie. She glanced over at the short, stout Hindu woman who walked at her side. For a few moments, she had forgotten Kasi's presence. A chilly breeze fluttered the edges of Kasi's sky blue cloak, revealing a glimpse of the brilliant orange sari beneath it. The old ayah was the nursemaid who had cared for the three Crompton sisters since childhood, giving them the love and guidance they'd needed.

However, Kasi had also had an uncanny way of knowing when any of them were up to no good. As a young girl, Lindsey had been half-convinced that the woman possessed the fabled power of the Evil Eye.

"Not wise?" Lindsey asked, striving for an innocent expression as they continued their slow progression past Mansfield's home. "I can't imagine what you mean."

"You plan mischief." Her leathery face stern beneath a knob of graying hair, Kasi jabbed her forefinger at Lindsey. "You tell me."

"Oh, pish-posh. We are merely enjoying a pleasant stroll through the neighborhood."

Kasi gave her a sour glare, one that demanded the truth.

"Oh, all right, if you must know, there's something I would very much like to do now that we are here. Miss Underhill told me that an old family friend lives on this street. I would like to pay a call on Miss Jocelyn Nevingford." Lindsey nodded at the town house right beside Mansfield's. "There's the place."

It was only a minor fib. The governess really *had* mentioned a tenuous connection between the Cromptons and the earl's young ward. But to obtain the actual address Lindsey had had to engage in a bit of sleuthing. A small bribe had sufficed to coax a footman into obtaining the information.

Kasi regarded her with raisin-eyed suspicion. "Memsahib not give consent for visit."

"La, there's no harm in stopping for a brief hello. In truth, it would be rude to pass by without any greeting when we're right here in the vicinity. And anyway, she's just a young girl around Blythe's age, so I can't imagine how Mama could possibly object."

Lindsey knew she was babbling. She did it to keep Kasi from getting a word in edgewise. And perhaps also to convince herself that she was making the right move. As they reached the town house, she steeled her nerves, marched up the front steps, and seized the lion's head knocker to give three hard raps on the door.

Huffing and puffing, Kasi caught up to her on the small porch. The old woman was mumbling under her breath, something about needing to pray to the Hindu god Shiva for guidance. But thankfully she made no further attempt to dissuade Lindsey.

An aging butler opened the door. Lindsey presented him with her card and asked to see Miss Nevingford.

His bushy white brows lifting in a faintly quizzical look, he invited Lindsey into a spacious foyer fashionably decorated with striped-green wallpaper and mahogany chairs. A grand staircase curved toward the receiving rooms on the first floor. The butler marched up the stairs and vanished. He returned a moment later to usher them up to a bright yellow-painted sitting room with tall windows that gave a view of the back garden.

A dainty blond girl lounged on a chaise by the fire, a white blanket arranged over her legs. The table beside her held a lap desk with a sketchbook and pencil. There was an almost ethereal quality to her slenderness, a fairylike delicacy to her face.

Surprise rippled through Lindsey. *She* was Mansfield's ward? This beautiful woman-child?

A plump elderly woman occupied a nearby chair, intent on mending the hem of a chemise. The plain brown dress and widow's cap marked her as a servant or perhaps a companion. She looked up to peruse Lindsey with a placid interest.

Miss Nevingford didn't rise to greet Lindsey but smiled dazzlingly and held out both hands. She had striking green eyes, deep and beautiful. "Hullo! How wonderful to have a visitor on such a dreary afternoon."

Lindsey was a bit taken aback by the display of friendliness from this waiflike stranger. Remembering her manners, she glided forward and briefly pressed the girl's soft hands. "It's a pleasure to meet you. Did you recognize my name, then?"

That pretty brow crinkled a bit. She glanced down at the card in her lap. "No, but . . . should I have?"

"My family, the Cromptons, are also from Lancashire. I'm given to understand that my parents were neighbors of your father's. I presumed you knew of the connection, Miss Nevingford."

"Oh, you must call me Jocelyn. And if you don't mind, I shall call you Lindsey. I know we are going to be fast friends. Fisk, will you ring for tea?"

The old woman rose obediently from the chair and hobbled over to tug on the bell rope before returning to her sewing.

Lindsey told herself to be thrilled at this opportunity. This was her big chance to dig up information. Yet something about the situation made her a trifle ill at ease. Perhaps it was the fact that Jocelyn seemed so overly eager for her companionship.

"I don't know how long I can stay," Lindsey said. "I only came for a moment to introduce myself."

"But you mustn't go away so quickly," Jocelyn insisted. "Pray, sit down so that we might become better acquainted. I have so few friends in town and it's been ever so dull, sitting here day after day, with only Fisk and my sketchbook for company."

Lindsey obediently perched on the edge of a chair near the girl. From the corner of her eye, she noticed that Kasi had settled down to wait on a stool beside the door.

Jocelyn's pale green gown enhanced her elfin appearance. She had the translucent skin of someone who seldom ventured outside. How different from Lindsey's upbringing. Despite Mama's scoldings, Lindsey and her sisters often had turned brown from the hot Indian sun.

"Surely you have many acquaintances," Lindsey said. "There must be girls that you attended school with, or who live here on this street. If you go for a stroll through the neighborhood, you're bound to make some new friends."

"A stroll?" Jocelyn lowered her chin, gazing at Lindsey with the solemn eyes of a china doll. "Oh, did you not know—? The doctors say I will never walk again. Ever since the accident last year, I have been crippled."

Shock held Lindsey immobile. A flush of mortification heated her cheeks. Of course, that would explain why Jocelyn hadn't arisen to greet her, and why she reclined with a coverlet over her legs.

How had Miss Underhill failed to mention such a momentous fact? Knowing her, she probably hadn't wanted to gossip.

"Forgive my thoughtlessness. I—I had no idea."

"Oh, it's quite all right," Jocelyn said with a wan smile. "I don't mind, really. Would you like to hear about the accident?"

"If—if you wish to tell me."

"Certainly. Friends share such stories, don't they?"

Lindsey managed a stiff nod. She felt swamped with guilt at deceiving the poor girl into thinking she had come here for such an altruistic purpose.

"It happened last November, while I was in living in Belgium. My father was a captain in the cavalry, you know. Mama and I followed the drum with him, traveling with him wherever his company went. There were times when we had to make do with living in a tent."

Lindsey struggled to imagine this refined girl living under such difficult conditions. She felt a sympathetic connection between them since she, too, had grown up in a different world than the rest of high society. "You must have visited lots of interesting new places."

"Yes—at least I did until my parents died." As if looking into the past, Jocelyn turned her head to stare out the window. "One evening, I went with Mama and Papa out to dinner at the mayor's house. On the way home, a terrible rainstorm blew up. The wind was howling, making the coach rock from side to side. Then from out of nowhere, a carriage came racing straight at us. I remember hearing a loud crash and being thrown about as the coach tipped over. And then . . . and then . . . there was nothing. . . ."

Biting her lip, she looked back at Lindsey, and her green eyes had a watery sheen. "When I awakened, my parents were dead and I was confined to bed, suffering the most unbearable pain from two broken legs."

Aghast, Lindsey groped for something to say. Mere words seemed inadequate. "I'm so sorry."

"Lord Mansfield took me in when I was left all alone. He said it was his duty. You see, he and Papa were the best of friends." A wry smile banished the sorrow from Jocelyn's face. "I daresay, I have been a millstone around the earl's neck."

"Why would you think that?"

"He's a bachelor and quite the wild rogue. It must be terribly difficult for him to be saddled with a cripple as his ward."

Lindsey gave him credit for taking in an orphaned girl, even if only out of obligation. Yet she bristled at the notion of him making Jocelyn feel unloved and indebted. "The earl ought to change his ways, then. It would behoove him to cease all his gambling and carousing at once."

Jocelyn leaned forward, interest shining in her eyes. "You sound as if you are acquainted with His Lordship, then."

The girl knew nothing about Lindsey's unconventional meeting with him—nor would she. "Only by the flimsiest connection. We were introduced at a party, that's all."

She was saved from further inquiry by the arrival of the tea tray, delivered by a footman who placed it on a table near Jocelyn. At the girl's behest, Lindsey sprang up to perform the role of hostess, pouring two cups of steaming liquid and adding a lump of sugar to both. She would have offered an additional cup to Fisk, but the plump old woman had dozed off over her sewing. As for Kasi, she only took food or drink prepared by her own hands, and anyway, the English rules drummed into Lindsey by Miss Underhill forbade treating a servant as an equal.

Once Lindsey had passed out the tea and slices of plum cake, she deemed it time to steer the topic to her purpose.

"I was wondering," she said. "Would you perhaps know of a maid named Nelda? Until very recently, she worked next door for Lord Mansfield."

Jocelyn frowned thoughtfully. "Nelda. Yes, I believe she's a dark-haired girl with the most unfortunate mole on her chin. Sometimes, when the other servants here were busy, she would help haul my bathwater from the kitchen."

"So you do know her!" Not wanting to appear overly enthused, Lindsey toned down her excitement. "Nelda is cousin to my abigail. The reason I brought up her name is that a few days ago Nelda went away without sending word to her family. You wouldn't happen to know where she's gone, would you?"

"Oh my. She left? Without a word?" Her eyes widening, Jocelyn set aside her teacup. "I hope she hasn't come to foul play. Especially considering . . ."

"Yes?"

Jocelyn glanced over at Fisk, who was snoring softly, her chin propped on her massive bosom. The girl fixed her guileless gaze on Lindsey and said in a confiding whisper, "I don't wish to alarm you, but there is a madman roaming the streets at night. Have you heard of the Serpentine Strangler? He has been murdering maidservants all over London."

Lindsey nearly choked on a sip of tea. "I'm aware of the case. There have been two victims, no more. But really, you shouldn't know of such sordid crimes. Who told you?"

"No one in particular. I have excellent hearing. People seem to think that being crippled means my senses are dulled. But it's really quite the opposite." A hint of slyness touched Jocelyn's smile. "I'm especially good at pretending to be asleep while the servants are gossiping. One can learn all sorts of interesting tidbits that way."

"I see. Well, I doubt Nelda has come to such an untimely end. She very likely found a better position in another house. It's just a matter of finding out where."

"Mmm. You could be right." Jocelyn swirled a dainty fingertip in the crumbs of plum cake on her plate. "And yet, considering that Lord Mansfield is such a wicked rake, I can't help but wonder. . . ."

His name poked like a thorn into Lindsey. "Wonder what?"

Jocelyn peeked from beneath her lashes. "Perhaps the earl had his way with Nelda. Perhaps she had conceived his baby, and he did away with her before the scandal could come to light. Perhaps she'll be found strangled like those other girls."

Lindsey almost dropped her cup. Jocelyn was worse than Blythe at wild speculations. Was it just that she had so much time alone here to dream up tall tales to amuse herself? Or had close proximity enabled her to know Mansfield's character better than anyone else?

The Earl of Mansfield couldn't possibly be the Strangler.

Yet Nelda *was* missing from his house.

And Blythe had reported that one of the murdered maids had been on her way to meet a gentleman lover.

Lindsey had a sudden, clear memory of Mansfield walking into Lord Wrayford's study accompanied by a comely maidservant.

The icy fingers of suspicion prickled her skin. She had assumed that he and the maid intended to engage in a sordid tryst. But what if he'd had an even more sinister purpose?

No. No, it was absurd. He was a peer of the realm, not a criminal from the stews of London.

She realized that Jocelyn was gazing avidly at her, awaiting her reaction. Good manners dictated that she chastise the girl for stepping outside the bounds of propriety.

With studied composure, Lindsey set down her teacup on the tray. "Don't be silly. That seems a rather dramatic accusation to make of your guardian."

Jocelyn ducked her chin. "Perhaps you're right. You must think I'm dreadfully ungrateful, don't you? To suggest such an awful thing about the man who has given me a home and shown me naught but kindness."

"I think you're bored and in dire need of an outing. You should ask His Lordship to remedy that situation straightaway—"

"Remedy what?"

The deep male voice startled her. Lindsey's heart gave a wild lurch. She glanced over her shoulder to see the menacing figure of Lord Mansfield looming in the doorway.

Handsomely groomed, he wore a tailored black coat and buff breeches with black riding boots. The pure white of his cravat set off the swarthiness of skin darkened from years spent in the sun. Despite his fine garb, he exuded an aura of toughness, perhaps because of the breadth of his shoulders or the hard contours of his scarred face.

He was not smiling. Rather, he looked as if he contemplated strangling her.

A shiver eddied through her. The hostility that emanated from him was a palpable presence in the air. Was he one of those high-and-mighty aristocrats who thought a commoner unfit to associate with his ward?

He strolled into the sitting room, his powerful figure making the walls seem to shrink. "This is quite a surprise, Miss Crompton. I had no notion that you were acquainted with my ward."

Her mouth felt too dry to form words. What was he doing here? And how much had he heard?

To buy time, Lindsey flung a question at him: "Do you always walk in unannounced and eavesdrop on private conversations?"

"There's a connecting door between this house and mine. I own both homes. Or didn't you know that?"

His cynicism made her nerve endings vibrate with discordant emotions. She felt defensive for being caught here, embarrassed that he might think she was trying to worm her way into his affections, and alarmed at the possibility of him guessing her true purpose here—to locate Nelda and to steal the IOU.

Then Jocelyn made matters worse by lying: "Don't be angry, m'lord. Lindsey and I have known each other for *ages*. You see, our families hail from the same area of Lancashire. We share a *long* history together."

"Indeed." Arching a skeptical eyebrow, the earl took up a protective stance at the end of the chaise. He glanced down at his ward as if to assure himself she hadn't been tainted by Lindsey's visit. "It seems your father would have mentioned such a connection to me."

"Why would he?" Lindsey said, recovering her aplomb. "I've lived most of my life in India. And what Jocelyn really means is that we have known *of* each other for years. I thought it only polite to renew the acquaintance in person."

"I see. You should be informed, then, that Miss Nevingford tires easily. The doctors have prescribed complete rest for her."

"All I *ever* do is rest," Jocelyn said with a pout. "I vow I'm not weary in the least—"

"It's all right," Lindsey said, forcing a smile. It was a difficult effort, considering the potency of her resentment toward Mansfield. "I really must return home anyway. Perhaps we'll talk again sometime. Good day."

Rising from the chair, she concentrated on keeping her

movements graceful to convey the message that she was leaving of her own accord and not because she had been intimidated into doing so. It was not an easy task. All the way to the door, she had the discomfitting sense of his eyes boring into her back.

For the umpteenth time, Edith Crompton twitched back the lace curtains of her sitting room and peered down at the cobbled street. People strolled the concentric walkways of the square, mostly fine ladies and gentlemen, out taking the air despite the overcast skies.

On any other afternoon, she would feel a righteous sense of superiority that *she* occupied the fine stone mansion at one end of Berkeley Square, while the aristocrats had to settle for the smaller row houses. Having once been a nameless girl in service, Edith had clawed and scraped her way into her current high position in society. Two qualities commanded respect from the nobility: bloodline and wealth. Edith could never claim the first, so she'd made certain she possessed more money than any of them.

But today she was preoccupied. Her sharp eyes scoured the pedestrians in a vain search. Hearing the click of the door opening behind her, she let the curtain drop and spun on her heel to face her husband.

"Where *is* that wayward girl?" she demanded. "She and Kasi departed two hours ago."

George Crompton ran his fingers through his sparse brown hair, and his weathered features wore a frown. He looked more annoyed with Edith than with their middle daughter. "Is *that* why you summoned me from my account books? Lindsey went for a stroll. There's no harm in that."

"No harm?" Edith felt about to burst with pent-up frustration. She paced back and forth, the elegant rose-striped gown swishing around her girlishly slender figure. "Lord Wrayford came to call in her absence. I had to listen to him ramble about the superiority of his hunting hounds for nearly an hour, all in the hopes that she would return promptly. Now he's gone and Lindsey has missed a prime opportunity to encourage his courtship."

George planted his hands on his hips, pushing back his coffee brown coat and revealing the paunch around his waist. "If the man has a serious interest in her, he won't give up so easily. Besides, are you certain she even wishes to marry him? I've never heard her say so, and he seems a rather havey-cavey sort of fellow to me, anyway."

"All young gentlemen enjoy their amusements. He'll settle down once they're wed." She took a step toward George. "As a matter of fact, I was hoping you would have a word with her."

"A word? About what?"

"Remind her that Wrayford is eminently suitable. With the death of his elder brother, he's now heir to the Duke of Sylvester. The old man won't last much longer, and then Lindsey will be a duchess." The fantasy buoyed Edith's spirits. "Just think, George, our grandchild could be heir to a dukedom!"

His face darkened. He took hold of her shoulders and gave her a hard shake. "You and your blasted ambitions! Did you learn nothing from the near disaster last year with Portia? Nothing at all?"

The previous season, their eldest daughter had been courted by the stately Duke of Albright, the match promoted and guided by Edith. But from the start, Portia had rejected his advances in favor of the notorious Viscount Ratcliffe. There had been a dreadful scandal with Portia running off with Ratcliffe, then Ratcliffe being thrown into prison for killing the duke in a duel. The resulting gossip and disgrace was something Edith hoped never to endure again.

And she wouldn't, if things went as planned this time.

Realizing she'd stepped over the line, she forced a conciliatory smile. George might be a malleable man, yet he had an iron streak that accounted for his incredible success in the business world. Since he controlled the purse strings, it wouldn't do for her to antagonize him.

She cradled his weathered cheeks in her palms. "Pray don't be angry with me, darling. I'm quite happy with the way things have turned out for dear Portia. Just think, we'll be holding our first grandchild in a few short months."

The reminder had the desired effect. George relaxed his grip on her shoulders, although he still regarded her warily. "Heed me well, Edith. Lindsey will have the final say in who she marries. I will not have you forcing her into a union she does not favor."

"Of course not."

Edith's expression turned calculating as she watched him stride out of the chamber. She would not relinquish this perfect opportunity to bolster her position in the very highest circles. When the time came, Lindsey would make the right choice.

Edith intended to make certain of that.

Chapter 6

Lindsey staved off boredom as she danced with Lord Wrayford. The hour was past midnight, and it would be embarrassing to yawn in the middle of a crowded ballroom. Not to mention unspeakably rude. Luckily, it was a country tune with two long lines of dancers. The complicated steps required the couples to be separated for short stretches of time while switching off with other partners.

That, at least, saved her the effort of making inane conversation with Wrayford. He was a dreary jackanapes who wasn't so much pursuing *her* as he was her dowry.

It was the second time this evening that Mama had arranged for him to partner Lindsey. The new pair of slippers pinched her toes and she'd wanted to sit this one out, but Mama would hear nothing of it. Lindsey hadn't dared press the issue. She had already earned a scolding for vanishing so long the previous afternoon.

Mama would be furious to learn she had gone visiting without her approval, and so Lindsey had sworn Kasi to secrecy. Admitting the truth would lead to awkward questions—such as why Lindsey had sought out the Earl of Mansfield's ward in the first place.

The thought of him stirred disquiet in the pit of Lindsey's belly. She hadn't seen him all evening, which was just as well. The less she encountered him, the better.

He represented to her all the prideful arrogance of the nobility.

The steps brought her face-to-face with Wrayford again. He had artfully styled sandy hair, pale blue eyes, and fair skin flushed from the exertion of the dance. The yellow coat he wore only made his complexion appear washed-out, as did the elaborate white cravat, which had more flounces than a peacock had feathers.

The previous year, Wrayford had courted Portia. Lindsey had thought her sister was exaggerating about his habit of ogling a lady's bosom. She had since discovered her mistake. Every time his avid gaze dipped to her blue muslin bodice, it made her skin crawl, as it did now.

"I vow, Miss Crompton, you are the very essence of beauty. The glow of candlelight surrounds you like a halo."

She forced a stiff smile. "Thank you."

Lud, what else was she to say to such a ridiculous statement? If the fool thought to win her over with puffed-up compliments and lascivious stares, he would soon find out the futility of his effort.

Placing her gloved hand in his, Lindsey turned in a stately circle around him in accordance with the dance. The throng of gentlemen and ladies in the ballroom held a number of familiar faces, although many of these aristocrats were still strangers to her. Papa's vast wealth may have purchased her entry into their elite circle, but it couldn't buy their approval. Most of the guests here believed that lineage trumped all other qualifications.

Not that Lindsey cared what they thought. If she could placate her parents by enduring this one season, then there might be a chance of winning her freedom. How lovely it would be to face a future of her own making, without a husband to dictate her every move. She could escape from this gilded cage of parties and shopping. She could fulfill her dream of setting up a small private detective agency, where she could solve mysteries for a genteel clientele—

She stumbled slightly, blinking at the spot where she had just seen him. Was that Mansfield's black hair and tall form? Or was she woolgathering? With the squeeze of people shifting this way and that, she couldn't be certain. But the mere thought of running into him made her feel flushed and agitated.

At least it had had one good effect: she was now wide awake.

The dance steps were drawing to a close. Lord Wrayford bowed deeply from the waist, revealing that he had carefully combed his hair to hide the bald patch at the back of his head.

Preoccupied, Lindsey curtsied by rote and spoke without thinking: "Do you know if Lord Mansfield is present tonight?"

"Mansfield? Why do you ask?"

"I—I had a question to ask of him. In regard to his ward."

Wrayford cocked a sandy eyebrow in a calculating stare. "Now that you mention it, I did catch a glimpse of him a few moments ago while we were dancing. If you'll take a turn around the room with me, I'll show you precisely where he is."

Grasping her elbow, he led her off the dance floor in the direction where she'd seen Mansfield. Lindsey tried to lag back, but Wrayford had a firm hold and she had to match his pace or risk creating a scene. The last thing she wanted was a face-to-face encounter with Mansfield.

Why, oh why, had she been so foolish as to bring up his name?

"This is hardly a convenient time to seek him out," she said. "My mother will be looking for me."

"Never mind that; we're almost there." Wrayford

brought her to a halt by the massive arch of the doorway. He nodded toward one of the marble pillars set at intervals around the ballroom. "Look, there's our quarry now."

His back to her, Mansfield stood half-concealed by a screen of ferns. There was no mistaking his lofty dark-haired form. A chocolate brown coat emphasized the breadth of his shoulders as he bent down to speak to a lovely brunette in a turquoise gown cut scandalously low at the bosom. They seemed to be having an excellent time laughing together, the lady casting coquettish smiles from beneath her lashes. She boldly walked her fingertips up the lapel of his coat, and Mansfield caught her gloved hand, turning it over to kiss her palm.

The sight caused an unsettling twist inside Lindsey. It was disgust, of course, for who else but the earl would dare to flirt so outrageously out in public?

"Do you recognize his companion?" Wrayford murmured.

The tickle of his breath on her ear startled her into taking a backward step. Wrayford stood mere inches from her, so close she could see a few pockmarks on his skin. "No," she said. "I'm afraid I don't."

"That doesn't surprise me. Her name is Lady Entwhistle, and she's hardly the sort that innocent young ladies should know."

Entwhistle. The name rang a faint bell, although Lindsey couldn't recall where she'd heard it. "What do you mean?"

"She's a widow who . . . how shall I say it? Who counts an inordinate number of gentlemen among her closest acquaintances."

His implication shocked Lindsey. She couldn't resist taking another peek at the couple. Still clasping Lady Entwhistle's hand, Mansfield kept his full attention trained on his companion. Their aura of intimacy filled Lindsey with an instinctive dislike of the woman.

And even more so of Mansfield.

"If her reputation has suffered," she asked Wrayford, "why has society not shunned her?"

"Her father was a marquess, and pedigree does allow for a certain leeway in conduct. Besides, she's well versed in pressing the boundaries of discretion. Come along now; I believe you've seen quite enough." Wrayford guided Lindsey back through the throng of people in the ballroom. "We are friends, are we not?" he asked, taking her hand and patting the back of it.

Still trying to recall where she'd heard of the woman, Lindsey had to cudgel her thoughts back to him. "Mmm."

Her lackluster response failed to deter Wrayford. "As such," he continued, "I feel compelled to warn you to keep your distance from the rogue. You can see the caliber of female that Mansfield prefers. He's a gamester and a rake who would think nothing of tarnishing a young lady's name."

The assessment irritated her, coming as it did from a man who stared at bosoms. A man who wanted her rich dowry in order to pay off his own gaming debt to Mansfield. Though, of course, Wrayford didn't know she was aware of his own foibles. "How are you privy to so much tittle-tattle about Mansfield? I thought he'd only just sold his commission in the cavalry. He wasn't even here in London until a few months ago."

Wrayford led her toward the front of the ballroom, where her mother sat and gossiped with a number of the other married ladies. "I have connections in the military. Wherever he was stationed, Mansfield was known as a ladies' man among all the foreign nationals. He left a string of mistresses all over the Continent. You would do well to stay clear of him."

"Thank you for enlightening me. I'll take your advice under consideration."

Her sarcasm sailed right over his styled sandy hair. Fervently he pressed his fingers to hers, his gaze flicking again to her breasts. "I'm always happy to serve you, Miss Crompton. I shall return you now, safe and sound, to the care of your dear mother."

"Actually, I'm a bit parched," she said, withdrawing her hand. "Why don't I wait right here while you fetch me a lemonade?"

"Your wish is my command."

Wrayford vanished into the crush of guests. The orchestra had set down their instruments for a much-needed respite. In the interlude, people were wandering over to the refreshment tables in the next room or gathering in clusters to chat.

Lindsey had no intention of standing in a corner like a wallflower. Nor did she want to return to her mother's protective custody. Instead, Lindsey set forth on a solitary stroll along the perimeter of the ballroom, wending irresistibly back toward the pillar where she had seen Mansfield and Lady Entwhistle.

Her goal was not to interrupt their conversation. Rather, she wanted to spy on them in the hopes of jogging her memory. There was something nagging at the edge of her mind, something concerning Lady Entwhistle.

A brown-haired man ventured into her path. "M-Miss Crompton?" He bobbed his head, a hesitant smile on his freckled face. "I-I must b-beg a moment of y-your t-time."

She swallowed a groan. Of all her suitors, he was the one who most elicited her pity for his painful shyness. His frayed cuffs and ill-fitting coat betrayed him as the purse-poor younger son of a baron. "Mr. Sykes. I trust you're having an enjoyable time this evening."

"Are-are-are you engaged for the next d-dance?" he stuttered, the words tumbling out in a mad rush.

Lindsey had partnered with him at another ball and still retained the painful memory of him stepping on her toes numerous times. "Hmm, I do believe—"

"Sorry, old chap, she's already dancing with me."

Mansfield appeared at her shoulder. Before she could do more than inhale a startled breath, he placed his hand at the small of her back and propelled her toward the row of glass doors that stood open to the darkness of the night.

The candlelit ballroom took on a jeweled brilliance. Lindsey was keenly aware of the hum of conversation all around her. His scent of spice was uniquely male compared to the floral perfumes worn by the ladies. The light pressure of his touch at the base of her spine seemed unbearably intimate. She knew it would be wise to pull away, yet the nudge of curiosity made her move forward in accordance with his direction.

A host of questions begged to be answered: How had he found her so quickly in this crowd? What could he want with her? And what had happened to Lady Entwhistle?

They reached the doors and proceeded outside onto a stone-flagged loggia with steps leading down into a garden. Lighted lanterns marked the pathways where a few couples strolled, arm in arm. Against the black velvet sky, the moon glowed silver behind a gauzy veil of clouds.

"I've been hoping to have a word with you in private, Miss Crompton."

His deep voice sent a shiver over her skin. Or perhaps it was merely the coolness of the evening air after the heat of the ballroom. "Oh? For what purpose?"

"I'll tell you in a moment."

Like a man on a mission, he steered her down the steps and to a bench beneath a trellis, where interlaced vines formed a pool of deep shadow. She made the mistake of sitting down on the cold stone seat. Mansfield remained standing, instantly making her feel subordinate to him.

He braced his hand on the trellis and stared down at her, his expession hidden in the gloom. "Now," he stated in an ominous tone. "I'd like the truth from you for once."

She arranged her skirts in a show of nonchalance. "The truth?"

"Precisely." He leaned closer, so that she could see the glitter of his eyes through the darkness. "Tell me the real reason you came to visit my ward yesterday."

His voice was as chilly as the night breeze. Had Jocelyn revealed her questions about Nelda, the missing maidservant?

Cautiously Lindsey said, "I thought I'd made my purpose quite clear. There's a connection between her family and mine. It was only polite to renew the acquaintance. Would you deny Jocelyn the hand of friendship?"

"Of course not. But she's underage and her companions are subject to my approval."

Lindsey took the remark as a jab at her commoner status. Irked, she went on the attack: "Then why is the poor girl sitting alone in that house, with only an elderly servant for company? Does she even *have* any friends?"

"Very few. She grew up overseas. And I brought her back from Europe less than two months ago."

"Very few," Lindsey mocked. "I'll presume that to mean *none*. Do you ever take her on outings, to places where she can meet people her own age?"

"She's frail and cannot be subject to excitement."

"Bah. She might develop a bloom of healthy color in her cheeks if ever you took her on a drive to the park."

He paced back and forth, his shoes crunching the gravel. "Who are you to pass judgment on my care? You know little of her medical condition. I would sooner trust the guidance of her doctor. And he has been adamant in his assertion that she's to be protected from any type of stimulation."

There was a thread of worry to his tone that made Lindsey soften her voice. Perhaps he did have a heart, after all. "And what is it he says? As the accident happened last autumn, her broken bones should be healed by now. Why has Jocelyn not resumed walking?"

"She suffers great pain whenever she attempts to put weight on her legs. And she's prone to bouts of weeping afterward."

The poor girl. "She seemed in excellent spirits to me."

"You aren't with her all the time," he snapped. "A deep melancholy affects her on occasion. In truth, she was quite despondent today after yesterday's upheaval in her routine. Which is why I must forbid you ever to return."

His ultimatum was a hot prod to her pride. Lindsey shot up from the bench to confront his menacing shadow. "So you don't approve of me, do you? You would sooner share the company of females like Lady Entwhistle."

"What the devil does she have to do with anything?"

"I saw you with her tonight. If you cared a whit for Jocelyn, you would make the effort to behave as a gentleman. You wouldn't consort with women of such dubious moral standards." She brushed past him, then turned back. "And I'll thank you not to curse in my presence."

His fingers closed around her bare upper arm, preventing her from storming away in a righteous rage. As he leaned forward to stare closely at Lindsey, a shaft of moonlight lent hard contours to his features. "You're jealous of my attention to Lady Entwhistle."

Nothing he said could have startled—or infuriated—Lindsey more. It was the tone of his voice as much as the content of his words. He sounded confident . . . cocky . . . *amused.*

She jerked at his hold. "Why, you vainglorious fool—"

"You're right; I must be a fool."

On that cynical statement, he pulled her deep into the shadows of the arbor and brought his mouth down on hers. Lindsey was too stunned to offer more than a token resistance. His arms held her tightly, trapping her hands against his broad shoulders. His aroma and taste, his sheer maleness, engulfed her senses. All at once, her anger and antagonism transformed into a heat that burned at her core.

Without thinking, she closed her eyes and succumbed to the pleasure of his lips gliding over hers. The warmth of his muscled body clasped to hers was a delight unknown until this moment. She reveled in it, pressing herself closer to him, hardly understanding the need that induced her to utter small throaty sounds of desire. On some deep level, she was aghast at her own behavior, yet the temptation to enjoy the moment overwhelmed her.

"Sweet Lindsey," he muttered, his breath hot against her skin. Then his tongue sought entry between her lips, exploring her mouth with a skill that had her melting in his arms. Nothing else mattered but to be held by him, to feel his hands stroking up and down her back. She ached for him to touch her more intimately, in ways no innocent young lady ought to contemplate. Unlike other girls her age, she knew a little of sexual matters from her time in India, where rules were more lax and where she often had eavesdropped on the raucous gossip of servants.

As abruptly as he'd grabbed hold of her, Mansfield lifted his head, his breathing harsh in the quiet night. She started to murmur a protest, but he placed his forefinger over her lips. There was a tension in his body, an alertness that penetrated her silken trance.

Voices emanated from somewhere nearby. The scuff of footsteps approached on a pathway.

A glimmer of sanity returned to her mind. She stood very still within the circle of his arms. Lud, there was a party in progress a short distance away. What had she been thinking, to permit him such a passionate kiss when anyone might happen by and see them?

What had she been thinking to grant this man a kiss *at all*?

Awareness of her wanton behavior bought a hot blush to her face. She hadn't been thinking, that's what. At one expert brush of his lips, all sense had flown from her brain. Even now, she reveled in the warmth of his body against hers. It shook her to realize how easily he'd aroused her base instincts—instincts that had lain dormant until this moment.

No wonder Mansfield was renowned for his prowess at seduction.

The chattering couple walked past the little arbor without spying them standing in the gloom. Lindsey had been waiting for the couple's voices to fade before wrenching herself from his arms. But Mansfield released her first. He stepped back, a tall black shadow in the gloom.

"You'll want to return to the ballroom before you're missed."

His formal tone nonplussed her; he might have been dismissing a disobedient child. Was he so unaffected by their fervent embrace? She told herself to go, to put as much distance between them as possible. Yet the devil of pride prodded her into asking, "Is that all you have to say for yourself?"

He didn't answer at once. Music from the ballroom drifted into the silence. The orchestra had begun playing again, and the dancers would be forming sets. She waited on pins and needles, wishing to her shame for some acknowledgment that he'd experienced the same all-encompassing thrill as she had.

"I'd advise you to make haste," Mansfield murmured. "Lady Entwhistle is due to join me out here in a few moments."

His cool words made her humiliation complete. He had subjected her to an ardent kiss merely to pass the time while he waited for his lightskirt.

Drawing back her arm, Lindsey slapped him.

She scored a direct hit despite the darkness. The force of the blow traveled up her arm. Her palm stung with satisfying pain.

Mansfield staggered backward a step. His hand went to cup his cheek. But he said nothing and sought no retaliation.

Wheeling around, Lindsey went marching back toward the house. The slap had served as a cathartic release of white-hot fury. In the absence of that high dudgeon, she felt forlorn and mortified, dangerously close to weeping. How he must be laughing at her. All the while, when she'd responded fervently to his kiss, he'd been toying with her for his own amusement.

Blast him to Hell!

And blast Lady Entwhistle!

Memory returned to Lindsey in a rush. Her footsteps faltered in the shadows of the loggia, and she stopped just outside the open doors that spilled golden candlelight from the ballroom.

She knew now with sudden, cold clarity where she'd heard the name before. The first maidservant killed by the Serpentine Strangler had been employed by Lady Entwhistle.

The significance of that fact chilled Lindsey to the bone. Because it was one more piece of evidence to link Lord Mansfield to the murders.

Chapter 7

Lindsey hadn't realized how badly the coarse weave of a servant's gown could itch.

Lifting the latch of garden gate, she paused a moment to roll her shoulders in an effort to relieve the prickly sensation along her back. She was accustomed to the finest silks and muslins, and linen chemises as soft as a cloud, not this cheaply made frock with its high, choking collar. Adding to her discomfort were the stiff leather shoes she'd borrowed from her maid. Since Flora had bigger feet, Lindsey had had to stuff the toe of each with a wadded handkerchief. As a result, her shoes made a clumping noise as she opened the gate and stepped into the damp garden.

The drizzling rain gave her an excuse to wear an old brown cloak with the hood drawn over her head. It reeked, rather unfortunately, of wet wool. Still, she had to congratulate herself on the perfection of the disguise. No one on the street had paid her the slightest notice as she'd trudged the three blocks from Berkeley Square to the mews behind Lord Mansfield's house.

Pursing her lips, she risked a glance from beneath the hood at the upper windows of his home. The draperies were drawn shut in all the chambers. At this early hour of seven o'clock, Mansfield would be fast asleep like most gentlemen of his ilk. Against her will, the image of him lying abed caused an irksome tension deep inside her.

Without a doubt, it was festering anger. He had tricked her for his own amusement, used his expertise as a seducer in order to humble her. Two days had passed since that ill-fated kiss, and she'd been fuming ever since. During that time, she'd also had to endure Lord Wrayford's cloying attentions under Mama's none-too-subtle encouragement. Lindsey needed the IOU that would implicate Wrayford as a gambler.

More important, she had made a promise to Flora to find Nelda. Lindsey had concocted a plan to borrow her maid's clothes and infiltrate Mansfield's house. So much depended on her success today.

Anyway, for all she knew, he wasn't even at home. Perhaps he'd spent the night with his mistress, Lady Entwhistle. Or perhaps he'd been out murdering another unsuspecting maidservant.

The sobering possibility stalked Lindsey's peace of mind. She was still struggling to reconcile herself to the mounting evidence against him. As much as she disliked Mansfield, it was difficult to place him in the role of cold-blooded killer. Surely peers of the realm didn't go around strangling women.

Yet Lindsey had witnessed for herself the sight of Mansfield entering the study at Lord Wrayford's house in the company of a pretty, blond housemaid.

Mansfield also had a direct connection to Lady Entwhistle, whose maid had been the first victim—Maria Wilkes, who purportedly had been on her way to meet a gentleman lover.

And Flora's cousin, Nelda, was still missing. She had vanished from this very house less than a week ago.

Time and again, Lindsey had found herself wondering if there might be some truth to Jocelyn's theory: *Perhaps*

*the earl had his way with Nelda. Perhaps she had con-
ceived his baby, and so he did away with her before the
scandal could come to light. Perhaps she'll be found
strangled like those other girls.*

A grim sense of purpose conveyed Lindsey through
the puddles in the garden and to a nondescript door,
clearly the servants' entrance. She rapped hard on the
wooden panel, and a moment later the door was opened
by a plump older woman in a black dress and white apron.
The ring of keys at her waist marked her status as the
housekeeper.

The woman critically looked Lindsey up and down,
nodded briskly, then motioned her inside the house.
"Come in, come in. Ye look a bit skinny, but praise God,
ye're 'ere at last. The place 'as been sorely neglected this
past week."

Startled by the hospitable reception, Lindsey stepped
into a narrow corridor. Obviously, the housekeeper was
expecting someone else. "I think—"

"I'm Mrs. Yardley and ye're the girl from the agency.
Come along downstairs, ye'll tell us yer name and meet
the staff. No sense in wastin' time chatterin' since there's
much work t' be done."

The housekeeper pushed open a door and headed
down a steep staircase that had a sharp turn. Lindsey had
no choice but to follow, ducking her head to avoid the low
ceiling. Disregarding her own advice, Mrs. Yardley continued to gabble as she descended the steps, and Lindsey
could only catch a word or two out of every three.

"Ye'll share wid . . . upstairs . . .'alf day off . . . third
Monday . . . watch 'Is Lordship . . . mind ye . . . no
flirtin' . . ."

They emerged into a long passageway with open door-
ways leading to various workrooms. Scurrying to keep up
with Mrs. Yardley's vigorous strides, Lindsey glanced into

the rooms as they passed, seeing a maid ironing diligently in one, a footman polishing silver in another.

The housekeeper sailed through a doorway and Lindsey found herself in a cozy kitchen with copper pots hanging from a rack and window slits set high in the stone walls. A coal fire burned merrily in the large stone hearth.

"Wait 'ere," Mrs. Yardley instructed, then vanished into an adjoining room.

A stout cook stood at the stove, stirring a pot, talking over her shoulder to a tiny young maid who sat at a long wooden table, paring potatoes and then tossing them into a basket. Both turned to stare, and Lindsey found herself subjected to another uncomfortably close scrutiny. Perhaps they thought it odd that she hadn't lowered the voluminous hood of her cloak now that she was out of the rain.

Mrs. Yardley bustled back into the kitchen, carrying a pile of clothing, which she handed to Lindsey. "'Ere's yer gown. 'Is Lordship ain't one to complain, not like some o' the Quality, but ye best keep yer apron spit-spot clean. We've standards in this 'ouse, we do."

Lindsey automatically held out her arms for the heap of folded garments. It dawned on her that the housekeeper assumed her to be a newly hired housemaid sent by an agency.

Nelda's replacement.

"This 'ere's Cook, and Essie, our scullery girl," Mrs. Yardley said. "An' ye're . . ." She looked expectantly at Lindsey.

"Sally." Lindsey blurted out the first name that came to her mind. "Sally Simmons."

Feverish thoughts raced through her head. Should she correct the housekeeper's mistake? Her original plan had been to pose as a relative looking for Nelda, in the hopes of eliciting information about the girl's disappearance.

But now Providence had dropped a golden opportunity into Lindsey's lap. In the maid's garb, she would have un-bridled access to the upstairs rooms. With any luck, there would be a chance to rummage through Mansfield's desk for the IOU that would implicate Wrayford as a gambler. In the process, she might just stumble across a clue that would shed light on whether or not Mansfield was the Serpentine Strangler.

Her heart pounded. Did she really dare do this?

Yes, but she could only spare an hour or two. Any longer and Mama would notice her absence at breakfast. After conducting a swift search here, Lindsey would have to contrive an excuse to quit her post.

And during her brief employment, she'd have to be extremely careful not to run into the earl. It was a daunting prospect, for he was certain to recognize her on sight. He was too observant a man for her to hope she'd fade into the background like other servants.

Yet how much danger was there, really? By the time he roused himself from his bed, she would be long gone.

Thane stood lathering his face by the washbasin in his dressing room. He rinsed off his hands and dried them on a linen towel. Then he picked up the long razor, tilted his head to study himself in the mirror, and carefully shaved his jaw.

The glass reflected the image of his manservant moving behind him, laying out various articles of clothing. Thane squinted at him and frowned.

"Not that blue coat," he barked. "It's much too fine. Something old and tattered. I must be incognito today."

Bernard snorted. "You own *nothing* old and tattered, my lord. If you did, what would that say about my competence as a valet?"

"Then choose one that's dark and nondescript. And procure some older garments today for my future use."

"Hmph. I was planning to visit your tailor to order some linen shirts. I'll seek out the ragman instead."

Bernard's sarcasm made Thane grimace. He could hardly chastise the man for insubordination when he owed Bernard for saving his life on the battlefield. Some debts could never be repaid.

In brooding silence, he concentrated on shaving another swath beneath his cheekbone. It wasn't anyone's fault but his own that he was in a foul temper this morning. He hadn't slept well. And not because he was worried about his task this morning of tracking down a potential witness to one of the murders in the stews of Seven Dials.

Rather, Miss Lindsey Crompton was the source of his ill humor. He had spent the night tossing and turning, continually waking up to find himself as hard as an adolescent boy having his first dream of a girl.

What a fool he'd been to lower his guard and succumb to the temptation to kiss her. He should have known it would be a mistake. But there was something about the little virago that stripped away all his common sense. She had been so fierce in her defense of Jocelyn, and so self-righteous in her criticism of his dalliance with Lady Entwhistle.

Since Lindsey could have no knowledge of his true purpose, he had leaped to the conclusion that she was jealous, that she wanted him for herself. The notion had spurred him to act on primitive instinct. For a few reckless moments, he'd lost his head and indulged his base nature. Her passionate response had pushed him to the brink of madness. Had no one come along, he might have laid her down right there on the stone bench and thoroughly compromised her.

Afterward, a shaft of moonlight had illuminated her face. He would never forget her dreamy expression, nor the hurt that had replaced it a moment later when he'd been so unspeakably cruel to her.

He had lied to her about Lady Entwhistle joining him out in the garden. He'd done so deliberately. Because it was the only way to put a damper on things that could never be.

He couldn't afford to lead Lindsey—or himself—astray. He needed to keep his mind focused on finding the Serpentine Strangler. The clock was ticking, a murderer was on the loose, and she was a prime distraction. If he continued to waste so much time obsessing over how she'd melted in his arms—

"Ouch, damn it!" A spot of red appeared on his cheek where he'd cut himself. He grabbed the towel and blotted the stinging wound. "Bring me a plaster, will you?"

Bernard produced the sticking plaster much too quickly. Which meant he must have anticipated the inevitability of its need. Scowling, Thane rinsed his face and patted it dry before leaning close to the mirror to dab on the white paste.

Holding out a pair of black breeches, Bernard observed, "If you'd permit me to shave you, in accordance with the tasks of a gentleman's valet, you would not have suffered injury."

"When I'm wizened enough to require a cane, I'll consider it." Thane stepped into the breeches and buttoned the placket. "Now, have you learned anything about the cravat I gave you?"

"No one recognized it, as you already know. But I intend to question the seamstresses used by the various tailors in town. One of them might recognize the stitching on the hem."

Thane looked at him in surprise. "The stitching? White thread is all the same, is it not?"

"The differences can be subtle. A millimeter more or less between stitches may possibly lead to identifying the person who did the sewing."

Pleased, Thane clapped him on the back. "Excellent. If you can come up with something tangible, it may prevent another murder."

"Not like that," Mrs. Yardley chided. "Up an' down, girl, up an' down."

Lindsey was on her hands and knees in the library. The fine Axminster rug had been rolled back and she was scrubbing the wood floor with a bucket of water, into which a dribble of powdered soda had been dissolved. What did the woman mean, "up and down"?

Wishing she'd paid more attention to the maids in her own house, she glanced up quizzically at the housekeeper who towered over her. "Mum?"

Mrs. Yardley uttered a huff and used her hands to demonstrate a smooth, straight-line motion. "Ye allus follow the direction o' the boards, not rub every which way like a Bedlamite."

"Oh . . . sorry."

Under the housekeeper's watchful eyes, Lindsey applied the brush diligently again according to instruction. Her back already ached. She had been at this and other tasks for what seemed like days, although the mantel clock had just now chimed eight. It seemed impossible that she'd walked in the door only an hour ago.

A strand of hair came loose from her mobcap, tickling her nose, and she blew it out of the way. If nothing else, she'd developed a new appreciation for servants.

"An' dry it straightaway, lest the boards warp. There, that's the way; go wid the grain. I declare, ye've 'ad no trainin' t' speak of. An' look at those soft 'ands, not a callus on 'em. I'll 'ave a word wid that agency, I will, fer sendin' us such a green girl."

Gritting her teeth, Lindsey polished the clean section of floor with a linen towel. It was ever so tantalizing being here in Mansfield's library, seeing the oak writing desk against the far wall, knowing the IOU might be hidden inside it. Being observed at her work had put a twist in her scheme. But she might as well play the scene to her advantage.

"Beggin' pardon, mum," she said, affecting a low-class accent. "Can ye tell me wot 'appened to the last girl?"

"I see ye're a gossip. Ye'd best apply yerself t' yer work."

Contrary to her earlier affability, Mrs. Yardley had become a hard taskmistress. She bustled around the room with a cloth in hand, dusting delicate vases and artifacts that she clearly didn't trust to the hands of the new maid.

Lindsey hoped to appeal to the woman's talkative nature. "But . . . was she let go?" she ventured. "I surely don't want t' make the same mistake."

"Hmph. Then don't be flirtin' an' carryin' on with flashy gents. That Nelda! Always 'ad a eye above 'er station, she did."

"Was she meetin' someone of the gentry, mum?"

"Now don't be puttin' words in me mouth." The housekeeper took down an enameled box and shined it with her rag. "Nelda liked a fellow wid a little polish t' 'is manners, is all."

Lindsey sat back on her heels to look at the housekeeper. "Ye . . . ye don't think . . . she could've been caught by the Strangler, do ye?"

Mrs. Yardley chuckled and shook her head. "I never said any such nonsense. She run off wid a fellow, she did. An' good riddance t' bad rubbish."

"But . . . who was he? Where did she go?"

Mrs. Yardley gave her a sharp look. "Ye're a chatter-box, ain't ye? If ye wants t' stay on, do yer work an' mind yer own business. Now, finish up that floor whilst I run down t' check on 'Is Lordship's breakfast. The master be up early today, and I want the place done spit-spot before he comes downstairs."

Lindsey froze at her scrubbing. Her eyes widened on the puddle of water beneath her brush. Dear God, Mansfield was *awake*?

The housekeeper bustled out of the library, the ring of keys jingling at her waist. Scrambling to her feet, Lindsey wiped her damp hands on her apron. She listened with her head cocked to the side until the brisk footsteps died away. To be certain she was alone, she ventured to the door and risked a peek out to check.

The ornate corridor was empty in both directions.

Lindsey eased the door partially shut, then turned to scan the room. Several comfortable chairs were scattered here and there, along with a table holding a globe of the world and an open dictionary on a wooden stand. Under less dire circumstances, she would have been interested in perusing the shelves filled with leather-bound volumes. Did Mansfield own any adventure novels, like the ones she enjoyed reading?

She doubted it. He was a cad who wiled away the hours by gambling and seducing women. He'd probably inherited this library rather than assembled the collection of books himself.

So why was he awake at so early an hour? Did he have an appointment to keep?

The answer didn't matter. She had a limited amount of time and needed to make the best of it.

Hastening toward the desk in the corner, she bypassed the bucket and brush, taking care not to slip on the wet floorboards. The borrowed shoes clumped and squeaked, and she had the irrational fear that the sound carried out into the corridor and up the stairs, alerting Mansfield to her presence. The thought of encountering him made her want to flee out the door at once.

Nonsense. She was here in his lair and there would never be a better opportunity to do her sleuthing. She wouldn't turn coward now.

Lindsey sat down on the chair in front of the kneehole desk, glanced over her shoulder, and then reached for the top drawer. *Locked!* She tugged in frustration on each of the three drawers and encountered the same result.

Did Mansfield have the key? Or was it on Mrs. Yardley's ring?

Another possibility occurred to her. In India, her father had had a desk similar to this one. When she was little, he had allowed her to conceal herself there while playing hide-and-seek with her sisters. It had been the perfect place to elude discovery.

Lindsey felt around beneath the knee opening. In the back was a high, narrow shelf. In triumph, she pulled out a small iron key.

She inserted the key into the hole and, in a moment, pulled open the top drawer. Inside lay a neat array of quills. A penknife for sharpening the tips. A blotter and sand. All ordinary items found in any desk.

The IOU was nowhere in sight.

But in the back lay a notebook and on top of it what looked like a clipping from a news sheet. She drew out the bit of paper and unfolded it. To her shock, she was gazing down at a recent news story about the second murder.

Why would a gentleman cut out and save an article about the Serpentine Strangler? It made no sense . . . unless he had a connection to the murders.

Perhaps the earl had his way with Nelda. Perhaps she had conceived his baby, and he did away with her before the scandal could come to light. Perhaps she'll be found strangled like those other girls.

Jocelyn's words came back to haunt Lindsey. She didn't want to believe it, but his possession of this clipping seemed to lend substance to the wild theory. It was certainly a damning piece of the puzzle.

Even as she was congratulating herself on her detective skills, a sound in the passageway caught her attention.

The heavy footsteps of a man.

Chapter 8

Thane pushed open the door to the library. Before he headed to the dining room for breakfast, he wanted to review his notes on the murders and organize his thoughts. God knew, his mind hadn't been focused on the task these past few days. He could make a serious mistake by chasing after false clues or arriving at a wrongful conclusion.

He was conscious of the time ticking away. His greatest fear was that the killer would strike again before Thane could apprehend him.

In the middle of the library, a maidservant was down on her hands and knees, her back to the door as she vigorously scrubbed the wood floor. Ordinarily, he wouldn't even notice her presence. But given his current ill humor, he was annoyed by the intrusion into his sanctum.

Making a detour around an area of damp floor, he headed straight to his desk. He sat down, then reached underneath the desk for the key.

It wasn't on the shelf.

Impossible. It was always on the shelf.

Frowning, he pushed back the chair and crouched down to see if the key had fallen to the floor. He couldn't make out much in the shadowy alcove, so he reached inside and patted the floorboards with his hand. From behind him came the splashing of water and the sound of more scrubbing.

Half-turning toward the girl, he said, "Excuse me. Have you been cleaning around this desk?"

She had shifted position so that her back was still toward him. A white mobcap covered her hair and hid her face from his view. Without looking up from her work, she muttered, "Nay, m'lord."

Now that was the truth. The hand he drew back was coated with dust. Disgusted, Thane slapped his palms together, then wiped them on his black breeches, leaving gray streaks that were bound to send Bernard into a bout of apoplexy.

Blast it. Where was that key? Had he mistakenly carried it upstairs with him the previous night?

No, that wasn't his habit. There wasn't any reason to think he'd done so. Besides, if he'd left it anywhere in his bedchamber, Bernard would have called his attention to it.

Determined to have the notebook that was locked in the top drawer, Thane sat down again on the chair and scanned the floor around the desk. Damn it, one of the other maids must have been in here this morning. The key could have been knocked somewhere out of sight.

He hated when things weren't in their proper place. The discipline of the military had instilled that quality in him. In times of war, a carelessly mislaid weapon could mean the difference between life and death.

Out of the corner of his eye, he noticed that the maid was inching her bucket closer and closer to the door. There was a furtive quality to her actions that caught his attention.

He narrowed his eyes at her. That voluminous cap on her head prevented him from catching more than a glimpse of her features. Like all maids, she wore a nondescript gray gown and white apron. She appeared to be slim and fit, which meant she was neither that tiny girl, Essie, from the kitchen, nor the pudgy one who cleaned the upstairs chambers.

"You," he said. "What is your name?"

She didn't answer at once, making him wonder if she'd even heard him. Then she murmured without turning her head, "Sally."

Sally? To his knowledge, there was no maid on the staff by that moniker. Then his frown cleared. She must be the new girl Yardley had told him about, Nelda's replacement.

At least that mystery was solved.

For no reason at all, he thought of Lindsey Crompton again. Like a nagging tooth, she was always lurking at the fringes of his mind. No other woman had ever spoken to him with such cheeky animosity. Their conversation about Jocelyn had been especially troubling.

Do you ever take her on outings, to places where she can meet people her own age?

That question stirred an unwelcome guilt in him. Was he wrong to have insulated his ward from the outside world? Maybe the doctors were mistaken and Jocelyn needed more interests in her life, rather than less. Maybe he ought to have created opportunities for her to form friendships with other young girls.

The problem was that he had no female relatives to guide him in the matter. His cousin, Edward, was married, but he and his wife made their home in the country. Thane himself had been gone from society for many years. The ladies he knew were either mere acquaintances or entirely inappropriate, like Lady Entwhistle.

If you cared a whit for Jocelyn, you would make the effort to behave as a gentleman. You wouldn't consort with women of such dubious moral standards.

He clenched his jaw at the memory of Lindsey's denouncement of him. There was an unfortunate grain of truth to her words. Having the responsibility of a young ward *did* require him to have a high standard of respectability. Maybe he ought to do as Uncle Hugo had ordered and take a bride.

No, not yet. Although he did intend at some future date to do his duty and produce an heir, it wouldn't be fair to betroth himself to an innocent young miss. For the moment, he needed to be free to pursue Lady Entwhistle, as he had done the previous evening, in order to determine if one of her many lovers had done away with Maria Wilkes.

At the top of his list of suspects was Lord Wrayford, a frequent occupant of Lady Entwhistle's bed. Thane had focused his attention on Wrayford because he also lived two doors away from Lord and Lady Farthingale, who had employed the second victim.

And now Wrayford was courting Lindsey Crompton.

Not for the first time, Thane found himself worried for her safety. If Wrayford was the Strangler, she could be in grave danger. For all her acerbic nature, she was an innocent when it came to recognizing true evil. Thane tried to console himself with the reminder that Wrayford needed her dowry, so surely he wouldn't harm her before they were wed.

But afterward? What better way to claim all her money for himself than to kill her?

The thought made Thane's blood run cold. Devil take it, he needed those notes. The sooner he solved this crime, the better.

He rose to his feet, intending to go ask Yardley about the key when the housekeeper herself came bustling into the library. The stout woman stopped by the maid and gave the girl a piercing stare before glancing over at him.

"M'lord, I didn't expect t' see ye in 'ere." She bobbed a curtsy almost as an afterthought.

"Have you taken the key to my desk?" he asked.

"The key, m'lord? Why, no, why would I?"

"It's missing from its usual spot. I'd like you to ask all the servants if they've seen it. If you can't locate it, then summon a locksmith. I've important papers and other valuables in there that I need to access."

Mrs. Yardley had the oddest reaction. Releasing a huff of breath, she planted her hands on her hips and spun around toward the new maid. Her venomous look could have slain a dragon at ten paces. "Sally! Stand up this instant. If indeed 'tis yer true name."

Sally had pushed her bucket almost to the verge of the doorway. Now she froze with her hand on the scrub brush. Her head was bowed, and Thane wondered what the devil was going on.

All of a sudden, the girl sprang to her feet. Half-tripping on her clunky shoes and long hem, she made a mad dash for the corridor.

Thane reacted on instinct. He lunged after her, bypassing Mrs. Yardley and knocking over a chair in the process. The brief falter had cost the girl her escape. He seized her by the waist before she even made it out into the passageway.

His mind registered the slenderness of her form as he spun her around toward him. With his arms acting as manacles, he locked her against the door panel. She must be a thief. He'd been right to sense something amiss. . . .

One look at her face left him thunderstruck. Framed by the droopy white mobcap, she had the fine features of a lady—a lady he knew well. He was gazing down into the defiant blue eyes of Miss Lindsey Crompton.

* * *

In short order, Lindsey found herself marched back into the library by Lord Mansfield. His fingers had a bruising grip on her upper arm, and his cold expression was etched in stone. There was absolutely no way to escape, trapped as she was by the oversized shoes and his superior strength.

He righted a straight-backed chair that had been knocked over and then pushed her down onto it. "Sit."

Lindsey obeyed, although pride kept her chin high. He had every right to be furious, she reckoned. She had invaded his house, tricked his staff, and tried to deceive him, too. Once he calmed down, maybe she'd have a chance to talk her way out of this dilemma.

Mrs. Yardley swooped after them. "I'm terrible sorry, m'lord. She said she was the girl from the agency."

"I said no such thing," Lindsey objected. "You assumed it."

Mrs. Yardley shook her finger at Lindsey. "An' listen to ye talk, all 'igh-an'-mighty. Ye came 'ere to steal 'Is Lordship blind, ye did. I thought there was somethin' fishy about ye. I knew it fer sure when I went downstairs and the right girl came t' the back door."

Now that was a contingency Lindsey hadn't considered. She had been forced to make up the rules as she went along, rather than planning ahead, as she preferred to do. If only the earl hadn't come into the library, she could have completed her search of his desk and then left the house before the woman's return.

"Go on back to your work," Mansfield told Mrs. Yardley. "I'll handle this matter."

"Best t' check 'er pockets fer gold, m'lord. She belongs in Newgate, she does. I've a good mind t' send a footman fer the Watch."

"You'll do nothing of the sort," he said. "Now, go and await my instructions. And kindly close the door on your way out."

Mrs. Yardley gave Lindsey one final piqued glare, then dipped a curtsy to the earl. She flounced out of the library and pulled the door shut with a self-righteous click.

Mansfield stood watching Lindsey. He placed his hands on his hips, pushing back his dark blue coat and making her uncomfortably aware of his powerful form. A shaft of morning sunlight illuminated his unsmiling face. The scar on his cheek would have lent him a sinister aspect except for the white spot of sticking plaster where he'd cut himself shaving.

It made him look human.

She would sooner believe him a fiend from Hell.

Abruptly he stepped forward and thrust out his hand. "The key."

Denials would serve no purpose. Keeping a wary eye on him, Lindsey reached into the pocket of her apron, found the small iron key, and dropped it into his palm.

"If you must know, I never looked in your desk," she fibbed, not wanting him to know that she had seen the clipping. If only she'd had a chance to look at that notebook, too. . . . "You came in before I had the opportunity."

He dropped the key into an inner pocket of his coat. "If you think that absolves you of guilt, Miss Crompton, you're sadly mistaken. You entered my house under false pretenses. You lied to Yardley. And you intended to steal something from me." He paused. "I presume it was the IOU."

Lindsey swallowed. He mustn't realize she was investigating Nelda's disappearance, too. Mrs. Yardley had claimed Nelda had gone off somewhere with her lover, but what if the woman had been misled by Mansfield? If he was involved in Nelda's mysterious vanishing, that in itself would be compelling evidence to prove he was the Serpentine Strangler. He may have disposed of her body in such a way that it had not yet been found.

She suppressed a shiver and forced herself to meet his gaze. "Yes, the IOU. I need proof of Lord Wrayford's perfidity so that I can convince my parents he'll make an unsuitable husband."

"Is there another man you wish to marry?"

"No, of course not. I . . ." Lindsey stopped herself from blurting out that she had a better plan for her life, one that did not involve consigning herself for eternity to the custody of any man. "I find most noblemen to be either condescending bores or unprincipled rogues."

Mansfield made no reply. His eyes narrowed, he walked back and forth like a restless tiger contemplating its prey. His plain garb belied the usual veneer of the sophisticated lord and made him look more like a ruffian from the streets.

As he paced, his calculating scrutiny served to magnify her trepidation. What was he thinking? Did he intend to wreak some sort of punishment on her? But what could he really do to her?

What, indeed.

Lindsey shifted on the chair as an alarming thought occurred to her. The Serpentine Strangler had attacked only maidservants. If Mansfield was the killer, then perhaps the sight of her in this mobcap and aproned gown would turn his mind to murder.

Her heart thrumming, she started to rise. "I must return home at once. My mother will be wondering where I am—"

"Sit down, Miss Crompton. Unless you wish me to inform your parents of your actions this morning."

The silken menace of his voice made her wilt back into the chair. She could imagine the fireworks that would ensue if Mama were to find out that Lindsey had come alone to a bachelor's house, especially one with a reputation as a ladies' man. And it would make matters even worse if

Mama knew that her daughter had demeaned herself to playact as a servant.

"You wouldn't dare do that," she challenged. "My father would be well within his rights to demand that you offer for me."

"Quite so."

His easy agreement worried Lindsey, as did the calculating smile that lifted one corner of his mouth. "You wouldn't wish to be forced into a marriage to me," she stated firmly. "I'm a commoner and far beneath your notice. So you had better let me go at once, lest you be caught in your own trap."

"As you yourself pointed out recently, I need to nurture a more respectable image for Jocelyn's sake. The best way for me to do so is to acquire a wife."

Lindsey clenched her fingers in the folds of her apron. *Dear God.* What was he saying? That he *did* want to be forced into wedlock—with her? "There are scores of blue-blooded debutantes making their bow this season. Choose one of them."

He stepped closer, towering over her. "Ah, but I have *you* right here, ensnared in my web. You've saved me the trouble of sorting through all the other prospects."

He was serious. Aghast, she shook her head. "I can't marry you. I won't. We are dreadfully ill suited."

"Not in all ways." He reached down to lightly caress her cheek with his fingers. "You enjoyed my kiss, Lindsey. We would meld well together in the marriage bed."

An involuntary shiver radiated over her skin, and she flinched away from him. Yet she could still feel the effects of his touch. It had ignited a burn deep inside her, while his dark, knowing gaze sparked the memory of being held in his arms.

Jumping up, Lindsey moved behind the chair, keeping

it between them as a shield. "You must be mad to think I would ever agree to such a scheme."

"Rather, it is the most logical of plans. You'll accept my proposal, or else I'll inform your parents of what happened here this morning and your father will force you into the marriage anyway. You really have no choice in the matter."

He had her backed into a corner. It would serve no purpose to involve her parents because the outcome would be the same. If they discovered what Lindsey had done, Mama would be in a cold fury, while Papa would give her that awful, censorious look of disappointment. She remembered their anguish the previous year when Portia had run off with Colin, Viscount Ratcliffe. Lindsey couldn't bear the thought of causing her family such shame.

But the alternative was to marry Mansfield.

He was too wicked, too dictatorial, too full of his own prideful superiority. He would never allow her the freedom to live her own life as she pleased. She would be trapped in a rarified world of parties and fashion and snobby aristocrats who would always regard her common background with disdain.

And that wasn't the worst of it. What if Mansfield really *was* the Serpentine Strangler?

No one would believe a peer capable of such heinous acts, least of all her parents, who worshipped the nobility. Lindsey needed proof positive that he was the culprit. . . .

An idea sprang full-blown into her head. Why not turn the tables on him, use the situation to her advantage? By stalling, she would gain the time to investigate him. Then once she'd exposed him as a criminal, there would be no question of a betrothal.

Lifting her chin, she met his watchful eyes. "All right,

I will yield to your proposal. But you must agree to one condition."

"You're hardly in any position to make demands."

"Nevertheless, I must insist that we delay announcing the engagement until the end of the season in June. People will gossip otherwise. It will reflect badly on the both of us—and on Jocelyn—if you don't spend time courting me first."

"Courting you."

"Yes. You'll have to act the swain, send me posies, ask me to dance, write me romantic poems."

Mansfield thinned his lips. His possessive gaze swept her servant's gown as if he was weighing a postponement against the prospect of immediate ownership of her.

"A fortnight and no longer," he countered. "And there will be no poetry."

"One month," she bargained. "You'll have to permit me to visit Jocelyn, too."

He continued to stare at her in that unnerving manner. "The middle of May, then. That should be sufficient time to satisfy the gossips. And to commence our courtship, I'll call on you tomorrow at eleven."

But he didn't.

The following morning, Thane crouched beside the corpse of a young woman. Dawn was a mere thread of luminosity to the east. Its light had not yet penetrated this thicket of willows along the banks of the Serpentine.

The ground was muddy, the shadows deep, the air heavy with the odors of lush earth and murky water. By day, this bucolic area of Hyde Park was a pleasant spot to stroll. But at this early hour, fog shrouded the pathways and caressed him with icy fingers.

The fair-haired maidservant lay sprawled on her side as if sleeping. Her arms were folded neatly, her eyes closed.

The white mobcap and stark black gown confirmed her menial status. The reddened ligature mark around her neck indicated that she had been strangled.

Although he knew it was futile, he pressed his thumb to the inside of her cold wrist. Then he glanced up at Cyrus Bott, who stood over him with a lantern. "No pulse, of course."

"Exactly as I told you, m'lord," Bott said gravely.

The Bow Street Runner had already been on the scene when Thane had arrived. A messenger from the magistrate had banged on Thane's door only twenty minutes earlier and a footman had come to rouse him from bed. Thane had thrown on whatever clothing he could find. His eyes still felt gritty with sleep. By contrast, Bott looked as dapper as ever, his blue coat neatly brushed, his neck cloth perfectly arranged.

Thane had known a few like him in the military, men who arose early to preen, men who met in secret with other like-minded fellows. Thane had never been able to fathom their peculiar tastes, but he could spot them a mile off.

The grizzled old watchman who had stumbled upon the girl shuffled closer. His fearful gaze flitted to the body. "Is it . . . is it the Strangler, then?"

"Indeed so," Bott confirmed. "Now, go along with you and wait at the Hyde Street entrance. You must direct the funeral dray here when it arrives."

"Aye, sir." The man looked around fearfully as he backed away, then turned and set off at a shambling trot for the lamp-lit street outside the park.

"I don't suppose there's any indication as to the perpetrator," Bott said, hunkering down on the other side of the victim. "No cravat left this time."

Studying her, Thane shook his head. "Although that would appear to be the likely murder weapon. And judging by the stiffening of her limbs, death occurred around midnight or shortly thereafter."

Yellow lamplight spilled over the body. Thane guessed her to be around eighteen to twenty. The same age as Lindsey Crompton.

The observation pushed past the wall of his detachment, and he felt an involuntary clench of horrified anger. He had coerced Lindsey into a betrothal in order to protect her from his prime suspect, Lord Wrayford. If the bastard had strangled this woman, Thane would make him pay.

Violent death belonged on the battlefield, not here in the middle of a city park. And certainly not to a young woman who'd had her whole life ahead of her.

There was only the slightest signs of a struggle, a few broken twigs and some gouges in the soil. She must have truly believed the man to be her lover until the moment when he'd looped his cravat around her neck. She would have fought back against her attacker, but it would have been too late to save herself.

Afterward, the killer had taken the time to arrange her in this slumbering pose. He had closed her eyes and crossed her arms over her breasts. Why had he bothered?

Cyrus Bott uttered an exclamation. He was peering into a thicket of reeds just behind her. Bending down, he snatched up something small and round, then held it out in his hand.

Thane took the object from him. As he turned it in his fingers, a grim sense of purpose filled him. It was a brass button, engraved with a crosshatch pattern, and of a quality only a gentleman could afford.

Chapter 9

Standing by the window in her chamber, Lindsey tilted the front page of the newspaper to catch the dull light of late morning. Her attention was absorbed by the report with its lurid headline: *Serpentine Strangler Strikes Again*.

The previous morning, a third maidservant had been found murdered in Hyde Park. Somehow the killer had managed to steal past the watchmen patrolling the area. The circumstances were much the same as the other two murders. Residents of the surrounding area, especially Mayfair, were warned not to venture out alone.

A disturbing bit of information concerned one of the previous murders. Apparently, a gentleman's cravat had been found at the scene of the crime and was presumed to be the murder weapon.

Flora tugged on Lindsey's sleeve. Her broad features were stark with worry. "Wot's it say, miss? Wot's it say? 'Tisn't Nelda, is it?"

Lindsey had nearly forgotten the presence of her abigail. Unable to read, Flora had risked dismissal from her post in order to smuggle the newspaper out of the breakfast room while the butler's back had been turned.

Lindsey's heart went out to her. "No, the poor girl wasn't your cousin. Her name was Clara Kipp. The article reports that she was employed by the Beardsleys."

Flora fanned herself with her apron. "Oh, praise the 'eavens. I mean, I'm sorry fer 'er an' all, ye know. But it'd be 'orrible if me cousin was killed by the Strangler." Her lower lip wobbled. "Oh, wot's 'appened t' Nelda? Wot's 'appened t' 'er?"

Lindsey wished she knew. Her worst fear was that Nelda was lying dead somewhere and no one had yet found her.

She placed a comforting hand on the maid's sturdy shoulder. "We've already discussed this. Lord Mansfield's housekeeper told me that Nelda went off with a man. Are you absolutely *sure* you don't know who he might be?"

The maid vigorously shook her head. "I only seen her once a month, on me 'alf day off. Mayhap 'e was a new fellow."

"Then let's pray she sends a message to you very soon." Lindsey hesitated. She hadn't told Flora that Mrs. Yardley had hinted that Nelda's mysterious lover was a gentleman. Nor did she intend to do so. "Have you heard any rumors below stairs of who the Strangler might be?"

"Nay, miss. Ye know I'd tell ye straightaway if I did."

"Well, keep your ears open, will you? If you hear anything suspicious, please don't hesitate to let me know."

The maid's swift agreement displayed the fear that must be running rampant among the staffs of the great houses in Mayfair. Not for the first time, Lindsey wished she were privy to all the information that the Bow Street Runners must have collected on each of the murders. She had precious little to go on, other than circumstantial evidence, such as that news clipping she had discovered in Mansfield's drawer and his being with the maid at Wrayford's house.

And if the Earl of Mansfield was responsible for Nelda's disappearance, Lindsey was at a loss for how to prove it. She had expected to have the opportuntity to question him, but two days had passed since she'd been forced into that dreadful bargain in his library and she had not heard a word from him. Nor had she seen him at the ball she'd attended the previous evening.

Had he reconsidered their courtship and betrothal?

Or had he failed to call on her as promised because he'd been caught up in murderous schemes? Because he had been too busy killing that third girl and then covering his tracks?

A distinctively sharp rapping on the door startled her from the gruesome thought. She shooed Flora toward the dressing room. "That sounds like Mama. Hurry, make yourself busy. And don't worry; if you were seen taking Papa's newspaper, I'll tell her I ordered you to do so."

With a grateful nod, Flora vanished into the dressing room.

Quickly Lindsey folded the news sheet and stuffed it beneath the gold-striped cushion of a nearby chair. She smoothed the bronze silk of her skirt and then went to open the door.

Her mother swooped into the bedchamber like a ship at full sail. Girlishly slender in a gown of apple green muslin, Edith Crompton looked more like an older sister than a mother. Her stylish russet curls showed no hint of gray, and emerald earbobs glinted at her lobes.

"Lindsey! I must have a word with you this instant. The most horrid event has transpired."

The grave look on her face boded ill. Mama seldom made reference to unpleasantries. Lindsey had taken a tray in her chamber, so she could only surmise that Papa must have told Mama about the murders while reading the newspaper over breakfast. "Do you mean . . . the Serpentine Strangler?"

Her mother's lips pursed. "Certainly not. Where did you hear that distasteful story, anyway?"

"Um . . ." Lindsey fumbled for an excuse that wouldn't

get Flora into trouble. "People were whispering about it at Lord Huntington's ball yesterday evening."

"Well! I do hope you didn't join in the gossiping. It is most unseemly for a young lady to discuss such sordid matters."

"But the maid was employed by the Beardsleys. I thought Mrs. Beardsley was your friend."

"That is neither here nor there. I'm more concerned about your future. Which at the moment appears to be in great jeopardy!"

"I beg your pardon?"

Scowling, Edith Crompton paced back and forth, her skirt swishing. "The Earl of Mansfield has come to call on you. He's waiting downstairs in the drawing room."

Lindsey's heart performed a cartwheel. So he hadn't given up on that wretched betrothal scheme, after all. A plethora of emotions assaulted her, a tangled mix of excitement and trepidation. She would as soon never see him again, yet she also itched to investigate his possible role in the murders.

Pretending disinterest, she strolled to her dressing table and toyed with a blue bottle of perfume. "Isn't it a bit early in the day? I suppose he wanted to arrive ahead of any other callers."

"I made it eminently clear to him that you are not receiving. But he insists that you agreed to let him take you out for a drive."

Agreed? What an accomplished liar he was! Yet she had no choice but to go along with his fib. "I'm sorry, Mama. I must have forgotten all about it."

Edith Crompton stalked to her side, seized the glass bottle, and set it down with a thump. "*Forgotten.* How did Lord Mansfield arrive at the notion that you would welcome his courtship, anyway? Never mind, I know the answer. You were seen leaving the ballroom with him the other night. The Duchess of Milbourne took great pleasure in informing me of that fact!"

Lindsey struggled against a blush. Was that all Mama knew?

She certainly hoped so. The betrothal would happen much sooner than the middle of May if someone had seen her locked in a passionate embrace with Lord Mansfield.

"We merely had a polite conversation," she said. "I've done the same with a good number of other gentlemen. Would you rather me be rude to the earl?"

Mrs. Crompton eyed her suspiciously. "He has a wicked reputation. I've heard that he keeps a fifteen-year-old girl in the house adjoining his. A girl who is of no relation to him."

Lindsey found the insinuation monstrous, even given her dislike for Mansfield. But Mama mustn't know that she'd met Jocelyn. "The girl is his ward. And I believe she's crippled, too. Surely you're not suggesting anything unseemly could be going on."

"One never knows with his sort. He must not be encouraged, do you hear me? Now, Lord Wrayford is due to arrive at any moment. I've asked him to come here in the hopes that you would go on a drive with *him*."

Nothing could be more unwelcome. Lindsey remembered the last time he'd taken her out in his carriage. He'd tried to plant a slobbery kiss on her mouth and she'd had to jam her elbow into his side to make him stop.

"Really, Mama! It isn't fitting to push me at Lord Wrayford. What will he think of us?"

"He has been most welcoming of my intervention. And you would do well to encourage him. He is the heir to the old Duke of Sylvester, after all, and very soon he will outrank Lord Mansfield."

"But . . . Lord Wrayford is a gambler. I heard some

ladies whispering that he owes large debts. That won't make Papa very happy."

"Nonsense, he's a fine, upstanding gentleman who will make you a duchess someday. Only think, your firstborn son will someday be a duke." Mrs. Crompton eyed her critically, then reached out to straighten the sleeve of Lindsey's gown. "Now, do come along, darling. You must tell the earl that you have made other plans."

Thane was sitting forward on an elegant but uncomfortable gold-striped settee, his elbows resting on his knees, when the sound of approaching footsteps came from the corridor.

He had been ruminating about the possible owner of the button found at the scene of the third murder. Cyrus Bott had handled the inquiries at various tailors' around town, while Thane had questioned the watchmen who had been on duty that night, only to learn nothing of value. Now, he banished all thought of the Strangler, sat up straight, and affixed a pleasant smile to his face.

But it wasn't Lindsey or her dragon of a mother who entered.

It was Wrayford.

Dressed to the nines in a pale blue coat and tan breeches, Wrayford carried a gold-topped walking stick that was pure pretension. His face had the florid complexion of a man who routinely imbibed too much drink. From his styled sandy hair to the polished tips of his brown shoes, he looked ready for courtship.

Wrayford stopped dead in his tracks. "You!" he exclaimed, his genial expression altering to suspicion. "What the devil are *you* doing here, Mansfield?"

Nothing could have been more providential. Thane had intended to seek him out for questioning later in the day. Now he had the chance to milk this opportunity for all it was worth. "I could ask the same of you."

"I'm here to take Miss Crompton out for a drive."

Thane stretched his arms out along the back of the sofa. "It seems you'll have to wait your turn, then."

Wrayford's face flushed a deeper red and his sandy brows lowered in a scowl. He stood there, nostrils flaring like a bull in a Spanish fighting ring. With an abrupt huff of released breath, he charged forward, gripping the stick like a cudgel. "Why, you knave—!"

Thane tensed his muscles without abandoning his relaxed pose. He was prepared to spring into action if need be. But Wrayford must have seen the menace in Thane's gaze, because he stopped short a few feet distant.

"This is deliberate," he snapped, shaking the cane. "You've no real interest in Miss Crompton. You're trying to stop me from paying off my markers."

"Don't be absurd. I certainly do want the thousand guineas you lost to me in that dice game."

"Blackguard! Then don't interfere with my courtship of her!"

"It may be best to lower your voice," Thane advised. "You wouldn't want Miss Crompton—or her father—to learn just how close you are to drowning in River Tick."

Compressing his lips, Wrayford glanced over his shoulder at the arched doorway and the empty corridor beyond it. Then he cast a spiteful look at Thane and hissed, "You're wasting your time here. Mrs. Crompton prefers *me* as a suitor."

"I very much doubt Mr. Crompton will be pleased to hear that news."

"What? You know I was referring to her daughter. And why are you poaching in *my* territory, anyway?"

"Maybe I've decided it's time I took a wife."

Thane pretended it was the most logical decision in the world when in fact it had been an act of supreme idiocy. He had embarked on the course on the spur of the moment, when he had caught Lindsey in his library, dressed like a maid and plotting to rifle through his desk for that damned IOU. Any lady who would go to such extreme lengths to rid herself of a suitor had to be nothing but trouble.

Yet there was something about her that robbed him of reason. Perhaps it was that lush mouth, so temptingly kissable, or her disdainful manner that challenged him to sweeten her disposition.

No, it was merely chivalry that obliged him to protect her from a suspected murderer. He need never go through with the betrothal if sufficient evidence to implicate Wrayford could be found.

Wrayford shook the walking stick. "Pick another girl. You don't need an heiress. You're well set for funds."

"Is that all she is to you—a bank account?"

"Of course not. She's a fine specimen of a female. Why else would a man shackle himself to such a proper young lady?"

"You seem more suited to a merry widow like Lady Entwhistle."

A crafty look entered Wrayford's pale blue eyes. "Speak for yourself, old chap. The two of you looked quite cozy at that ball the other night. Miss Crompton had some choice words to say about your little tête-à-tête."

Had she?

Thane could well imagine Lindsey denouncing him. But he could hardly correct her mistaken assumptions. She mustn't know the real reason for his conversation with Lady Entwhistle, that he had been gathering information about the woman's various lovers.

"Have a seat, Wrayford. We'll let Miss Crompton make

her own decision." Thane deliberately eyed him up and down. "That's quite a handsome cravat you're wearing. Where do you purchase your neck cloths?"

"Eh?" Taking the bait, Wrayford sank into a chair and cast a prideful glance down at the elaborate folds of white linen. "At Stapleton's, of course."

Thane knew the establishment. If Bernard could connect the cravat left at the second crime scene to Stapleton's, that would help build a case against Wrayford.

"Did you tie it yourself, or is that the work of your valet? Perhaps I'll send my man, Bernard, over to study his technique."

"Not a chance. My valet will never give up his secrets. Too bad you'll never be able to duplicate this style."

Damn. It would have been helpful for Bernard to have the chance to search Wrayford's dressing room for a coat that was missing a brass button with a crosshatch pattern. From information he'd coaxed out of Lady Entwhistle, Thane knew that Wrayford had a taste for maidservants and bondage. But was there a connection between him and the third victim?

Thane was casting about for a way to ask Wrayford how well he knew the Beardsleys when the approach of footsteps again drew his gaze to the doorway. Mrs. Crompton swept into the drawing room with Lindsey lagging a few steps behind.

As Thane rose to his feet, Wrayford leaped out of his chair and rushed to bow over Lindsey's hand. "My dear, you look utterly charming today, as always."

For once, Wrayford spoke the truth. Lindsey Crompton was a goddess in bronze silk that skimmed her body and hinted at womanly curves. The color enhanced the richness of her upswept brown hair, while the scoop neckline revealed a tantalizing glimpse of beautiful breasts—a portion of her anatomy that Wrayford had noticed, too.

The damned lecher was gawking.

Fists clenched, Thane started forward. In three steps, he caught himself short. What the devil was he thinking—to knock Wrayford to the floor right here in the drawing room? That would make a fine impression on the ladies.

He forced himself to relax, to lower his head in a bow. "Miss Crompton. It's always a pleasure."

Extracting her hand from Wrayford's, Lindsey afforded Thane a guarded smile. "Lord Mansfield. How good of you to call."

Good? So, aloofness was the game she intended to play. "Surely you've been expecting me. We spoke the other day of going for a drive."

She regarded him impassively. "Did we? I . . ."

"I'm afraid my daughter is not allowed to make promises to gentlemen without my permission," Mrs. Crompton said. "Whatever she said to you must be rescinded."

"Quite so," Wrayford interjected. "I'm sure Miss Crompton would far rather go for a drive with *me*."

"Perhaps," Thane said, "we should allow the lady to choose for herself. If she's to be known as someone who does not keep her word, it should be by her own decision."

He looked straight into Lindsey's beautiful blue eyes and she met his gaze without flinching. It was impossible to read her thoughts. Would she call his bluff?

He'd never had any real intention of tattling to her parents about her intrusion into his house. What kind of man would he be to force a lady into marriage by such dastardly means?

But she had believed his assertion that morning in his library, and he hoped she still did now. Claiming her for himself was the best way to keep Wrayford at bay. Despite Lindsey's conviction that the IOU would bring her salvation, Thane seriously doubted that learning of Wrayford's massive gambling debts would deter

Mrs. Crompton from an ambition to marry her daughter to a duke's heir.

Lindsey slid a glance at her mother. Then she gave Thane a cool nod. "You're quite right, my lord. It seems I must honor my promise to you."

Chapter 10

Lindsey could feel her mother's angry stare boring into her back as Mansfield helped her up into his open phaeton. It took a bit of maneuvering with her skirts to achieve the high perch. Primly she settled herself on the leather cushions while he untied the reins and then leaped up beside her.

As he directed the black horse away from the curbstone, she caught one last view of her mother standing in the doorway, Wrayford glaring over her shoulder. A perverse sense of liberation made Lindsey smile and wave good-bye. It was unkind of her to feel so pleased at thwarting her mother's wishes—and Wrayford's. Yet Lindsey experienced a buoyancy of spirit nonetheless.

"It appears your mother doesn't approve of me," Mansfield said. "I suspect there'll be a price to pay when you return home."

Amusement glinted in his keen dark eyes. The warmth there caught Lindsey off guard, causing an unexpected clutch inside her bosom. Blast him, he wasn't the charming man he appeared to be on the surface. He was a cad who would stoop to blackmailing a lady into marriage. A rogue who flirted with loose women like Lady Entwhistle.

A villain who might well be a murderer.

"Mama has her mind set on a match with Lord Wrayford," Lindsey said, folding her gloved hands in her lap and striving for a casual demeanor. "I could discredit him as a gambler if only I had the proof that you took from me."

"Forget about that IOU. It will serve to discredit *me* as a gambler, too, when I seek the approval of your parents. Besides, Wrayford will cease to be of any importance once you and I announce our betrothal."

Lindsey pursed her lips and pretended an interest in the passing row of elegant houses. Clearly, the earl believed she was quaking in terror at the prospect of him revealing the truth about her stealing into his home, clad as a maidservant. He presumed her to be cowed and intimidated at the notion of facing her parents' wrath.

That had been her initial reaction.

But Lindsey had conquered her fear of being forced into a hasty marriage. Now that she'd had ample time to reflect on the matter, she had no intention of going through with any wedding. She was determined to stand her ground. No matter what brouhaha the earl might stir with Mama and Papa, no matter how dire the threat of scandal, she would refuse to speak her vows to a man she barely knew.

A man who might have strangled three maidservants.

How incongruous it was to ponder such a horror as she sat beside him, the well-sprung carriage gently rocking along the cobbled street. With the sun shining and a gentle breeze stirring the ribbons of her bonnet, it seemed impossible that he could have any part in such dark deeds. Nevertheless, she was pretending to go along with his courtship scheme because it offered her the opportunity to investigate him. He had too many uncanny connections to the murders—and she didn't believe in coincidences.

The very first time Lindsey had met him, Mansfield had been in the company of a pretty maidservant.

At another ball, she had seen him flirting with Lady Entwhistle, who'd employed one of the victims of the Serpentine Strangler.

And Flora's cousin, Nelda, had mysteriously vanished from his household—although, to be fair, her body had not been found. Did Mansfield know what had happened to her? Had he played a role in her disappearance?

Had he kept that news clipping so he could revel in his notoriety?

Somehow, Lindsey had to uncover the truth.

The earl slowed the phaeton to allow an elderly couple to hobble across the street. When he clucked softly, the horse resumed a brisk trot, its glossy black mane swinging. The harness jingled in rhythm with the clopping of hooves.

Abruptly Mansfield startled Lindsey by transferring the ribbons to one hand and reaching over to cover her hands in her lap. "You needn't look so worried," he murmured. "As we become better acquainted, you'll see that I'm not an ogre."

The warmth of his fingers made her heart beat faster. Those persuasive brown eyes invited her to lean toward him—but she held herself rigidly upright. "You sound very certain of yourself."

Smiling, he withdrew his hand. "You'll have to judge for yourself. However, women usually find me to be considerate."

"Considerate? You were supposed to call on me yesterday, not today."

His eyes narrowed ever so slightly, rendering his gaze unreadable. "I must beg your pardon. There was an unexpected business matter that required my full attention."

Lindsey bit her lip to keep from asking him if he'd

been hiding out after strangling a maidservant. "It was remiss of you not to have sent word to me."

"You're entirely right. It shan't happen again. Now, if we're to be engaged soon, perhaps you ought to tell me about your family. You have two sisters, do you not?"

"Yes," she said, relieved to change the subject. "Portia is the eldest. She married Viscount Ratcliffe last year and they're expecting their first child in a few months. Blythe is sixteen and still in the schoolroom. She's already begging Mama to make her debut next spring, although Papa wants her to wait another year."

"Hmm." Mansfield narrowed his eyes at Lindsey. "Perhaps you'll do me a favor."

"What do you mean?"

"Blythe is nearly the same age as Jocelyn. I'd like for you to bring her to visit my ward."

The invitation took Lindsey aback. "But you won't allow anyone to call on Jocelyn, remember? The doctors said she might become overwrought."

"I've reconsidered the situation since we last spoke. And I've decided you're right, it would do her good to have a friend or two."

He had heeded her advice? The notion gratified Lindsey, but only for a moment. The last thing she needed was for Blythe to get in the way of her sleuthing. "I rather doubt Mama would permit such a visit, since she's so set on me marrying Wrayford. She won't want to encourage any connection to you."

"Then I shall have to charm her into changing her mind."

Hands loosely on the reins, Mansfied looked utterly confident as he turned his gaze ahead to the street. The scar on his cheek was hidden from her view. Unlike other gentlemen who were out and about, he wore no hat and his black hair was tousled, a lock falling down onto his brow. His aura of brooding intensity brought to mind a fallen angel.

Awareness of him as a man hummed through her veins. She had little use for romance, so why did he fascinate her so? Perhaps because she couldn't quite grasp his true character, and curiosity had always been her bane. Somehow she had to expose him as a conniving rogue.

Lindsey drew a deep breath. "I've been wondering. . . ."

He cast an inquiring glance at her. "Go on."

"The other morning, your housekeeper was expecting a maid from an agency. She told me I was replacing a servant named Nelda."

"And?"

"Well . . . I was curious as to what happened to Nelda."

"Happened?" He frowned, his voice turning cool and dismissive. "She left, as servants are wont to do. I don't keep track of the staff. Mrs. Yardley might know—you may ask her if you like."

Lindsey found the subtle chilling of his demeanor highly intriguing. As a child in India, she had taught herself to notice nuances of character. She'd spent much of her time lingering in the shadows, eavesdropping on the conversations of the adults and observing the petty spats between the servants. Now she had the distinct impression there was more to the story than Mansfield let on.

His inscrutable expression was difficult to read, though. He had no nervous mannerisms like evasive glances or foot tapping, as she'd seen in other people. Of course, she was fast learning that he was an extremely shrewd man unlike anyone else she'd ever met.

What was he hiding?

As Mansfield drove along the residential street, she caught tantalizing glimpses of movement inside the windows. So many people, so many different lives. Where did the next victim of the Serpentine Strangler work? In one of these aristocratic homes?

According to the newspaper report, the killer had throttled his victims to death with a cravat. Lindsey's gaze slid to Mansfield's neatly tied white neck cloth, and she shuddered to imagine it being used to choke one of those poor women.

As they neared a busy intersection, she made a swift decision. "Pray don't take me to the park. I would prefer to visit a friend instead."

He glanced at her. "A friend."

"An acquaintance, really." Lindsey deemed it best not to claim *too* close of a relationship, since she only knew the girl as the daughter of one of Mama's circle, someone who had made her debut the previous year with Lindsey's older sister, Portia.

"Who?"

Lindsey watched him closely. "Perhaps you know her. Miss Frances Beardsley."

One of his eyebrows arched as he looked at the street ahead. "Beardsley," he mused. "The name sounds familiar. . . . You must forgive me. I haven't been back in society for very long."

Had that been a flash of guilt on his face? It was gone so swiftly Lindsey wasn't certain. "You may have seen her name in the newspaper this morning."

Mansfield's mouth twisted. "Do you read the newspapers, then? I can't imagine your mother approving of such racy behavior."

Was he teasing? Or attempting to distract her? And why was she staring at his lips and remembering the taste of his kiss?

"Never mind Mama. The Beardsleys employed a maid by the name of Clara Kipp. She was found murdered yesterday morning in Hyde Park. I should like to offer my condolences."

"Ah, now I recall the story. She was attacked by the villain they're calling the Serpentine Strangler."

His face indicated only sympathy mixed with a trace of revulsion. It was exactly the reaction Lindsey would expect of a well-mannered gentleman. Yet there was a tension about him that would seem to hint at deeper knowledge of the case. If he was the killer, he must have made contact with the maid during a visit to the Beardsleys' house. When else would he have done so?

Lindsey decided to risk one more question. "I wonder . . . is it possible that Nelda might have been a victim of the Serpentine Strangler, too?"

Mansfield subjected her to a hard stare. "Is that what's made you on edge today? You may set your mind at ease. If she'd been murdered, her remains would have been discovered by now."

"But if her body was well hidden . . ."

"Nonsense. The Strangler left his three victims in the middle of Hyde Park. He obviously wanted them to be found. And that's quite enough wild speculation. Crime is hardly an appropriate topic to be discussed during a courtship."

Lindsey opened her mouth to deny they were courting. But she swallowed the words. How could he be so certain about the murders anyway? Had the newspaper specified exactly where in Hyde Park the poor women had been found? She couldn't recall.

Noticing that Mansfield had turned the horse onto Albemarle Street, she exclaimed, "I thought you weren't acquainted with the Beardsleys! So how do you know their address?"

He shrugged. "The newspaper must have mentioned the street. I presume you know the number?"

Lindsey did, from the endless rounds of calls she had made with her mother to all the finest homes in Mayfair. "It's the house with the ornate entryway," she said, pointing discreetly. "The third one from the end."

Although the hour was still early for visiting, a coach already waited out front. To her dismay, it bore the silver thistle insignia of the dukes of Milbourne.

Oh, no. Mama had cultivated an acquaintance with the elderly duchess, who was one of society's biggest gossips. Being seen here with the Earl of Mansfield would be a declaration of their courtship. And besides, Mama likely would find out that they'd come here.

Why, oh why, hadn't she considered that possibility?

As he drew up behind the coach, Lindsey said hastily, "There seems to be another visitor. Perhaps it would be best for me to return at another time."

"Nonsense. We're here already. It'll only take a few moments for you to pay your respects."

He jumped down and went to secure the horse to an iron post, leaving her to fume on the high seat. What an arrogant, dictatorial man! He was supposed to defer to a lady's wishes, rather than override her decision. But short of making a nasty scene on a public street, Lindsey had to exit the phaeton.

Climbing down, she felt with her slippered toe for the iron step. Two strong hands seized her by the waist from behind. As the earl easily swung her to the ground, momentum caused her to brush against his muscled form.

The contact was a jolt to her senses. A whiff of spice stirred the mad impulse to follow the scent to its source, to press her lips to his throat. It brought to mind that searing kiss out in the garden when she'd been held within the circle of his arms.

Now, his fingers brushed caressingly over her abdomen.

Instantly her legs turned to molten wax and she might have stumbled if not for his firm hold on her.

"Don't *do* that," she muttered through gritted teeth.

Pulling free, Lindsey summoned all of her dignity and marched toward the front door. His low chuckle grated on her nerves. Strolling at her side, he murmured, "Come now, Miss Crompton. It isn't as if I've never before touched you."

"This is a public street," she hissed. "You will keep your hands to yourself."

"And when we're alone? Will you allow me liberties then?"

His dark eyes laughed down at her. He looked breath-stoppingly handsome in the sunlight, his chocolate brown coat a perfect match for his eyes. But she was too clever to fall for his dangerous charm.

She grabbed hold of the brass knocker and rapped hard. "I'll allow you to treat me as a lady."

"I believe—"

Thankfully, the door opened and cut off his words. A footman admitted them into a luxurious entrance hall cluttered with Greek statuary and tall columns. A few minutes later, they were led upstairs to a crimson and gold drawing room, where the ancient, horse-faced Duchess of Milbourne sat across from plump Mrs. Beardsley and her frivolous blond daughter, Miss Frances Beardsley.

Mrs. Beardsley, who resembled an overstuffed pouter pigeon in gray silk, fluttered forward to greet them. "Why, this is a surprise!" She looked expectantly at the doorway. "And where is your mother today, Miss Crompton?"

"I'm afraid she had other calls to make."

Lindsey hoped they wouldn't question the lame excuse. It was one thing to accompany Mama and sit quietly listening to the chatter of the ladies. It was quite another to face three avid-eyed gossips while in the company of an infamous gentleman.

Enthroned on a blue chair, the Duchess of Milbourne wrapped her gnarled fingers around an ivory-topped cane. She looked up her long nose at the earl. "Ah, Mansfield. How is Hugo these days? Have you been to Oxfordshire yet to visit him?"

Mansfield bowed over her hand. "Indeed I have. My uncle is as cantankerous as ever."

"His rheumatism, no doubt. You should encourage him to take the mineral waters at Bath." Her sharp blue eyes pierced Lindsey. "As for you, Miss Crompton, I'm surprised at Edith's lenience. In my day we never allowed young bucks to escort unmarried ladies on their calls."

Lindsey dipped the obligatory curtsy. "I'm sure you're right, Your Grace. But I trust it will be acceptable since our families have become such fast friends."

"Hmm." She glared from Lindsey to Mansfield and back again. "Nevertheless, I would have expected Wrayford to accompany you."

"I outfoxed the poor fellow by arriving earlier than him," Mansfield said. "As the Bard once wrote, all's fair in love and war."

Love? Lindsey gritted her teeth. Blast him for pretending to be the smitten swain. He was merely using her to provide himself with a semblance of respectability.

In the midst of her incendiary thoughts, he steered her to a chaise, applying subtle pressure to her arm and compelling her to take a place right beside him. She perched rigidly on the edge of the cushion, her hands folded in her lap, a polite smile fixed on her lips. So much for sitting in a chair across the room in the hopes of fostering the illusion that they were *not* a couple.

The three ladies watched avidly. The duchess was the one who had relayed the gossip to Lindsey's mother about

Lindsey venturing into the garden with him a few nights ago. But had anyone see him kissing her? She certainly hoped not.

"*I* never go out without my mother," said Miss Frances Beardsley. She leaned toward Mansfield, her face framed by a halo of blond curls and the gauzy pink dress clinging to her bosom. "That way, there is never the slightest hint of impropriety."

Mrs. Beardsley gave her daughter a doting smile. "You are indeed the essence of modesty, my dear. Of course, *you* have had the benefit of the very best English upbringing."

Frances batted her pale lashes at Mansfield. "For a lady, there is no substitute for proper instruction in the womanly arts."

Lindsey refrained from rolling her eyes. She couldn't help wondering if what her sister Blythe had heard was true, that Frances had been caught kissing one of the footmen. Not that Lindsey would ever lower herself to their level of malicious gossip. The Beardsleys never missed a chance to make snide remarks about the Crompton girls' having grown up in India. Frances Beardsley had played the very same tricks on Lindsey's sister Portia.

"How very fortunate you are," Lindsey said with a hint of sarcasm that she knew would fly right over the girl's head. "While you were studying with dancing and pianoforte masters, *I* was learning to track a tiger through the jungle and to ride on the back of an elephant."

"Indeed!" exclaimed the Duchess of Milbourne. "It is hard to believe Edith would permit such abominations."

Mrs. Beardsley gasped. "How very primitive. Why, I don't know how she bore such a life for so many years."

"With great enthusiasm, one would hope," Mansfield said. "There's a fascinating world out there. It would benefit all young ladies to have firsthand knowledge of it. I'm sure Miss Crompton could tell us many interesting tales about her life in India."

He turned to study her, a half smile crooking his mouth. All three ladies leaned forward in disgusted expectation.

Lindsey found herself caught in a quandary. She could regale them for hours with stories about watching the monkeys playing in the banyan trees near her house, baking in the heat of a sun so bright it hurt the eyes, or spying on the wizened holy men who performed strange rituals before statues of Hindu gods and goddesses. Sometimes that life seemed like a magical dream to her, as if it had happened to someone else.

But she hadn't come here to talk about herself.

"Perhaps another time," she said. "Mrs. Beardsley, I hope you'll forgive my forwardness, but I came to offer you my condolences. It must have been a terrible shock to learn about the tragedy that befell your maidservant."

The atmosphere in the drawing room altered abruptly, as if a chill wind had leached every vestige of warmth from the air.

Frances uttered a squeak of dismay. Leaning close to her mother, she said in a loud whisper, "I told you, Mama, everyone will be visiting today, wanting to talk about that horrid event. I don't know if I can bear it."

"Shh, darling," her mother said, reaching over to pat the girl's hand. "It is dreadful, to be sure, but we must face the tittle-tattle with our heads held high. It is hardly our fault that that one of the staff was foolish enough to be nabbed by the Strangler."

The duchess thumped the tip of her cane on the floor. "The chit ought never have been sneaking out at night to meet her beau. If she came to a bad end, she has only herself to blame."

During the exchange, Lindsey had been keeping a surreptitious eye on Mansfield, hoping to spot some indication of his culpability. But his face revealed only thoughtful interest in the flow of conversation.

His gaze on their hostess, he said, "Are you quite certain she was going out to meet a man? Did she say so?"

"Say so, my lord?" Mrs. Beardsley repeated, fanning her plump face with a lacy handkerchief. "Why, how would I know? I would hardly engage in chitchat with a servant."

"Clara brought me my hot chocolate every morning," Frances piped up. "But she never spoke except to apologize once for forgetting my extra pot of cream."

He cocked an eyebrow. "Perhaps she confided in one of the other servants. Did she have any particular friends on the staff?"

Why was the earl pursuing the topic? Lindsey wondered. Was it idle curiosity . . . or did he want to ascertain if anyone knew he himself had romanced the maidservant in secret and lured her to her death?

"That vile Bow Street Runner might know," Mrs. Beardsely said with a sniff. "He interviewed the staff for hours. Why, I needed a whiff of hartshorn afterward, to recover from my distress."

"A Runner?" Lindsey's ears perked up. Ever since arriving in London, she had heard tales about the exploits of that famous band of detectives. They worked on cases assigned by the chief magistrate at Bow Street. She felt a keen stab of envy at the thought of having the freedom to solve crimes. What a curse it was to be born female! "Who was he, if I might ask?"

"I believe his name was Cyrus Bott." Mrs. Beardsley spat out the name like a curse. "A low sort, with the pretensions of a gentleman. He dared to infer that I permit my staff to leave this house at will."

The duchess snorted. "Commoners! They've no inkling of how to comport themselves around their betters."

Cyrus Bott. Lindsey committed the name to memory.

Somehow, she had to figure out an excuse to talk to him, to learn what he knew about the Serpentine Strangler. The trouble was, Mama would be livid if Lindsey lowered herself to speak to Bott. She was likely to find herself locked in her chamber, as Mama and Papa had once done to Portia, after she had gone off with the wicked and handsome Lord Ratcliffe.

"And what is worse," Mrs. Beardsley went on, "a nasty reporter came nosing around the kitchen yesterday. If not for his poking and prying, we might have been spared that dreadful notice in the newspaper. He harangued my servants with questions. He even had the temerity to follow one of the maids above stairs, to the corridor outside this very room."

"Good heavens!" exclaimed the duchess, her narrow face flushed with outrage as she clutched her cane. "Ever since the revolt in France, the riffraff have become entirely too bold. I hope you had one of the footmen throw him out on his ear."

"Luckily, Lord Wrayford had come to call," Frances said, with a sly glance at Lindsey. "He chased the man out of the house. It was truly quite heroic of him."

Clearly, she hoped Lindsey would be distraught at the news of Wrayford's visit. Mama had dropped plenty of hints among her friends that she was set on Lindsey making a match with him.

But Lindsey was only half-listening.

Out of the corner of her eye, she saw that Mansfield had straightened up. An aura of alertness radiated from him, and his eyes were intent on Frances.

"Wrayford was here?" he asked. "Tell me, does he often—"

Whatever the earl had been about to ask was cut off as a footman entered the drawing room to announce the arrival of another visitor. White-haired Lady Grantham, another of Mama's acquaintances, hobbled into the chamber, and Mrs. Beardsley rose to greet her.

Lindsey found herself intrigued by the muscle that tightened in Mansfield's jaw. Why did he look inordinately perturbed by the interruption? What was so important about his aborted question? Did he merely see Wrayford as a rival for her affections?

Or was it something more?

Chapter 11

"You received another bouquet from Mr. Sykes this morning," Blythe announced the moment Lindsey walked into the breakfast room the next day. Her sister was sitting with their father, who was absorbed in his newspaper. "I'm afraid it's daisies again."

"Mmm." Lindsey headed to the sideboard to add toast and sausage to her plate. She had no interest in the stuttering young man whom she'd briefly seen at a party the previous night. Her thoughts, as always, were on Mansfield. He had not attended, much to her frustration. Where had he spent the evening?

"I wouldn't care for a man who only sent me daisies," Blythe said, taking a dainty sip of tea. "I would vastly prefer roses or lilies . . . or, better yet, jewelry. Diamonds, to be specific."

"Don't be absurd. A young lady cannot accept jewelry from a suitor." Lindsey brought her plate to the table. "By the by, where is Mama today?"

"I hope she's getting dressed, since we have a big day planned."

Their father looked up from his newspaper. A pair of spectacles perched on the end of his nose, he gave Blythe an absentminded smile. "Actually, I'm afraid she awakened with a megrim. She'll be remaining abed this morning."

Blythe let her fork clatter to her plate. "Papa! I've been sitting here for ten minutes already and you never even told me that."

"You didn't ask."

"But what about the shopping trip? Mama promised to take Linds and me to Regent Street this morning."

"It shall have to be postponed. You're not to disturb your mother until the afternoon."

"But—"

"No complaining, child," George Crompton said, drilling her with a glare that hinted at his success in the business world. "You should show a bit more sympathy for your mother's plight. Be a good girl now and let me finish my reading before I have to leave for the docks."

Rattling the newspaper, he nodded to a footman to refill his cup of coffee.

Blythe pursed her lips and lapsed into pouting silence. She picked up her fork and trailed the tines through the remains of egg yolk on her plate. Since she wasn't yet allowed to wear her hair up, she had tied back her auburn curls with a vivid ribbon that matched her best blue gown.

Lindsey felt a flash of sympathy as she took the seat opposite her sister. *Poor Blythe.* She was usually the last one to come down to breakfast—except on shopping days. How she must have been looking forward to escaping the stern tutelage of Miss Underhill for a few hours.

Lindsey, on the other hand, regarded the cancellation as an unforeseen blessing.

Spreading plum jam on her toast, she contemplated the prospect of a free morning, unencumbered by obligation. There were so many actions to be done in regard to solving the murders, she hardly knew where to begin. Surreptitiously she peered at her father's newspaper to see if there was any new information about the crimes. But the headlines on the front page dealt with a problem at the Bank of England, a rash of burglaries in Covent Garden, and a trade agreement with Italy.

Lindsey needed to learn more information about the victims of the Serpentine Strangler, to see if there might have been a connection among them. Having discovered what little she could from the Beardsleys, she hoped to sleuth in the fine houses where the other two murdered maidservants had worked. With all the society obligations that usually filled her days, she might never have a better opportunity than right now.

But Blythe's woebegone face brought on an attack of conscience. Lindsey understood exactly how it felt to be underage and confined to the schoolroom. Perhaps there was a way to accomplish more than one objective today.

She waited until her father set down the newspaper to slice the kippers on his plate. "Papa, might I be allowed to take Blythe out? Kasi could come along with us to chaperone."

Blythe's drooping posture perked up at the prospect. "Why, what a brilliant notion!"

George Crompton cast a distracted glance from one sister to the other. "Your mother makes these decisions. She'll be better within a day or two."

Clasping her folded hands to her bosom, Blythe gave him a soulful look. "*Please,* Papa. I *never* have a chance to go out. If I have to spend one more moment confined in this house, I vow I shall *die*."

A wry twinkle entered his brown eyes, and his mouth eased into a smile. "Indeed? Well, then, to spare myself the expense of a funeral, I suppose I must concede. Now cease your chattering lest I, too, end up with a megrim."

A mere half an hour later, a footman admitted Lindsey and Blythe to the sitting room at Jocelyn's town house. A week had passed since Lindsey's last visit and it was as if nothing had changed here. Fisk, the elderly companion, still sat snoozing in the chair by the fire. Her chin was propped on the brown fabric stretched over her ample bosom, and a white widow's cap crowned her gray hair.

Jocelyn lay on a nearby chaise, a blanket draped over her legs. She was drawing in a sketch pad on her lap desk. If not for the fact that she wore a yellow gown today instead of green, Lindsey would have thought the girl hadn't stirred an inch.

A glow of delight lit Jocelyn's elfin face as she set aside her artwork. "Lindsey! I was afraid you'd never come back!"

At the sound of her voice, Fisk gave a loud snore and came awake with a start. She blinked her bovine eyes in bewilderment. "Aye, miss. Wot is it?"

"I've visitors," Jocelyn said with a smile. "You may go on down to the kitchen until I ring for you."

Fisk obediently pushed up from the chair and lumbered off, bobbing a curtsy to Lindsey and Blythe on her way out. The servant gazed askance at Kasi, her round form swathed in a rich purple sari, who already had settled herself on a stool by the door.

The aging Hindu servant gave Fisk an unblinking stare that as children Lindsey and her sisters had dubbed the Evil Eye. Clearly alarmed, Fisk made a wide berth around her and vanished out into the corridor, the sound of her footsteps fading away. Lindsey considered chiding Kasi, but the old ayah was already irked at being coerced into keeping this visit a secret from Lindsey's parents.

Turning her attention to Jocelyn, Lindsey said, "I've brought my sister Blythe this time. You're almost the same age and I thought you might enjoy meeting each other. Blythe, this is Miss Jocelyn Nevingford."

Blythe glided to the chaise to shake the girl's hand.

"Hullo. We decided to come and visit you instead of going to the shops."

"Oh!" A look of sheer envy shone in Jocelyn's green eyes. "Do you mean Bond Street? Or Regent Street—or both? I would love to go there if only I could. Please sit down right here and tell me, what is it like?"

"It's wonderful. Did you know there is a shop entirely devoted to corsets? And another that deals only in fans?" Blythe plopped down on a stool beside the chaise and launched into a detailed description of the best milliners, shoemakers, and glove purveyors that were frequented by the upper crust.

Hiding a smile, Lindsey took the wing chair that Fisk had occupied. No one would guess she'd had the very devil of a time convincing Blythe to forgo the shopping expedition in favor of calling on an invalid. Blythe had had her heart set on finding a new straw bonnet to match one of her pelisses. Unlike Lindsey, who found the whole process tedious, her sister could spend hours examining bolts of fabric, selecting a fan, or poring over the latest issue of *La Belle Assemblée* to determine the most flattering style of gown.

Yet Blythe had been generous enough to postpone the trip. She now looked to be having great fun, chattering with Jocelyn as if they were fast friends.

"It's truly dreadful about your accident," Blythe was saying in her usual forthright manner, "but I don't believe that being crippled should keep you from going to the shops."

Jocelyn gave a wistful sigh. "But how would I ever manage? And I couldn't bear to see people pointing at me and whispering."

"Oh, pooh. They'll do no such thing. And even if they did, well, Lord Mansfield is your guardian, is he not?"

"Yes, but—"

"Then he can carry you inside. There are always chairs and chaises to sit upon. The shopkeeper and her assistants can bring over items to show you. And should anyone dare to say an unkind word, the earl will set them straight. Don't you agree, Linds?"

Both girls looked at her for guidance.

Lindsey hesitated. She didn't want to raise Jocelyn's hopes only to see them dashed. The truth was, she couldn't guess how Mansfield would react to such a proposition. He remained an enigma to her, an amiable gentleman one moment and a brooding misogynist the next.

Was he the Serpentine Strangler? The only proof she had was circumstantial, mere conjecture. Somehow, she had to put her hands on some irrefutable bit of evidence to link him to the crimes. . . .

"I would hope so. However, his consent must be sought before any promises of outings are made." Casually she added, "By the by, is he at home today?"

"I don't believe so," Jocelyn said. "I saw him from the window when the footman was carrying me downstairs two hours ago. The earl was mounting his horse by the stables."

"No matter," Blythe said. "Linds can ask him the next time he comes to take her for a drive. Perhaps we can all go to the shops together. There now, the matter is settled."

Jocelyn tilted her head to the side and stared at Lindsey. "Has he really taken you out for drives? When you were here last, I thought you didn't like him very much. Is he courting you now?"

Lindsey fought back a blush. She had to offer some semblance of explanation, since she intended to spend time in his company in order to investigate him. And then there was the sticky problem of his resolve to announce their betrothal in less than a month's time. "In a manner of speaking, yes. But so are a number of other gentlemen—including Lord Wrayford."

"The Earl of Mansfield is the handsomest of the lot," Blythe said, clasping her hands to her bosom in rapturous admiration. "He's tall and dark and broad of shoulder, with the most gorgeous military bearing to his walk."

Lindsey frowned. "How on earth would *you* know that?"

"Oh, I watched him from the top of the stairs yesterday when you were leaving with him." Blythe waggled her eyebrows. "You're not the only one who spies on people."

"Then we have that in common, too," Jocelyn said in a confiding tone. "I adore eavesdropping on the servants. Especially when they think I'm asleep."

Lindsey seized the opportunity to change the subject: "Speaking of which, have you perchance learned anything more about Nelda? You know, my maid's cousin, the servant who vanished."

"Oh my, I'd almost forgotten about her," Blythe said. "She was employed by Lord Mansfield, was she not?"

Jocelyn nodded. "As you know, he lives in the house right beside this one. There's a connecting door, so I've met most of his servants." To Lindsey she said, "I've asked a few questions here and there, but no one seems to know what happened to her. Yet there are some peculiar aspects to her disappearance. . . ."

"Such as?"

"While I was napping here the other afternoon, the housekeeper came in to have a little chat with Fisk. They were whispering about Nelda having had a sweetheart and how she often bragged he was a fine gentleman. And they were wondering . . ."

Lindsey reflexively leaned forward in her chair. "Go on."

"They were wondering if she might have been nabbed by . . . the Serpentine Strangler."

Blythe gasped. "How horrible!"

It would be worse than horrible if Mansfield was the killer, Lindsey thought. The possibility made her blood run cold. "Did they have any idea who he was?"

Jocelyn solemnly shook her head. "No, I'm afraid they didn't. In truth, I'm certain they had no notion at all, or they would have said so. And yet . . ."

"Yes?"

"I've a suspicion His Lordship might know what happened to Nelda." Glancing at the open doorway, she lowered her voice to a conspiratorial murmur: "You see, after you left last time I remembered something rather peculiar. At the very same time that Nelda disappeared, the earl went away for two days."

Lindsey clenched her fists in her lap. "Where did he go?"

Deep in thought, Jocelyn tapped a slim forefinger against her chin. "I'm not quite certain. Although I do recall hearing Bernard speaking to Lord Mansfield out in the corridor."

"Who is Bernard?"

"Lord Mansfield's valet. I gathered that the earl had important business to attend to in the country."

"Do you mean at his estate?"

The girl shrugged. "I'm afraid I don't know."

It might be nothing out of the ordinary, Lindsey told herself. Most noblemen owned rural properties that required oversight from time to time. And there could be any number of other reasons for a gentleman to leave London for a short time, such as a duty visit to a relative—or a tryst with his paramour.

She thinned her lips, remembering how he had flirted with Lady Entwhistle at the ball on the same night he'd kissed Lindsey in the garden. Her wayward mind conjured up the image of him embracing the older woman in a bedchamber. Lindsey had to stop her imagination from running wild. It was too disgusting, too infuriating, too . . . embarrassing.

There was little reason for him to leave town with Lady Entwhistle, anyway, when they could easily arrange an assignation at her residence. Frowning, Lindsey pondered the fact that at least one of the murdered maids had been throttled with a gentleman's cravat. Was it merely a coincidence that Mansfield had left at the same time Nelda vanished?

Or was there a sinister purpose to his actions?

A wealth of auburn curls slipping over her shoulders, Blythe leaned forward on the stool to stare with widened eyes at Jocelyn. "Are you implying that *Lord Mansfield* abducted Nelda? And that *he* could be the Serpentine Strangler?"

Casting a sidelong glance at the girl, Jocelyn plucked at the blanket on her lap. "I haven't the slightest idea. But anything is possible, isn't it?"

Blythe blew out a breath. "What humbug! Why, I've never heard anything so preposterous in all my life. The earl is a war hero. He's far too refined to be a common murderer."

Jocelyn lifted her chin. "He killed soldiers during the war, didn't he? So perhaps murder means little to him. Did you ever consider that?"

"Shooting an enemy on the battlefield is a far cry from strangling maidservants in London. For heaven's sake, he's a peer of the realm. It's ridiculous to suspect him!"

"Hmph. Well, *I* think *I* know him better than *you* do. And if *I* say he's behaving suspiciously, then you ought to listen to me."

Their squabbling reminded Lindsey of growing up

with two sisters. It hampered her ability to focus her mind on the case. Besides, she was beginning to suspect that Jocelyn loved the drama of being in the middle of controversy.

Lindsey clapped her hands. "That's enough, both of you. It's all useless conjecture. And it's wrong of us to gossip when Lord Mansfield isn't even here to defend himself."

Her waiflike features taking on a woebegone expression, Jocelyn lowered her gaze. "I'm sorry," she said meekly. "I'm not being a very polite hostess, am I?"

"Since he's your guardian, we ought to afford him more courtesy. As for you, Blythe, I don't want any of this speculation to go beyond these four walls." The last thing Lindsey needed was for her nosy sister to inveigle herself into the investigation. "If you breathe a word of our conversation here to anyone, I won't take you on any more outings. Is that clear?"

Scowling, Blythe crossed her arms. "I'm not a tattletale, and you know it."

Lindsey deemed it wise not to remind her of the time she'd told Mama about the stash of adventure novels underneath Lindsey's bed. Better Lindsey should change the topic of conversation to something that had been weighing on her mind. "I'll take you at your word, then. Jocelyn, there's a rather delicate matter I should like to discuss, and I hope you don't find my inquiries too intrusive. You see, I wanted to find out a bit more about your injury."

Jocelyn eyed her warily. "What did you wish to know?"

Lindsey pondered how to frame the subject, then decided it was best to be blunt and forthright. "Did your legs heal properly? Are they whole and straight, rather than crooked?"

Nodding, the girl blushed a delicate shade of pink. "Y-yes."

"You do have sensation, don't you? You can feel heat and cold, or the prick of a pin?"

Another tentative nod.

Lindsey found that encouraging. "Then are you certain you cannot walk at all? Not even to take a few small steps?"

Alarm widening her eyes, Jocelyn shook her head. "Oh, no, I could *never* manage that! It would hurt terribly! I've no strength whatsoever in my limbs."

"But can you stand, at least? What if you leaned on me?"

Lindsey arose and came forward, but the girl shrank back on the chaise. "No! No, I couldn't possibly. The doctors told me never to attempt it lest I fall and hurt myself."

The sheen of unshed tears in her eyes proved that Jocelyn had a deep-seated fear that would be difficult to overcome. Yet it was disturbing to think of this vibrant young girl sitting here day after day, dependent on servants and the occasional visitor, cut off from the activities that she ought to be enjoying.

Lindsey perched on the edge of the chaise, near Jocelyn's feet. "Shh. Pray, be still and listen to a story about a girl I knew in India. She was a servant, no older than you. One day, she was sitting on the rim of a dry well when she lost her balance and tumbled down into it. Like you, she broke both of her legs."

"Farah!" Blythe exclaimed. "That was the most dreadful accident. I remember how Mama wouldn't let us go see what was happening."

Lindsey kept her gaze on Jocelyn, who was listening with an intent, if somewhat dubious, expression. "It was quite fortunate that some men heard her and they were able to pull her out with ropes. She was forced to lie abed for many weeks afterward while her bones healed. At last, when it was time for her to get up, she couldn't manage to do so. Her legs had become weak, and her muscles were puny from lack of use."

Jocelyn plucked fretfully at the fringed edge of the blanket. "Why are you telling me this? It's gloomy to hear about someone else who is crippled like me."

"Oh, but Farah isn't crippled, at least not anymore. You see, she recovered the ability to walk."

"Indeed so," Blythe added. "When last I saw her, she was running along the docks, waving good-bye to us as our ship set sail."

Jocelyn lowered her chin. "Hmph. You're just trying to make me feel bad. Why are you being so mean?"

Lindsey scooted forward to take hold of Jocelyn's hand. "No, you've mistaken us completely," she said. "Rather, I'm wondering if you, too, can learn to walk again."

Wistfulness in her eyes, Jocelyn glanced out at the sunny garden. "I heard the doctor talking to Lord Mansfield outside this room one day, not long after we arrived in London. He said it's improbable that I'll ever regain use of my legs." She returned her gaze to Lindsey. "Anyway, this Farah is a servant and a native girl at that. *I* have a far more delicate constitution than her."

The girl's fingers felt warm and strong despite their dainty appearance. "Do you trust me?" Lindsey asked.

Jocelyn bit her lip. "I suppose so."

"Then let me explain how Farah improved. It was my ayah, Kasi, who helped the girl's muscles regain strength. Kasi accomplished it by massaging Farah's legs every day."

Lindsey nodded at the old Hindu nurse. She was half-afraid Kasi might refuse to cooperate. On the walk here, Lindsey had had to use considerable persuasion to convince the ayah to give her assistance.

Thankfully, Kasi appeared more biddable now. She rose from her stool and trotted forward, the gold-embroidered purple sari swishing around her plump form. Her raisin brown eyes regarded Jocelyn with the softness of compassion.

Lindsey reached for the white blanket. "If it meets with your approval, she'll demonstrate the method to you."

Jocelyn gasped, slapping her palms down to hold the coverlet in place. "You mean . . . right now? Aren't you going to ask Lord Mansfield's permission? He would want to have the approval of my physician."

Lindsey already knew what the earl would say. His pronouncement echoed in her memory. *You know little of her medical condition. I would sooner trust the guidance of her doctor. And he has been adamant in his assertion that she's to be protected from any type of stimulation.*

Unfortunately, the physician sounded like a strict curmudgeon who would never consider any homespun treatment that didn't appear in his medical books, especially if it was administered by a foreigner. And there could be little doubt that Mansfield would concur with whatever the doctor proclaimed.

Yet the diagnosis kept Jocelyn confined and helpless— and that was something Lindsey could not abide. If there was any chance at all that the girl could recover, Lindsey firmly believed it was worth pursuing.

"Lord Mansfield needn't know," she said. "We'll keep it our little secret until you've made sufficient progress in regaining your strength. Don't you think it would be a wonderful surprise if you were to stand up one day and walk to him?"

A tentative smile bloomed on Jocelyn's lips, and she gave a small nod. "I do want to . . . but . . ."

"Linds is right; you must at least attempt it," Blythe urged. "Just imagine yourself strolling with me from shop to shop on Bond Street. We could try on all the gowns at the dressmaker's. It will be great fun."

While Jocelyn was distracted, Lindsey drew off the blanket. She pushed up the girl's yellow skirt, discreetly avoiding staring at those thin shrunken limbs, encased in white silk stockings. Kasi bent over the chaise, her brown hands massaging Jocelyn's calf in smooth strokes.

"Gently now," Lindsey warned, "until she grows accustomed to it. Does it hurt, Jocelyn?"

The girl shook her head as she watched dubiously. After a moment she added, "But do you really believe this will work?"

The hopeful look she aimed at Lindsey broke her heart. "There's no guarantee, but it's certainly worth the effort, don't you think? Now, you'll need to have someone rub your legs like this at least twice a day. I'll find Fisk so that Kasi can teach her how to do it for you."

"The bell rope is over there," Jocelyn said, nodding toward the fireplace.

Lindsey went to tug on the braided cord. Little did anyone know, she wanted to slip out of the room for a short while. She cast about for another reason. "It might be soothing if I were to read to you to help pass the time. If you'll excuse me, I'll find a book. Blythe, stay here and talk to Jocelyn while I'm gone."

Lindsey hastened from the sitting room and shut the door behind her. Thankfully, the corridor was empty in either direction, the only observer an old-fashioned lady in a portrait on the opposite wall who appeared to be staring balefully at her. Lindsey aimed a distracted frown at the painting before setting out to have a look through the rooms on the side adjacent to Mansfield's town house.

According to Jocelyn, he'd gone out this morning. That meant there was little risk of an accidental encounter. She would never have a better opportunity to find a piece of evidence that proved Mansfield was the Serpentine Strangler.

But time was of the essence. If she was gone more than ten or fifteen minutes, Jocelyn might send a servant in search of her.

Her slippers tapping on the marble floor, Lindsey peeked into an elegant blue dining chamber and then a formal drawing room. A housemaid who was polishing the baseboards gave Lindsey a curious glance before returning to her labor.

Intent on her quest, Lindsey hastened down a back staircase to the ground floor. She struck gold in the first room to her left. It was a library that looked very similar to the one in Mansfield's residence, with windows facing the back garden, cozy groupings of chairs, and an array of tables for writing. Here, at last, she spied the object of her search.

On the far wall stood the connecting door that must lead into his house.

Chapter 12

As he descended the stairs on his way to the library, Thane was in a foul humor. Nothing whatsoever had gone according to plan today. Having risen early, he had visited Bow Street to speak to the chief magistrate, only to discover the man was tied up in a court hearing.

Next, he'd paid a call on the employers of the second murdered maidservant, Dorothy Huddleston. But Lord and Lady Farthingale were indisposed with a matching case of the chills.

Finally, he had returned home to see if Bernard had discovered anything about the latest victim through the network of below-stairs gossip. However, he had gone out on an errand and no one on the staff knew precisely when he'd return.

Thane decided he might as well use the time to check on Jocelyn. He normally did so at least once a day, but of late he'd been sorely neglectful of his ward. Even though he hardly knew how to make conversation with a fifteen-year-old girl, she was always delighted to see him and crestfallen at his departure. His actions—or lack thereof—stirred an uncomfortable feeling in him that he acknowledged was guilt.

Her father, Captain James Nevingford, had been Thane's best friend since their early days together in the cavalry. Even after all these months, it was still wrenching to think that James and his beloved wife, Sarah, were gone forever. Before Waterloo, James had secured Thane's promise that in the event of his death, Thane would see to the care and education of his only child, Jocelyn. The terrible irony was that James had survived the rigors of the battlefield only to die in a carriage accident in Belgium that left his daughter crippled.

Accordingly, Thane had obtained the best physicians for Jocelyn. Once her bones were healed sufficiently for her to make the sea voyage across the Channel, he had brought the girl here to London and consulted with one of the king's own doctors, who had examined her wasted muscles. Thane had been told that due to the strain on her delicate nature, she likely would never walk again. He had attempted to compensate for the grim prognosis by supplying Jocelyn with every creature comfort: a fine home, plenty of books and games, art lessons every other afternoon, and a host of servants to attend to her every need.

Do you ever take her on outings, to places where she can meet people her own age?

Lindsey Crompton's sharp question continued to gnaw at him. Perhaps she was right, he had not done enough to secure Jocelyn's happiness. That could be why his ward often had days when she was petulant and moody. He himself would behave like a caged bear if forced to sit day after day within four walls, never getting out to experience the world.

It was time he rectified the matter.

Striding into the library, he headed toward the connecting door. A fine Aubusson rug muffled his footfalls. This room brought to mind the memory of discovering Lindsey here, garbed as a maidservant and scrubbing the wood floor.

He wasn't sorry for using the incident to coerce her into the promise of a betrothal. Her actions had been reckless, her mission to steal the IOU foolish. It was highly unlikely that securing proof of Wrayford's debt would deter Mrs. Edith Crompton from the ambition to see her daughter marry the heir to a dukedom. Society swarmed with ruthless mothers intent on matchmaking. And Lindsey was too naïve to know how to stop Wrayford from taking advantage of her.

Once the blackguard had secured her hand—and her fortune—in marriage, he could set the stage for murder. A convenient fall down the stairs, a dose of arsenic in her food, and her immense dowry would belong to Wrayford with no strings attached.

Thane clenched his jaw. Never would he allow such a crime to transpire—even if it meant having to wed her himself. Lindsey Crompton might be clever, but she was a babe in the woods when it came to dealing with scoundrels like Wrayford. She could have no notion that the man might very well be the Serpentine Strangler.

Or even that the scapegrace led a secret life that would put any decent lady to the blush.

Reaching the connecting door, Thane turned the knob. There was no need to knock, since Jocelyn spent her days upstairs in a cozy sitting room. She seldom had visitors, which meant only he and the servants frequented the ground floor.

He pushed open the door and stepped into a library that was similar to his own. The main difference was the contents of the shelves. While he owned an extensive collection of legal treatises, weighty biographies, and volumes on battlefield history, for Jocelyn he'd provided an array of educational and inspirational books more suited to a young lady, along with a few novels, including those by the Prince Regent's favorite, Jane Austen. Any book Jocelyn desired could be fetched by Fisk or one of the other servants.

The room was dim and quiet, the chairs empty, and the hearth cold. A pair of large oak tables provided places to sit and write in comfort. But almost immediately Thane sensed he wasn't alone.

He had taken only two steps when his peripheral vision caught sight of someone standing to the left of him. Turning sharply, he stopped dead in his tracks.

Miss Lindsey Crompton was perusing the shelves.

Or at least she was pretending to do so. Her head was tilted slightly so she could observe him from the corner of her eye. An upsweep of dark chestnut curls revealed the swanlike curve of her neck. Slim and feminine, she wore a pale blue gown with a scoop neckline that revealed a tantalizing hint of her charms.

His gaze lingered a moment on those mounds of creamy flesh. He had to tamp down a surge of lust and force his eyes back to hers.

"Well, well. This is quite the surprise."

"Oh! Good morning, my lord. I do hope you don't mind my coming to visit Jocelyn without first asking your permission. I was just now seeking a book to read to her." She plucked a volume at random from the shelf and riffled the pages. "This one looks interesting."

She was talking too fast and her manner had a skittishness that stirred his suspicion. "I didn't see your carriage out front," he said.

"I walked here in the company of my sister and my maid Kasi. It's a lovely day for a stroll, sunny yet brisk and cool."

Thane took a step closer. The light allure of her perfume distracted him, but only for a moment. Her presence so near the connecting door was too convenient to be mere coincidence.

He took the book out of her hand and scanned the cover. "This is a geography text. It's for Jocelyn's schooling, not for pleasure reading."

Those blue eyes rounded. "I was hoping to show her where I grew up in India. And I thought she might like to point out to me where she's lived, since she and her mother followed the drum."

While talking, Lindsey lowered her lashes slightly. That siren aura of mystery didn't fool him—at least not for longer than one overheated moment of fantasy in which he envisioned their naked bodies entwined in wild passion.

He replaced the book on the shelf. "Enough with the fibs. You were planning to sneak into my house again, weren't you? Don't deny it. You still want that blasted IOU."

She elevated her chin. "Believe what you will, my lord. It matters naught to me."

Thane was accustomed to women flirting with him, paying him deference, or at the very least treating him with the proper respect due his rank. He had never before met a lady who cared so little for his regard.

Nor one he so dearly wanted to tame.

Half-irritated and half-amused, he closed the gap between them, crowding her against the bookshelf. He braced his arms on either side of her so that she was trapped in place. "I see you've learned little from that time when I caught you snooping in my house. You're still as audacious as ever."

Her breath caught in a little gasp that was pure enticement, although he was sure she didn't mean it that way. Lifting her hands, she pushed against his encircling arms. "And you're still as overbearing. Now kindly keep your distance."

With any other female, Thane would have heeded her

wishes and stepped away. But Lindsey Crompton impaired his ability to think rationally. He was too enamored by the feel of her womanly form brushing against him.

He bent his head closer, the better to breathe in the intoxicating scent of her skin. "I must warn you to cease your wriggling," he murmured. "With the wrong man, such careless behavior could result in retribution."

She regarded him challengingly from beneath the screen of her dark lashes. "Oh? I would have called *you* the wrong man—"

"Precisely."

His mouth stopped her tartness with a kiss. Before she could recover from that strategic move, he pulled her flush against him. She uttered a muffled protest as he caught hold of her rounded bottom to keep her from squirming free. Then he mustered all of his seduction skills to woo her.

The softness of her lips belied the rigidity of her body, but gradually the resistance ebbed from her. To his great satisfaction, she slid her arms around his neck, lifted herself on tiptoe, and returned his kiss with fervor.

God help him. He had bedded a lot of women in his time, he had experienced all manner of sensual moves, but nothing stirred him as much as Lindsey Crompton's fingers in his hair, her slim body pressing against his. She was such a mix of contradictions, both cold and hot, with a feisty manner that boded ill for any man who treasured peace in his life.

Not that he cared much for tranquility at the moment. He hungered for a bout of hard, wild, animal rutting. With Lindsey. Only Lindsey.

It was the last coherent thought he had for a time, as Thane lost himself in tasting her, in learning every inch of her shapely figure, at least as much as her gown would allow. The kiss went on and on, but it was no longer enough;

it was a mere sample of the banquet that he craved. His mouth traveled down the fragrant curve of her throat and thence to her bosom. Cursing the barrier of fabric that guarded her silky skin, he walked his fingers along her low-cut neckline and then dipped inside to explore the uncharted territory of her breasts.

A small moan of enjoyment eddied from her. She tilted her head back against the bookcase, resting her hands on his shoulders in a move that was unbearably erotic. With her eyes closed and her lips parted, she looked like a goddess offering him his most carnal desire. Drunk on her wine, he moved his mouth along the edge of her bodice to lap her sweetness. All the while, he worked his finger inside her tight corset until he could stroke the nub of her breast. The action elicited a whimper from her that drove him wild.

"Beautiful," he muttered, "you are so very beautiful." He wanted Lindsey naked in bed, her legs parted to receive him. Compelled by the dark delirium of passion, he walked her backward to the nearest table and levered her down beneath him.

Gasping, she attempted to roll away. "Stop! You cannot . . . oh!"

He distracted her by continuing his erotic play with her breasts. "Shh. We're promised to each other."

She shook her head. "No . . . we aren't . . . this is wrong."

The fevered yearning in her eyes told a different story. She found as much pleasure in this romp as he did. "Nothing could be more right. Let me make you happy, Lindsey. Trust me, darling."

He subjected her to another deep, drowning kiss. Driven by reckless need, his fingers shifted to the hem of her skirt to delve beneath it. He shaped his hand around her slim calf, sliding upward over silken warmth until he found the garters that held her stocking in place. Thane didn't stop there; he was too focused on his quest, too keen on discovering—

A sharp jab to his gut jolted him back to reality. "Ouch—blast it!"

Self-preservation overruled the command of his loins. Thane jumped up, grabbing for the back of a chair to steady himself. He stood there, breathing hard, unable to comprehend anything but the sight of Lindsey half-lying on the table with her lips reddened and her skirts in disarray.

Then he noticed the metallic glint in her hand. A silver letter opener.

He instantly regained his mental acumen. Lindsey had attacked him with that puny weapon. She must have grabbed it from the table. While they were in the middle of their passionate kiss.

Scowling, he rubbed the sore spot in his belly. There was no blood; she'd only bruised him. Too bad for her, his coat was well made and the blade too dull. "What the devil—! Why did you stab me?"

"I warned you to stop." Lindsey slid to her feet, the letter opener gripped in her hand. "And if you dare to assault me again, I'll use this where it hurts the most."

He had faced the enemy in battle without flinching. He had fought in hand-to-hand combat when his horse had been shot out from under him. Yet Lindsey's threat made his manhood shrivel. He didn't doubt she meant every word. The little termagant looked fierce enough to carve him into pieces.

"Assault? You enjoyed that kiss as much as I did."

She shook her head fiercely. "You're mistaken."

Her blush gave her away, he noted. How swiftly he had forgotten she was a maiden who had little experience with passion.

Thane fought to get his emotions under control. The galling truth was, she'd had every right to attack him. He had been ready to mount her here in the library where anyone might have walked in on them. Never in his life had he treated a lady so shabbily, especially one he had sworn to protect from bounders and blackguards.

Bloody hell. He had never been threatened in the midst of a seduction before, either. Usually his women begged him for more.

Frustrated by unslaked desire, he stepped away from her. "Pray forgive me. You may put that ridiculous weapon down. I've no intention of causing you harm. Come, I'll escort you back upstairs."

"That won't be necessary," she said stiffly, side-stepping his reach and edging toward the door, her fingers still gripping the letter opener. "I can find my own way."

Thane prowled after her. He harbored as much mistrust of her as she exhibited toward him. Good God, *she* was the one who'd intended to go snooping in his house—again.

"Nevertheless, I'll accompany you," he said. "I need a word with Jocelyn."

Lindsey came to an abrupt halt in the doorway of the library. "No."

"No?"

"She and Blythe are having a pleasant chat. You *did* want your ward to have friends her own age, did you not? It's best to leave them alone together."

Once again, he had a suspicion that Lindsey was hiding something. "A brief interruption will hardly destroy their friendship. What I have to say won't take but a few moments."

He brushed past Lindsey and headed for the stairs. The patter of her footsteps trailed behind him. "What do you mean to tell her?" she asked, her voice echoing in the marble corridor. "Perhaps I can convey the message."

Something was up; he could sense her nervousness. She didn't want him to visit Jocelyn . . . but why the hell not? "It's a matter I'd like to broach to her myself, so I can gauge her reaction."

"I don't understand. Is it a secret?"

"It won't be soon."

He started up the stairs, ignoring the polished oak balustrade and taking the risers two at a time. There was really nothing covert in what he wanted to ask Jocelyn, yet he was curious to discover what had Lindsey in such a lather.

Upstairs, he strolled down the corridor and gave her a chance to catch up. He glanced back to see her half-running with her skirts hiked just enough for him to catch a glimpse of trim calf. The memory of that silken warmth likely would torture him in the nights to come.

He arrived at the sitting room to find the door closed. Odd that, for it was usually open. He was reaching for the knob when Lindsey thrust herself in between him and the door. To his annoyance, she still clasped the letter opener.

"Must you walk so fast, my lord?" she complained loudly. "It isn't very well mannered of you to leave me lagging behind."

Damn, she looked gorgeous with her cheeks flushed and a few chestnut curls dangling loose from her usually prim hairdo. "Call me Thane," he murmured. "After what we just shared there's no need for formality between us."

Her blue eyes flashed beneath the dark wings of her brows. "I hardly think that's appropriate. And as I told you, there's no need to disturb Jocelyn and Blythe. I'm sure you have much more important things to do than talk to a pair of juvenile girls."

Lindsey had raised her voice. It occurred to him that

she was sending a warning to Jocelyn and Blythe inside the sitting room. Why? So they'd have time to cease whatever they were doing?

He'd had enough of these games.

Thane reached past her and turned the knob. Pushing open the door, he leaned close and whispered, "By the by, you may wish to fix your hair. It's in a bit of a muss from our kiss."

In the time-honored manner of all women, she lifted her hands to survey the damage. As she did, he deftly snatched the letter opener away and stepped into the sitting room.

Late-morning light poured in from the tall windows that overlooked the rear garden. To his surprise, there were four females present, not just two. Jocelyn reclined on the chaise with the other three surrounding her. She looked perfectly normal, sitting up with the usual white coverlet over her legs.

The girl standing at the head of the chaise had to be Blythe. She gave him a rather saucy smile, her auburn curls tied back with a blue ribbon that matched her dress. At the foot of the chaise hovered Mrs. Fisk. Other than a swift look at him, she kept her gaze downcast.

A plump foreigner in an embroidered purple wrap stood right beside Jocelyn. What had Lindsey called her Hindu maid? Kasi, he remembered.

Jocelyn glanced up at Blythe, who very slightly shrugged her shoulders. Thane had the clear impression he was missing something. Something vital.

He walked closer. "What's going on here?"

"Hullo, m'lord," Jocelyn said. "I wasn't expecting you this morning. Why do you have a letter opener?"

Thane hadn't realized he was still holding it. Placing it on the nearest table, he said, "Never mind that. Now, answer my question. What have you been doing?"

Lindsey appeared at his side. "Nothing, as well you can see. They were simply chatting. It's about time Jocelyn had visitors to keep her entertained."

"Are you Lord Mansfield?" Blythe chirped, stepping forward to dip a curtsy in front of him. "It's such a pleasure to meet you. I'm Lindsey's sister Blythe."

He gave her a nod. As much as he planned to win over Lindsey's family, he knew a distraction technique when he saw one.

Proceeding straight to the chaise, he noticed that Kasi was holding Jocelyn's hand, palm up. He aimed a stern look at his ward. "You're involved in some sort of mischief. I command that you speak the truth at once."

"Oh dear, you've caught me," Jocelyn admitted sheepishly. "Kasi was reading my palm. I asked her to tell my fortune, so please don't be angry with her."

"Reading your palm."

Jocelyn's green eyes sparkled. "Yes, and I must say it was most enlightening. Kasi said I'm destined to have a very exciting life filled with lots and lots of adventures."

The hard core of suspicion in him melted into something softer. It had been forever since he'd seen Jocelyn so animated. Not since before the death of her parents. She had always been an ethereal fairy child who delighted in simple joys, watching the flight of a butterfly or tumbling in the grass with a puppy.

That carefree girl was crippled now, denied a normal life, and it would be cruel to allow her to be misled by a fortune-teller. Yet he lacked the heart to discourage Jocelyn. Was it really so wrong for her to dream about exciting adventures?

Warm fingers closed around his wrist. He blinked down at Kasi, who was placing his hand, palm up, in hers. In a singsong voice, she said, "I read your fate, sahib."

He tried to pull free. "I've no use for such nonsense."

Kasi held firmly to his wrist. Her raisin-eyed stare had a curiously mesmerizing effect on him. "Be still, sahib. You must not run from your destiny."

Crouching close to his hand, she ran her stubby forefinger over the lines and whorls of his palm while muttering to herself.

Thane found himself gazing down at the knob of graying black hair on the top of her head. Run? Did she think him some sort of coward? He was caught in a quandary. It seemed rude to make an issue of wresting his hand from this batty old woman, so why not humor her?

Then he noticed that all eyes were upon him. Blythe and Jocelyn wore identical looks of expectation, Fisk was smiling fondly, and Lindsey stood watching with her arms crossed. Her teeth sank into her lower lip as if to bite back a smile, and the sight immersed him in the memory of kissing that lush mouth. He wanted to taste her again, and this time, he'd move more slowly and coax her. . . .

Kasi's melodic voice lured him out of the fantasy. "You live far away for many years," she said, "but now you come home to stay. You leave England no more."

"Someone told you about my military service." He frowned at Jocelyn, Blythe, and then Fisk, but they shook their heads. Lindsey shrugged as if to say it hadn't been her, either.

"Long ago, you a very lonely boy," Kasi continued, tracing the long line that bisected his palm. "No parents, no family, no love."

Thane stiffened. How could she possibly have known about those harsh years with Uncle Hugo—unless Fisk had been gossiping. He aimed a glare at Fisk, but his old nurse held one hand to her fleshy cheek, her expression openly mystified.

Kasi went on, "You a man of great passion, like the

god Shiva. You destined for one love . . . only one . . . and soon she will be yours."

His gut tightened involuntarily. Lindsey was watching him, her lashes half-lowered, her expression unreadable. The moment spun out into an eternity. For once, he wanted her to look him straight in the eye, so he could see into her mind and fathom her thoughts.

Then he realized the girls were giggling behind their hands, glancing from him to Lindsey and whispering to each other.

Thane felt the creep of a dull red heat up his neck. He snatched back his hand from Kasi. "Rubbish. This is naught but a parlor game."

Seemingly unperturbed, the Hindu woman pressed her palms together and bowed. "I pray to Shiva you find your destiny, sahib."

Destiny be damned. Too bad she hadn't foretold something useful, such as the identity of the Serpentine Strangler. Or where the villain would strike next. *That* information would have been well worth his while, rather than some claptrap about love.

He stepped toward his ward. "Jocelyn, I came here for a reason. I would like to take you out for a drive tomorrow afternoon."

Nothing could have been better designed to divert her attention. Her face suffused with radiance, she clasped her hands to her bosom. "Truly?"

The glow in her eyes made him regret never having taken her on an outing before now. "Be ready right after luncheon tomorrow. We'll take a turn around the city in the landau so you can see the Green Park and St. James's Palace."

"Can Blythe and Lindsey come along, too?"

"What a capital notion!" Blythe said. "I'd like that very much!"

Lindsey directed a warning frown at her sister. "No, Mama will never approve. And you've lessons tomorrow, remember?"

"But that isn't fair—"

"I'm sorry, you know it isn't possible." Her gaze flitted to Thane in what struck him as a strangely calculating look. "I, however, would be pleased to accept the invitation."

Chapter 13

Early the following afternoon, Lindsey peeked out into the upstairs corridor to make sure no one was around. Only then did she step out of her bedchamber. It was vital to avoid being waylaid by her mother, who at breakfast had announced a schedule of afternoon calls to several of society's top hostesses. If all went well, Lindsey intended to escape the duty visits.

For that purpose, she needed to keep a watch out the front window.

She hastened down the marble stairs to the first floor, which was usually deserted at this time of day. The series of chambers along the ornate corridor was designed for entertaining large crowds. To her right loomed the vast ballroom, dim from the drawn draperies, while to her left lay the state dining chamber, which could seat well over a hundred guests. Only a few sounds disturbed the silence: the faint patter of her shoes, the ticking of a clock in the gold drawing room, and the muted buzz of conversation drifting up from somewhere on the ground floor.

She tiptoed to the filigreed iron railing of the grand staircase and risked a quick peek into the entrance hall. A blue-liveried footman stood on duty by the double front doors. Unfortunately, the talkers were out of sight, although the pair sounded like a man and a woman. Was it Mama and Papa? Or gossiping servants?

Their words were too muffled for Lindsey to discern— yet an inexplicable tingle of nervousness prickled her skin.

She ducked into the larger of the two drawing rooms and hastened to the bank of windows that overlooked the square. Parting the heavy brocade draperies, she peered down through the wavy glass at the street. Ladies and gentlemen strolled the pathways of the parklike square, while the occasional fine carriage trundled along the cobblestones.

She could see no black landau carrying Mansfield and a young blond girl. Then again, it was a full quarter hour before the appointed time.

What if he rescinded his offer to take his ward on an outing? Jocelyn would be crushed. Lindsey wished she had more faith that he would hold to his promise. But her suspicions of him ran too deep. She of all people knew he could not be relied upon to behave as a gentleman of honor.

Let me make you happy, Lindsey. Trust me, darling.

A blush suffused her from head to toe. She had spent the night tossing and turning, burning with the carnal memory of his embrace and her own ardent response to it. At first she had capitulated to the kiss as a means to delay him from going upstairs. She hadn't wanted him to find out about the treatment that Kasi was giving to Jocelyn's withered limbs for fear he would forbid it. Yet Lindsey's acquiescence had altered swiftly into illicit pleasure, especially when he had slipped his hand inside her bodice and stroked her bare breasts. And sweet heaven, she'd been spellbound when he'd reached beneath her skirts, his fingers stopping short of touching her in the most shamefully wicked manner.

The memory made her weak all over, and she caught hold of the window frame to steady herself. In a very short time, Mansfield had made her crave his caresses. She had been wild for him, ready to follow her reckless desires wherever he might lead her. Then a sobering thought had cut through her passion: Was this how he had charmed those maidservants before he'd strangled them? By seducing them with his skillful touch? In horror, she'd snatched up the letter opener and struck at him.

You enjoyed that kiss as much as I did.

She ought to be angry at Mansfield for making such a blunt statement. It was hardly gallant of him to point out her embarrassingly wanton response to his touch. However, Lindsey had never been one to mince words or deny the truth. In the heat of the moment, she had wanted his seduction with all her heart and soul. How had he overcome her defenses when she had believed herself immune to male persuasion? When she had every reason in the world to mistrust him?

Those relentless questions had nagged at her for half the night until at last she'd fallen into a fitful sleep. With the light of day, she was no closer to finding any answers. The Earl of Mansfield remained an enigma to her. A part of her wanted to believe him to be an admirable man, yet another part—her logical half—fretted about the mounting evidence that pointed to him as the Serpentine Strangler.

On the night they'd met, she had caught him escorting a comely maidservant into the study at Wrayford's house, presumably to engage in an illicit tryst.

A few nights later, she'd witnessed his flirtation with Lady Entwhistle, who had employed the first Strangler victim.

Then there had been the matter of the clipping about the murders that she'd found in his desk drawer. If he wasn't guilty, what possible reason could he have for keeping the news article?

Most damning of all, Nelda had vanished from his house. Jocelyn had said that at the same time as the maid had disappeared Mansfield had taken an overnight trip.

Where had he gone? To dispose of Nelda's dead body?

Lindsey tightened her grip on the window frame. Leaping to conclusions wouldn't solve the mystery. She had to probe deeper to uncover the truth, and this outing was a prime opportunity. She needed to shadow the earl in the hopes that he might be tricked into dropping a clue about his culpability.

And she was concerned for Jocelyn's safety, too.

Thus far the murderer had shown an affinity for lower-class women, yet it would be a dangerous mistake to underestimate him. If Mansfield was indeed the killer, then he must be made to realize that Lindsey intended to keep a close watch on Jocelyn. It was the only way to protect the girl from harm.

Footsteps approached from the passageway. Lindsey spun around to see her mother step into the doorway of the drawing room. Mrs. Edith Crompton looked trim and fresh in a green-and-white-striped gown, her russet hair stylishly arranged.

"Ah, there you are, my dear." Smiling, she playfully shook her forefinger. "Naughty girl, you were to wait in your chamber for my summons."

The bantering note in her voice served as a warning to Lindsey. It blunted the surprise as Lord Wrayford stepped into sight just behind Mrs. Crompton.

Nevertheless, Lindsey's heart plummeted. This was a complication she had hoped to avoid. It was obvious from their smirks that the two of them had something planned. Was it Wrayford and her mother that she'd heard talking downstairs earlier?

Wrayford looked entirely too confident as he swaggered forward to bow over her hand. He was the consummate dandy in a pale yellow coat with a frothy cravat and tan breeches. As usual, he addressed her bosom rather than her eyes.

"Miss Crompton, you are a vision of beauty. I am most delighted to find you alone, without a crowd of suitors. May I remind you, you owe me a drive in the park."

She extracted her hand from his. "I'm afraid you've arrived at an inconvenient time."

His gaze snapped to her face. "Sorry?"

"My schedule is rather full today. Perhaps you could return another day."

"Lindsey!" her mother exclaimed, rushing forward to join them. "Such rudeness is not to be borne. You must apologize to your guest and accept his invitation at once."

Lindsey firmed her lips. She resisted the urge to peek out the window in the desperate hope of seeing Mansfield drive up to the house. Not, of course, that his arrival would matter one whit now. Judging by the determination on Mama's face, there would be no dissuading her from playing the matchmaker.

In bitter frustration, Lindsey realized she'd been outmaneuvered. Her own wishes were for naught. She would have to do as her mother wanted. The last thing she needed was to waste the afternoon in the company of a colossal bore like Wrayford.

Unless . . .

An idea sprang into her mind, a plan that would enable her to investigate the murders while placating her mother at the same time. Feverishly Lindsey considered all aspects of the scheme. It might just work. As the old adage went, every dark cloud had a silver lining.

* * *

Edith Crompton stood beneath the grand portico and watched as Lord Wrayford helped Lindsey up into his smart yellow phaeton. The girl had been rebellious at first yet ultimately had acquiesced. A sense of deep satisfaction filled Edith. At last her long-held dreams were coming to fruition. She must make certain there were no further impediments to a betrothal between Lindsey and Lord Wrayford.

Nothing would cement her position in society more than having her middle daughter marry the heir to the Duke of Sylvester. The previous year, Portia had wed a mere viscount, having scorned the hand of a duke amid a firestorm of scandal. Edith was determined to prevent any such event from happening this time. To that end, she had taken a bold step today. She had summoned Lord Wrayford and struck a bargain with him. If he was able to coax Lindsey into an engagement within the next month, Edith would provide him with a bonus payment in addition to Lindsey's enormous dowry.

Considering the pitiful state of his finances, Wrayford was in full agreement with her proposal. Any slight misgivings Edith felt were vanquished by the thought of the enhanced status the family would gain as a result of the grand connection. Unfortunately, George wouldn't approve of her manipulative tactics—he was very protective of their daughters—which was why he need never learn all the particulars.

A flurry of movement from behind her distracted Edith. Out of the corner of her eye, she spied Kasi coming out of the house. A thickset figure clad in bright yellow silk, the old Hindu woman lumbered past Edith and headed toward the phaeton.

Edith seized the ayah's arm, grabbing her from behind in such a way that it wouldn't be apparent to any watchers.

"Stop," she hissed through gritted teeth. "Where do you think you're going?"

Kasi tugged at her hold. "Missy need protection."

"Nonsense. It's perfectly acceptable for them to take an unchaperoned drive to the park."

"He is bad man."

The ayah made another attempt to wrench free, but Edith had learned a few tricks of her own during her hardscrabble youth. She dug her fingers into the soft area beneath the woman's arm. "Don't be absurd. And stop fighting me. You'll make a spectacle before all the neighbors."

Then it was too late for any interference as Lord Wrayford picked up the ribbons and the phaeton set off down the cobbled street. Cognizant of any watching eyes, Edith released the servant. A few pedestrians strolled the pathways of the square, but thank heavens, it didn't appear that anyone had noticed her little tussle with Kasi.

The Hindu fixed her with a hard stare, and the accusation in those inscrutable brown eyes shook Edith. She was well aware that the woman knew too much about her and George and their time in India. That was why Edith had brought Kasi to England, where she could be watched closely. The past must be left buried lest the family suffer dire consequences.

Edith would never, ever allow that to happen. She had not achieved entry to high society without having strength of will.

"Follow me," she told Kasi. "I want a word with you in private."

But no sooner had Edith turned toward the house when she caught sight of a landau heading down the street on the opposite side of the square from where Lord Wrayford's carriage had disappeared. Something made her pause to observe its approach.

A coachman sat on the high seat, driving a matched pair of blacks. With a shock, Edith recognized the gentleman riding in the back. Her sharp eyes could just make out his boldly handsome, scarred face. A young woman, bundled in blankets against the cool spring weather, perched beside him.

Edith amended her order to Kasi: "Go to my boudoir at once. I'll see you there shortly."

The Hindu bowed and disappeared into the mansion. Edith proceeded inside as well, for the earl must be coming here to call and she did not wish for their conversation to take place outside on the steps. She instructed the footman on duty in the entrance hall to send any visitors to her in the green sitting room.

Who was the girl with Lord Mansfield? His ward?

Pursing her lips, Edith headed for the chamber down the corridor, her footsteps ringing on the marble floor. If he was intending to introduce Lindsey to his ward, then he must be very serious indeed about winning her hand. And there were already signs that Lindsey harbored a preference for him.

No wonder the little minx had been watching out the front window of the drawing room. Lindsey must have been intending to sneak out of the house to join him. She had taken a shine to Lord Mansfield, and that was something Edith could never allow.

"If you don't mind," Lindsey said, "I should like to make a stop on our way to the park. A brief detour to your home."

Lord Wrayford's pale blue eyes bugged out as he swung to stare at her. He fumbled the reins, causing the bay gelding to swing his head from side to side and snort a protest. "What's that you say? You want to go to my *house*?"

"Yes. You see, at your ball, I lost one of my best diamond earbobs. Do you know if any of your maids might have found it?"

"Uh . . . not that I've been informed."

"Well, it may have rolled out of sight beneath a piece of furniture. In truth, I believe I may know exactly where I dropped it. I hope you won't mind my taking a quick peek."

He arched his sandy eyebrows. "Certainly not, Miss Crompton. Your wish is my command!"

As he returned his attention back to the street, Lindsey caught the occasional calculating glance he sent her way. Of course, the buffoon must be pondering how to use her request to his advantage. He would see it as a chance to compromise her, to force her hand in marriage. Too bad for him, she had no intention of letting that happen.

Striving for serenity, she kept her gloved hands folded in her lap as he turned the phaeton onto Bruton Street with its row of stately redbrick residences. Had Mansfield arrived at her house yet? Would he—and Jocelyn—be disappointed to find her gone?

Lindsey banished the troubling thought. At present, she had more important things to occupy her, the first of which was gaining entry to Lord Wrayford's house and accomplishing her purpose there without his interference.

Midway along the block, he stopped the carriage and clambered down to secure the reins. Lindsey quickly descended from the high perch before he could come around to help her. She shuddered to imagine his hands on her waist, the way Mansfield had done when he'd assisted her.

Not that she wanted the earl touching her, either. All men liked to show their superiority over women and to keep them as possessions. Lindsey had no intention of spending her life under the rule of any male.

She glided to the iron post where Wrayford was

securing the leather ribbons. "Thank you for being so kind. Now I must ask you to wait right here."

"What?" he said, his florid face exhibiting displeasure. "I thought you said you wanted to have a look around my house."

"It's best that I do so alone. If you accompany me, people will find out and gossip. They'll spread rumors and ruin my good name. You wouldn't wish to embroil a lady in scandal, now would you?"

Wrayford looked as if he would relish doing just that— and much more. His detestable gaze kept flitting to her bosom. With the corners of his mouth turned downward and his lower lip jutted out, he resembled an overgrown schoolboy who had been denied a sweet.

"No one will know if we hurry on inside very quickly," he countered, grabbing for her arm.

She pulled free. "It's too late. The neighbors are already watching us. Just now I saw someone peering out the window across the street. If you dare to follow me inside, you'll ruin not just me but your own standing in society as well."

"Oh, balderdash. It was probably a servant."

He swung his head around to inspect the opposite house and Lindsey seized the opportunity to mount the three steps to his porch. She rapped hard with the brass knocker. The claret red door swung open to reveal a tall footman in green livery with shiny brass buttons.

"Good morning," she said. "Your master has granted me permission to fetch something that I left here. He'll be waiting for me outside."

The servant bowed, revealing the top of his curly white wig. "Aye, m'lady."

As she stepped into the shabby foyer, she cast a glance over her shoulder. Much to her relief, Lord Wrayford paced back and forth beside the carriage. He was sulking, his arms folded and his chin lowered in displeasure. Lindsey suspected she had only a limited amount of time before he would lose patience and come after her.

The footman shut the door. Continuing with her ruse, she explained, "I lost a diamond earbob during Lord Wrayford's ball. The last time I recall noticing it was when I went to his study. I'd like to have a look around there."

"Aye, m'lady."

Like most footmen, he was a young, handsome man, but his blue eyes were vacuous, his features devoid of intellect. He just stood there, staring dumbly at her.

"Will you be so kind as to show me to the study?" she prompted.

"Oh . . . aye, m'lady."

He plodded off down a dim corridor, and Lindsey followed at his heels. She already knew the way from her previous visit here. But she needed to question one of the staff and this footman would have to do.

He led her inside the shadowy room, then turned as if to leave.

"What is your name?" she asked.

"Me? Buttery, miss. Buttery, I am, but don't serve me up on toast." Blushing, he ran his finger under his high collar. "'Tis a jest me mam used t' say."

Lindsey smiled politely. "Do open the draperies, Buttery. I'll need the light in order to see."

As he went to do her bidding, Lindsey strolled around the shabby study, making a pretense of peering beneath the chairs, then under the old desk where she had found the IOU on that fateful night when she'd met Lord Mansfield. The stale odor of tobacco smoke permeated the air. As the draperies were drawn back, daylight illuminated the shelves of musty, ancient books.

"There was a maidservant I encountered here on the

evening of His Lordship's ball," Lindsey said. "I wonder if you might know her name. She was quite pretty, about my height, with fair hair."

Lindsey burned to question the woman who had been with Lord Mansfield that night. He'd had his arm around her as he'd ushered her into the study. Clearly expecting the room to be deserted, he had brought the woman here in the midst of a party.

Why?

Her stomach twisted. He must have wanted to engage in a tryst—because what other purpose could there be for a gentleman to seek out the companionship of a comely maidservant?

Unless he also intended to murder her. . . .

The footman furrowed his brow. He stared up at the yellowed paint of the ceiling as if searching the cobwebs of his mind for the identity of the woman. "Must've been Tilly, I s'pose."

"If it isn't too much trouble, I'd like a word with Tilly. She might know what happened to my diamond earbob."

"Are ye sayin' . . . she nicked it?"

"No, of course not. I'm certain it was merely mislaid. But since she passed by this room at the same time as I did, I thought perhaps she might have seen where the earbob dropped."

The excuse sounded impossibly contrived, yet Buttery didn't question it. He continued to stand there, gazing at Lindsey and shifting from one foot to the other.

"Well?" she prompted. "Will you please go and ask Tilly to come here at once?"

Slowly, he shook his head. "Can't, m'lady. 'Tis impossible. Ye see, Tilly's gone."

Foreboding slid down her spine. "Gone where?"

"Dunno." He shrugged his shoulders. "She quit 'ere the day after the ball."

Chapter 14

"I'm afraid my daughter must have changed her mind about your invitation. She isn't at home today."

Elegant and slender, Mrs. Edith Crompton sat embroidering a handkerchief by the hearth, her dainty fingers drawing the white thread in and out of the linen square. An expression of tranquil politeness graced her face, as one would expect of any lady of society. Yet as she glanced from her sewing to him Thane recognized the hardness of resolve in the arch of her brow and the firmness of her chin. He found himself admiring her iron will even as he silently cursed her determination to bar him from Lindsey's company.

Clearly, he had a rocky road to travel before he won over Lindsey's family.

"May I inquire where she's gone?" Thane asked. "Perhaps she means to return in time for our appointment."

"Hardly," Mrs. Crompton said with studied sympathy. "In truth, you've only just missed her. A few minutes ago, she went for a drive with Lord Wrayford."

His gut tightened with alarm. "With Wrayford? Good God!"

So he'd been right to think he'd glimpsed that villain's fancy yellow phaeton leaving the square. Blast himself for a fool! He ought to have had the sense to give chase.

Not, of course, that the cumbersome landau could have kept up with the lighter vehicle. And he had Jocelyn to consider, who was waiting outside with the coachman.

Mrs. Crompton frowned. "I'm sorry if you consider Lord Wrayford to be a rival for my daughter's affections. But that is no excuse for you to use our heavenly Father's name in vain."

"I beg your pardon." Thane took a step toward her. "Tell me, where were they heading?"

"I hardly think that is any concern of yours."

"It is indeed my concern. You see—"

Running his fingers through his hair, Thane bit off his words. No doubt Mrs. Crompton already knew Wrayford was a philanderer who would never keep his marriage vows, a gamester who would squander Lindsey's fortune within a year. Maybe she didn't care so long as she could purchase a ducal coronet for her daughter.

However, the woman couldn't possibly know that Wrayford was under suspicion of murder. Or that Thane was compelled to keep the investigation a secret until he could find irrefutable proof of Wrayford's culpability.

Mrs. Crompton let the embroidery fall to her lap. "Let me be quite frank, my lord," she said, fixing him with a resolute stare. "I wouldn't recommend your pursuing Lindsey any further. Her schedule is quite full, and I rather doubt she'll be interested in seeking your company anytime in the near future. You see, she informed me this very morning that she wants nothing more to do with you."

Thane stood stock-still. Had Lindsey confessed to her mother about his attempt to seduce her? Surely not. Mrs. Crompton had to be spinning a tall tale in order to discourage his courtship.

Yet Lindsey had been furious with him the previous day, angry enough to strike out at him with that blasted letter opener. She must have accepted his invitation out of kindness toward his ward and then had second thoughts. Apparently, not even her charitable feelings for Jocelyn could induce Lindsey to spend a few hours in his company. And now, to avoid him, she had gone off with Wrayford.

The sharp teeth of guilt nipped at Thane. By his own actions he may have inadvertently pushed her into the arms of a killer.

Lindsey sent Buttery below stairs to fetch the housekeeper, since pulling the bell rope would summon only a maid and waste precious minutes. With Lord Wrayford impatiently waiting outside with the carriage, Lindsey couldn't afford any delays.

She paced the threadbare rug in the study while considering the troubling new development. Another servant associated with Mansfield had vanished under peculiar circumstances. Lindsey herself had seen fair-haired Tilly in his company on the night of Wrayford's ball.

Her disappearance was too significant an event to be mere coincidence. Not when the same thing had happened to Nelda.

Yet a part of Lindsey balked at believing Mansfield was capable of cold-blooded murder. He had served honorably in the cavalry for many years. He had shown true concern for Jocelyn and had showered his ward with all manner of luxuries. For the most part, he had behaved as a proper gentleman—except when it came to seducing women.

Memory swept her into the quagmire of bodily desire. From the moment he had taken her into his arms, she had been wild for his kisses, eager for his touch in places that made her blush to recall. No other man had ever had so profound an effect on her. It was as if the earl had administered a love potion that had erased all her reason and logic.

Now, in the light of day, troubling questions nagged at her: Didn't his skill at seduction enhance his likelihood as the murder suspect? Could he have had the same effect on other women . . . like those maidservants? Had he romanced them with sweet lies, enticed them into sin, and then lured them to their death?

The very real possibility of that scenario made Lindsey shudder. Her hand strayed to her throat. It would have been so simple for him in the heat of the moment to untie his cravat and then wrap it around the neck of his victim . . . or to wrap it around *her* own neck.

"Aha! I've found you!"

The sudden boom of Wrayford's voice gave Lindsey a start. She whirled around to see him grinning in the doorway. She'd been so lost in thought that the approach of his footsteps had failed to register on her consciousness.

His presence here boded ill for both her investigation and her reputation.

"Go back outside," she ordered. "If any of the neighbors are watching, they'll spread gossip about me and ruin my good name."

He made a dismissing gesture with his hand. "Let the small-minded busybodies say what they will. If there is the slightest smear to your character, I shall gladly protect your honor."

Wrayford swaggered toward her. In his dandified yellow coat and elaborate neck cloth, he more closely resembled a deceitful scapegrace rather than the guardian of a lady's virtue. The calculating look in those pale blue eyes alarmed Lindsey.

She deemed it prudent to retreat behind a wing chair. "The best way for you to protect me is to return to the carriage in accordance with my wishes."

"Nonsense. It's quite rude of me to stand by idly when I could be here, offering my assistance. Have you found the earbob that you lost?"

"Not yet. I've summoned your housekeeper to help me. She should arrive at any moment."

Instead of being discouraged, Wrayford came right up to Lindsey, stopping so close she could smell the cloying odor of his cologne. "Confess the truth now, my dear. There isn't really a missing jewel, is there?"

His question threw her off kilter. How could he possibly know it was a ruse? Was he merely guessing because her fib had been transparent? Or had he somehow figured out that she suspected Lord Mansfield of murder?

"I . . . don't know what you mean."

"Of course you do, my darling." Reaching out, he fingered a curl of her hair that had escaped her feathered bonnet. "You knew all along that I would follow you inside here. Because you *wanted* me to come to you. It was all part of your plan."

"Plan?"

"Yes, you intend to trap me into wedlock. I've enough experience with women to know false modesty when I see it. In truth, you aspire to be Duchess of Sylvester as soon as my grandpapa takes to his deathbed."

Wrayford made a grab for her. Lindsey escaped him by moving to the other side of the chair.

"That may be my mother's wish, but it certainly isn't mine. I've no interest whatsoever in becoming your wife."

He took a step closer, and again she eluded him, keeping the chair between them. "Don't be coy," he said. "I recognize a come-hither look when I see one."

"You couldn't be more wrong. I want no part of you. Now stay back or I'll scream."

He thrust out his lower lip in a pout. "Please, Miss

Crompton, you mustn't deny me. Pray, fulfill my heart's desire. Give me a kiss, now there's a good girl."

He lunged again, this time catching hold of her sleeve. As she jumped back, Lindsey's heel caught the hem of her skirt and caused her to stumble. Wrayford took instant advantage by clamping his arms around her from the side so that her shoulder was jammed into his chest. The awkward position made it more difficult for her to wrench free.

Though her arms were locked at her sides, she managed to drive her elbow into his stomach. "Beast! Let me go!"

Wrayford grunted but held on. Despite his soft appearance, he proved to be as strong and tenacious as a bulldog.

He loosed a nasty chuckle. "You're a feisty one. Exactly the way I like my females."

His mouth swooped down toward hers. She quickly turned her head, so that his slobbery lips met the back of her neck. Disgusted and alarmed, she glanced around but could spy no handy weapon like a letter opener anywhere in sight. Perhaps, if she were facing him, she might be able to manage the trick that Kasi had taught her—

The jingle of keys in the doorway caught her attention. A fleshy woman peeked inside, a mobcap perched on her head and her dark eyes like currants in a doughy face.

The housekeeper.

"Help!" Lindsey called. "He's attacking me!"

Wrayford snarled over his shoulder, "Go away, Lambkin. You aren't needed here."

The woman vanished from sight at once, abandoning Lindsey to Wrayford's villainous clutches. Clearly, there would be no aid from any of his servants. She was on her own.

Lindsey forced herself to go limp. Her best hope was

to convince him that she had given up the fight, so that he might relax his guard. To enhance the aura of defeat, she let herself quiver a little as if in fear.

"Oh my," she murmured. "No one is willing to help me. Whatever am I to do now?"

"Give me a little taste of your sweetcakes, that's what," Wrayford said, turning her in his arms to face him. "It's only fair that a man should sample the wares before buying them, eh?"

Lindsey clenched her teeth to keep from retorting that as the heiress, *she* was the one doing the purchasing.

But she needed to play the damsel in distress. "You're a cad for saying such things to a lady of virtue. My mother warned me never to let any man touch me."

"Bah, the two of you planned this ruse of the lost earbob. Although I'll wager your mama never told you that the real jewel lies within my breeches."

Cackling at his crude jest, Wrayford leered down at her bosom.

While he was distracted, she seized her chance and brought up her knee to connect with his groin. She scored a direct hit despite the hindrance of her skirts.

Wrayford howled and his hold slackened. She gave him a mighty shove so that he fell backward. He stumbled against the bookshelves and dislodged several volumes that crashed to the floor. Moaning, he bent over, his hands cupping the front of his breeches.

"Argh!"

Amazed at how well the trick had worked, Lindsey sprang toward the door of the study. She had no intention of waiting around for Wrayford to recover. "I'm borrowing your carriage," she said over her shoulder.

His face a mask of agony, he glanced at her. "Wha—?"

"Never fear, I learned how to handle the ribbons in India. Now, do have a pleasant afternoon!"

Chapter 15

Thane craned his neck to see the street ahead as the burly coachman drove the landau through the elegant district of Mayfair. The open coach trundled along at a sedate pace that set Thane's nerves on edge. He despised being relegated to a seat back here like a doddering old uncle. If not for his need to chaperone Jocelyn, he would have leaped up to the front, grabbed the ribbons, and urged the horses to a faster pace.

Where the devil had Wrayford taken Lindsey? The villain's phaeton had been heading north, rather than west to Hyde Park, which was the usual destination of courting couples out for a drive. On the off chance that the two were calling on a noble household, Thane had instructed the coachman to conduct a methodical sweep of every street in the area.

"How much farther is it to St. James's Palace?" Jocelyn asked.

Thane flashed a distracted smile at his ward. She was all bundled up against the cool spring day, with a straw bonnet framing her delicate features and a blanket over her useless legs, which were propped on a stool. Pencil in hand, she had been doodling faces in the sketch pad in her lap.

"It'll be a little while yet," he said. "I thought you might enjoy a tour through Mayfair first, to see all the fine houses."

"Oh, yes, it's all been very interesting, especially the people. I'm certainly glad I brought paper and pencil. Although I daresay I could draw better if it weren't so bumpy traveling over the cobblestones. Do you suppose we could slow down?"

"We'll stop soon enough, I promise you. Then you'll have plenty of time to sketch."

They wouldn't stop until he'd located Wrayford and Lindsey—if indeed the task was even possible. The couple could be any number of places by now. After all, they'd had a good fifteen minutes' head start.

Worry thrust Thane to the precipice of patience. If Wrayford really was the Serpentine Strangler, Lindsey could be in grave danger. As strong and capable as she was, she could have no notion of how to handle the murderous villain. Even a sharp letter opener might not stop a madman who was bent on killing her.

He realized that Jocelyn was talking. "I do wish Lindsey or Blythe could have come with us today," she said plaintively. "It would be so much more fun if I had a friend along."

Thane awkwardly patted her gloved hand. Lindsey was right; he ought to have allowed Jocelyn to associate with others her age. "It's been rather lonely for you, hasn't it?"

"Perhaps they've changed their minds about liking me," Jocelyn fretted. "I hope that isn't the case. Do you suppose they'll come back to see me sometime?"

"If they don't," he teased, "I'll kidnap them in the dead of night. I'll bring them to you and stand guard at the door so they can't escape."

Jocelyn's green eyes widened. "Truly?"

She looked as if she didn't quite know whether or not

to take him seriously. Sometimes he forgot how young and easily influenced his ward could be.

He tweaked her pale cheek. "No, of course not, silly. But I can certainly deliver your invitation to them to visit."

Just then, the coachman turned the landau onto Bruton Street. Looking ahead, Thane forgot all else as he spied the familiar yellow phaeton far down the street, parked in front of Wrayford's town house.

Alarm choked Thane. Bloody hell! He should have thought of coming here first. A man as evil as the Serpentine Strangler would suffer no qualms over taking an innocent young lady to his home in the middle of the day.

His mind worked feverishly. Lindsey knew better than to go unchaperoned to a gentleman's house. How had Wrayford managed to bamboozle her? Whatever it was, he must have thrown all caution to the wind. At this very moment, he might be choking her to death with his cravat as he'd done to those other women. . . .

Thane had one hand on the door of the landau. He was half out of his seat, ready to dash to her rescue, when he spied the object of his thoughts. Lindsey Crompton emerged from Wrayford's house and hurried forward to unloop the reins of the phaeton. Oblivious to the approach of the landau, she clambered up onto the high seat and drove away from them.

Alone.

Luckily, Jocelyn didn't appear to notice. She'd bent her head down over her sketch pad, her pencil moving in swift strokes as she drew an old gentleman walking briskly along the foot pavement.

Thane was at a loss for what to make of Lindsey's actions. He was thankful she appeared unharmed, surprised that she could handle such a fancy rig, and astonished to realize she must be stealing it from Wrayford. What had happened to make her behave so outrageously? Even more puzzling, she was heading east, away from her home.

Where the devil was she going?

He briefly considered stopping at Wrayford's house to demand answers from the villain. But first things first.

Thane leaned forward to address the coachman: "Follow that yellow phaeton. And if you value your position, do not let it out of your sight."

Upon reaching her destination, Lindsey handed a coin from her reticule to a scruffy young urchin on the street. She promised him another if the carriage was still there when she came out. Thieves and pickpockets abounded in the area of Covent Garden. But if she lost courage now, there might never be another opportunity.

Taking a deep breath, Lindsey walked into the stately stone building. She found herself in a large room with long wooden benches and groups of milling people who were waiting to see one of the magistrates. Various officials in white wigs scurried to and fro, and for a moment she stood there, drinking in the hectic scene.

This was Bow Street Station, home to the famous Runners. Lindsey had been fascinated by those valiant detectives ever since the age of fourteen, when she'd happened upon a tattered English book at a stall in the bazaar in Bombay. It had been a lurid adventure story in which a Runner had played a role as the crime-solving hero. The novel had been confiscated by her mother, who'd declared such reading beneath contempt for a lady. But Lindsey had never lost her secret desire to emulate the Runners, no matter how imprudent or impossible that goal might be.

Upon her arrival in London two years ago, she'd made a point to find out the location of Bow Street Station. Once, she had even glimpsed its imposing edifice on her way to Drury Lane Theatre. But this was the first time she'd dared to venture inside. Mama would have her head on a platter if she knew Lindsey had come here.

And no wonder. All manner of criminals were brought here to stand before one of the magistrates in the court-rooms. There were also witnesses to crimes and people who'd come to visit their loved ones being held for ar-raignment.

Several occupants of the waiting room had turned to gawk at her. Their expressions ranged from curious, to envious, to downright hostile. She spied a bearded man with a patch over one eye and blackened teeth, a harried woman with a swaddled baby on one hip and a toddler clinging to her ragged skirts, and a skinny hunchback with a porkpie hat and a sinister glare.

Lindsey hadn't felt at all troubled as an Englishwoman strolling down a street thronging with dark-skinned Hin-dus. Yet in this place she found herself discomfited by the scrutiny of her fellow Londoners. She imagined seeing herself through their eyes: a fine lady in a costly blue gown and copper-hued pelisse, her fashionable straw bonnet decorated by an elegant peacock feather. Given time to plan ahead, she would have donned a cheap disguise. But this rare chance had presented itself and she wouldn't turn back now.

Lifting her chin, she headed toward the clerk's desk at the side of the chamber. Her heart was thudding, her palms damp within her gloves. Never in her life had she done anything so outrageous. If her parents found out, at best she'd be locked in her bedchamber for the next year. At worst, she'd be married off to the highest bidder—likely Lord Wrayford, who offered a duchess's tiara.

Had he recovered from her attack yet? Would he go straight to her house and tattle to Mama? Would he reveal that Lindsey had the audacity to steal his carriage and go off on her own?

The thought made her anxious. It was imperative that she finish her business here and be gone before anyone found out what she'd done.

A burly, balding man in a dark coat sat on a stool at a tall desk. His weathered features bespoke a world-weary outlook on life.

"Good afternoon, sir. I'd like to speak to Mr. Cyrus Bott." It was the name Mrs. Beardsley had mentioned, the Runner who had questioned Mrs. Beardsley's servants after her maid had been murdered by the Serpentine Strangler.

The man didn't bat an eye; he just came out from behind the desk. "Aye, miss. Follow me, then."

Relieved to escape the gawkers, she scurried to keep up with him. They proceeded down one barren corridor, then another, their footsteps echoing. At the end, he jerked his thumb toward a narrow stairway. "Top floor, second door on yer left."

He turned on his heel and trudged back toward his post.

Lindsey looked up uncertainly at the towering stairwell. Could she really do this? She must. It was now or never.

She mounted three flights of stairs and found herself in a cramped attic corridor. Light filtered through a small window at the far end. The floorboards creaked underfoot as she walked down the passageway. Locating the room, she took a deep breath for courage and then knocked on the half-closed door.

A quick tapping of footsteps sounded inside, then the panel swung open to reveal a dapper young man with neatly combed dark hair. He wore a tailored brown coat, white linens, and tan breeches.

Surprise flitted over his face before he inclined his head in a respectful bow. "Have you taken a wrong turn, my lady? May I escort you to the proper office?"

"I was directed here by the clerk downstairs." His genteel appearance wasn't what she'd expected of a Bow Street Runner. The faint aroma of sandalwood emanated from him. "Are you Mr. Cyrus Bott?"

"I am indeed. And you are . . . ?"

She had no intention of telling him her real name. "You may call me"—she glanced at the color of his coat—"Miss Brown. I'm told you're investigating the case of the Serpentine Strangler."

His limpid blue eyes widened slightly. "Indeed so. Although I cannot imagine what a fine lady as yourself would know of such a sordid matter."

"I . . ." Lindsey paused. Could she really say what needed to be said? She was taking an enormous step from which there would be no turning back. But she had to speak out; lives were depending on her. "I may know some information vital to solving the case," she stated. "You see, I've a strong suspicion as to the identity of the Serpentine Strangler."

"Stop right here," Thane ordered.

The coachman obligingly drew the landau to a halt half a block away from the yellow phaeton. Flummoxed, Thane watched Lindsey bend down to speak to a street urchin and then vanish into Bow Street Station.

Of all the destinations she could have been heading, this was the very last place he would have expected her to visit. Refined ladies did not set foot among the common riffraff. Her behavior was so wildly out of the norm that he needed a moment to ponder.

Wrayford must have attacked her. She must have come straight here in order to report him to the authorities. That was the only explanation that made any sense—indeed the only explanation he could fathom at all.

But why had she not gone home, as most young ladies

in such a dire situation would have done? Was she afraid her mother wouldn't believe her? Perhaps. Yet Lindsey had to know that the chief magistrate would immediately contact her parents. So there was nothing to be gained by putting her reputation further at risk in coming here.

For that matter, how the devil had she known where Bow Street Station was located?

"Where are we?" Jocelyn asked. "Why have we stopped here?"

He glanced distractedly at her, his gaze flicking at the sketchbook in her lap. "To give you a moment to draw without the carriage rattling."

Jocelyn tapped the tip of her pencil against her chin. "Hmm. Is that the entire reason? I do believe we have been following Lindsey all this time."

The alertness in her eyes handed him a fresh complication. He could see that fobbing her off with a fib wouldn't work. "That's very observant of you."

"I often notice things that other people miss," she said airily. "All artists do. It's bred into my nature to see details."

How adorably sweet Jocelyn could be. A flash of fondness swept away his concern—but only for a moment. "I'm afraid Miss Crompton may be in a spot of trouble. I'd like to offer her my assistance. Will you stay here and draw for a few minutes? The coachman will protect you in my absence."

Lindsey took the only chair in the tiny office. Although the place was meticulously neat, the windowless room had to be smaller than one of the linen closets in her house. The sole contents of the office included a shelf of books and a writing desk barely large enough to hold paper, pens, and inkpot.

Cyrus Bott remained standing, his hands clasped behind

his back. His deferential bearing posed no threat, yet she felt a trifle awkward having to look up at him. The close quarters added to her underlying sense of anxiety.

Or perhaps it was just the suspicions weighing on her mind that made her ill at ease. Had she been right to come here? What if there was a rational explanation for Mansfield's suspicious behavior?

"You have information about the Strangler," the Runner prompted.

"Yes. I believe I do." Lindsey knew she had to speak out if lives were to be saved. Yet the words lodged in her throat. "I beg your pardon. This is difficult for me."

"Do take your time, Miss Brown. It cannot be a simple task for a fine lady such as yourself to venture into a place as sordid as this. If I can help alleviate your fears in any way, pray let me know."

His kindness was an unexpected blessing. She had imagined the Bow Street Runners to be a bold and dangerous lot, brawny men who were rough around the edges, since they dealt with criminals who roamed the dark stews of the London underworld. But if she'd passed Cyrus Bott on the street, she would have mistaken him for an ordinary gentleman. There had to be reassurance in that thought.

Lindsey moistened her lips. "There is a certain gentleman, a suitor of mine, who has been embroiled recently in suspicious behaviors. The first time we met, he was in the company of a maidservant named Tilly who has now vanished."

"Vanished?" He gave a start of surprise. "Where was she employed?"

"At Lord Wrayford's house on Bruton Street. I must add that the gentleman to whom I refer also employed a maid named Nelda who disappeared a fortnight ago. No one in his household seems to know what happened to the girl. And . . . and this gentleman departed on an overnight trip at the same time she went missing."

"I see." Hands behind his back, Bott paced slowly back and forth in the narrow space. "As I'm sure you're aware, servants do come and go for various reasons. They usually move on to other posts. Unless there is direct evidence connecting this man to one of the murders, I cannot attribute these events to anything but coincidence."

Lindsey didn't dare reveal that she knew from personal experience Mansfield was also an accomplished seducer. "I also took the liberty of searching his desk one day. In it he had a news clipping about the murders."

"Hmm. A bit unusual, but there could be an explanation. Perhaps he harbors an interest in crime stories. People are often fascinated by lurid events."

"Let me add, he's acquainted with Lady Entwhistle, who employed the first murdered maidservant. I've seen them together myself, at a society ball. They were very . . . close. That means he may well have been in Lady Entwhistle's house and had contact with the victim."

Bott stopped, his eyes boring into her. "Indeed? If what you say is true, it will call for an investigation. You must give me a name. Who is this gentleman you suspect of being the Serpentine Strangler?"

Lindsey swallowed. The whole point of her coming to Bow Street Station was to gain help from the Runners in uncovering the truth. To catch the killer before he struck again. So why was she hesitating? Why did she wish she'd never obeyed the impetuous notion to come here?

More to the point, why did the memory of Mansfield's kiss clutch at her heart?

She mustn't allow her private weakness for him to interfere with justice. It would be terribly wrong to withhold his identity when those two maidservants had disappeared into thin air. Dear God, how horrifying it would be if someone else died because of her dithering.

"His name is—"

The creak of a floorboard out in the corridor startled her. She jumped, half-turning on the chair toward the open doorway.

Thane froze in place. Barely breathing, he pressed himself to the peeling green paint on the wall. Damn himself for creeping closer. He knew the old floorboards made noise, yet the tale Lindsey was relating had him disbelieving his own ears.

Three quick steps sounded, then Bott poked his well-groomed head out of the office. He stared at Thane, one eyebrow arching.

Thane pressed a forefinger to his lips.

The Runner scowled slightly and gave an almost imperceptible nod of understanding. Then he vanished back into the office.

"No one's there, Miss Brown. This is merely an old building, and I often hear such sounds. Now, do tell me the name."

There was a short silence before Lindsey spoke. "Yes, well . . . his name is . . ."

Thane cocked his head to hear better.

"Lord Mansfield."

It took a moment for her declaration to register. Then Thane clenched his teeth to hold back a huff of incredulity. He wanted to hoot with laughter. *What the devil—?* Was she accusing him of being Serpentine Strangler as some sort of twisted revenge for that hot kiss they'd shared?

Or did she truly believe it?

She must, for she'd attributed the disappearance of

Tilly and Nelda to him—and rightfully so, although she'd leaped to the wrong conclusion for his actions. She'd also placed a wildly mistaken meaning on his flirtation with Lady Entwhistle.

Of course, Lindsey was unaware that he'd been investigating Wrayford's connection to the merry widow. No one in society knew of Thane's secret business in assisting the Runners.

He wanted to march into the office and give her a hard shake to restore the common sense she'd clearly lost. It infuriated him that she actually believed him capable of committing those vile murders.

At least now her past actions made sense. No wonder she had been trying to invade his house. She hadn't been looking for the IOU but for evidence to implicate him.

Yet when he had kissed her she had melted in his arms. His seduction skills had overcome even her suspicions—if only for a few wildly enjoyable moments. If the circumstances weren't so dire, he might find her misconceptions somewhat amusing.

Inside the office, they were concluding their meeting.

"I warn you," Bott was saying, "I must have irrefutable evidence of his culpability. One cannot arrest a member of the Quality on the basis of mere anecdotal evidence."

"Oh, certainly! That's why I asked you to look into Nelda's disappearance, as well as Tilly's. Oh . . . and please do promise me you won't tell Lord Mansfield where you heard about this."

"I won't, Miss Brown. Your secret is safe with me."

Miss Brown. The little minx at least had had the sense to use a pseudonym. If anyone discovered she'd come alone to Bow Street, driving a stolen phaeton and associating with Runners, her reputation would be in tatters. In spite of his anger, he had to acknowledge Lindsey's fearless, intrepid spirit.

"Thank you," she told Bott. "And I'll be sure to send word to you of any further evidence I can gather on my own."

Her words jabbed into Thane, causing him to stand up straight. Like hell she would investigate the murders!

"That won't be necessary," Bott said, his voice taking on a pompous tone. "No fine lady should dirty herself with common police work. Such affairs are best left to the proper authorities."

The chair legs scraped slightly as she rose to her feet. "We'll see," she murmured.

Scowling, Thane retreated to the staircase. He had to get out of here before she caught him eavesdropping. But as God was his witness, he'd make certain Lindsey Crompton kept her nose out of the dangerous matter of the Serpentine Strangler.

Chapter 16

"M-Miss Crompton, w-will you honor m-me with this d-dance?"

Lindsey had just escaped a dull conversation with a stuffy middle-aged baron when she found herself facing Mr. Sykes.

With his shaggy brown hair, freckled face, and warm brown eyes, he brought to mind an eager puppy. His ill-fitting russet coat and frayed cuffs revealed the purpose behind his dogged pursuit of her. As a younger son, he desperately needed to wed an heiress.

On occasion, Lindsey accepted his invitation, although unfortunately his skill at dancing matched his ability to speak clearly. "Thank you, but—"

At that moment, Lindsey spotted Lord Mansfield making his way toward her through the throng of guests. He was easy to spot in the multitude of aristocrats, since he was half a head taller than most of the other men present. Even from a distance, the sight of his scarred, handsome features caused her heart to lurch.

He was gazing straight at her.

A fit of nerves tied her stomach into knots. Had he been contacted by Cyrus Bott? Did he know that she'd accused him of murder? Lud, she couldn't face him. Not here, in front of all these people.

She turned to Mr. Sykes and tucked her gloved hand into the crook of his arm. "I'd be pleased to accept."

His spaniel eyes lit with adoration. "Oh! M-my dear M-Miss Crompton, y-you have made m-me the h-happiest of men."

"I'm very glad. Now do come along."

She half-dragged him to the dance floor, where other couples were forming long lines, the men on one side, the ladies on the other. At least the separation gave her an excuse to avoid making small talk. Within moments, the orchestra in the corner of the ballroom struck up a country tune and she had the freedom to ponder while performing the orderly steps of the dance.

What a coward she'd proved to be. After that interview with the Bow Street Runner, Lindsey had expected to feel relieved at the burden of worry that had been lifted from her. She'd thought to relax, knowing she had acted appropriately in relating her suspicions to the proper authorities. Instead, she'd been wracked with guilt. She'd gone over and over the evidence, but now it all seemed weak and circumstantial.

What if Mansfield was tossed into prison—and he was innocent of any crime? What would happen to Jocelyn? Mansfield had said the girl didn't have any blood relations who could take her in.

Surreptitiously Lindsey kept a watch for him, but he had vanished into the horde of guests. That fact did little to ease her tension. As she performed the dance, she braced herself to feel the tap of his fingers on her shoulder. It would be just like him to appear out of nowhere.

Nothing happened.

Down the line, she saw many familiar faces, but no Mansfield and no Lord Wrayford, either. Since attacking her two days ago, Wrayford had avoided her company. After leaving Bow Street Station, she'd deposited his pha-

eton at a public stable and sent a note as to where to retrieve the vehicle. To her mother she'd told a fib about
enjoying their ride in the park. The news had made Mrs.
Crompton happy for a time, but tonight, during the coach
ride here to the party, Mama had fretted about his neglect
of Lindsey.

At least Wrayford hadn't tattled on her. Maybe he'd
been too embarrassed to reveal that a lady had bested
him, and in such a humiliating manner. With any luck,
the incident would mark the end of his interference in her
life.

As the dance ended and Mr. Sykes escorted her back
to her mother, Lindsey glanced across the crowded ballroom and stopped short. Mr. Sykes stuttered something,
but she paid him no heed. Her attention was focused on
the arched doorway.

Mansfield stood in the large foyer just outside the ballroom. He was speaking to a maid who carried a silver
tray of champagne glasses. After a moment, he walked
alongside the servant in the direction of the grand staircase, where they vanished from sight.

Lindsey's breath froze in her lungs. All of her suspicions of him returned in full force. What in heaven's
name was he doing with that maidservant?

"Is-is s-something wrong?" Mr. Sykes asked.

"No, of course not." She glanced toward her mother,
who was holding court with several other older ladies
seated in chairs near a stand of palms. Their heads were
bent close while they shared tidbits of gossip. "I merely
saw someone I know."

He bowed over her hand. "It-it has b-been a delight.
M-May I c-call on you tomorrow?"

"I'm afraid you'll have to obtain permission from
Mama," Lindsey said, knowing that her mother would
consider the penniless younger son of a baron eminently

unsuitable. "Now, if you'll excuse me, I must have a word with my friend."

Lindsey scurried toward the gilded arch of the doorway. To avoid being delayed by any acquaintance, she kept her head down slightly while making her way through the crush of guests. People thronged the grand lobby, most of them strolling toward the supper room where a midnight buffet was laid out.

She went against the flow toward the staircase that curved downward to the ground floor. All the while, she kept a sharp eye peeled for Mansfield. At the carved oak balustrade overlooking the entrance hall, she glanced down and spied him.

He was alone now, striding rapidly toward the rear of the house. Once again, he vanished from her view.

Without conscious decision, Lindsey went flying down the staircase, clutching her pale blue skirt to keep from tripping. At the bottom, she followed in the direction he'd been heading and caught sight of him at the end of the long passageway. There he opened a door and disappeared through it.

Was he intending to meet that maidservant? Had they planned a rendezvous in some deserted place, as he'd done with Tilly?

Alarm spurred Lindsey on a swift journey along the arched corridor. On either side, the chambers were dimly lit, since most of the guests were upstairs in the reception rooms. Reaching the door, she opened it and was startled to find herself outside on a loggia that ran along the back of the house. There were lanterns strung through the trees, but with supper about to begin, no guests strolled the pathways.

Where was Mansfield?

A tall shadow at the back gate caught her eye. As he stepped through the opening, a shaft of moonlight revealed the distinctive features of his scarred face.

She shivered, as much from a sense of sinister fore-boding as from the chill of the evening air. Logic fought a battle with her imagination. Maybe she was mistaken to think he'd made plans for a tryst. Maybe he'd tired of the party and intended to return home or to pay a visit to his club.

Yet a nagging fear persisted in her. She'd never forgive herself if there was another murder and she had the means to prevent it. The maid could have slipped out a different door in order to meet him elsewhere. The woman's life could be in jeopardy.

Lindsey headed through the garden in pursuit. Her slippers made a muted crunching sound on the crushed oyster shells of the path. Anxiety tightened her stomach. If only she'd taken the pistol, the one Mama kept in her night table, the one Lindsey had borrowed the previous year and lent to her sister Portia, who'd promptly used it to shoot Colin in the arm. What an uproar that had been!

The memory usually brought a smile to Lindsey's face, but not tonight. Tonight she longed fiercely for the protection of a weapon.

Yet the lack of one didn't deter her, either.

Quietly she opened the garden gate and stepped through it. Gloom shrouded the mews, and the scent of horse drop-pings perfumed the night air. In a nearby stable, a horse snorted, then settled down.

Which way had Mansfield gone? Was it possible he merely intended to fetch his mount and in a moment she'd hear him riding away?

Her eyes were adjusting to the lack of light. To the left she glimpsed a black shadow far down the alleyway. Good heavens, he was moving away from her at a rapid pace.

Even as she plunged through the darkness in hot pur-suit, Lindsey wrestled with a mountain of qualms. She oughtn't be doing this. Oh, she was going to be in such awful trouble if her mother found out she had left the ballroom on this wild chase. All manner of terrible things could happen to a woman who ventured out alone at night. Footpads and robbers roamed London, hunting for easy prey. This time, she might not be so lucky in subduing her assailant as she'd been with Lord Wrayford.

Ahead of her, Mansfield passed through another gate. The creak of the hinges carried through the hushed air. Afraid she might miss him, Lindsey made haste, stumbling on a stone and biting her lip to keep from crying out. Luckily, the gate stood ajar and she was able to slip noiselessly through the opening.

She found herself in a darkened garden three doors away from where the ball was being held. Taking refuge behind a tree trunk, she studied the scene. Lamplight glowed in several of the windows. A winding pathway led through clumps of overgrown plants and shrubbery. She could just make out the black figure of Mansfield striding toward the house.

Lindsey wracked her brain to remember who lived here. She had visited most of the better families in Mayfair, but apparently this house didn't belong to one of them. Yet there was something about the location that nagged at her memory. . . .

The distant scuff of a footstep yanked her attention to the veranda. A rear door opened, and the faint light revealed a tall, dark form entering the house. *Mansfield*. She hesitated no more than an instant before scurrying in his wake.

Many times in her daydreams she had fancied herself on a clandestine mission such as this one, creeping through the gloom while tracking a dangerous murderer. But reality had its drawbacks. The murky darkness beneath the trees made it difficult to see. Once, she bumped her knee against a stone bench alongside the path. Brambles snagged her hem several times, forcing her to stop and carefully unhook herself lest she face awkward questions later from Mama about her ruined skirt.

Reaching the rear door at last, Lindsey cupped her hands and peered through the glass. A long, dim corridor stretched out before her. About midway down, candlelight shone from a room.

Had Mansfield gone in there?

Hoping to peek into a window, she made a detour around to the side of the house. But the pitch-darkness meant the draperies must be drawn.

Blast! She simply had to find out what he was doing. If he was up to no good, then by the heavens, she must find some way to stop him—or at least to send word to Bow Street Station. If it turned out to be nothing, she could retreat from the house and return to the party with no one the wiser.

She eased open the back door and stepped inside, standing in the darkness a moment to get her bearings. The corridor ahead was deserted, but voices and laughter emanated from somewhere. There seemed to be several people present.

She took that as an encouraging sign. Surely Mansfield wouldn't murder a maidservant in the midst of a group of witnesses. Perhaps finding out who he'd come here to join would give her a clue as to his purpose.

Lindsey crept closer, thankful for the dancing slippers with their soft kid soles. She hugged the wall, staying to the shadows in case someone suddenly ambled out into the corridor.

The closer she drew, however, the more she realized the voices were coming from elsewhere. From upstairs?

She peeked into the room. A fire burned low in the grate. On a table, a lamp cast pale illumination over a sitting room. No one occupied the chamber.

Lindsey walked onward, following the echo of distant revelry. She kept alert for any sign of Mansfield's dark figure. But the entire ground floor appeared to be deserted.

Arriving at the gloomy foyer, she took a quick glance around and then started up the staircase. Her heart thudded against her ribs. If she was caught here, she might be taken for a thief. A scandal would ensue, one that would land her in hot water with her parents. Yet she couldn't stop now, not until she discovered Mansfield's reason for coming here.

He must know the person who lived in this house, else why would he have walked right inside? Was it possible he had arranged to meet his paramours here? She'd heard whispered gossip of gentlemen keeping such a place for their mistresses. They certainly couldn't bring fallen women home and still maintain their respectability.

Upon reaching the next floor, she found herself in a corridor lit by an occasional candle in a wall sconce. A patch of light radiated from the room nearest the staircase. So did the voices, which were louder now.

She tiptoed closer to see who was present. At the doorway, she moved her head slightly forward and risked a look inside.

A foursome sat playing cards at a table by the fire, three gentlemen and a dark-haired lady whose back was to the door. Lindsey recognized two of the men as disreputable scapegraces known for their gambling debts. Her eyes widened on the third one—Lord Wrayford.

Lindsey shrank back out of sight and flattened herself against the wall. *Good heavens!* If he saw her here, she'd be in trouble for certain.

And where was Mansfield? Was he sitting out of sight,

an observer to the card game? Surely so, because where else would he have gone?

"Aha!" Wrayford declared from inside the room. "Now there's the winning card."

A burst of male laughter rang out. "Go on, m'lady," one of the other men said. "You lost the wager fair and square, and now 'tis time to pay the piper."

"Oh, I'll pay with pleasure," came her dulcet tones. "And by the end of it, all three of you will be begging for mercy."

Chortles and hoots followed her declaration.

Taking advantage of the noise, Lindsey eased herself to the edge of the doorway again. The brunette had risen from the table and draped herself across Lord Wrayford's lap. She was playfully unbuttoning his coat to much raucous encouragement from the other two gentlemen.

Her identity hit Lindsey at once. Lady Entwhistle!

No wonder Lindsey had had the vague sense that she ought to know this place. Upon learning that the first murdered maid had been employed by the widow, Lindsey had obtained Lady Entwhistle's address. She would have known the house at once had she approached it from the street instead of the mews.

A coquettish smile on her face, Lady Entwhistle licked her forefinger and then trailed it along the edge of her extremely low-cut bodice. Lord Wrayford watched the action with an avid leer.

"Now, there's my sweetcakes," he said. "I do believe I shall enjoy a little bite or two."

Growling, he buried his face in the valley of her breasts while the other men guzzled brandy and cheered.

Lindsey's stomach curdled with revulsion. *What a nasty scoundrel!* To think Lord Wrayford had presented himself to her parents as an upstanding suitor. After his attack on her, and now this disgusting display, she would never marry him no matter how much Mama schemed and scolded.

And now Lindsey could see why Lady Entwhistle had a bad reputation. The woman was making a spectacle of herself. Her behavior was far more outrageous than the time when she'd been at that ball with Mansfield a few weeks ago, flirting openly with him, touching his chest and making come-hither eyes at him.

The memory caused an unpleasant wrench inside Lindsey. How unnerving to imagine Mansfield inside that room, watching as Lady Entwhistle and Wrayford engaged in a bout of kissing and caressing. Did these aristocrats have no shame?

Just then, one of the other men jumped up and started to unbutton the back of Lady Entwhistle's gown. The widow did a sinuous movement of her upper body and her bodice drooped, exposing a portion of her lacy corset. The man began to crudely fondle her breasts, but Lord Wrayford shoved him back.

"Get away with you, Skidmore," he irritably told the other man. "She's mine. I won the round and I won't have you cheating."

Skidmore shook his fists. "You dare to call me a cheat? I'll meet you at dawn. Pistols or swords, take your choice."

Lady Entwhistle gave a throaty laugh. "Patience, gentlemen. You'll all have your turn. In the meantime, it might be best if Wrayford and I retired to my bedchamber to enjoy our pleasures in private."

Lindsey ducked back out of sight. They were going to catch her out here!

She beat a hasty retreat, deeming it time to flee the house and return to the ball. Heading toward the stairs, she glanced back over her shoulder. In the same instant, something moved in the darkened stairwell that led to the upper floors.

A shadowy figure grabbed her from behind and yanked her hard against his chest. A masculine hand clamped over her mouth to stifle her yelp. She knew him at once from his scent and the strength of his body.

Mansfield!

Chapter 17

"Minx," he whispered, his voice a mere thread of sound in her ear. "What the devil are you doing here? You're going back to the party at once."

Lindsey wanted to retort that she'd meant to do just that. But with his hand over her mouth, she could utter only garbled nonsense. She needed to tell him that Lady Entwhistle and Lord Wrayford were about to walk out into the passageway.

Apparently, Mansfield had not made his presence known to the others. Was he, too, spying on them?

If so, why?

Lindsey wriggled and fought against his hold. But his arms were iron bands enclosing her. He started to urge her toward the downward flight of stairs. Then the tapping of footsteps coming from the card room must have alerted him to the imminent danger.

"Blast," he muttered.

He hauled Lindsey up a few risers into the shadows of the upper stairwell. Here they were out of sight of the doorway. She squirmed against him, trying to signal that they couldn't stay here, that Lady Entwhistle and Lord Wrayford would catch them at any moment.

Yet where was there to hide?

The pair had walked out into the corridor. The sounds of their kissing and giggling drifted up the stairwell.

Lady Entwhistle let out a playful squeal. "Please, sir, you mustn't ravish me! Why, I've my reputation to consider."

Wrayford gave a raspy chuckle. "You know how much I like that game," he said. "You play the pretty maid. I'll be your lusty master and chase you into the bedchamber."

"Mmm." Her voice took on a high-pitched, beseeching tone: "Me mam raised me to be a good girl. Pray don't steal my virtue."

"Disobedient chit! If you refuse to submit, I shall tie you to the bedposts while I have my way with you."

Mansfield's arms tensed around Lindsey. In a flash, she found herself towed up the staircase and hauled through the nearest doorway. The oil lamp that burned on a table revealed a large canopied bed and various pieces of dainty white furniture. From the collection of perfume and cosmetic bottles on a dressing table, Lindsey realized this must be Lady Entwhistle's chamber.

Mansfield must have come to that conclusion at the same time as she did because he cursed under his breath and brought her to a crashing halt, his hand still over her mouth.

Pivoting on his heel, he made a move to leave. But it was too late.

The tramp of running footsteps drew nearer, along with Lady Entwhistle's squeals of sham alarm.

Lindsey didn't need any urging to hide. In unison, she and Mansfield dashed into the safety of the adjoining dressing room. She had a quick view of several wardrobes, one with a myriad of gowns spilling out. Then he shouldered the door shut and plunged the room into total darkness.

They stood there, breathing hard. Relieved at their close escape, Lindsey ceased fighting. There was no purpose, since they were stuck in here together. Oddly enough, they had become comrades against a common enemy.

The constriction of his hold eased. His lips close to her ear, he murmured, "I trust you won't scream for help."

When she shook her head, he withdrew his hand from her mouth. She turned in his arms to face him, but his expression was lost to the gloom.

Her voice low, she hissed, "What were you thinking, to grab me like that?"

"The more pertinent question is: why did you follow me here?"

"I . . ." Lindsey had no ready excuse. He couldn't possibly guess that she suspected him of murder. Or that she'd reported him to the authorities. "I was curious to know where you were going, that's all."

"Indeed?" He gripped her shoulders and gave her a little shake. "Did no one ever warn you about the danger of venturing out alone at night? Or going uninvited into strange houses?"

"*You* certainly let yourself in here. Why were *you* hiding in the stairwell without Lady Entwhistle's knowledge?"

He hesitated. "I was returning something I'd borrowed from her. Other than that, the matter is of no concern to you."

He was lying; Lindsey could sense it in her bones. So what *was* his true purpose here?

She was distracted by the patter of footsteps outside the door to the dressing room. The sounds of a mock chase came from the bedchamber, with Lord Wrayford barking out commands and Lady Entwhistle playing the coyly virtuous maid.

Despite the peril of discovery and the embarrassing

romp going on out there, the situation struck Lindsey as humorous. Her governess, Miss Underhill, had never tutored her in the proper etiquette of how to behave when trapped in a closet with a man while a tryst ensued in the next room. A giggle escaped her, and she had to clap her hand to her mouth. Luckily, the clamor those two were making drowned her out.

An answering chuckle rumbled from Mansfield. She could feel it vibrate in his chest as he held her loosely in his arms. They stood close for a few minutes, listening to the silly scuffle outside and struggling to contain their laughter.

Bending closer, he spoke softly into her hair: "There's no other way out of here, you know. This dressing room has only the one door. We shall have to wait until they're finished."

"I'm afraid you're right."

They were imprisoned here together in the pitch-darkness. Why wasn't she terrified?

Mansfield could very well be the Serpentine Strangler, yet for some peculiar reason she felt safe in his arms. She tried to reason it out. Perhaps he had this reassuring effect on all women. Perhaps that was how he had lured those maidservants to their death.

However, that line of argument now struck her as nonsensical. Maybe it was their shared laughter, or the fact that they were cellmates in this luxurious prison, but for whatever cause, her mistrust of him had eased.

At least for the moment.

"Since we may be here for a while," Mansfield whispered, "we might as well sit."

He guided her down to the floor and settled her against him, his arm looped around her waist. It seemed the most natural thing in the world for Lindsey to rest her head in the crook of his shoulder. It occurred to her that he hadn't known the location of Lady Entwhistle's bedchamber. Had she been mistaken, then, to assume they were lovers?

The sounds of revelry continued, muted by the closed door. It was a lucky thing she couldn't make out their conversation. The situation was awkward enough already.

Mansfield found her hand in the darkness and stroked it. "There's one good outcome to this," he whispered. "You've discovered what a cad Wrayford is. He's only pursuing you for your money."

"Hmm. That's quite a compliment."

He squeezed her fingers. "This is no jest," he muttered urgently. "You cannot allow him to court you any longer. Promise me you'll refuse all his invitations. Don't go anywhere alone with him."

Lindsey had learned that lesson all too well. But there was no way she could tell Mansfield about the incident in Wrayford's house. He might take it into his mind to confront Wrayford. And then Mansfield might discover that she'd stolen the phaeton. If he ever learned where she'd gone . . .

"You'll have to convince my mother of that," she said lightly. "Mama has her mind set on making a match between me and Wrayford."

"I know. She told me so herself."

Surprised, Lindsey angled her head back and tried to see him, but the shadows were too thick. "What do you mean? When?"

"The day Jocelyn and I were to take you out for a drive. Your mother made it quite clear that I was to stay far away from you." He paused, then added in a softly calculating tone, "Which leads me to wonder if you asked her to do so."

There was an underlying accusation in his voice that set her heart to beating faster. A thread of fear stitched her lungs, squeezing her of air.

How much did he guess? Was he aware, after all, that she suspected him of murder?

Wrayford's triumphant hoot penetrated the door. He must have caught Lady Entwhistle, for she uttered a mock cry of surrender. The bed ropes squeaked loudly from the force of their activities.

Lindsey blessed the darkness for hiding her blush. She certainly didn't want to picture what those two were doing, so she focused on her whispered conversation with Mansfield. "I never told my mother any such thing. Although if I may add, I'd rather remain a spinster than marry you—or any other nobleman."

She braced herself for his anger. But he merely continued to stroke her hand. "Why?" he asked. "Why are you so dead set against a future that most other ladies aspire to gain?"

Because she yearned to fly free of the gilded cage where she'd been locked since childhood. Because she wanted to be independent, unencumbered by the expectations of society. Because she dreamed of setting up a discreet agency where she could devote herself to solving mysteries for genteel clients.

"I don't wish to spend my days shopping, planning menus, and calling on gossips and snobs."

"Fair enough. When you're my wife, I'll absolve you of those duties."

The prospect of marriage to Mansfield plunged her into a quagmire of longing, and she grabbed desperately for the safety of resistance. "I never agreed to wed you."

"You agreed to a betrothal. May I remind you, our month is rapidly drawing to a close."

"And may I remind *you,* my promise was made under threat of blackmail."

"Hmm. Then I shall have to find a better means of persuasion."

Tipping up her chin, he subjected her to a light, teasing kiss. She could have drawn away, but the brush of his lips felt too wonderful. One of her hands rested on his chest, where her palm absorbed the strong beating of his heart. It was no use denying the fact that she desired him. When his tongue probed for entry, she parted her lips and slipped her arm around his neck to draw him closer.

Oh, he did know how to please a woman. Being caught here in the dressing room gave them the luxury of time to kiss and caress. He continued to explore her mouth while his hand wandered up and down her bare arm, then along the curve of her waist and hip, sending a delicious shiver through her. He seemed far more in control tonight than during their last passionate encounter in the library of Jocelyn's house, when Lindsey had fended him off with a letter opener.

She traced the long, thin scar on his cheek. "Is this the legacy of another disgruntled woman?"

He chuckled. "Hardly. It was an unfortunate encounter with a French bayonet."

"You never speak of the war. What was it like?"

"Hell on earth." He nuzzled her hair, whispering, "I vastly prefer Heaven on earth here with you."

She should laugh at such outrageously romantic blather. But common sense fell prey to the pleasure that wrapped around her. And her imagination ran wild at the suggestive sounds coming from the bedchamber.

The rhythmic rocking of the bedsprings, the moans and groans of excitement, now made her burn with unladylike zeal—for Mansfield. It was shocking to realize that she ached to do that same carnal act with him. She wanted it so much her entire body hummed with need.

Through the gloom, she traced his lips with her fingertip. "You cannot expect me to believe such overblown flattery."

"Mmm. If you prefer, there's no need to talk at all."

Much to her delight, his mouth took hers in another drowning kiss that left her gasping. She moved her hands over him, sliding them inside his coat and relishing the firm muscles of his chest and the narrow slope of his waist. He was like a furnace, radiating the heat of passion.

Bending his head, he ran his tongue along the bare skin above her décolletage. She bit back a moan and buried her hands in the thickness of his hair. His warm breath stimulated her skin, the sensation traveling down to the throbbing center of her body.

The darkness of the dressing room enhanced her awareness of him. With every breath, she drew in his spicy scent. Moving against him brought her into contact with hard contours of his body, so harmoniously paired with her own softness. How was it that no other man had ever made her feel so alive?

She'd always scorned women who fawned over men. They seemed like silly twittering birds begging for a crumb of affection. It had been something of a shock when, the previous year, her otherwise rational sister Portia had succumbed to the charms of Colin, Viscount Ratcliffe. That they were happily wed and expecting their first child had left Lindsey with a vague sense of perplexity.

But now she was beginning to understand the power of bodily desire. Especially when Mansfield slid his hand beneath her skirts.

She forgot all else as he worked his way upward, over stocking and garter. A part of her was scandalized, yet a fevered anticipation robbed her of breath. She found herself shifting restlessly against him, tugging up her gown to allow him better access, shameless in her fervor. When his finger slid into her damp heat, she moaned from sheer bliss.

"Shh," he murmured.

A tenuous grip on reality alerted her to the need for quiet, and she buried her face against his chest. Mansfield continued to ply her lightly, rubbing and stroking, seeming to know precisely how to feed the heat inside her. Lindsey hardly knew what she craved, except that she could happily endure this torturous delight forever. She clung to his shoulders, needing him as her anchor, as her purveyor of pleasure.

His touch became deeper, more rhythmic, until she feared she might die of pleasure. Each caress sent her closer to the verge of madness. Needing surcease, she pressed herself against his hand. "Oh, Mansfield . . . please . . ."

"Lindsey, you're mine. Mine alone . . . never forget that."

His voice barely registered as a powerful rush of bliss swept through her body. It was so intense, so startling, that she arched back, crying out in sheer wonder. Quickly he caught her close, holding her face to his neck while the marvelous sensations ebbed away, leaving her replete and happy.

Only then did she sense Mansfield's alertness. Against her ear he murmured, "Hush, darling. They've heard us."

From the bedchamber came the sound of upraised voices. The bed ropes squeaked. Heavy male footsteps hit the floor and stomped toward the dressing room.

Awareness returned to her with a shock. She struggled to slow her breathing, to think coherently. If they were found here like this, with her clothing in disarray . . .

She tried to get up, but Mansfield clasped her close, not allowing her to move.

The footsteps proceeded past the dressing room to the outer door, where Wrayford shouted something unintelligible.

His face buried in her hair, Mansfield whispered, "He

thinks it was one of those other two buffoons, spying on them."

Lindsey nodded wordlessly. *Oh, thank heavens.* After a moment, a door slammed, the footsteps went past, and the bed creaked again.

All the while, she was keenly aware that Mansfield's hand still lay beneath her skirts, his finger resting casually in her most intimate folds. A little aftershock of pleasure rolled through her. How amazing that he could coax such a surfeit of sensations from her body.

And no wonder girls were warned never to allow a man's touch. Lindsey had a sinking suspicion it could become addicting.

What little she knew about mating came from her time in India, where such matters were not so strictly hidden as in England. Once, not long before her family's departure, she had wandered into a Hindu shrine dedicated to the worship of Shiva's lingam. Women praying for fertility had placed garlands of marigolds before the stone statue of an erect male member. Their willingness to kneel in supplication to a symbol of raw masculine dominance had disturbed her greatly. It had seemed humiliating for any female to prostrate herself in such a manner.

But now, the memory thrust Lindsey into the throes of a new temptation. Mansfield had not achieved his own pleasure. As he kissed her brow, she let her hand slip down to the waistband of his breeches—and lower. She found the hard swelling shape of him and cupped him in her palm.

A tremor coursed through his body. He sucked a breath through his teeth, then reached down and dragged her hand away. "My God . . . don't do that."

Suddenly uncertain, she flushed at her own boldness. "I'm sorry. I only wanted . . ."

"I want it, too," he whispered roughly. "You cannot imagine how much."

From outside the dressing room came the groans and cries of repletion. The screeching of the bed ropes finally came to a stop.

Mansfield's face moved in a grimace that she felt against her cheek. He continued, his voice a mere breath of sound, "But not here. Not now. When we make love for the first time, I'll have you in my bed . . . as my wife."

His declaration stirred Lindsey in a way that left her restless and confused. She wasn't supposed to trust him at all, let alone fall prey to his charm. "It's wrong of you to coerce me."

To her surprise, he chuckled softly. "Haven't you learned? Coercion can be quite a delight." Beneath her skirts, he lazily fingered her again, igniting a pulse of hot sensation in her core. "Or perhaps you'd prefer to cling to your plan of remaining a spinster."

His amusement spurred a quick, rash answer: "Yes, I *would*."

"I see." His tone smug, he withdrew his hand from beneath her gown, much to her discontent. "Well, then, it seems you won't be needing me anymore."

Chapter 18

The following morning, Thane was tying his cravat in front of the pier glass when a sudden rapping on the door caused him to yank too hard and put the knot askew. "Come in," he snapped.

Bernard entered the bedchamber. The valet looked as well-groomed and composed as ever, albeit with a distinct spring to his steps. That hint of jauntiness only fed Thane's grouchy mood.

"It's high time you returned."

Unperturbed, Bernard bowed. "Good morning, my lord. I must humbly beg pardon for my tardiness. My pocket watch stopped."

Thane knew exactly why the fellow had forgotten to wind his watch. A miasma of contentment oozed from Bernard. He'd been given leave for an overnight conjugal visit, a circumstance that only served to remind Thane of his own unsatisfied lust.

Peering into the mirror to straighten the crooked folds of the cravat, he made a stab at civility: "How is the wife faring?"

"Quite well, thank you. A bit prickly, but that is only to be expected of a woman in her delicate condition."

Bernard strolled into the dressing room, leaving Thane alone with his brooding thoughts. He could hear the valet whistling under his breath in an uncharacteristic breach of protocol. Clearly, Bernard had enjoyed a much more satisfying night than Thane. If only he himself could feel so at peace with the world.

Good God, now he was envying his servants.

Only a few short weeks ago, he would never have imagined himself wishing he was married with a little one on the way. Having grown up under Uncle Hugo's strict rule, Thane had never known the closeness of family life. He and his timid cousin Edward had been like oil and water. There had been no one to mourn Thane when he'd run off to join the cavalry, where he had found camaraderie in an itinerant military life. The only women he'd known had been camp followers and the occasional daughter of a local landowner, and none had stirred more than a passing carnal interest in him.

Now he acknowledged a twinge of emptiness. Meeting Lindsey had caused Thane to take a hard look at his solitary future. He found her boldness and vitality a welcome contrast to the ranks of insipid young debutantes. The two of them shared a penchant for adventure and a disdain for the vanities of high society. Once he'd overcome his anger at her for following him to Lady Entwhistle's house, he'd felt a certain admiration for Lindsey's courage in tracking down a murderer—even if she believed that villain to be him.

Thane scowled at the thought. Whatever false logic Lindsey had employed to convince herself of his culpability, deep down she had to be aware of her mistake. Otherwise, she wouldn't have lowered her guard in so spectacular a manner. Her uninhibited response to his touch had revealed the passion hidden behind that cool exterior.

She had driven him mad with desire. He had spent half the night tossing and turning, finally resorting to his hand to relieve his pent-up frustration. But that was a poor substitute for having Lindsey in his bed. In his fantasies, he was back in that pitch-black dressing room with her, only this time he let her unbutton his breeches. This time he allowed Lindsey to pleasure him as he'd done to her. And this time he pushed her down onto the floor and mounted her, riding hard until they both reached the peak of bliss—

"Ahem."

He realized that Bernard stood before him, holding a fresh length of linen. Thane glared at him. "What?"

The valet lowered his gaze to frown at Thane's throat. "You cannot mean to go out with your neck cloth in so disastrous a condition, my lord. Unless you wish for my reputation as a gentleman's gentleman to fall into complete and utter ruin."

"Don't be theatrical."

Nevertheless, Thane ripped off the ruined cravat and tossed it onto a nearby chair. He looped the fresh linen around his neck and then shifted impatiently from one foot to the other while Bernard deftly tied it.

The valet's precise movements reflected years of discipline in the military. Thane admonished himself for his testiness when he owed the fellow a debt of gratitude for saving his life. The two of them had survived many a battle together, equals in fighting a common enemy. Thane knew of no one he trusted more.

"Regarding cravats," he said in a more modulated tone, "have you found out who stitched the one used in the murders?"

"I've visited a number of tailors, and as yet no one recognizes it."

Thane had known that hope was a long shot. "Try some of the gentlemen's emporiums along The Strand. The villain might have purchased his neck cloths from a lesser-known establishment."

"I will indeed—and the button you found beside the third victim, as well. By the by, did you learn anything of importance from Lady Entwhistle yesterday evening?"

Thane had learned he was a glutton for punishment. He had been trapped for the better part of an hour with the most desirable woman in the world, yet he had stopped himself from taking the ultimate prize. He didn't know if that made him a hero . . . or a damned fool.

One thing was certain: the episode had been a huge distraction from his investigation. He'd been following a hunch that Lady Entwhistle might be in cahoots with Wrayford in regard to the murders. The first victim had been in her employ, and given her penchant for playing nasty games, it was possible she had provided Wrayford with a handy place to conduct his romances with the slain maids. Those two were precisely the unscrupulous sort to get their jollies out of seducing and then strangling vulnerable women.

He realized Bernard was waiting for an answer.

"She was entertaining Wrayford, along with two other scapegraces. There wasn't sufficient time for me to conduct a thorough search of her house."

However, he'd had ample time to conduct a thorough search underneath Lindsey's skirts. He'd been so enthralled they had almost been discovered in flagrante delicto. Despite the risks, he had burned to take Lindsey right there on the floor of the dressing room, and damn the consequences.

"Will you be calling on Miss Crompton today?" Bernard asked.

Thane jerked his head back. He hoped to God that a flush didn't give him away. "Miss Crompton? Why the devil would you bring up her name?"

The valet cocked an inquisitive eyebrow. "You mentioned her while you were dressing yesterday, my lord.

You were intending to determine a time when she might accompany you and Miss Jocelyn to the shops."

Thane had completely forgotten. "I did encounter her," he admitted grudgingly, "but there was no opportunity to ask. I'll have to do so another time."

The prospect of seeing Lindsey again sent a jolt of heat to his loins. The trouble was, Mrs. Crompton had forbidden the courtship. She had made her ambitions quite clear to Thane. If he called at their house, the footman stationed at the door would be instructed to tell him that Lindsey was indisposed. Likewise, any notes he posted to her were likely to be delivered to Mrs. Crompton instead. Lindsey would be kept insulated from any contact with him.

Perversely, Thane relished the challenge. He resolved to glance through his stack of invitations and determine which society gatherings Lindsey likely would attend in the coming evenings.

And when he did arrange a clandestine meeting, they wouldn't be heading to the shops. That was merely a cover for his true purpose. Lindsey suspected he'd done away with the maids Tilly and Nelda.

It was time he set her straight.

"You've driven him away," Mrs. Crompton whispered. "I demand to know precisely what you said to him."

Lindsey gave her mother an innocent look. "I cannot imagine, Mama. Perhaps he's simply lost interest."

She sat on a gilt chair in between her parents in the ballroom at the Marchioness of Wargrave's house. Her father was engaged in conversation with the elderly gentleman beside him. At the front of the chamber, a stage had been set up with white columns, statuary, and clumps of ferns to simulate a Grecian temple. A low hum of conversation blanketed the ballroom as everyone awaited the imminent arrival of a famed soprano.

Lindsey saw her mother cast yet another worried glance toward Lord Wrayford, who sat with Miss Frances Beardsley at the front of the chamber. Much to Mama's aggravation, a vast fortune mattered little when it came to protocol. The Cromptons' common lineage had consigned them to the back rows of the audience.

"He ought to have invited you to sit with him," Lindsey's mother muttered. "He promised . . ."

"Promised what?" It incensed Lindsey that Mama and Lord Wrayford had formulated a secret pact behind her back. Wrayford had admitted as much himself that day she'd gone to his house. Was she to have no say in the matter of her own future?

"Hush," Mrs. Crompton whispered. "The performance is about to begin."

A dark-haired woman mounted the steps to the stage. Her coppery gown shimmering in the candlelight, she struck a pose beside a column with both hands clasped to her bosom and her face raised to the heavens. After a dramatic pause, she launched into a song with tones so pure Lindsey felt a prickling over her skin.

Or perhaps it was something else that caused the chills. From the corner of her eye, she noticed a tall man in the doorway. Angling her head ever so slightly, Lindsey saw him more clearly.

Mansfield.

Her heart launched into a mad drumbeat that drowned out the smooth clarity of the opera singer's voice. Fixing her attention on the stage, Lindsey sat rigidly in her chair, her gloved hands clenched in her lap. Three nights had passed since that erotic episode with Mansfield in the dressing room at Lady Entwhistle's house. All the while, Lindsey had been on pins and needles, both dreading and anticipating when he would walk back into her life again.

One fact was certain: she had not succeeded in banishing the memory of her shamefully wanton behavior.

What had she been thinking, to grant him intimacies that belonged only to a husband?

She hadn't been thinking, that's what. The power he wielded over her heart and mind defied explanation. Mansfield was a charmer; she had known that from their first meeting. But her sister Blythe was the one who fawned over men, while Lindsey had always been scornful of such romantic nonsense. So how was it that he had coaxed such a sinfully glorious response from her body? It was almost as if Mansfield had cast a spell that erased all her common sense.

She couldn't concentrate on the musical performance when he stood only a few yards behind her. Had he come here on purpose to seek her out? Or was his presence merely a coincidence?

She didn't believe in coincidence. Especially not when it came to Mansfield.

Ignoring her better judgment, Lindsey risked another glance over her shoulder. The moment she did so, he lifted his hand slightly and beckoned to her.

Her heart lurched again, and she wrenched her gaze back to the singer. Thankfully, Mama was engrossed in watching the stage, as were all the guests around them. No one else had noticed Mansfield.

Blast him for motioning to her as if she were a servant trained to do his bidding. And blast herself for feverishly casting about for an excuse that would enable her to slip out during the performance. It was preposterous even to contemplate such a discourtesy.

Yet the knowledge of his presence burned into her. Instead of heeding the sweetly melodic voice of the singer, Lindsey entertained a vision of Mansfield's arms enclosing her, drawing her against his muscular body, pressing his mouth to hers in a passionate kiss. . . .

Lindsey opened her fan and waved it to cool her flushed face. Then she realized he would know she was over-heated and lowered it to her lap again. *Botheration!* It didn't matter what the cad thought of her.

Mansfield was an expert seducer who knew precisely how to tempt a lady into sin. He had offered only a flimsy excuse for snooping in Lady Entwhistle's house, saying that he'd come there to return something. Lindsey knew he had to be lying. Otherwise, he would have knocked on the front door like any other gentleman.

For the past three days, she had wracked her brain to conceive of a logical reason for him to be creeping around in the dark. Her obsessive thoughts kept going back and forth on a well-trod path. Had he intended to carry on a tryst with Lady Entwhistle, just as Lord Wrayford had done?

Or worse, had Mansfield meant to seek out one of the female servants—in his guise of the Serpentine Strangler? After all, Lady Entwhistle had employed the first murdered maid.

Staring ahead at the stage, Lindsey tried to reconcile that horrible possibility with the tender man who had kissed her senseless. He had known two maids who had disappeared—Nelda and Tilly—and Nelda had bragged of having a gentleman lover. On the strength of that knowledge, Lindsey had gone to the Bow Street Runners. Ever since, she had agonized over her decision and prayed for a happy conclusion. If only Cyrus Bott could discover their whereabouts, then Mansfield's name would be cleared.

Meanwhile, Lindsey felt weighed down by her secret. She could only imagine Mansfield's reaction if he knew she'd reported him to the law. If he was guilty, he might well seek revenge. And if he was innocent, he would be wounded by her colossal lack of faith in him.

For the remainder of the set, Lindsey kept her eyes trained straight ahead, pretending that he didn't exist. At last the singer concluded the first portion of the program, and Lindsey joined in the polite applause.

As the aristocrats began to leave their seats to seek refreshments during the interval, Mrs. Crompton caught hold of Lindsey's elbow and urged her to her feet. Lindsey's father made to stand up as well, but her mother said, "There isn't any need to disturb yourself, Mr. Crompton. We'll return in a few minutes."

Papa gave Lindsey a quick smile and a nod. "Off to gossip, are you? Pray behave yourselves." He and the stoop-shouldered older man resumed their conversation about the shipping trade.

"Come along," Mama commanded. "We only have a few minutes."

Clutching her closed fan, Lindsey allowed her mother to herd her down the row of chairs and into a broad aisle. She scanned the throng of elegant gentlemen and ladies. But Mansfield's tall figure had vanished from sight.

Where had he gone?

She realized that Mama was steering her toward Lord Wrayford, who was strolling in their direction with Miss Frances Beardsley on his arm. The girl resembled an elaborately decorated confection with pink bows festooning her sleeves and waist and a matching ribbon threaded in her blond curls.

Under her breath, Lindsey hissed, "Please, Mama. We mustn't intrude on them."

"Nonsense, this is your chance to charm him," Mrs. Crompton whispered back. Her agreeable smile widened as they reached the pair. "Why, my dear Lord Wrayford.

How very pleasant to see you here. And Miss Beardsley, I trust you've enjoyed the performance thus far?"

Frances made a show of clinging to Wrayford's arm. Unfortunately for her, he wore a coat in a garish shade of mustard yellow that jarred with her aura of syrupy sweetness. "It was eminently satisfactory," she purred, "especially considering our prime position in the front. So, Lindsey, how was it at the back of the chamber? I do hope your view wasn't too terribly impaired."

"I've always believed that the view is not as important at a concert as the quality of the sound," Lindsey said. "A fine soloist is much better appreciated from the vantage point of a slight distance."

Frances curled her lip. "Well! I found the company more stirring than the singer."

She batted her pale lashes at Wrayford. But he was too busy leering at Lindsey's low-cut bodice to notice.

Lindsey snapped open her fan to block his view. "Did you?" she said in a bored tone. "How very remarkable."

She considered adding a yawn for effect, but Mama was already frowning slightly at the flow of conversation.

"I'm looking for your mother," Mrs. Crompton said to Frances. "Do you happen to know where she's gone?"

"She was here with us a few moments ago," Frances said, making a vague wave toward the guests who were heading toward the refreshment tables. "I believe she went that way."

Mrs. Crompton stepped forward to take firm hold of the girl's arm. "Do show me if you will."

"But Lord Wrayford and I were—"

"He'll accompany Lindsey. Now come along at once. You simply must tell me who made that deliciously dazzling gown of yours."

Frances snapped at the bait. As they walked away, she

launched into a rhapsody about the superiority of her seam-
stress.

Lindsey found herself alone with Wrayford. He regarded her with wary resentment, hardly a surprise, since
at their last face-to-face meeting she'd left him doubled
over in pain. Thank heavens he had no idea that she'd
witnessed his erotic romp with Lady Entwhistle.

Lindsey leisurely waved the fan to keep her bosom
hidden from his gaze. "I trust you've collected your phaeton."

He folded his arms in the manner of a sulky boy. "I did
indeed. Though since you'd stolen it, you ought to have
paid the stable fee."

"Consider it the price of attacking a lady." She glanced
around to see that most of the guests had trooped out to
the dining chamber for the refreshments, leaving the ballroom nearly empty. "Shall we join the others? I perfectly
understand why you've no interest in pursuing your courtship of me. As far as I'm concerned, we may deem your
agreement with my mother null and void."

Turning, she strolled toward the open doorway. He
didn't follow at first; then the hurried tapping of his footsteps caught up to her. "Now, Miss Crompton, pray don't
be hasty. Why, thoughts of you have occupied my every
waking hour. I vow you are the most ravishing creature
ever to walk the face of this Earth."

She burst out laughing. "How preposterous. I suspect
you told that very same lie to Miss Beardsley."

"Jealous, are you?" He watched her with a lordly confidence in his own superior birthright. "It could have been
you sitting up front with me. Perhaps if you apologize
nicely, I'll reconsider our estrangement."

From the avaricious look in his eyes, she knew he still
coveted her dowry. But he also craved a sop to his over-
weening pride.

He would have neither from her.

"Heaven forbid I should ever come between you and Miss Beardsley." Lindsey paused, then couldn't resist adding, "Or between you and Lady Entwhistle."

Wrayford started visibly. His pale blue eyes widening, he fingered the folds of his elaborate cravat. "Lady Entwhistle? Why, I hardly know the woman."

"Hmm. There's a rumor flying around that you were seen departing her house a few nights ago."

"Bah. You shouldn't heed such silly gossip." His clammy fingers wrapped around her upper arm. "Come, my pretty, we'll find a quiet corner and have a pleasant little chat. You may beg my forgiveness for your mistreatment of me, and if you're lucky I shall be generous enough to grant you clemency."

During that absurd speech, he steered her out the door and toward an alcove featuring a life-size marble statue of the goddess Athena. Lindsey considered yanking free, but she disliked making a scene while guests strolled the grand hall with its frescoed ceiling and massive chandelier.

A man stepped out from behind a bank of ferns. "Wrayford. I see you're coercing women again."

With a jolt, Lindsey found herself looking up at Mansfield. Her pulse sped up at the sight of him. He embodied the essence of masculinity in a chocolate brown coat, snowy white cravat, and fawn breeches. She yearned to catch his eye, but his hard gaze was focused on her companion.

Wrayford glowered. "Go find your own female. I'm sure Miss Crompton would be alarmed to learn how many hearts you've broken all over the Continent."

Mansfield quirked his mouth in a way that resembled a snarl more than a smile, the expression enhanced by the thin scar that bisected his cheek. "Better broken hearts than a trail of debts. Now, you will allow me to have a word alone with Miss Crompton."

A look passed between them, and Wrayford's tough stance wilted. With gutless bravado, he told Lindsey, "Your mother will hear about this outrage!"

He turned and stomped off into the throng of guests. Mansfield placed his hand at the small of her back, guiding her into the alcove so that they stood behind the potted ferns. The light pressure of his fingers conveyed a possessiveness that should have irked Lindsey but instead thrilled her to the core.

"Perhaps we should find someplace more private," she murmured.

His mouth softened into a cocky grin. "I'd like nothing better than to ravish you, but now is hardly the appropriate time."

A hot blush swept her cheeks. "I didn't mean . . . it's just that we mustn't be seen together."

His expression turning serious, he took hold of her hand and gently squeezed her fingers. "Never mind the secrecy. Now, tell me, why were you in Wrayford's company? You should know better after witnessing his depravity the other night."

"My mother orchestrated the meeting. She's bound and determined that I should marry him."

"And I am bound and determined that you shall marry *me*." His thumb rubbed her palm in such a way that she felt the effect in a more intimate place. "Promise me you'll keep your distance from him in the future."

"You know I daren't thwart the wishes of my parents. I'll avoid Wrayford whenever possible, but I can guarantee you no more than that." She paused, then added, "Not that I owe you any such pledge."

Mansfield eyed her with a lazy smile. "In a matter of days, our month will be up. Then I'll speak to your father about our betrothal. That should put a permanent end to Wrayford's pursuit of you."

The reminder of their bargain ignited both alarm and longing in Lindsey. There were so many aspects to him that remained a mystery to her. Logic told her if there was anyone she needed to fear, it was Mansfield himself.

Yet his stroking of her hand spread a shivery pleasure throughout her body. With every breath, she inhaled his uniquely masculine scent. She had to struggle to keep her thoughts focused. *I am bound and determined that you shall marry me.*

Was he merely in competition with Wrayford? Or did Mansfield want to claim her because he felt a deeper, richer emotion . . . like love? That second possibility filled her with a yearning so intense it frightened her.

He glanced beyond her shoulder. "Hmm. It appears we've been noticed."

Lindsey turned her head to look. Through the screen of ferns, she spied her mother bearing down on them like a ship at full sail. "Oh, no. Lord Wrayford must have tattled."

"There can be no doubt about that. Now, hold up your fan."

Mystified, she obeyed, raising the open fan to her bosom.

Under its concealment, Mansfield tucked a folded bit of paper in between her corset and her skin. The boldness of his action caused her to gasp. The pleasure of his touch coursed over her skin, flashing downward to nestle low in her belly. It brought to mind the first time they'd met, when he'd plucked the IOU out of her bodice.

"Read my note later," he murmured, as his fingers gave her soft breasts one last, loving stroke. "And dream of me."

Chapter 19

Two mornings later, a bell jingled overhead as Lindsey entered the dressmaker's shop. On the brisk walk here, a sense of urgent anticipation had spurred her steps. Kasi had grumbled about the rush for the entire five blocks from their house.

Resembling a ripe mango in her yellowish orange sari, the ayah planted herself just inside the door. "Memsahib not like this," she warned for the umpteenth time.

"Mama need never know. And please do be a dear and purchase the items on her list."

Lindsey was too preoccupied to pay the servant any further heed. The broad brim of the straw bonnet framed her face as she surveyed the small establishment. Located on a lane off one of the fashionable shopping streets, this store was unfamiliar to her. Shelves of colorful fabric filled one wall. Here and there, glass cases contained buttons, lace, and other trimmings. Rolls of ribbons dangled their colorful streamers from the ceiling.

At this early hour, only a few people browsed the merchandise. A maid in a drab brown cloak was making a purchase from a shop clerk. By the light of the bow window, two ladies were paging through a book of patterns.

Anxiety twisted Lindsey's stomach. She was a full quarter of an hour late to the appointment because Mama had summoned her for a lecture on their plans for the day. She'd been instructed to fetch several items and return immediately so as not to delay the scheduled round of afternoon calls.

Mama knew nothing of Lindsey's planned rendezvous with Mansfield.

Had she missed the meeting because of her tardiness? Surely not, for he'd taken the trouble of seeking her out at the musicale and slipping that note into her bodice. The brief message had conveyed an invitation to come here this morning. She doubted he would give up on her after a mere fifteen minutes.

She started toward the clerk behind the counter, intending to make inquiries once the woman finished her transaction. But the sound of girlish giggling drifted from the rear of the shop, followed by the deep tone of a man's voice.

Her heart aflutter, Lindsey veered in that direction. She proceeded through a doorway and entered a small corridor with curtained dressing rooms on either side. Parting the drapery of one, she smiled.

Jocelyn reclined on a chaise with a copy of *La Belle Assemblée* lying open on the lap of her pale green gown. She wore her long blond hair caught back with a ribbon. Her eyes bright with mirth, she watched as Mansfield struck a pose, pretending to model a frilly yellow dress that he held up to his chest.

Neither of them noticed Lindsey.

"What think you of this one, m'lady?" he asked. "Every fashionable girl owns at least a score of gowns in this style."

"Take it away," Jocelyn said with an imperious wave of her hand. "Heaven forbid I should look like everyone else."

Mansfield tossed it over a chair. "I do beg your pardon.

Perhaps another will suit m'lady's impeccable tastes. This one looks fetching when worn with a fancy bonnet."

He snatched up a feathered hat and jammed it onto his dark head, then grabbed a cherry pink gown from a hook on the wall. As he swung back toward Jocelyn, he spied Lindsey and stopped, clutching the dress to his front.

A faint dull flush swept his scarred face. With his brown eyes fixed on her, he looked charmingly discomfited. The sight of those masculine features framed by the dainty bonnet made her laugh.

She pushed aside the curtain and stepped into the dressing room. "My, this is a surprise. I was expecting the Earl of Mansfield, rather than *Lady* Mansfield."

Recovering his aplomb, he dipped an exaggerated curtsy. "I'm ever so pleased you could join us today, Miss Crompton. Perhaps you can offer better advice on fashion than I."

"Lindsey!" Jocelyn cried out. "I was so afraid you'd forgotten all about me."

Lindsey went to give her a hug. "I'm terribly sorry to be late. I wouldn't have missed this outing for the world."

"But where is Blythe? Did she not come with you?"

"I'm afraid she had a French lesson this morning. Now, what in heaven's name is going on here?"

"Lord Mansfield is most comical, isn't he? He's been showing me some of the selections."

"So I see. Although I must say, I do prefer him as a man."

"That's a relief," Mansfield said.

He whipped off the bonnet, leaving his black hair in attractive disarray. Tossing the gown and hat onto a chair, he aimed a dazzling smile at Lindsey, one that made her legs turn to molten wax. "I'm afraid I wasn't a very successful salesman, anyway. Miss Finicky turned down all my choices."

"I'll thank you to call me Miss Nevingford," Jocelyn said with an exaggerated sniff. "And you looked ridiculous. I do believe it was a ploy to discourage me from squandering your coin."

"Oho, so now I'm an evil pinchpenny, am I? Well, I shall have to prove you wrong by purchasing an entire new wardrobe for you."

"Hurrah!" Jocelyn clapped her hands. "You are my witness, Lindsey. He has promised to buy me anything I please."

Their bantering warmed Lindsey's heart. She had been troubled by the aloofness that Mansfield had exhibited toward his ward, worried that Jocelyn had been given all creature comforts yet lacked the love of a father figure in her life. Now her eyes sparkled and her cheeks glowed. Clearly, the girl had blossomed under Mansfield's paternal care. It reminded Lindsey of how dearly she herself treasured the attention of her father on those rare occasions when he could wrest himself away from business affairs.

The lone clerk came bustling into the dressing room, clutching several rolls of fabric. Clad in an aproned gown of dark gray, the nondescript woman managed to curtsy without dropping her burden. She looked only a decade older than Lindsey, yet years of labor already had worn grooves into her plain features.

"Forgive me, m'lord. The proprietor was taken ill today and there's no one to help out."

"Never mind, I quite understand," Mansfield said as he turned to Lindsey. "This is Miss Valentine. She's been kind enough to assist us."

The clerk gazed adoringly at him, then quickly glanced away when she caught Lindsey's eye. That glimpse of raw attraction shook Lindsey. Did he have this effect on all women?

Surely he must. The appealing combination of a hand-some face, a lofty title, and a benevolent manner was part of his allure.

His lethal allure—perhaps.

Unwilling to dwell on morbid speculation, Lindsey focused her attention on Jocelyn. She stepped forward and took a bolt of delicate rose fabric from the clerk. "This shade would look lovely on you, Jocelyn. Shall we go through the fashion book together and choose a style of gown?"

"Oh, yes, please!"

Miss Valentine fetched a straight-backed chair for Lindsey, then the bell tinkled out in the shop and the clerk excused herself to answer the summons.

Lindsey was aware of Mansfield watching them indul-gently as they pored over the periodical. Jocelyn had very definite opinions on the mode of her gowns, preferring those with subtle adornment to more elaborate designs. Lindsey found their chitchat quite comfortable, for it re-minded her of being with her sisters. She was relaxed and happy, at least until Jocelyn called over her guardian to grant his final approval of her selections.

Lindsey's heart beat faster as Mansfield walked to them. He stopped so close she could have reached out and touched his buckskin breeches. What would those firm muscles feel like under the exploration of her fingers? She wanted so badly to know.

Appalled with herself, she gripped the edge of the book and forced her gaze to remain on the page. Tempta-tion loomed at the corner of her eye. Afterward she could not have identified the particular gown in the sketch had her life depended upon it.

Miss Valentine returned to the dressing room to take Jocelyn's measurements, and Mansfield tactfully retreated out to the main area of the shop.

"Are you able to sit up straight for me, Miss Nevingford?" asked the clerk.

"I'm afraid that's impossible," Lindsey answered for her.

"Actually, I *can*," Jocelyn said.

To Lindsey's surprise, the girl used her thin arms to lever herself into an upright position on the chaise. Her useless legs, the dainty feet housed in slim green slippers, dangled an inch or so from the floor.

Was she doing her daily exercises, as Kasi had instructed? Mrs. Fisk, Jocelyn's old companion, had been instructed in how to help her. Lindsey wanted to ask but couldn't do so now, not with Mansfield lurking nearby. He mustn't learn of the scheme when he'd been so adamant about Jocelyn following the doctor's strict instructions. Only time would tell if the repetitive movements would strengthen Jocelyn's legs and allow her to walk again.

Miss Valentine took the petite girl's measurements, exclaiming over the slenderness of her waist and shoulders. "'Tis a pity indeed that you cannot walk," she said with a cluck of her tongue. "All the gents would fight for the privilege to dance with you, I'm sure."

"Oh, I'm far too young to make my debut," Jocelyn said breezily. "And when the time comes, I daresay I shall hold court while my suitors crowd around me." She peered closely at Miss Valentine. "That's a lovely pin you're wearing. Do *you* have a beau?"

The clerk blushed, her chapped fingers going to the dainty stickpin tucked in the folds of her fichu. "Oh, no, miss, this isn't from a suitor. My late father had it specially made for my mother a long time ago. A heart for a pretty Valentine, he used to say."

Lindsey took a closer look. The dull gold stickpin had a heart fashioned out of tiny ruby red chips.

How observant of Jocelyn to have noticed it. "What a beautiful heirloom," she said. "You must treasure it greatly."

"Aye, miss, I do."

They agreed upon a schedule for Miss Valentine to deliver the gowns; then Mansfield came into the dressing room to gather Jocelyn into his arms. He lifted her easily and carried her out into the shop, where a lady and her maid examined the buttons displayed in a glass case.

Kasi rose from a stool by the door and stood patiently waiting, holding a package wrapped with string. Thank heavens, she must have purchased the items on Mama's list.

Lindsey didn't want the morning to end. Since she wasn't expected back home for another hour, she cast about for a reason to delay the departure. "Jocelyn, do you wish to look at any of the ribbons or trimmings?"

"Oh, not today," Jocelyn said. "I'm tired of being indoors. I would very much like to go for a carriage ride."

She and Mansfield exchanged a glance. A silent communication passed between them.

Then he looked at Lindsey. "We would be honored if you would join us."

"I . . ." Yearning kept the automatic refusal glued to her tongue. The warmth in those chocolate brown eyes called to her, tempting her to risk any consequences in exchange for a few more minutes in his presence.

"Say yes," he commanded. "We'll only be gone a short while. Besides, you owe us a carriage ride after reneging last week."

"You do indeed," Jocelyn added, thrusting out her lower lip and looking woebegone. "I hope you won't disappoint me yet again."

Looking from one to the other, Lindsey laughed. "All right. But Kasi will accompany me. And I must return home in an hour, or Mama will worry."

"Fair enough," Mansfield said. "My landau is parked around the corner. Shall we go?"

As they walked out of the shop, the impact of his smile warmed Lindsey through and through. She shied away from examining the pleasure she found in his company. There would be time enough later to do so. All she wanted was to enjoy the outing.

Kasi fell into step beside her. For once, the old woman didn't scold or complain. Rather, she trudged along in stoic silence, her enigmatic gaze trained on Mansfield.

The sunshine made Lindsey glad for the bonnet that shaded her eyes. Only a few pedestrians and carriages roamed this sleepy lane, which was tucked away from the hustle and bustle of nearby Bond Street. Carrying Jocelyn, Mansfield led the way past the bow window with its display of ribbons and lace, and around the corner of the brick building.

There a black landau sat waiting with a blue-liveried coachman sitting on the box. A footman opened the half door, and Mansfield entered first, since he had to settle Jocelyn on the cushions.

While she waited with Kasi, Lindsey happened to glance down the narrow alley. Her heart skipped a beat.

At the far end, a man leaned against the brick wall and watched them. There was something eerily familiar about him. Despite the cap that he had pulled down low over his brow, she recognized that lanky figure and debonair garb.

It was Cyrus Bott, the Bow Street Runner.

Chapter 20

Hiding her alarm, Lindsey accepted Mansfield's help while stepping into the landau. For once she felt no attraction, only the cold shroud of dread. She avoided his eyes for fear he might guess something was amiss.

Dear God! Bott must be shadowing Mansfield in an effort to prove he was the Serpentine Strangler. When she'd informed the Runner about the two maids who had disappeared, she had expected him to make a few inquiries below stairs. She had hoped and prayed that he would discover that it was all a mistake, that Nelda and Tilly had merely taken posts elsewhere.

Lindsey had *not* intended for Bott to spy on the earl. It was far too risky. If Mansfield noticed the man and then found out she had alerted the law, he would be furious with her.

She sat down beside Jocelyn while Kasi settled her bulk on the other side of the girl. Watching the earl adjust the blanket over the girl's legs and then hand her a sketch pad and pencil, Lindsey had the awful sense that she'd misjudged him. Surely a man who had taken a crippled girl under his wing, a man who would treat his ward with such thoughtful care, could not be guilty of the heinous crime of murder.

The more she came to know Mansfield, the less she

was able to view him in the role of the Serpentine Strangler, who had killed three maidservants in the dark of night. There had to be rational explanations for all the events that had stirred her suspicions.

And if indeed he was innocent of the charges, he would be more than angry to discover what Lindsey had done. He would be horrified—and wounded—by her utter condemnation of his character.

As the vehicle began to move, she clenched her gloved fingers in her lap. Mansfield sat on the opposite seat with his back to the horses, allowing Lindsey to look ahead as the landau proceeded down the alleyway. But she couldn't quite see around the horses and the coachman on his high box.

She took a deep breath to quell her panic. If he spotted Bott, Mansfield wouldn't know him, anyway. Unless, of course, the Runner had been nosing around Mansfield's house and asking questions of his staff. . . .

Then they were passing the place where she had seen Bott, and to her vast relief he was gone. She couldn't spot him anywhere, not even when the coach emerged onto the main street. Here throngs of pedestrians strolled along the foot pavement, looking in shop windows, while street peddlers shouted out their wares of hot pies and oranges on the corner.

It was foolish to be so fearful, she told herself. Bott would take great care to keep Mansfield from guessing that he was being watched. The Runner must have ducked into one of the many stores or joined a group of people as cover. A skilled detective knew many ways to be unobtrusive about collecting information.

Yet only when the landau had gone several blocks down the crowded street did she allow herself to relax against the cushioned leather seat. The fine-sprung coach rocked only slightly over the cobblestones, the motion not disturbing Jocelyn, who was idly sketching a likeness of Miss Valentine. On the other side of her, Kasi folded her stubby fingers over her mango orange sari as she observed the hustle and bustle of the thoroughfare.

Lindsey glanced at Mansfield to find him watching her, one eyebrow cocked. The cool breeze had tossed a lock of dark hair onto his forehead, enhancing his rakishly attractive looks.

"Who did you see?" he asked.

"I beg your pardon?"

"You seemed to be looking for someone you knew back there," he said. "I merely wondered who it might be."

"Oh! No one. I—I was just remembering that I forgot to purchase a length of Belgian lace for my mother."

"Ah. Perhaps you can apply to Miss Valentine and ask her to send it." He leaned forward, his hands clasped loosely. "Now, you haven't even asked where we're going."

It was an enormous relief to change the subject. "Where are we going?"

"For a drive around the outskirts of Hyde Park. Jocelyn will enjoy seeing the fine houses on Park Lane."

The girl raised her head. "Actually, I prefer to draw people. So it doesn't matter to me where we go so long as we're outdoors."

Mansfield chuckled. "I'm glad you're so easily pleased, sprite. Then you won't mind if we make one brief stop along the way."

"Stop?" Lindsey asked.

"Yes." His gaze touched her, slid away, then returned. "At my uncle's house."

Intrigued, Lindsey leaned forward slightly. "I didn't realize you had any relations in town. Perhaps I know him. What is his name?"

"The Honorable Hugo Pallister, and you won't have met him, since he isn't in London. It's been many years since he's come here."

She remembered Mama's friend the Duchess of Milbourne asking after a Hugo who lived in Oxfordshire. What had Mansfield said in reply? *My uncle is as cantankerous as ever.*

Apparently, the two of them had a strained relationship. Lindsey found herself keen to ferret out why.

"Since you were away in the cavalry," she said, "you must not have seen him very often over the years. He's your father's brother, is he not?"

"His twin, actually. I grew up in his household in Oxfordshire after my parents died." Mansfield compressed his lips and looked out at the passing street. His posture clearly discouraged any further questions.

His reticence only intrigued her all the more.

Since Mansfield's father had possessed the title, Hugo would have been the second born of the twins. Therefore, Hugo would have inherited the earldom if a certain nephew hadn't stood in the way. Could that be the source of Hugo's cantankerous nature?

It was ridiculous to speculate. Lindsey knew little of the man, except that one-word description. Yet he was a part of Mansfield's life, and for that reason she burned to know more.

"How old were you when you lost your parents?" she asked.

He glanced at her. "Five years. I've been told they both fell ill of a fever."

The news caused a softness of sympathy in her breast. She remembered what Kasi had proclaimed while reading his palm: *Long ago, you a very lonely boy. No parents, no family, no love.*

Lindsey had always known the warmth and security of

family. It was a revelation to think of him as a small orphaned boy thrust into his uncle's household. She wanted to question him further, but since Jocelyn had lost her parents only the previous year, Lindsey didn't want to pursue the matter for fear of bringing back sad memories. "I'm sorry."

"Don't be. I scarcely remember them."

His dismissive manner warned her to change the subject. "Why do you need to visit your uncle's house?"

"As I was leaving this morning, I received a message from the steward, asking me to approve a few expenditures. It shouldn't take more than a few minutes. Ah, here we are."

Directly across from Hyde Park, the landau drew up in front of a stately stone residence with tall pillars flanking a carved portico. Rows of fanlight windows lent a graceful splendor to the façade, and the brass fittings on the dark green front door gleamed in the sunshine.

"What a lovely place!" Lindsey exclaimed. "I've noticed it on drives to the park, but I never knew who lived here."

"This is Pallister House." He paused, eyeing her. "Would you care to take a quick tour? I'm sure Jocelyn and Kasi wouldn't mind waiting."

"Go ahead," Jocelyn said, waving her pencil. "There's so much more to draw out here than inside a dusty old house."

"The place had better not be dusty," Mansfield said in a mock-threatening voice. "Or I shall have a stern word with the housekeeper."

The footman opened the door and stood back impassively. Mansfield descended from the coach and then held out his hand to assist Lindsey.

She hesitated a moment before grasping it. What harm could there be in going inside the house with him? He could hardly be planning to ravish her while Jocelyn and Kasi waited outside. And even with the family not in residence, there must be a skeleton staff of servants on duty to keep the place tidy.

As they walked toward the marble portico, she said, "Pallister House . . . with that name, shouldn't it belong to you, as head of the family?"

He shrugged. "Such a large pile is highly impractical for a bachelor household."

He had dodged the question rather than answered it directly, she noted. "Did you ever come here as a youth?"

"Once or twice. Enough to know my way around."

Extracting an iron key from an inner pocket of his coat, he bent down to insert it in the lock. Then he frowned at her and said, "It's already unlocked. The maids must have been polishing the brass this morning."

He turned the handle and opened the door. His hand at the small of her back, Mansfield ushered her into an impressive foyer lit by sunshine streaming though the tall windows. The place had the musty, forlorn air of a house that had been closed up for years, devoid of family members to lend it brightness and life.

Her footsteps echoed on the checkered marble floor. She tilted her head back to gaze at the high domed ceiling, then the gracefully curving staircase with its intricate oak railing.

"So you visited here as a boy," she mused. "Did you ever slide down that banister?"

"More than once. And each time, it was well worth the paddling I received in return."

She laughed. "I'm imagining you as a very naughty child who often fell into trouble."

"That is unfortunately true," he said with a wry twist of his mouth. "Now, I would like to take a look around, to make sure everything is in proper order. Shall we?"

His hand again rested at the small of her back as he steered her down an ornately decorated corridor. The warmth of his palm seeped into her, stirring her blood. She found herself wishing he would spirit her into one of the deserted rooms they were walking past, to press her down onto a chaise and subject her to a steamy kiss and a long bout of bodily exploration.

Lindsey drew a shaky breath. Heaven help her if he guessed the disgraceful direction of her thoughts. It was shocking indeed for a young lady to harbor such fantasies about a man who was not her husband.

When we make love for the first time, I'll have you in my bed . . . as my wife.

He had murmured that to her while they were trapped in the dressing room at Lady Entwhistle's house. He wanted to marry her, and she had only to voice her acceptance. But her suspicions of him formed an insurmountable barrier between them. And she didn't *want* to marry a nobleman anyway. She had sworn to herself—

Mansfield stopped walking, bringing her to an abrupt halt. His grim expression startled her. "What is it?" she asked.

"Shh."

He cocked his head in a listening pose. Then Lindsey detected what she'd been too self-absorbed to hear earlier. Voices emanated from somewhere toward the end of the long passage. There was another sound, oddly enough, the heavenly music of a harp.

"Wait here," he ordered.

Without further ado, Mansfield went striding down the corridor, his footsteps sharp and decisive. Lindsey stood still for no more than half a minute. Then curiosity had the better of her. She needed to know what put that forbidding look on his face.

His tall figure was already vanishing through a doorway

at the rear of the house. Picking up her skirts, she ran after him, her slippers making a whispering sound on the marble floor. Reaching the spot where he'd disappeared, she peeked into a spacious sitting room with a bank of windows that framed the green of the garden.

Several people were gathered in a group near the fireplace. An older man with a curled gray wig and weathered face occupied a wing chair, his stockinged feet elevated on a stool. Across from him sat a younger version of himself, a gentleman with prematurely balding russet hair and rather nondescript features. A plump brown mouse of a lady sat by a gilded harp by one of the windows, her fingers frozen on the strings, while two boys played jacks at her feet.

Mansfield stood in front of the assembly, his back to the door and his fists planted on his hips. Everyone's attention was fixed on him.

". . . might have warned me you were coming here," he was saying. "You never leave Oxfordshire."

Oxfordshire. Was the older man Hugo? The uncle who had raised Mansfield since the tender age of five?

He must be, Lindsey realized in shock.

"Pray forgive me," Hugo said, his voice sour as he glared up at his nephew. "I was unaware of the need to submit my activities to you for approval."

"I'm speaking of common courtesy," Mansfield snapped. "It would have been decent of you to send word to me of your expected arrival. But apparently you didn't intend for me to know of this visit at all."

"What, will you toss us out of the house, then? By gad, perhaps you'd prefer that we move to the Pulteney Hotel."

So this mansion *did* belong to Mansfield, Lindsey thought. Why had he said that it was his uncle's?

"Please don't quarrel," said the younger man. Shifting in his seat, he kept his chin tucked low in a wary look.

"You mustn't blame him, Thane. He only wanted to be with his grandsons. This trip to London was entirely my doing."

"Yours?" Mansfield said with a hint of contempt.

"Yes, we're here to celebrate John's seventh birthday. He begged to go to the Tower zoo."

The older of the two boys, a towheaded tyke in short pants, sat back on his heels. "That's me!" he proclaimed. "Mummy said it's my birthday all week long!" Then, before Lindsey could duck out of sight, he pointed straight at her. "Who's she?"

Everyone turned to stare at her.

Embarrassed to be caught eavesdropping, Lindsey stood rooted to the floor. It was horribly rude of her to listen in on their private family discussion. Nothing could have made matters worse . . . except what Mansfield did next.

He strode forward, took hold of her arm, and compelled her toward the group. Without any warning, he told a bald-faced lie. "This is Miss Lindsey Crompton. My fiancée."

She sucked in a breath. "No!" Glancing around at the mystified faces of his relatives, she modified her tone: "What I mean is, we are *not* officially engaged."

"I have yet to speak to her father, so we would appreciate your discretion in the matter," Mansfield said smoothly. "Lindsey, this is my uncle Hugo and my cousin Edward. In light of the irregular circumstances, I'm afraid I haven't yet made the acquaintance of Edward's wife and children."

Edward cleared his throat. "Dinah, pray meet my cousin Thane . . . er, Lord Mansfield . . . and Miss Crompton. John is my eldest son and the younger boy is Hugo."

Mansfield bowed to the mousy lady at the harp, who bobbed a shy curtsy. "My pleasure, ma'am," he said. "And Hugo must be named for his grandsire, how splendid."

The note of cutting sarcasm in Mansfield's voice caught Lindsey's attention. It was clear he felt animosity toward his uncle, but that was no reason to mock a young child. Luckily, the boys were oblivious to the strained atmosphere in the room, having returned to their game of jacks.

"At least you've taken my advice to acquire a wife," Hugo told Mansfield. "It's about time you ended your ne'er-do-well ways and settled down."

Lindsey saw Mansfield's face darken and intervened to ward off another round of insults. "Sir, I do believe his reputation as a rogue is much exaggerated," she said with a little laugh. "He's been the perfect gentleman toward me. Now, did you have a good journey? I confess that since I was raised in India, I've never had occasion to visit Oxfordshire."

"It was a miserable trip, jolting around in a box for hours," Hugo grumbled, "which is why I seldom come to the city anymore. But I will concede, you've traveled a sight farther than I have."

"Around the tip of Africa and through several fierce storms," she said. "My family made the voyage two years ago."

Edward regarded her with admiration. "I cannot imagine what that must have been like, Miss Crompton. I prefer to have solid ground beneath my feet."

At that moment a maid pushing a tea trolley entered the room. The boys jumped up to crowd around her, peering to see what was on the tray. "Mummy, where's my birthday cake?" John cried.

Dinah scurried forward to steer them away. "Boys, do behave yourselves," she murmured. "John, you'll have your cake for supper."

Hugo watched his grandsons indulgently. Affection for them gleamed in his rheumy blue eyes. However, when he noticed Lindsey's gaze on him, he worked his face into a fierce scowl. "Well, don't just stand there gawking, miss. You're giving me a crick in my neck. Sit down and drink a spot of tea, if you must."

Lindsey welcomed the opportunity to quiz Mansfield's uncle further, yet the thought of Jocelyn and Kasi waiting out in the landau gave her pause. "Thank you, but I couldn't possibly. My mother is expecting me back home soon."

Beside her, Mansfield moved restlessly. "There aren't enough cups anyway," he said. "While I'm sure Tilly would fetch more, she and the other servants must be very busy with all the unexpected company."

Tilly?

Lindsey looked sharply at the maidservant. A few curls of blond hair showed at the edge of the slender young woman's mobcap. Her rosy skin and pleasing features struck a shocking chord of recognition in Lindsey.

Dear God. She was the very maid who had accompanied Mansfield into the study at Wrayford's party all those weeks ago.

Chapter 21

Tilly bobbed a curtsy. "I'd be more'n 'appy to oblige, m'lord."

Thane paid her little heed. He closely watched Lindsey for a reaction. Had she recognized the servant? She must have, because her gaze was trained on the girl.

His purpose in coming here had been fulfilled—albeit not precisely in the manner he'd intended.

"Never mind," he said. "I'm afraid Miss Crompton and I must take our leave now."

Thane bowed to his family when he wanted to grind his teeth instead. In light of his uncle's unannounced visit, it irked him to have to show politeness to the man. To think that he had traveled to London and taken over this house without even bothering to notify Thane!

Uncle Hugo afforded him a cool nod in return. "If you like, you may join us for dinner on the morrow."

The invitation caught Thane off guard. For the barest instant he felt like a boy again, yearning for approval where none existed. But, of course, his uncle had issued an obligatory offer, nothing more. The truth of that was evident in the sour set of his mouth and those sharply judgmental eyes.

"Thank you, but I've already made other plans," Thane said. "Good day."

With that, he guided Lindsey out of the sitting room and into the corridor. Anger drove his steps. He still reeled from the shock of hearing those voices and then walking in on that cozy family scene. Finding his uncle in town so unexpectedly—and seeing timid Edward after all these years with a wife and children in tow—had knocked Thane off kilter. If he hadn't stopped here today, they might have come and gone without him being the wiser. *Blast them all!*

"Slow down," Lindsey said. "*You,* at least, aren't hampered by a skirt."

He realized that while caught in his own morbid thoughts he'd been half-carrying her along the passageway. He moderated his pace. "Forgive me. I was preoccupied."

Her keen blue eyes regarded him. "Of course you were. Your family came to town and they didn't bother to tell you. Anyone would be distraught under such circumstances."

"Distraught?" He loosed a harsh laugh that echoed in the cavernous corridor. "You couldn't be more mistaken. They mean nothing to me."

"Then why are you behaving like a tiger with a thorn in your paw?"

"Because I've a right to know who's trespassing on my property, that's why."

"Trespassing, is it? You told me earlier that this is your uncle's house."

Thane found himself caught in a fib. He had needed an excuse to bring her here and to take her down to the kitchen where he'd made prior arrangements to run into Tilly—so that Lindsey would realize he was not a cold-blooded killer.

He had to offer some explanation, no matter how lame. "Uncle Hugo was my guardian when I was a child. It always *seemed* as if he owned the place. I've been gone all these years, so I've never had occasion to stay here."

"Hmm." She eyed him suspiciously, then glanced back over her shoulder as if to make certain no one had come out into the passageway to listen. "Nevertheless, *trespassers* is hardly a fitting way to describe your family. Why do you despise them so much, anyway? They seemed like rather pleasant people to me."

"Pleasant?" The sharp teeth of resentment gnawed at him. "Only to the casual observer. The truth is, my uncle is a harsh man who never let me forget that I was living under his sufferance. There's no love lost between us."

Lindsey frowned thoughtfully, gazing up at him from beneath the brim of her bonnet. "All the more reason for you to mend fences with him. You really should join them for dinner tomorrow."

"What? Hell, no!" They had reached the entrance hall, and he stopped abruptly to confront her. "I'd rather be spitted on a French bayonet and roasted over a bonfire."

"Shh. Keep your voice down. I'm only saying that things may be different now that you're an adult. Perhaps you should renew your acquaintance with your uncle, rather than let yourself be bound by the pain of the past."

Thane raked his fingers through his hair. She couldn't possibly fathom the pointlessness of what she suggested because she knew nothing of his childhood. His uncle had no real interest in renewing their acquaintance. Discovering the family celebration in progress here had only served to prove that. Thane was the outsider, and by God, he wouldn't behave like a little boy with his nose pressed to the sweetshop window. "I've told him no, and that's that."

Lindsey regarded him with a mixture of sympathy and disappointment. "Well. Do as you please, then. And by the by, you are *not* to tell people that we are betrothed. I can't imagine what induced you to utter such a brazen lie to your family."

On that abrupt statement, she wheeled around and marched toward the front door. He stood transfixed by the sight of her in high dudgeon, her hips swaying, her heels kicking up the hem of that slim blue skirt. A hot rush of desire poured through him, a salve to the corrosion of anger.

To hell with quarreling. That wasn't what he wanted to do with Lindsey Crompton.

Thane caught up with her in two strides. Placing his hands on her shoulders, he swiveled her around to face him. Sunlight through the window shone on the rich chestnut curls beneath her broad-brimmed bonnet. His thumbs stroked the bare softness of her neck.

"Our month will soon be up, that's why," he murmured. "It's time for us to announce our engagement."

"And if I say no? Will you tell my father that I stole into your house, dressed as a maidservant?" Her eyes big and blue, she shook her head. "You might have fooled me a few weeks ago, but not anymore. You aren't a tattler."

She was right; he'd never had any intention of following through on that threat. His resolve to court her had begun as a ploy to protect her from Wrayford. Now, however, his feelings for her had grown into something deeper and richer, something he preferred not to analyze.

Especially when she looked so delectable.

Bending down, he nuzzled the velvety softness of her cheek. She smelled tantalizing, like sun-warmed flowers. "You gave me your word. You said you would agree to the betrothal."

She sent him a coy look through the veil of her lashes. "I made that promise under duress. You offered me no choice in the matter."

"I'm giving you the choice right now, then." His lips

wandered over her face, while his hands slid downward to trace the womanly curves of her body. "We can be husband and wife . . . if you so desire."

Although she didn't say yes, she rewarded him with a shiver and a sigh. Her hands had crept inside his coat to lie against his shirt. That one small action filled him with passion and he prepared to renew his assault with a kiss.

But as he leaned closer, the casement clock in the nearby library bonged the hour. With a gasp, Lindsey drew back, looking charmingly flustered. "Is it one o'clock already? Lud, I really *must* be going."

Thane leashed his frustration. He'd already learned the folly of trying to impose his will on Lindsey. Besides, with visitors just down the corridor, this was hardly a suitable setting for romance.

As she turned to the door, she paused to give him a guarded look over her shoulder. "That maid . . . the one who brought in the tea tray . . . she looked rather familiar. I wondered . . . is she the same one you were with at Wrayford's ball?"

Pleased by the question, he pretended to ponder. "Tilly? Now that you mention it, yes."

Lindsey's gaze faltered as if she were having trouble meeting his eyes. "I don't understand. I thought she was employed by Wrayford."

"She was, but something happened to her there and she was in rather desperate need of a new position."

"Desperate?"

"You don't want to know. It's rather indelicate for a lady's ears."

She swung to face him again. "I don't care a fig for proprieties. Tell me."

"As you wish, then. I discovered that Wrayford had attempted to ravish Tilly against her will."

That was only half the story. Once he'd found out

about Wrayford's unrelenting lecherous pursuit of the maid, Thane had been afraid that she would become the Serpentine Strangler's next victim. Her testimony had been a boon to his investigation, too. Tilly had provided him with valuable information about Wrayford's habits, including his penchant for forcing young maidservants into his bed and his frequent inclusion of Lady Entwhistle in threesome romps.

Lindsey appeared somewhat subdued, frowning at a point just over his shoulder, and he had the uncharitable hope that she was suffering from a well-deserved case of guilt.

"I see," she said. "That was very kind of you to help her."

"You sound surprised." He gave her a stern stare. "When you saw her with me that night, did you perchance assume *I* was engaging in a tryst with her?"

"Oh! Well . . . actually, I didn't know what to think."

Thane played the gallant gentleman, reaching around her to open the door. But he couldn't resist twisting the knife: "It's good to know you didn't believe the worst of me, darling. Because you see, I'd be quite miserable to find out otherwise."

Lindsey experienced another shock upon arriving home. In her bedchamber she found her maid, Flora, waiting, all aflutter, a look of great excitement animating her plain features. "Oh, miss! Miss! Ye'll never guess wot's 'appened. Me cousin Nelda's come t' call on me!"

"Nelda? When?"

"This very mornin', miss. She come prancin' into the kitchen, proud as ye please. She weren't dead a'tall. She run off to be married!"

"Married." Lindsey slowly untied the ribbon beneath her chin and removed her bonnet. She could scarcely believe the news, coming so close upon her discovery that Tilly, too, had not been spirited away and murdered by Mansfield. "Why did Nelda not send word to you? She must have known you would worry."

Flora took the bonnet and laid it on the bed, then helped Lindsey slide her arms out of her pelisse. "Nelda don't know 'er letters, so she couldn't write. And she's been ailin', too." The maid leaned closer in a confiding manner. "She be in the family way, ye see. 'Tis why she had t' wed in haste. If not fer 'Is Lordship, she'd be—" She clapped her hand over her mouth. "Oh, wasn't supposed t' tell ye that part."

His Lordship?

The fire of curiosity burned in Lindsey. She took hold of Flora's sturdy shoulders. "I want the truth. Lord Mansfield helped her, didn't he?"

The maid nodded, her blue eyes bright beneath the crown of her white mobcap. "Nelda said 'twas to be a secret. Ye see, she married 'Is Lordship's valet, Mr. Bernard. And Mr. Bernard bein' a fine gent 'isself, well, the earl wanted t' keep matters quiet-like. T' protect Mr. Bernard's reputation, ye see. The earl bought them a neat little house in Chelsea, where Nelda's been livin'. I'm t' go visit 'er on me next day off."

"I'm glad everything's turned out so well."

As the maid fairly skipped into the dressing room with the pelisse and bonnet, Lindsey leaned against the cherrywood bedpost. Although she was happy to hear the missing girl was alive, she felt sick at heart. Nelda's lover had not been Mansfield but rather his valet. As the earl's personal manservant, Bernard would be at the top of the hierarchy below stairs, which explained why Nelda had bragged of being courted by a fine gentleman.

Lindsey had misinterpreted everything. She had

assumed the worst without any evidence. She'd been all too ready to cast Mansfield in a dastardly role—

A knock on the door interrupted her morbid thoughts. Before she could take more than a step to answer the summons, her mother walked into the bedchamber.

Perfectly groomed in a stylish gown of moss green with thin white stripes, Edith Crompton looked ready for an afternoon of social calls. Her hair was drawn into an elegant waterfall of russet curls, while emeralds glinted at her ears. However, her chilly expression did not bode well for pleasant chitchat.

"Lindsey, I'd like a word with you at once," she said, before reversing course and leaving the bedchamber.

Lindsey's stomach contracted. Did Mama know where she had gone this morning? Surely not.

Unless Kasi had told her. But why would the ayah betray her? Such a confession would only invite Mama's wrath, and Kasi had more sense than to do that.

Reluctantly, Lindsey trailed her mother out of the bedchamber and down the passageway. So much for her hope to have a few minutes alone to ponder all the momentous events of the morning. In addition to the discovery of Tilly's and Nelda's whereabouts, Lindsey had gained a tantalizing glimpse into Mansfield's past. It had been a revelation to meet his family, especially his ill-tempered uncle Hugo.

How difficult it must have been for a lonely little boy of five to come under the guardianship of such a curmudgeon. The very fact that Hugo had come to London for a family party without notifying his nephew spoke volumes. No wonder Mansfield had lashed out in anger; she had glimpsed the wounded look in his eyes that he'd tried so hard to hide.

She couldn't help but wonder why he had taken her to Pallister House in the first place. The situation now seemed like a deliberate orchestration of events. He had talked her into going for a drive, casually requested the stop, and urged her to accompany him inside. He must have been planning something that had been interrupted by the presence of his family—but what?

Had he merely wished to avail himself of a private moment with her? So that he might persuade her to marry him?

We can be husband and wife . . . if you so desire.

A delicious shiver enveloped her. Lud, she couldn't possibly be considering his offer. She had no interest in wedlock, and especially not to a nobleman. It would mean being trapped in the gilded cage of endless society events, gossip, and shopping. Ever since she had arrived in London, her fondest dream had been to set up an agency to solve mysteries for highborn clients who desired discretion.

Although perhaps *that* was the future she needed to reconsider. Today she'd learned just how badly she'd failed at sleuthing.

Discovering that both Tilly and Nelda were alive and well had struck the final blow to Lindsey's theory that Mansfield was the Serpentine Strangler. Instead of doing away with Tilly, he had helped her find another post. He had shown kindness and consideration, just as he'd done for Nelda when she'd discovered herself pregnant out of wedlock.

It's good to know you didn't believe the worst of me, darling. Because you see, I'd be quite miserable to find out otherwise.

The memory of his words made her squirm. She felt dreadful for misjudging him, for branding him as the perpetrator of such a heinous crime. And she flogged herself with the whip of ill-begotten pride. How could she fancy herself a detective when she had leaped to such a wildly inaccurate conclusion based on flimsy circumstantial evidence?

Lindsey knew the answer. She had allowed her imagination to be carried away because she'd been utterly determined to dislike Mansfield. She had so feared the power of her attraction to him that she'd been ready to believe him capable of murder. . . .

"What is the matter with you?" Mama snapped from the doorway of her boudoir. "Don't just stand there, child; come in here at once."

Lindsey realized that she'd absentmindedly stopped in the middle of the upstairs corridor. Gripping her skirts, she went into the room and braced herself for a lecture. Whatever rebuke Mama had to say couldn't surpass the scolding that Lindsey knew she richly deserved.

As always, a faint floral scent hung in the air, the aroma that belonged to her mother. A dressing table with an oval mirror held an array of blue and green vials. In the corner by the window, a rose pink chaise provided a place for Lindsey's mother to lounge when she suffered from her occasional megrims. In such an instance the draperies would be drawn and the family warned not to disturb her.

Judging by her stern expression, Lindsey half-wished now was one of those times.

Mama shut the door with a decisive click. Turning with a whisper of silk skirts, she clasped her hands in front of her. "I will not mince words," she said. "I was watching out the window a few minutes ago. Imagine my astonishment when I saw you and Kasi stepping out of Lord Mansfield's landau."

Lindsey blinked in surprise. Since they'd walked to the dressmaker's shop, he had offered them a ride home. But he'd left them off at the far corner of the square rather than risk discovery. "You must have had your nose pressed right up to the glass to see that."

Mama's lips formed a thin line. "Then you will not deny it."

"No, I shan't." It felt oddly freeing to speak her mind, almost as if it were an atonement for what she'd done to Mansfield. "The earl is a fine gentleman and I see no reason why he shouldn't court me."

But he might change his mind if he knew the full extent of her mistrust of him. What would he say if he discovered the truth, that she had believed him a murderer?

Mrs. Crompton glared. "You speak as if this . . . *courtship* has been going on behind my back for quite some time."

Lindsey raised her chin. "If you must know, I've been to visit his ward several times. She and I have become good friends."

"Friends. What do you know of this girl, this cripple? Who are her people? You could be ruining our position in society by associating with riffraff."

"How ludicrous, Mama. Miss Nevingford is gently born. Her father and the earl were great friends in the cavalry. She hails from Lancashire, just as we do."

The news put an arrested look on her mother's face. She stood frozen, as if she were staring right through Lindsey and into the past. "Nevingford? Are you certain that's her name?"

"Yes. Miss Jocelyn Nevingford." Lindsey fancied her mother's face had gone pale, or perhaps it was merely a trick of the light. "Do you know the family?"

Mrs. Crompton glanced away. "The name sounds vaguely familiar, that's all. It's been a very long time since your father and I lived there, and I can't be expected to recall every servant or neighbor."

"Oh, I'm sure they weren't servants." Lindsey took a step toward her mother. "Perhaps you'd like to meet

Jocelyn. She's very friendly and you could ask her about her connections—"

"No! That is absolutely out of the question. You are not to associate with that girl ever again."

Mama's frigid expression stunned Lindsey. She'd never seen her mother look so determined, so unbending. "But you don't even know Jocelyn."

"This isn't about the chit; it's about Lord Mansfield. You are not to encourage him any longer. It is Lord Wrayford that you will marry. Then someday you will be the Duchess of Sylvester."

Lindsey curled her fingers into fists at her sides. "I most certainly will *not*! He's a gambler and a cad. Even worse, he's known for chasing after the serving girls and forcing them to lie with him."

"Then it is up to you to mold him into a tolerable husband. That is what all ladies of high station must do when they wed. Now, go to your room and reflect upon what I've said."

Lindsey's heart raced in panicked disbelief. Mama meant every word. There would be no persuading her otherwise. This time, she would not back down or heed any arguments to the contrary.

But Lindsey could match her mother in icy demeanor.

"Pray remember this as you spin your schemes, Mama: You cannot force me to walk down the aisle at St. George's. And I will never do so with Lord Wrayford."

Edith watched her daughter stalk out of the boudoir. Only when she was gone did Edith allow her stiff spine to sag as she sank down onto the chaise. She pressed her fingers to her temples. The ache there foretold the onset of a megrim, but she took deep breaths to calm herself in the hopes of willing away the pain.

Lindsey was proving to be an even more willful child

than Portia had been. Neither of them appreciated Edith's effort to fortify her daughters' position in society. They had been raised with too much luxury. They had never known poverty or privation.

But Edith had. A lifetime ago, she had labored for a living at a fine manor house in Lancashire. She had worked her fingers to the bone as a maidservant. Had it not been for her seizing a fortuitous opportunity and moving with her master and mistress to India, she might still be condemned to that hardscrabble existence.

This new development frightened her to the point of illness. If she and George were found out . . .

Groping for the handkerchief that was always on the nearby table, she took the folded square of lace and dabbed her brow. *Nevingford!* The name was a knife in her heart. Squire Nevingford had been a neighbor, a blustery fellow who had spent an entire winter trying to coax fifteen-year-old Edith into his bed. He had been besotted enough to possibly remember her if ever they were to come face-to-face.

Was he related to Jocelyn Nevingford, possibly her grandsire? If so, surely he would have taken in the orphaned girl. Perhaps he was no longer alive, then. Edith knew it was shameful to pray for someone's death, but she offered up a brief entreaty anyway.

In the meantime, she dared not take any chances. Lindsey's association with the girl—and with Mansfield—must end.

Once and for all.

Chapter 22

Lindsey only agreed to go on the picnic to escape her mother's sharp eyes. Now, as the small party sat on a blanket beneath the shade of an oak tree, finishing a repast of cold meats and cheeses, the insipid company made her sorely regret her decision. Not even the cloudless day and the warm sunshine could lift the yoke of her worries.

Mama had kept her under close guard for the previous four days, forbidding any excursions to the shops and even banning strolls through the neighborhood. At several parties, she had ordered Lindsey's dance partners to return her immediately after the music stopped. At home, there was always a footman on sentry duty, waiting in the corridor outside her bedchamber and discreetly following her from room to room.

The near imprisonment might have been bearable if Lindsey had been able to see Mansfield. But he had not appeared at any of the society events she'd attended. It was as if he had dropped off the face of the earth.

Where had he gone?

Perhaps his absence was for the best. Lindsey wasn't certain she was ready to face him quite yet. The burden of guilt weighed too heavily on her. She dreaded his reaction to finding out how badly she'd misjudged him. It would be a terrible blow to him, especially in light of how he'd been mistreated by his own family. She found herself praying that he would never learn the truth.

Yet an innate sense of justice urged her to confess, no matter how difficult the task might be. She had debated the dilemma countless times since their last meeting.

Should she tell him—or not?

If only Portia was there to advise her. But her sister was in Kent, awaiting the birth of her first child. And Blythe was too young and capricious to act as a proper confidante. Lindsey had to make the decision on her own. At least she'd managed to smuggle out a note to Cyrus Bott, the Bow Street Runner, telling him that the missing maids had been found and he was to call off his investigation of Mansfield at once.

She crumbled a half-eaten slice of cheddar on her plate. Had she been too late in notifying the Runner? Maybe Mansfield already had caught Bott spying on him. In such a case, Mansfield might well use his lordly authority to force the Runner to reveal who had informed on him.

The notion made her queasy. Perhaps that was why she hadn't seen him since the outing at the dressmaker's shop. He was furious about her betrayal. So furious he had changed his mind about wanting her as his wife. She ought to be relieved . . . and yet she felt wracked by the longing to feel his arms around her again.

"W-would y-you care f-for some cake, M-Miss Crompton?"

The voice of Mr. Sykes broke through her reverie. She blinked and saw his brown spaniel eyes watching her with puppylike devotion. He looked incongruously formal in this bucolic setting, with his top hat and white cravat, his black boots buffed to a high sheen. He held out a slice of poppyseed cake on the blade of a silver server.

Forcing a smile, she nodded. "Thank you, that's very kind."

"I've had enough cake myself," Lord Wrayford declared. "Let's see what other goodies we have in here." He knelt beside the picnic basket and rummaged through it, then pulled out a bottle of champagne. "Why, fancy this. There's nothing like some bubbly to add good cheer."

"Ooh, do pour me a glass," Miss Beardsley said, running the tip of her tongue over her lips. "I'm ever so parched."

Wrayford stared at her mouth. "It would be my pleasure."

He returned his attention to the bottle. The cork gave way with a loud pop, and champagne foamed from the opening.

Miss Beardsley snatched up a flute, leaned close to him, and made a drama out of catching the drips. "Do have a care, my lord. Just look at all the lovely drink you're wasting."

His gaze flicked to her bosom, where the flower-sprigged green muslin hugged her breasts. "Mmm, mmm. Lovely indeed."

While Miss Beardsley continued to giggle and simper, he slid a sly glance over at Lindsey, as he'd done several times during the picnic meal. He was so transparent in his attempt to make her jealous that she feigned a yawn in hopes of setting him straight.

What a disgusting toad.

When she'd agreed to go on this picnic, there had been five couples planning to attend. Mama had given permission for Mr. Sykes to be Lindsey's partner, despite the fact that as the younger son of a baron he was a highly ineligible suitor.

Lindsey had seen right through the maneuver. Her mother knew Lindsey would never consent to being paired with Lord Wrayford, so she had accomplished the next best thing by throwing them into a situation where they would be together for hours. Lindsey hadn't objected to Wrayford's inclusion in the party because there would be plenty of other young people present.

However, when she and Mr. Sykes had arrived at the rendezvous point that morning, Wrayford had announced that three of the couples had cried off for various reasons. Lindsey had a strong suspicion the cancellations were Mama's doing, and she had been tempted to withdraw herself. But although irked at the way she'd been manipulated, Lindsey had deemed a day outdoors better than another boring afternoon of formal calls to the ton.

In two separate carriages, they'd set out on a southward course into a pastoral area where Wrayford claimed to know of the perfect picnic spot. Conversing with Mr. Sykes had been no ordeal since he was polite, if rather awkwardly spoken. She had spent the long drive telling him about India in order to spare him the need to talk. On the way home, though, she really would have to make it clear that her heart lay elsewhere.

The ache inside her breast confirmed that truth. For better or for worse, her heart belonged to Mansfield. Her yearning for him had become an ever-present companion, as real as the grass beneath her skirts and the sheltering branches overhead.

Sipping champagne, she leaned back against the trunk of the oak tree. Miss Beardsley was flirting with both Wrayford and Mr. Sykes now, brushing up against both men as if by accident, batting her lashes, and asking them to fetch her more tidbits from the basket. She was a Lady Entwhistle in the making, Lindsey suspected.

Bored with their antics, she closed her eyes and thought of Mansfield. The memory of their kisses flowed like honey through her veins. How she wanted to be with him again, to be held in the circle of his arms, to know that he could forgive her. . . .

She must have dozed off, because when next she opened her eyes the sunlight had diminished and the basket and blanket were gone.

Wrayford stood over her. "Wake up, sleepyhead," he said, his vulgar gaze roving over her prone form. "There's a storm brewing and we'd best be on our way."

He held out his hand, and she reluctantly allowed him to help her to her feet. The sky had darkened from more than the lateness of the afternoon. Black clouds gathered to the east, and a brisk wind set the oak leaves to dancing.

As they walked past a clump of gorse bushes and headed toward the two vehicles, she realized to her surprise that Miss Beardsley had taken her place beside Mr. Sykes in his carriage. The blonde was leaning against him, making a laughing grab for the ribbons and cajoling him to let her drive.

Clearly, she'd drunk too much champagne.

Lindsey frowned at them, then at Wrayford. "What's going on here? I'm riding with Mr. Sykes."

"The rest of us agreed to switch partners," Wrayford said with a sly smile. "We were hoping you'd be a sport about it."

"I'm sorry, that wasn't our arrangement. Besides, I left my reticule in there."

She marched toward Mr. Sykes's carriage, but it was too late.

"See if you can catch us," Miss Beardsley called over her shoulder. "Tallyho!" She snapped the reins and the brown horse set out at a brisk trot over the grass to the road.

Leaving Lindsey alone with Wrayford.

"I've finally found a match for the button," Thane said in Bott's tiny office on the top floor of Bow Street Station. He'd gone up to check with the Runner after giving the news to the chief magistrate. "We have my valet to thank for doing the legwork."

Seated at his tidy writing desk, Bott cast a skeptical look at Thane. "A match? You've had better luck than I, then. But does it allow us to identify the Strangler?"

"It sets another piece of the puzzle in place." Thane tossed the brass button to Bott. "As you know, the cross-hatch markings on it are unusual. I've narrowed the field down to only one shop on Bond Street that carries it—by chance, my own tailor. My suspect also orders his clothing from there."

Wrayford had run up a sizeable bill that was in arrears. Close scrutiny of the shop's records had revealed that he owned a morning coat with those very buttons, purchased the previous year.

"Who is he?"

Thane hesitated, reluctant to divulge the name until he had more definitive proof. But Bott was, after all, a fellow officer. "Lord Wrayford, of Bruton Street. That information is privileged between you and I, of course."

"Certainly."

Thane paced back and forth in the confines of the minuscule space. "For the past month, I've been investigating Wrayford. He has a reputation below stairs for seducing maidservants. And he's carried on a long-standing illicit relationship with Lady Entwhistle, who employed the first victim."

Bott pursed his lips. "Now that you mention it, there was talk of him when I interviewed the staff at Her Lady-ship's house. But several of the maids offered other possibilities, including a gentleman named Skidmore."

He was one of the scoundrels who had been playing cards with Lady Entwhistle on the night Thane had been trapped in the dressing room with Lindsey. "Freddie Skid-more is too stupid to have planned three murders without being caught. Besides, the other day I rode down to his country house in Wimbledon and verified a rumor that he was out of town at the time of the last murder."

Looking a trifle miffed at Thane's success, Bott carefully deposited the button in one of the cubbyholes of his desk. "Well, that's a step in the right direction. But you'll need irrefutable evidence before obtaining a warrant for his arrest. Any case against the nobility must be unassailable."

"I'll get the proof; you can be certain of that."

Weeks ago, he'd assigned Bernard the task of befriending Wrayford's valet, but thus far Bernard had been unsuccessful in convincing the man to let him have a look at Wrayford's wardrobe. So Thane would try another tack. When next he ascertained Wrayford to be engaged at Lady Entwhistle's, Thane would find a way to steal into Wrayford's house and conduct the search himself.

Perhaps tonight . . .

"And what of Miss Brown?" Bott asked.

"Miss Brown?"

"The lady who came here a few weeks ago to report *you* as the Strangler." Bott peered closely at him. "If indeed that is her real name."

Thane gave him a lordly stare. "Forget about Miss Brown. I'll handle her myself."

Thoughts of Lindsey energized him as he took his leave and headed down the long flight of stairs. As he emerged out into the teeming traffic on Bow Street, he noticed the wind had picked up. Heavy gray clouds had begun to pile in the sky, carrying the chilly portent of rain.

Thane swung onto his mount. He was too engrossed in his favorite obsession to pay more than passing heed to the weather. These past four days, he had deliberately kept his distance from Lindsey. She had needed time to assimilate the truth about him, to fully realize her mistake in believing him to be a murderer.

And perhaps, Thane admitted, he'd also wanted to penalize her for branding him such a dastardly character. He had wanted her to suffer a little. The irony was, their separation had punished him as well. Because of her, he'd endured sleepless nights and unending frustration.

He'd had quite enough of it all. Although it was over a week shy of their agreed-upon month, there must be no more delays.

Anticipation flourished in him. He had a few hours before conducting his clandestine activities at Wrayford's house. That should give him ample time to have a firm talk with Lindsey's mother—and to secure Lindsey's father's blessing for the marriage.

"Can you not drive a bit faster?" Lindsey asked. "It's growing dark and we're soon to have rain."

She sat huddled in the seat, wishing for a heavy cloak instead of the light pelisse that covered her muslin gown. When they'd set out in late morning, the sun had been shining from a clear blue sky. Now the swollen charcoal clouds threatened an imminent shower.

Yet Wrayford behaved as if they had all the time in the world.

"I daren't press the gelding too hard," he said. "I do believe the fellow is favoring his left front leg, don't you?"

Lindsey peered ahead into the gathering dusk. The chestnut horse trotted down the dirt road, hooves clopping and mane swinging. "It must be your imagination. I can't see anything wrong."

"Well, you don't know old Zanzibar the way I do. He might have picked up a small pebble. We'd best proceed carefully."

From Wrayford's too-hearty manner, Lindsey suspected

that it was all a ploy. He had something dastardly up his sleeve; there could be no doubt about it. Bitterly she acknowledged that this excursion must have been designed to trap her alone with Wrayford. It wouldn't surprise her in the least to learn that Mama's fingers were in the thick of the scheme. Since Lindsey had stated her opposition in no uncertain terms, she must be maneuvered and forced into the nuptials.

A part of her resisted believing that her mother could be so cruel. But Mama had made her ambitions eminently clear: *It is Lord Wrayford that you will marry. Then someday you will be the Duchess of Sylvester.*

Lindsey had been too preoccupied with thoughts of Mansfield to fully recognize the plot until it was too late. However, she'd experienced a vague uneasiness. The feeling had induced her to steal the pistol from her parents' bedchamber, where Mama had kept it out of habit from their days in India, when she had mistrusted the natives.

Unfortunately, Lindsey's reticule concealed the weapon and it was in Mr. Sykes's carriage somewhere along the road ahead. At the rate Wrayford was driving, they would never catch up.

No doubt that was the plan.

She surreptitiously eyed him. Gusts of wind buffeted his sandy hair and exposed the bald spot that he had combed over. He was not a large man, but he was as thick and stout as a tree trunk. It was unlikely that he could be pushed out of the carriage, even if she were to catch him by surprise.

He must be intending to stop somewhere along the road, she surmised. There was nothing wrong with his horse, but Wrayford needed to fabricate an excuse to delay their journey. The impending storm only bolstered his luck and conspired against her.

Once the rain began and darkness fell, the driving would

become difficult. They would be forced to take refuge in an inn—or perhaps somewhere else he'd arranged.

Her stomach twisted into a knot. No wonder Wrayford kept casting furtive glances at her, his mouth twisted in a cunning smile. He believed he had won. He must be congratulating himself on his scheme to take control of her sizeable dowry. He knew as well as she the ramifications of her spending an unchaperoned night in his company. It didn't even matter if he tried to force himself on her or not.

She would be ruined.

Chapter 23

A short while later, a few fat drops of rain began to spatter them. The phaeton had a small roof, but with the open sides it would provide scant protection in a downpour.

"Oh, blast," Wrayford said, cocking his head to peer up at the darkening sky. "I'm afraid we are about to be drenched, Miss Crompton. It would behoove us to find a place to shelter."

"We're in a predicament, to be sure. I don't suppose there's an inn anywhere close by?"

Lindsey had decided to go along with his ruse. With her pistol gone, she had only her wits and the element of surprise on her side. Better to let him play out his hand and hope that she could thwart him accordingly.

"A friend of mine owns a hunting box in the vicinity," Wrayford said. "I'm sure he wouldn't mind if we took refuge there."

"How fortunate. But it's growing dark. Are you quite certain you'll be able to find it?"

"Never fear. I've stayed there many a time, hunting for pheasant." He pointed ahead at a stone signpost that was barely visible in the gathering gloom. "We'll turn at the crossroads. Then it's no more than a half mile down the lane."

Lindsey had no intention of meandering off into the

countryside with the villain. At least here on the main road there was a chance of encountering another carriage— although the impending storm seemed to have driven everyone else indoors.

A chilly gust of wind raised gooseflesh on her arms. Bitterly she imagined Mama at home by a warm fire, aware that she'd sent her daughter off to be compromised. Would she pass the time writing out the guest list for the wedding? Was she already relishing her moment of triumph in marrying off her middle daughter to a duke's heir?

Not even an earl was quite grand enough to suit her mother's monstrous ambitions.

For a fleeting moment Lindsey entertained a fervent wish that Mansfield would come charging out of the darkness to save her. She ached to feel the security of his arms around her again. But he hadn't approached her for the better part of a week. What if he had changed his mind about wanting her as his wife?

A flurry of raindrops felt like cold tears on her cheeks and lashes, but she blinked them away. Now was not the time to wallow in despair or self-pity. Stranded out here in the rain, she could count on no one but herself.

Wrayford kept his attention on the dirt road as they approached the turn. He was leaning forward slightly, the better to see through the twilight. Upon reaching the signpost, he clucked to the horse to make haste around the curve.

He must be anxious to reach their destination. She felt surprisingly calm and clearheaded. Considering the low blow she'd delivered to him the last time they were alone, she doubted he would force himself on her. It would be enough for him to keep her out all night. Then, when he escorted her home in the morning, her parents would insist upon a betrothal. Mama would make certain Lindsey was forced into the marriage.

It was now or never. Taking advantage of his pre-occupied state, she lunged toward Wrayford and snatched the reins right out of his hands.

He jerked his head around. "Wha—?"

Lindsey gave him a mighty shove toward the side of the carriage. Caught off guard, he slid on the leather seat. His top hat went sailing into the darkness. Much to her regret, he managed to grab hold of the post that supported the roof.

In cold determination, she seized the buggy whip from its holder and beat him around the chest and shoulders. Wrayford thrust up both his hands to protect his face.

"Stop, you little bitch," he roared. "Have you gone mad?"

"Yes, I *am* mad. Lecher! How dare you think to abduct me!"

Luck had failed her numerous times that day. But now fortune blessed her. At that very moment, the startled gelding careened off the road. The wheels of the phaeton hit a rock or a rabbit hole, she didn't know which.

The vehicle tilted drunkenly. Lindsey caught the side and held on for dear life. But Wrayford wasn't quick enough. She had one last glimpse of his startled face as he plummeted from the carriage, yelping all the way.

There was no time to reflect upon her success. Having somehow managed to hold on to the reins with one hand, she focused her attention on bringing the runaway horse under control. It took a few minutes, but a firm grip on the ribbons soon had him quieted enough to slow down to a walk. Through the murky dusk, she guided the still-skittish horse back onto the road.

Lindsey needed the time to compose herself, as well. She felt shaky and weak, scarcely able to believe she'd actually won her freedom from Wrayford.

Had he been injured in the fall? Or killed?

She would have to check—from a distance, of course. He mustn't have the opportunity to seize her again. Another such scuffle might not turn out so well. Her heart was still beating like the drumming of hooves.

Then she realized it *was* hooves that she heard.

As she neared the place where Wrayford had fallen, a horseman rode straight at her from down the road. He drew up beside the phaeton, and her beleaguered heart leaped in recognition.

"Mansfield! What on earth are you doing here?"

He looked extremely imposing in a greatcoat and knee boots, a broad-brimmed hat covering his hair. Controlling his frisky black mount with an easy tug of the reins, he peered closely at her. "Lindsey, thank God! Are you all right?"

"Perfectly so. Now answer my question!"

His mouth twisted in a wry grin. "I came to save you. But apparently my gallantry isn't needed here."

Lindsey smiled giddily back at him. "Oh, but it *is*. Pray go over there and see if Wrayford has broken his neck."

She pointed with the whip to the shadowed area of the meadow where a loud groaning could be heard.

"Tumbled out of the carriage, did he? Too bad I missed it. That must have been quite a spectacle to see."

Turning the horse, Mansfield picked a path through the darkened shrubbery.

Rain fell more thickly now, and she huddled on the seat and tried to stay dry. The earl was a black shadow in the half-light as he leaned down to speak to the fallen man. Wrayford's whiny voice drifted across the meadow, although she couldn't make out more than a word here and there. Mansfield spoke sharply in return, then wheeled his horse back around and cantered to her.

"He's suffered a few bruises but doesn't appear to have any broken bones," Mansfield said. "More's the pity."

Beset by a belated attack of conscience, she said, "The storm is growing worse. Now that you're here, should we help him back to the carriage?"

"Hell, no. Let the rat drown."

Mansfield swung out of the saddle and tied his horse to the back of the phaeton. Then he leaped up onto the seat and shrugged off one arm of the greatcoat. Gathering her close, he wrapped the coat around her so they were snuggled together in a cocoon.

He felt marvelously warm. She burrowed into his side, resting her head in the hollow of his shoulder. The occasional raindrop still struck her face, but she no longer cared. Let the heavens pour snow and hail. It didn't matter so long as she was close to Mansfield.

He took the leather reins from her, and as they drove off, Lindsey could hear Wrayford shouting after them. He sounded more infuriated than injured.

"I suppose he can walk to the hunting box," she said. "He said it's only half a mile."

"So that's where the craven bastard was taking you. My God, he could have murdered you."

In the gloom, Mansfield's expression looked grim, almost cruel. The intensity of his pronouncement made her shiver. Why would he make such a theatrical statement? Surely he couldn't really believe it. His angry declaration must stem only from concern for her.

Wanting to soothe him, she stroked her hand over his midsection. "Wrayford wants my dowry, that's all. I wouldn't be of much use to him dead."

Mansfield sat silent for a moment, staring out at the lashing rain. Then he cast a grave look down at her. "Listen to me, Lindsey. I'm going to tell you something that you mustn't share with another living soul. Do you promise?"

Mystified, she said, "Of course."

"There are things you don't know about Wrayford. For some time now, I've been keeping a close watch on him. I've reason to believe he may be the Serpentine Strangler."

She stared up at him in stunned disbelief. "But . . . how can that be? He's merely a . . . a buffoon."

Mansfield shook his head. "Don't underestimate Wrayford. He's notorious for using dastardly tricks to lure young maidservants into his bed. He also has a close connection to each of the Strangler's victims. The first maid worked for Lady Entwhistle, the second for a neighbor who lives two doors away from him, and the third for the Beardsleys. It's only a matter of finding a definitive piece of evidence that will link him to the murders."

Pellets of rain struck Lindsey, but she took no heed. Lud, could she have been any more wrongheaded? She had never even considered Wrayford, perhaps because he didn't seem clever enough to plot a series of murders.

But Mansfield knew him better. Mansfield had been investigating the scoundrel all along.

The last pieces of the puzzle fell into place. No wonder Mansfield had kept that clipping about the murders locked in his desk. No wonder he had flirted with Lady Entwhistle—he must have been coaxing information from her. And no wonder he had continually warned Lindsey against associating with Wrayford.

All these weeks, she had branded Mansfield as the murderer. She had wanted to believe the worst of him because he was so dangerously tempting. With his wicked charm, he posed a threat to the future she had planned for her life, the cherished wish to gain the freedom to determine her own destiny.

But now her eyes had been opened. And the irony was, she wanted to be right here, cozied up with him, feeling the strong beating of his heart beneath her palm. Because she had fallen in love with him. Completely, madly, irrevocably in love.

The certainty of her feelings warmed her through and through. She wanted to be his wife, and yet she had betrayed his trust in the most unforgivable manner.

He deserved the truth. Even if it meant turning him against her.

Taking a deep breath, Lindsey struggled to find the right words. "Mansfield, I—"

"Thane," he corrected. He placed his gloved hand over hers and smiled down at her through the gloom. "It's time you addressed me with less formality."

"Thane," she murmured. "Though perhaps you won't like me very much in a moment. You see, I've something to confess. I . . . I thought for a time that *you* were the Strangler."

Her stomach in knots, she watched as his smile faded. He cocked an eyebrow, his expression one of cool lordly pride. The clopping of the horse hooves and the tapping of the rain filled the excruciating silence.

When he said nothing, she swallowed hard and continued, "It was because of Nelda and Tilly. When they both disappeared, I feared you'd done away with them. I . . . I even went to Bow Street Station and reported you to the Runners. I'm sorry for that . . . you can't imagine how much."

"Indeed."

His neutral tone told her nothing. She laced her fingers in her lap, wanting to touch him but no longer deserving of that right. "Please try to understand. It was just that I was so determined to find some reason to deny my attraction to you. I didn't want to admit that I could feel so drawn to any nobleman. There's no excuse for what I did, and I won't be surprised if you can never find it in your heart to forgive me—"

"I knew what you'd done," he broke in.

"I beg your pardon?"

"I saw you driving Wrayford's carriage. I followed you to Bow Street that day, *Miss Brown*."

Lindsey's jaw dropped. He could have no knowledge of the pseudonym she'd used unless he'd spoken to Cyrus Bott. All these days she had agonized over her impetuous behavior and Mansfield—Thane—*had already known*.

Yet still he had pursued her.

She felt like a fool—a very blissful fool. "Is that why you took me to Pallister House? You wanted me to know that Tilly was still alive? And Nelda—you must have told her to contact my maid Flora so I'd realize she, too, was unharmed."

He shrugged. "I could hardly let you go on thinking ill of me, now could I? That would only guarantee you'd never accept my marriage proposal."

Tears welled in her eyes. She pressed her face into the crook of his neck and dropped a kiss there, breathing deeply of his familiar spicy scent. "Oh, Thane, I don't deserve to be your wife."

"What, a girl who has the courage to knock a grown man out of a carriage? You're exactly the one for me." A thread of rough emotion in his voice, he tilted her face up to him. "If you hadn't stopped Wrayford, we wouldn't be here together right now. I'd never have found you in time."

Lindsey shuddered to think of what might have transpired had she failed. Thane wouldn't have known they'd left the main road. He would have pressed onward in the wrong direction in the vain quest to track them down.

His protectiveness stirred a soft tenderness in her, and she ran her fingers over his bristled jaw. "By the by, how *did* you find out where I'd gone today?"

He glanced down at her, his expression unreadable,

then looked back at the road. "I went to see your parents this afternoon."

She tilted her head back to look at him through the gloom. "You spoke to Mama?"

"Regrettably, I never had the chance. Kasi spied me in the entrance hall and told me where you'd gone—and with whom."

"Bless her for that," Lindsey said fervently. "But why did you go to my house in the first place?"

"To inform your mother that her interference is pointless. And to request your father's permission to marry you."

She took a shaky breath. It was humbling to know Thane had never wavered in his devotion to her, not even when he'd learned of her duplicity. She hardly dared to hope it meant that his feelings for her ran deep. . . .

Before she could manage a reply, he pointed to the road ahead. "There's an inn where we can stop. We daren't go on any farther. It's become too dark to see the road."

Lindsey spied the dim glow of a light through the veil of rain and darkness. Her heart began to beat faster. "By all means, we should take shelter for the night."

"Yes." He paused, then added, "If there aren't two rooms available, I can always sleep in the stables."

Lindsey felt as if she were standing on a precipice. She could retreat to the safety of her girlish fancies. Or she could become a woman by taking the plunge into a future of her own choosing.

Lifting her hand, she caressed his cheek. "I've a better idea," she murmured. "We can register as Mr. and Mrs. Pallister."

Chapter 24

A short while later, Lindsey found herself ensconced in the best room the inn had to offer. A crackling wood fire helped to dry her damp hair, while the cheery yellow glow chased the gloom into the corners. The low, sloped ceiling and curtained windows created a cozy retreat that was dominated by a four-poster bed.

Thane had left her alone for a few minutes while he saw to the horses. He'd said little to her in front of the fawning innkeeper, a stout, genial man who had been eager to offer the best accommodations to a gentleman and his lady wife. A maid had delivered a tray of bread and cheese, but Lindsey was too edgy to eat.

She hungered only for Thane.

Sitting by the fire, she'd already removed the pins from her hair. The maid had unbuttoned her, and Lindsey had shed both gown and corset, draping the dress over a chair by the fire to allow the rain-soaked hem to dry. Now, clad in only her chemise, she arose to prowl the small confines of the room.

Her gaze flitted to the bed with its claret red hangings and plump pillows. How amazing to think that she would sleep there with Thane tonight. The prospect stirred a plethora of emotions in the pit of her stomach: nervousness, desire, *impatience*.

Whatever was keeping him?

Rain tapped on the darkened windowpanes, a lonely sound that stoked her yearning for him. All of her life, she had been taught that no decent young woman behaved with wanton disregard for propriety. A lady must be modest, well mannered, and . . . boring. Lindsey smiled to imagine how the gossipy old biddies of society would squawk if they knew the premier heiress of the season had freely chosen to ruin herself with a rogue.

Any doubts she'd harbored about Thane had melted away the moment he'd appeared out of the darkness, riding to her rescue. She felt only a slight twinge of regret at giving up her dream of opening a private detective agency. Spinsterhood might have brought her freedom, but it would deny her a life with Thane . . . a life without love.

Her smile faded. *Did* he love her? His actions would suggest so, yet he had not spoken the words. When first he had proposed the betrothal scheme all those weeks ago, he'd said that he needed a wife in order to foster a more respectable image for Jocelyn's sake.

Was that still his sole purpose? Lindsey fervently hoped not. She wanted him to love her for herself.

A light knock sounded on the door. A moment later, Thane stepped into the bedchamber. He closed the door and stood there in the shadows, staring at her.

Her heart thumped against her rib cage. She was keenly aware of her nudity beneath the linen chemise. Perhaps she'd been too forward in removing her gown. For all she knew, there might be some sort of protocol to follow when disrobing. Or had he expected her to be in bed already, waiting for him there?

His gaze fixed on her, he removed his greatcoat and hat, letting them fall without a care. Then he peeled off his coat and waistcoat as well. His boot heels sharp against the wood floor, he came striding forward, a buccaneer in his billowy white shirt and buckskin breeches. The desire burning in his dark eyes made her melt.

Reaching out, he combed his fingers through the cascade of her hair. "Beautiful," he murmured. "My God, you are so very beautiful."

He smelled of rain and spice, a heady combination that made her dizzy. The bout of nerves she'd felt earlier transformed into a powerful yearning that unfurled throughout her body.

"You are, too," she murmured.

Bracing her hands on his shoulders, Lindsey raised herself on tiptoes and brought her mouth to his. He responded instantly, his arms enveloping her and his tongue aggressively seeking hers. His kiss swept her out of the chill of darkness and into a realm of light and warmth. Clinging to him, she lost herself to the sultry heaven of arousal.

His hands skimmed down her back, molding their hips together so that she felt the imprint of his manhood, thick and hard against the muslin chemise. His virility made her aware of the perfect way their bodies complemented each other.

The kiss tapered off to tiny licks, to moist lips rubbing back and forth. She loved the mastery of his mouth, the tenderness of his touch. It made her eager to be lying in bed with him, kissing and caressing beneath the covers.

She took his hand and led him over to the chair by the fire. "Sit down, and I'll help you with your boots."

His eyes shone with amusement and something else, something that promised pleasure. "Yes, my lady."

"I'm hardly behaving as a lady," she said, bending over him to yank off one tasseled knee boot. "My old governess would be quite appalled to see me now."

"Mmm."

Working on the second boot, she looked up to find him staring down into her gaping bodice. A flush tingled through her breasts and made them ache. She loved the hunger in his eyes, for it was reserved for her alone. With her palms on his knees, she leaned over him, teasing him with a better view. In a sultry tone, she asked, "Is that all you have to say?"

He shook his head. "Let me add, you take my breath away."

On that thrilling statement, he caught her by the waist and pulled her onto his lap so that she sat straddling him. The scandalous position drew her chemise up to the tops of her bare thighs. She could feel him beneath her, his breeches the only barrier to the joining of their flesh.

Her pulse quickening, she looped her arms around his neck. "My dear lord," she whispered. "You've become quite adept at tempting me into sin."

"I've only just begun."

He began to kiss her again, gently at first, then with increasing fervency. His tongue eased her lips apart and he tasted her deeply as if she were a feast to a starving man. His seductive manner emboldened her to act on her own desires. She tugged the shirt from his waistband and slipped her hands under it, the better to feel the hard-muscled heat of his chest.

He did the same with her chemise, delving beneath to cup her bare bottom and glide over smooth flesh. Sweet heaven, how she ached for his caress. Yet he seemed content with a leisurely exploration, oblivious to the way he was driving her mad.

"Please," she murmured, swiveling her hips to encourage him. "Won't you touch me . . . as you did before?"

He shifted his hand tantalizingly close. "I want your promise first."

"Promise?" she asked in a daze.

"That you'll marry me." Ever so lightly, he flicked his finger over the nest of tight curls. "I'll bribe you with this if that's what it takes."

He spoke lightly as if in jest, but she saw a moody vulnerability in his gaze. Did he truly believe she still needed an inducement?

He must. Considering his cold upbringing and his years in the military, Thane very likely had never been the recipient of love. Nor could he have any notion of what he meant to her. These past few weeks, she had hidden her feelings for him out of misguided fear and foolish denial.

Lindsey took his face in her palms, pressing her forehead to his. Then she looked deep into his eyes so that he could see to her soul. "Of course I'll marry you. I wouldn't be here with you otherwise. I love you, Thane. More than you can imagine."

His lashes dipped slightly, as if he couldn't quite allow himself to believe her. Then he wrapped his arms around her, clasping her very close, his lips in her hair. For a long moment, their hearts beat as one and she fancied a vast welling of joy encircled them.

"When?" he muttered against her ear. "How quickly can you plan our nuptials?"

She laughed. "I don't know; I hadn't thought about it. But considering what we're doing here, it had best be soon."

"Agreed." He brushed back a strand of her hair, laying kisses over her face. "After I take you back to London tomorrow, I can apply to the bishop for a special license. Then it's only a matter of choosing a time and place."

Lindsey caught her breath. "Oh, Thane. We could be wed in a day or two."

"Yes." His dark eyes searched hers. "Unless, of course, you prefer a formal affair at St. George's with all of society in attendance."

The previous summer, Portia and Colin had celebrated such a grand wedding. As much as Lindsey had enjoyed being her sister's maid of honor, she dreaded all the fuss and the myriad details of preparation.

She gave a firm shake of her head. "None of that matters to me. It would make me so happy to be your wife as soon as possible. Although I cannot imagine being more blissful than I am right now."

A brash grin crooked one corner of his mouth. "I can."

Sweeping her up into his arms, he carried her to the bed. The world tilted dizzily and she found herself lying on the mattress, the sheets cool against her fevered back. He bent over her, brushing a kiss across her lips before stepping back to draw off his shirt.

Turning onto her side, Lindsey watched in fascination, admiring the ripple of muscle across his chest and arms, the flatness of his belly. She marveled at the broad-shouldered perfection of his form. In India, she'd seen shirtless men on the street, but none of them had stirred her blood like her husband-to-be.

Husband. Never would she have dreamed a month ago that Thane would capture her heart so completely. Now she felt a zeal to join her life with his, to speak her vows to him, to claim him as her own.

Quite casually he unbuttoned his breeches and stepped out of them. The glow of the fire illuminated him in full male glory, and the sight stirred a pulse of raw desire deep inside her. The sensation of throbbing dampness grew between her legs. It was carnal passion, a passion she felt for no man but him.

He sat on the edge of the bed, unashamed in his nakedness. Shaping his hand around her breast, he idly plied the tip through the thin fabric of her chemise. His serious eyes met hers. "I've dreamed of this moment," he said. "But I don't want you to be afraid."

"I could never be, Thane. Not with you."

To prove it, she glided her fingers down his shaft. How very hot and hard he felt, yet silken to the touch. He sucked in a breath, letting her explore him at will. His face reflected both torture and intense pleasure. Purely on impulse, she leaned forward and pressed a kiss to him.

"Vixen!" Pushing her back against the pillows, he came down over her. "We'll savor each other, not see this matter to a swift conclusion."

He kissed her again in a long and leisurely feast of the senses. All the while, she let her hands roam to acquaint herself with his body. After a time, he drew back to slowly strip off her chemise, nuzzling the skin he exposed. He dropped the garment to the floor and then lay beside her, running his fingertips over her naked curves.

His eyes alive with smoky fire, he leaned down and took her nipple into his mouth. At the swirling of his tongue, she threaded her fingers in the thickness of his hair to encourage him. The ribbon of desire inside her pulled taut, tugging at her loins. When he turned his attention to her other breast, she moaned from a blend of enchantment and frustration. Why was he tormenting her? He must know where she craved his attention most. Oh, how she burned to repeat the rapturous moment he'd shown her only once before.

"Thane, please . . . oh, *please* . . ."

"Shh, darling," he said hoarsely. "You'll have your fill of pleasure tonight. I promise you that."

He smoothed his hand down her belly, and she parted her legs in breathless anticipation. At long last, his finger slid into her damp folds to play with her, lightly at first, then with increasing intensity. His stroking ignited a firestorm that centered in her core. She lay back, consumed by the torturous excitement that had her panting and pleading, her hips moving in search of surcease.

His ministrations stopped abruptly. Bemused, she looked down to see him bend his head to her, and then his tongue caressed her as he'd done to her breasts. The shock of his action swiftly faded beneath a wave of scandalous delight. He seemed to know exactly how to drive her to the brink of madness. Within moments she tumbled into a vast pool of bliss, sobbing out his name.

While she lay dazed and happy, Thane enveloped her with his body and slowly penetrated her. She clung to him, gasping, instinctively lifting her hips to ease the sting of his entry. The slight pain was surpassed by the marvelous sense of him inside her. She wanted to weep from the joy of it. Nothing in her life had prepared her for this feeling of voluptuous fullness, of knowing they were joined as one.

Kissing her brow, he held himself still. "How perfect you are," he murmured hoarsely. "I swore . . . I wouldn't make love to you until we were married. But you're irresistible."

The firelight illuminated the tension on his scarred face, reminding her that he had delayed his own satisfaction for her sake. Craving his enjoyment, she undulated her body to draw him even deeper into herself. His heartfelt groan rewarded her. The desire she'd thought slaked now returned to torment her again, even more intensely this time.

He began to move within her, and together they found a rhythm that pulled her ever deeper into the dark throes of passion. They kissed and caressed until she lost the capacity to think, until she was slick with perspiration and half-sobbing for release. When the storm broke, the pressure of his thrusts transported her from one glorious spasm to the next. Through the cloud of her own rapture came his cry of release.

Lindsey drifted back to an awareness of him sprawled

over her. Against her breasts, the beating of his heart gradually slowed to a normal pace. Contentment spread like warm honey through her limbs. She felt replete and drained, unable to string two thoughts together.

After a time, he shifted position slightly so that he lay beside her, his arms still cradling her close. The fire had died down and the chamber had grown darker. Listening to the rain pattering on the windowpanes, she marveled at how cozy and right it felt to be lying here with Thane. Never had she imagined that lovemaking could be so wonderful.

Releasing a contented sigh, she trailed her fingers through his hair. He was watching her in the semi-darkness. "Heaven on earth," she murmured.

He flashed her a cocky grin. "You're not sorry, then, that you gave up on your spinsterhood?"

"That was the dream of a very foolish girl." Lindsey stretched against the sheets, entangling her legs with his. "I'm amazed at how natural it feels to lie here with you like this."

"We belong together, that's why. For always."

Thane meant every word. No other woman had stirred such a sense of possessiveness in him. Gazing into her lovely face, he felt a clench in his chest, a richness of emotion that he didn't care to examine. He knew only that he wanted to keep Lindsey with him forever, that he would kill any man who dared to touch her. . . .

He inhaled sharply as her fingers drifted down to his groin. She looked like a goddess of love with her bare-breasted beauty, a sultry wisdom in her eyes. Aiming a flirtatious smile at him, she asked, "Will we make love again?"

Chuckling, he brushed back a strand of chestnut hair from her cheek. "Have pity; you've drained all my strength. At least give me a chance to recover."

She continued her bold exploration, exhibiting an uncanny gift for finding his most receptive places. Hell, every part of him was receptive to her. She could arouse him with just a glance.

"How long must I wait?" she asked.

In defiance of human limitations, his body was recovering with spectacular swiftness. "With you, apparently no time at all."

Pulling Lindsey close, he kissed her again, a long and leisurely feast of the senses. He couldn't get enough of her. The stirring of primal urges caused a rush of irresistible heat to his loins. But he wouldn't hurry, not when the long night ahead promised them many hours of pleasure.

He concentrated on stoking her passion, controlling himself even when he was buried deep inside her again. This time, they made love slowly, touching and whispering sweet nothings, gazing into each other's eyes. It surprised him to realize he enjoyed their bantering as much as the physical act itself. With all other women, he had never wanted to linger as he did with Lindsey. The closeness of their minds and souls unleashed a world of incomparable pleasure that went on and on.

Beset by idyllic exhaustion afterward, he held her in his arms. Her eyes drifted shut as she snuggled against him, her arm slipping around his waist. "Mmm," she murmured, her lips against his throat. "I do love you, Thane. So very much."

In lieu of a reply, he brushed a kiss across the top of her hair. He couldn't speak; his throat felt too taut. No one had ever spoken those words to him until today, and her declaration discomfited him.

Something soft and powerful tightened his chest. Was it love? He couldn't be certain. He knew only that he wanted to keep her close like this for the rest of their lives.

Her breathing became even as her body relaxed into

slumber. But despite his physical satiation, Thane found himself alert, unable to shake the irrational fear that he might lose her somehow. He would never forget the sick dread that had spurred him on the hard ride to find her today. If not for her intrepid actions, she might have been the next victim of the Serpentine Strangler.

The notion made his blood run cold.

The dying fire cast flickering shadows over the wall. Cradling her in his arms, he stared at the night-darkened window. Wrayford was out there somewhere. With any luck, he would catch a chill and die. Of course, that would rob Thane of the satisfaction of smashing his fist into the man's face. He would have done so tonight if the man hadn't already lain moaning on the ground.

Lindsey stirred slightly, sighing in her sleep. Awash with tenderness, Thane carefully arranged the blankets over her. She would be his wife and he would protect her with his life. Wrayford would never again have the opportunity to trap her.

But who would the villain turn his attention to next?

The question kept Thane awake long into the night. He couldn't shake the uneasy sense that he was missing some vital clue. And that if he failed to solve it, Lindsey might yet be in grave danger.

Chapter 25

Lindsey stepped though the open gate and into the small garden. It seemed surreal to be back in London after such an eventful change in her life. At this early hour, wispy streamers of mist still clung to the rosebushes. She loved the strength of Thane's hand gripping hers as he drew her down the winding stone path toward the town house beside his.

Marveling anew at the night they'd shared, she drank in the sight of him, so tall and masculine. They had arisen before dawn to make love one last time. It had been a swift, hard coupling, for he had been determined to make haste back to the city.

The roads had been muddy, which had slowed their progress. The hour was nearing eight, and she knew he was concerned for her sake that a nosy neighbor would spy their arrival. His protectiveness only endeared him to her all the more.

What did a little gossip matter, anyway? She felt so absurdly happy that she would have announced their imminent nuptials on every street corner.

Upon reaching the veranda, he opened the door and allowed her to precede him indoors. The house lay silent, the corridor deserted. At this early hour, Jocelyn would still be asleep in her chamber and the servants were likely below stairs, preparing for the day.

After a quick glance around, Thane drew her into a study that overlooked the garden. He took her into his arms, his hands cupping her face and his thumbs tracing her cheekbones. "Are you certain you want me to leave you here with Jocelyn?"

"It's either that or go with you to procure the special license."

He frowned down at her. "Certainly not. But there's still time for me to take you home. I don't care to worry your parents unduly."

It was Mama's own fault for sending Lindsey off on that picnic with Wrayford. But Lindsey didn't want to think about that now. "I'll send a note to my father," she promised. "However, I shan't tell them where I am. Mama would drag me home and imprison me in my bedchamber. That's what she did last year to my sister Portia."

"Hmm. I'll concede to your superior knowledge of them. But this will certainly get me off on the wrong foot with them—if I haven't done so already."

"They'll come around eventually," she assured him, reaching up to stroke his bristled cheek. "Especially when they realize how very much there is to love about you."

Thane's hard features took on a hint of vulnerability that melted her heart. Drawing her close, he kissed her soundly and thoroughly, stirring all the beautiful longings that only he could fulfill. Then with a regretful look, he pulled back.

"I'm going next door to make myself presentable for the bishop. If all goes well, I should return within a few hours." He ran his finger over her damp lips. "You'll be safe here until then."

"Most certainly."

"If you require a bedchamber, there are several empty ones upstairs."

She took his hand and planted a kiss in the palm. "That's very kind of you, my lord."

"You can have breakfast with Jocelyn. She should be waking up soon. Just tell her—"

"I know what to tell her," Lindsey said with a laugh. "Now do run along. We will be needing that special license straightaway."

His reluctance to depart was a balm to her heart—especially since he had not said he loved her. But surely his actions showed that he cherished her, and she must trust that eventually he would voice the words she so longed to hear from him.

He brushed his lips over hers one last time, then turned and strode out into the corridor. She stepped to the doorway and watched as he headed down the passageway and disappeared into the library, where the connecting door led to his house.

Lindsey leaned against the door frame and smiled like a besotted fool. Only a few short weeks ago, Thane had kissed her in that very library and she'd fended him off with a letter opener. How long ago that all seemed now!

Now she had shed the vestiges of girlhood and become a woman. She had been a wife to him through the joining of their hearts and bodies. It was stunning to think that their lovemaking might have already borne fruit. She smoothed her hands over her midsection, imagining herself carrying Thane's baby. The awe-inspiring thought brought a rush of tenderness and reaffirmed her resolve to marry him.

Deciding to freshen up, Lindsey found the back staircase and mounted the steps. She encountered no one on the way. How lonely it must be for Jocelyn to have only Mrs. Fisk and the other servants for company. Once

Lindsey and Thane were wed, all that would change. She would spend time every day with the girl and invite Blythe over to visit often. Mama could no longer object to the acquaintance; she would have to accept the marriage or lose face in society.

Buoyed by the thought, Lindsey tiptoed down a carpeted corridor upstairs and peeked into an open doorway to see a comfortable bedchamber decorated in blues and whites. She went inside and quietly closed the door. It would cause fewer questions if she didn't make her presence known for a little while yet. No one must guess that she'd just spent the most sinfully wonderful night of her life.

Then she caught sight of herself in a pier glass and laughed out loud. With her bonnet askew, she resembled a ragamuffin. Her gown was sadly wrinkled, the hem damp and somewhat muddied from stepping in puddles.

In front of the dressing table, she removed the bonnet and tidied her hair. Perhaps she'd wait a little while longer before writing that note to her parents. It would serve Mama well to worry a bit. Although perversely, she owed her mother a debt of gratitude. If Wrayford had not made the abduction attempt, then Thane would not have come riding to her rescue.

The image of him appearing out of the gloom on horseback made her heart clench. Welcoming the opportunity to savor all the memories, she wandered to a chaise, stretched out, and closed her eyes. A blissful relaxation bathed her. The pleasant ache between her legs gave testimony to the numerous times she and Thane had made love during the night. They'd taken turns waking up in the darkness to stroke and caress each other. There had been a dreamlike quality to it all, the most lovely dream she had ever known. . . .

* * *

Lindsey awakened to the muted chime of the ormolu clock on the mantel. For a moment she didn't recognize her surroundings. Then a quick perusal of the blue and white bedchamber released a flood of remembrance.

This was Jocelyn's house. Thane had left her here while he had gone to obtain the special license.

She squinted at the gold hands of the clock and then sat up straight. Lud, it was noon already. She'd slept for four hours. Papa must be frantic. Had Mama admitted to him her scheme to marry off their middle daughter to Wrayford?

Lindsey doubted it. Mama would hide the truth from him as long as possible.

She snatched up her bonnet and left the bedchamber. Swinging the straw hat by its ribbons, she hastened downstairs to seek out Jocelyn. At least the lateness of the hour would make her excuses simpler. Since no one had spied her as yet, she could claim to have stopped here while out on a walk. Jocelyn needn't know that Lindsey had napped in one of the bedchambers.

But when she entered the sitting room, the chaise where Jocelyn always sat was empty. The white blanket that usually covered her legs lay neatly folded on a cushion.

Jocelyn could be anywhere in the house, in her bedchamber for a visit to the necessary, in the dining room eating luncheon, or perhaps in another room, diligently at work with her art master. It might be best to wait right here for her. Meanwhile, the girl's lap desk would have paper and pen inside for Lindsey to use for her note.

Had Thane returned yet?

The thought of him proved an irresistible distraction. Abandoning her plan to linger, Lindsey took the back stairs down to the library on the ground floor, where she intended to use the connecting door. It might be too forward of her to visit his town house unchaperoned, but she no longer cared about her reputation. She needed to see him again, to find out if he'd succeeded in obtaining the special license. With any luck, they might speak their vows this very day. And then they would be together tonight and all the nights for the rest of their lives. . . .

An odd muffled thumping noise came from within the library. Thinking there was a servant at work, Lindsey stepped into the open doorway. She stopped, stupefied, her gaze riveted on the sole occupant of the room.

Clad in a pale green gown, her blond hair tied back with a ribbon, Jocelyn was standing up. Even more amazingly, she was using a cane to make her way toward the mantelpiece, where a coal fire hissed on the hearth.

"Jocelyn! You're walking!"

The girl gave a start of surprise, thrust one hand behind her back, and nearly toppled over in the process. Lindsey rushed to offer support, slipping her arm around the girl's slender waist.

"Lud, I can scarcely believe my eyes!" Lindsey exclaimed. "This is wonderful news. Why didn't you tell me? But you ought to have someone here with you. Where is Fisk? What if you were to fall down?"

Jocelyn promptly burst into tears.

Remorse swept through Lindsey. "Oh, you poor darling. I didn't mean to bombard you with questions. You must have overtaxed yourself. Here, let me help you to a chair."

"No, you don't understand!" Jocelyn said, wrenching away and nearly stumbling. Desperation shone on her tear-stained face. "I've something I must burn—and quickly."

"Burn? What do you mean?"

"The diary. I have to get rid of it before that awful man comes back."

Jocelyn showed her a small leather-bound volume that she held half-hidden in the folds of her dress. Leaning on the cane, she limped again toward the fire.

Perplexed, Lindsey hastened forward and gently pried the book from the girl's dainty fingers. Taking hold of her arm, she guided Jocelyn to a chair. "You aren't burning anything until you explain matters to me. Now, sit down. You'll tell me exactly what's going on here."

Jocelyn tensed as if to protest again; then all the fight drained from her and she sank into the chair. Her shoulders drooped in a pose of abject misery. "Oh, Lindsey, something dreadful has happened," she said, her green eyes shimmery with tears. "I can scarcely believe it. I—I don't know even where to start."

Lindsey pushed an ottoman closer. She perched right in front of Jocelyn, placed the small book in her own lap, and then took hold of Jocelyn's hands. "Start at the beginning, of course. What's happened to make you so overwrought?"

Jocelyn drew a deep, shaky breath. "A—a man came to call on Lord Mansfield this morning. He looked like a gentleman; that's why I didn't realize who he was at first. I—I saw him from the window."

"Do you mean . . . you *walked* to the window?"

Jocelyn nodded. "I've been practicing every day and doing my exercises. I wanted to surprise you."

"You certainly accomplished your purpose. Now, do tell me what happened to upset you."

"The man . . . he was next door for only a short time. Then a little while later, I overheard Fisk chatting to one of the maids out in the corridor. She said . . ."

"What? What did she say?"

Jocelyn tightened her grip on Lindsey's hands. "Last night, there was another murder by the Serpentine Strangler. He left the . . . the body in Hyde Park, the same place as all the others. Oh, Lindsey, you won't believe who was killed . . . it was Miss Valentine."

Chapter 26

The cold fingers of shock crept down Lindsey's back. She pictured the plain, dark-haired woman who had given Thane a look of admiration. "The clerk from the dress shop?"

Jocelyn nodded. A tear slipped down her pale cheek. "The man who came to see His Lordship was a Bow Street Runner. The maids were saying that . . . that he intends to arrest Lord Mansfield for murder!"

Lindsey sat frozen. A Runner who was dressed like a gentleman could only be Cyrus Bott. But she had sent notice to him that he was to cease investigating Thane because the two missing maidservants had been found. So why would Bott make such a threat?

Because he had seen Thane visit the shop? Bott *had* been lurking outside in the alley there, watching him.

But such flimsy circumstantial evidence was hardly cause to arrest Thane. Perhaps Jocelyn had mistaken the purpose of Bott's visit. The girl had a flair for the dramatic. Maybe he had merely come to consult with Thane. After all, Thane had mentioned he was trying to find evidence to prove that Wrayford was the killer.

She rubbed the back of Jocelyn's cold hand. "Don't worry, darling. Lord Mansfield is not a murderer. You may be absolutely certain of that."

"But-but I heard he didn't come home last night," Jocelyn said shakily. "The maids were whispering about that, as well."

Lindsey fought back a blush. She couldn't reveal that she knew precisely where he'd been. "I'm sure there's a very good reason. Gentlemen often stay out until dawn. He could have been at a party or at his club. You mustn't leap to conclusions."

"But I'm *not*." Jocelyn glanced at the open doorway and lowered her voice to a whisper: "I feared that awful man might come back and search through His Lordship's belongings. So I sent Fisk away and made the footman carry me down here. Then I went next door and looked through his desk in the library. And I found this."

She took the small volume from Lindsey's lap. "Look, it's Miss Valentine's diary."

A sick dread in her stomach, Lindsey opened the book. On the flyleaf, in spidery handwriting, was the inscription *Miss Harriet Valentine.*

She stared in perplexed shock. Why would Thane have this diary in his possession? Had the shop clerk given it to him for some unknown purpose?

A more logical explanation occurred to her. Perhaps upon leaving here this morning Thane had learned the news about the murder. Instead of obtaining the special license, he had changed his plans and gone to Miss Valentine's place of residence, where he had procured the journal as evidence. Then he must have brought it back and secured it in his desk with no one the wiser.

Yes, that must be it. There was no other viable reason for him to possess the diary of the dead woman. Lindsey flipped through the pages to see tiny, precise script that filled every inch of the precious paper. Perhaps Thane hoped to find something written here that would connect Wrayford to Miss Valentine.

"Don't you see?" Jocelyn said urgently. "Someone must be trying to *make* Lord Mansfield look guilty. And that's why I have to burn it before that nasty man returns."

Lindsey couldn't break her promise to Thane. He didn't want people to know that he was trying to find the Strangler. "I'm sure there's a rational explanation for the diary being in his desk. In the meantime, it would be wrong to destroy a valuable piece of evidence."

"But I *must*. His Lordship will be thrown into *prison* if I don't. And then what will happen to me?"

Lindsey's heart went out to the girl. Leaning forward, she embraced Jocelyn. "Is that what's worrying you? I give you my word, in such an unlikely event, I'll watch after you, darling. You won't ever be left to fend for yourself."

"You—you would do that?"

"Of course. We're the best of friends, aren't we? And Lord Mansfield won't be jailed, you'll see. This is just a terrible misunderstanding. It will all be sorted out, I'm sure. In the meantime, I'll keep the diary and make certain no one but the earl sees it."

Jocelyn bit her lip and nodded, although she still appeared somewhat apprehensive. Lindsey rang for tea, and after fetching the girl a drawing pad and pencil she sat down at one of the tables to compose a brief note to her parents.

In it, she wrote that Wrayford had attempted to abduct her but that she had eluded him and was now safe from harm. She would be returning home shortly and would explain everything.

Deciding that the missive would reassure them for the time being, Lindsey sanded the ink and folded the paper, sealing it with a blob of hot wax. Then she went to the entrance hall and handed it to the footman on duty at the front door. He was to slip it through the mail slot at her house without telling anyone who had asked him to deliver it.

Only then did Lindsey allow herself to contemplate the latest murder. Walking slowly back to the library, she was struck anew by the horrifying death of Miss Valentine. It was one thing to read about the Serpentine Strangler in the newspaper and quite another to have known one of the victims herself.

Last night, Wrayford had been miles away in the country without any means to travel. Didn't that eliminate him as the murderer?

A possible scenario occurred to her. Wrayford had been in a rage at her for pushing him out of the carriage. What if he'd hitched a ride in a passing vehicle and returned to London in the wee hours of the night? What if he'd then taken out his anger at Lindsey by strangling Miss Valentine?

Gripped by a cold shudder, Lindsey rubbed her arms. She didn't want to think that she might have been the impetus for murder. It was just too horrifying. Now, more than ever, she wanted Thane to return, to see if he knew any additional details. In the meantime, she could read the diary herself to see what information it might contain to implicate Wrayford.

As she neared the library, the sound of voices caught her attention, one male and the other belonging to Jocelyn. The girl sounded distressed again. Was she upset with the footman who had delivered the tea tray?

The tea cart was there all right, but not the footman.

Lindsey was startled to see a visitor in the room. He stood a short distance from Jocelyn, who was still sitting in the chair. Astonishingly, she brandished her cane like a sword.

"Mr. Bott!" Lindsey exclaimed. "Whatever are you doing in this house?"

"Miss Brown," he said, bowing to her. "I wonder if you might reassure Miss Nevingford that I intend her no harm."

"Why did he call you Miss Brown?" Jocelyn asked.

"I'll explain later," Lindsey said. "Now, do put down that weapon. There's no need for it."

As Jocelyn reluctantly lowered the cane, Lindsey's mind raced. Bott must have come through the connecting door from Thane's residence. Was he looking for evidence to prove Thane's guilt?

Dear heaven. She had left the diary lying out in plain view on the oak table where she'd written the note to her parents. Although there had to be a logical explanation for its presence in Thane's desk, it would serve no purpose to court trouble. She should ask Bott to follow her into another room. But that would require him to walk right past the diary.

Lindsey opted to move in the opposite direction from the table, so that Bott would keep his attention on her. The ploy worked. As she walked to the connecting door, he swung to face her, his back to Jocelyn.

He looked like a typical gentleman in the dark blue coat with the brass buttons, his cravat neatly tied beneath his chin. There was nothing remarkable about his wavy brown hair and even features; he was someone she might pass on the street and never really notice. Of course, that made him ideal for detective work.

"I can't blame Jocelyn for being alarmed," she said. "It's highly inappropriate for you to intrude here."

He ducked his chin. "Please accept my sincerest apology. I *did* knock before entering."

"I only said come in because I thought you were one of the servants," Jocelyn said with a sniff.

Bott glanced over his shoulder at her before returning his attention to Lindsey. "Forgive my imposition. It's just that I'm investigating a rather urgent case. I thought perhaps Miss Nevingford could supply me with information as to Lord Mansfield's whereabouts."

"She doesn't know where he is," Lindsey said. "She hasn't seen him today. You would be better off asking His Lordship's valet."

Behind the Runner, Jocelyn rose to her feet, using the cane as leverage. Her purpose quickly became clear to Lindsey. The girl was making her way toward the diary. How foolish of her to take such a risk! Didn't she realize she would only draw his attention?

"I'm afraid the fellow wasn't very cooperative," Bott said ruefully, his blue eyes on Lindsey. "He seems to have taken an unfortunate dislike to me."

"No doubt he sees you as impertinent for lingering around His Lordship's house. I would think the best course of action for you is to leave a note for the earl and then return to Bow Street to await his summons."

She was babbling, hoping the Runner wouldn't look over his shoulder. Jocelyn had nearly reached the table.

Lindsey went on, "I do believe you should leave now. There can be no further purpose for you here. Good day, Mr. Bott." She stepped aside to give him access to the connecting door. "I would suggest you go out the same way you came in."

"Perhaps you wouldn't mind answering one last question. Do you know where Lord Mansfield was last evening?"

She kept her face impassive, although her heart thudded hard against her ribs. "Why would I? I'm merely a visitor here, a friend of Miss Nevingford."

He looked at her closely. "But when you came to see me, you seemed to have particular knowledge of—"

Jocelyn uttered a muffled cry. She'd caught the tip of her cane in the rug and stumbled against the table. The diary slipped from her fingers and tumbled to the floor. Lindsey rushed to her aid, but Bott arrived there first. Clutching the table for support, Jocelyn tried to reach down for the journal, but he took it up in his hands.

"What's this?" he asked, scowling as he opened the fly-leaf. His fingers visibly tightened around the diary. "Why do you have a book belonging to Miss Valentine? Did His Lordship ask you to hide this for him?"

"Leave her be," Lindsey began.

At that moment, the connecting door opened and Thane strode into the library. He appeared angry, his mouth set in a grim line as he glared at the Runner. "Bernard told me you were here—"

Thane stopped abruptly. "My God," he said, his gaze honing in on Jocelyn. The severity of his countenance softened with wonder. "You're standing up."

Jocelyn lifted her chin proudly. "I can walk now. I've been practicing for weeks. See?"

Using the cane, she took a few tottering steps. But as she passed Cyrus Bott, she turned suddenly and attempted to snatch the diary out of his hands.

The Runner held resolutely to the small book. Their silent tug-of-war lasted the space of only a few seconds.

Both Thane and Lindsey rushed toward them. "What the devil are you doing?" he demanded. "If she wants the book, then by God give it to her."

Bott stepped back with the journal in his hands. "No. This is evidence against the Serpentine Strangler."

"Evidence?" Thane repeated with a questioning frown.

"Yes indeed. This diary belonged to Miss Harriet Valentine. She was strangled to death last night and left in Hyde Park."

Thane's dark eyes widened as a fleeting surprise played across his face. It was clear he'd known nothing of the murder. Then a stony bleakness thinned his mouth. "Miss Valentine . . . that name sounds familiar."

Lindsey's heart sank. So she'd been wrong to believe he'd found the diary himself. That could only mean someone really *was* trying to implicate him as the murderer.

She touched his arm. "She's the clerk at the shop, remember? The place where Jocelyn ordered her gowns."

"She was *murdered,*" Jocelyn cried, her beseeching eyes on Thane. "And this dreadful man is trying to blame it all on *you.*"

Thane aimed a lordly stare at Bott. "Is that so?"

The Runner gave him a wary look in return. "I've had certain suspicions these past weeks. It seemed a bit odd to me the way you, a nobleman, came to the magistrate to offer your assistance. And the diary does put you in a rather unfavorable light, my lord, seeing as it was discovered on the premises here."

Thane swung toward Jocelyn. "Where exactly did you find it?"

"I-I don't know. It-it was just lying about somewhere."

Going to her, he placed his hands on her shoulders and bent down to look deep into her eyes. "The truth, sprite. You won't help me by spinning tall tales."

A tear trickled down her cheek. "In-in your d-desk. Someone hid it there to-to make you look guilty."

His expression grim, he turned to the Runner and held out his hand. "Let me see the diary."

"I'm afraid that's impossible," Bott said, tucking it into an inner pocket of his coat. "You know the rules. I'm obliged to turn over all evidence to the magistrate. He'll want to see you, too."

Alarmed, Lindsey stepped to Thane and looped her arm through his. "This is all a terrible mistake. Lord Mansfield cannot possibly have committed murder last night. You see—"

"You will not involve yourself in this matter," Thane interrupted. "It is no concern of yours."

"But—"

"You heard me. I will brook no interference."

The cold harshness of his voice silenced her. Clearly, he didn't want her to provide him with an alibi because her reputation would be ruined in the process. She understood that, yet his gallantry might land him in prison.

Her fears were confirmed at once.

An apologetic look on his face, Cyrus Bott addressed Thane: "Lord Mansfield, I'm afraid I must arrest you for the murder of Miss Harriet Valentine."

Chapter 27

Thane sat on a wooden bench in a room the size of a linen closet. He leaned forward, his elbows on his knees, his hands clasped in front of him. The only light came from a small barred window mounted high in the wall. Every now and then he could hear sounds outside the locked door, the shouts of other inmates or their pounding on the wall.

He understood their frustration. Imprisonment filled him with impotent wrath.

An hour had ticked slowly past, then another, until now he cursed his willingness to cooperate. He ought to have insisted on being allowed to wait in one of the offices upstairs. But he'd been determined to show he had nothing to hide.

Bott had been contrite about the need to follow the rules. Since the chief magistrate was in the middle of a court session, Thane was to be held in a private cell only for a brief time. Unfortunately, that estimate had proved to be grossly understated. It took all of his self-control to keep from banging on the door and demanding his release.

Thane was confident that this mess would be straightened out once he spoke to the magistrate. What the devil was delaying Smithers?

Thane itched to take action in solving the case. Instead, he'd had nothing to do but reflect. A gruesome thought had continued to plague him. While he and Lindsey had been enjoying the most erotic night of their lives, another woman had been murdered. Miss Valentine, that mouse of a clerk from the dress shop.

Why her? Had she been chosen on purpose? Because she had a connection, however tenuous, to him?

It certainly would seem so. He'd been set up, no doubt about it. The mysterious appearance of the diary in his house proved as much.

Wrayford could have found a way back to London, perhaps by flagging down a vehicle on the main road. He had been in a towering rage, and the clerk would have made an easy target. But how would Wrayford know Thane had ever been to the dress shop?

That was something Thane couldn't explain—and he didn't believe in coincidences. There was also the matter of the diary. Before departing for Bow Street he had made inquiries, but none of his servants had seen Wrayford that morning. Yet someone had stolen into the house to plant the journal.

Was he wrong to believe the Serpentine Strangler was Wrayford?

The possibility chilled Thane. Wrayford certainly was the most likely suspect. He'd had clear connections to the first three victims. But this new development seemed to cast doubt on Thane's conjecture. Would Miss Valentine still be alive if he'd arrested Wrayford the previous evening—or would she have died anyway?

Thane clenched his jaw. Speculating accomplished nothing. He had not possessed sufficient proof to apprehend the man, so it was a moot point. And at the time, he had been thinking only of Lindsey.

Lindsey. When she had invited him to pose as her

husband, the temptation had been too great to resist. Their experience at the inn had been an unparalleled delight, like nothing he had ever known. Her soft declaration of love had stirred a powerful yearning in his soul, lending an amazing depth to their closeness in bed.

He remembered her anguished face as she'd watched him being taken away to Bow Street. What was she doing now? Had she returned to her parents' house? He hated to think of Lindsey out there, alone and unguarded, with a killer on the loose. Her dragon of a mother would have no compunction about letting Wrayford into the house.

His gut tightened. He ached to protect her, to hold her in his arms, to tell her that she was his very life, the breath in his body, the blood in his veins. This wrenching need he felt for her could only be love. What a fool he'd been not to recognize the truth and voice his feelings to her when he'd had the chance. . . .

An iron key rattled in the door. Thane jumped to his feet as the solid wood panel swung open.

Josiah Smithers walked into the cell. A portly man, the chief magistrate wore the tightly curled wig and black robes of his profession. Gazing over the pair of gold-rimmed spectacles perched on the end of his bulbous nose, he studied Thane with a look of disgruntlement.

In his hand, he clutched the small leather-bound diary.

"I'm sorry you've been obliged to wait so long, my lord. An unexpected visitor delayed me."

"Never mind; I'm glad you're finally here," Thane said. "Has anyone gone to verify Lord Wrayford's whereabouts? It's essential to find out where he was last night."

"Bott left a short time ago to check on him."

Smithers paced slowly back and forth in front of the door. Thane glimpsed a husky guard lurking out in the corridor. There was something in the way Smithers was studying him, with a hint of suspicion, that hit Thane like a sucker punch.

"I trust you realize I had nothing to do with Miss Valentine's murder," he said. "You have my word that I've never seen her diary before today. Someone is framing me for her murder."

Smithers pursed his lips. "I'm given to understand that last week you went to the shop where she was employed."

"Yes. My ward needed to order a few gowns." Thane had also wanted an excuse to rendezvous with Lindsey. He wondered suddenly if she might have mentioned visiting the dressmaker's to Wrayford while they'd been on that picnic. "Wrayford must have somehow found out about my visit there."

"According to Cyrus Bott, you never went home last night," the magistrate said. "Can you account for your whereabouts, perhaps give me the name of a credible witness who can vouch for you?"

Lindsey could. But Thane would not subject her to undue scrutiny that would ruin her in the eyes of society. He wouldn't allow anyone to put a sordid connotation on their tryst. It was a private joy that would only be sullied by exposure to the outside world.

"No," he stated. "I cannot."

"Cannot? Or will not?"

Thane stared stonily back at him.

Smithers sighed. "Your reticence is quite admirable, my lord. However, you should know that a short while ago, Miss Crompton came to my office to plead your case. That's what delayed me. She vows she will swear in court under oath that you were with her all night."

Thane averted his eyes. He didn't want the man to glimpse the rush of wild emotion in him. Blast Lindsey for disobeying him! At the same time, he felt a leap of exultation that she would fight for him.

He turned a cool façade to the magistrate. "I'll deny it. She's merely trying to secure my release. Be forewarned, I will not have her testifying on my behalf."

"You are right to oppose it," Smithers said. "A lady has no place in a public court of law. As for your innocence, I would very much like to believe you, my lord. When you first came to see me, you appeared to have a genuine desire to help solve these crimes."

"As I still do. But I won't accomplish anything locked up here."

The magistrate grimaced at the small journal in his hand. "Unfortunately, this diary contains a rather disturbing passage. Bott pointed it out to me before he left."

"He's certainly a fast reader. May I see?"

Smithers hesitated, then handed it over. "It's at the very end, my lord. And it implicates you by name."

Stunned, Thane riffled the pages until he found the last entry. The cramped, spidery script was difficult to read. But the reference jumped out at once.

Lord Mansfield came to me last evening. Oh, what delight, what joy I found in his embrace. . . .

His teeth clenched, he scanned the rest, a flowery tribute that thoroughly incriminated him as her secret lover. No wonder Smithers regarded him with keen distrust. Any court would convict a man on such damning evidence.

Thane held the diary up to the inadequate light from the high window. After studying the book for a few moments, he said, "There appears to be a slight discrepancy in the ink compared to the previous page. And the penmanship looks very similar, but it isn't exact. You can see it in the formation of several of the characters."

"You're suggesting it's a forgery?"

"I know it's a forgery. Someone added this entry to make me look guilty."

As he spoke, Thane's mind raced. Such a clever piece of counterfeiting seemed beyond Wrayford's capabilities—or any of his dissolute companions', for that matter. And none of them had visited Thane's house that morning.

Only one man had come to call. One man whom Thane had never in his wildest speculations had reason to consider a murderer. But now it all made a horrible, twisted sense.

He shoved the diary back into the magistrate's hand. "When exactly did Bott depart from here?"

"Perhaps twenty minutes ago," Smithers said with a startled look. "He and Miss Crompton went to see Lord Wrayford."

Lindsey had borrowed Thane's carriage to go to Bow Street Station. Now, in order to avoid drawing attention from any passersby, she had allowed Cyrus Bott to drive the vehicle along the outskirts of Mayfair. Thankfully, her bonnet had a wide brim that helped shield her face from view. In late afternoon, many people were out strolling or driving, and she didn't want any acquaintance to flag them down. Nothing must delay her in this quest to clear Thane's name.

A kernel of dread lodged in her stomach. She had thought to win his freedom by confessing they'd spent the night together. However, the chief magistrate had been polite but firm in his refusal to accept the alibi. The officious man also had declined to allow her to see Thane, proclaiming it too dangerous for a lady to visit an accused murderer. Her next best hope was to wrest a confession from Lord Wrayford.

By heaven, she would choke it out of him if need be.

The villain must be trying to pin the murder on Thane in order to rid himself of a rival for her hand in marriage.

"Here is Bruton Street, my lady," Bott said. "Which house is it?"

"Midway down, the one with the claret red door."

Bott had been scrupulously polite. He had ceased his attempt at small talk when she'd given him cold answers. Lindsey had little desire to chitchat with the man who had arrested Thane. But she also recognized the need for a Bow Street Runner to be present when she confronted Wrayford. Bott would serve as both a witness and an officer to cart Wrayford off to prison.

She would take great pleasure in clearing Thane's name. It was evident from Bott's smug expression that he believed they were on a fool's errand.

Her mind dwelled a moment on his zeal to charge Thane with murder. There was something odd about their encounter in the library this morning, something that hovered at the edge of her mind. Things had happened so quickly there had been little time for reflection. When Jocelyn had dropped the diary, Bott had picked it up. He'd opened the flyleaf to read the name inscribed inside. And then—

The memory flitted away as Bott drew the horse to a halt in front of Wrayford's residence. While he went to tie the reins to an iron post, Lindsey climbed down and hurried to the tall brick town house. She lifted the brass knocker and rapped hard on the door.

In a moment, she found herself facing the same vacuous young footman as the last time she'd been here. "Good afternoon, Buttery. May we come in?"

The white-wigged servant bowed. "Aye, m'lady." He stepped aside so that she and Bott could enter.

"I wish to speak to your master," she said. "Will you inform Lord Wrayford that I'm here?"

The footman frowned, glancing upstairs. "Can't, miss. The master told us not t' wake him. 'Twas past noon when he come home, ye see."

"Pray fetch him anyway. I need a word with him at once."

"But he'll be angry—"

"Go," she said firmly. "Or I shall march upstairs myself and do it."

Buttery hesitated, then with obvious reluctance trudged toward the staircase.

Untying the ribbons of her bonnet, Lindsey was unnerved to find Cyrus Bott standing directly at her side. She caught a flash of something in his blue eyes, a disdainful enjoyment as if he relished the scene to come when she would be proved wrong about Wrayford's guilt.

"Follow me," she snapped. Pivoting on her heel, she marched into a small visitor's parlor off the entrance hall. She took off her bonnet and tossed it onto a chair. Then she swung around to address him: "Lord Mansfield is innocent. I've vouched for his whereabouts myself. The true Serpentine Strangler will not be captured if you make up your mind prematurely and cease to look for him."

"With all due respect, my lady, all the evidence points at the earl. You yourself believed so for a time."

Her heart wrenched at the reminder of her own perfidy. "I was mistaken. And evidence can be fabricated."

A slight smile touched his mouth. "That's extremely doubtful in this case. Forgive me for being indelicate, but Miss Valentine named the earl in her diary. Her final entry describes their affair in detail."

Lindsey experienced a knell of shock. She hadn't known that detail. Dear God, no wonder the magistrate had been reluctant to accept her testimony. "I'm sure that close inspection will reveal it to be a forgery. Lord Mansfield couldn't possibly have killed her."

The Runner shrugged. "That will be for a court to decide."

He strolled to a gilt-framed mirror near the window, peering at himself and flicking a piece of lint from his dark blue coat. Frowning, Lindsey watched him straighten an imaginary wrinkle in his cravat.

"You're rather young to be a Runner, are you not? Just how many murder cases have you solved?"

"None as important as this one. It will be quite a feather in my cap." In the mirror, a gleam appeared again in his eyes although his expression remained sober. "I'm sorry, my lady. I'm sure this is a very difficult circumstance for you, given your close relationship with His Lordship."

Lindsey scarcely heard him. He stood in a shaft of light from the window. As he arranged his cravat, a stickpin inside the folds of white linen glinted dully. She took a few steps closer. The gold pin was crowned by a heart fashioned from tiny chips of ruby red stone.

Where had she seen it before?

Then it struck her. Miss Valentine had worn that very pin on her collar. She'd said that her father had had it specially made for her mother.

A cold chill coursed through Lindsey, raising gooseflesh on her arms. Had Bott stolen it from Miss Valentine's body at the scene of the crime?

Or . . . was he the one who had strangled her to death?

Chapter 28

Lindsey's mind raced. Once again, she thought back to the moment when Jocelyn had dropped the diary and Bott had snatched it up. He had opened the book to the flyleaf and read Miss Valentine's name aloud. . . .

He had not flipped through the other pages, Lindsey was certain of it. Yet a few moments later he had referred to the book as *a diary*. How had he known that?

Unless he had already read the contents. Unless he had forged the entry about Thane and then, early that morning, left the diary in his desk, where Jocelyn had found it.

Her heart beating faster, Lindsey stared in disbelief at the stickpin. Bott had been lurking in the alley outside the dress shop, too, on the day Lindsey had gone there to meet Thane and Jocelyn. . . .

"Is something wrong?" Bott asked.

She glanced up to find him watching her. "No. I—I was merely wondering what was keeping Lord Wrayford. Perhaps I should go see."

Lindsey started toward the door, but Cyrus Bott stepped swiftly to block her departure. "That would be most improper," he said. "Ladies do not chase after gentlemen in their bedchambers. Only the lowly riffraff behave that way."

"Like maidservants?" she asked. "Or perhaps shop clerks?"

She observed him closely. Perhaps she'd been too bold, yet she couldn't be in any real danger, not with servants in the house. At any moment Wrayford should be coming downstairs, too.

Cyrus Bott stood in the doorway, studying her. "You'll think me forward for saying this, but you're a very beautiful woman, Miss Crompton. And you're a commoner like me. Perhaps at some future time, you might possibly consider . . ."

He reached out as if to touch her hair, but she flinched. Never had she been so repelled or so frightened by any man. It was a struggle to keep her expression cool. "You are being impertinent, Mr. Bott. Now kindly move aside."

"I'm sorry, but that's impossible," he said. "I saw you looking at my stickpin. You've guessed everything, haven't you?"

There was a hint of mournfulness in his expression, as if he regretted being exposed as a killer. Her mouth felt dry as dust. "Everything?"

"You know about Miss Valentine. Let me assure you, she was merely a hussy who would lift her skirts in exchange for a bit of flattery. Her death is of no consequence."

He spoke in a normal conversational tone. They might have been talking about the weather, or a neighbor's new dog, rather than a horror so palatable Lindsey could taste bile just thinking about it.

"So you strangled her," she whispered. "As you did those other women."

"Don't waste your pity on them. They were whores, human weeds. The world is better off without such vulgar creatures."

"They were women who worked hard for a living. Like

anyone else, they had hopes and dreams. You robbed them of their life. Why?"

He shrugged. "It's tiresome to be chasing after petty thieves, year after year. If ever I hoped to advance in my profession, I needed to work on a much bigger case." His mouth tightened. "Lord Mansfield should never have interfered. They were *my* murders, not his."

Bott had committed the crimes for the glory of solving them. It all made a hideous sort of sense. He had romanced the maids, lured them to their deaths, and then planted the forged entry in the diary to implicate Mansfield.

"I see," she murmured, stalling for time.

Where was Wrayford? She needed him or Buttery or both of them to come charging down the stairs right now. At the moment, she would welcome either buffoon so they could help her ward off this madman.

Bott frowned at her. "You're going to tell on me, aren't you," he stated.

"No! I wouldn't do that. It will be our secret."

"Lying whore. You'll tattle to protect Mansfield."

In a flash, his face took on the look of a snarling beast. He lunged at Lindsey, spinning her around so that she faced away from him. She cried out, but his hand clamped over her mouth and muffled the sound. With his foot, he kicked the door shut.

She struggled with all her might, trying to jam her elbow into his side and stomp on his instep, but he reacted with wiry quickness. Thrusting her facedown on the floor, he held her in place with his body.

Lindsey could scarcely breathe. He had a sinewy strength that belied his slight appearance. And he seemed to possess an uncanny knowledge of where she would attempt to hit him next.

She could feel him tugging one-handed at his cravat,

cursing as the cloth caught on Miss Valentine's stickpin. In a panic, she realized he intended to strangle her.

She bucked and fought to no avail. A moment later, the stickpin went bouncing across the rug, landing under a chair in front of her.

He shoved the cravat beneath her chin to encircle her neck. To do so, he had to release her mouth, but it was too late for her to scream. The cloth tightened, cutting off her air. Black dots swirled before her eyes.

Somehow, in the midst of her terror, she managed to free one arm. She scrabbled desperately for the pin. Her fingers closed around it, the tiny stones of the heart digging into her palm. A swirling fog threatened to swamp her senses. With the last of her strength, she thrust her arm back, the sharp pin aimed straight at his face.

Bott howled, releasing her at once. His weight left her, and the deadly tension around her throat vanished.

Gasping for air, she rolled over to see him rocking on his knees, moaning. His hands covered his eyes. Blood seeped through his fingers.

A commotion sounded out in the entrance hall. Scrambling to her feet, Lindsey hurried to wrench open the door that Bott had shut. She expected to see Wrayford or Buttery but instead found three other men who were fanning out to search the house.

"Thane," she cried out.

He pivoted on his heel, the grimness of his expression transforming into joy. He half-ran across the foyer to haul her close in a fierce embrace. "Thank God, you're safe. *Thank God.*"

She clung to him, shaky and weak in the aftermath. "It was Cyrus Bott all along," she said. "He's the Strangler. He killed those women."

"I know. He forged a portion of the diary to point the blame at me." Thane gently tilted her chin up, his gaze scouring her. His jaw hardened as his gaze met hers again. "Your neck is red. The bastard tried to strangle you just now."

"Yes."

The horror of it washed over her anew. From the safety of Thane's arms, she saw the other two men, both burly officers, go into the sitting room to take hold of Bott. He was moaning and crying, his hand cupping his eye. She averted her face, sickened by his pain in spite of herself.

Thane tucked her face in the crook of his neck while the men escorted Bott out of the house. Thane's hand rubbed soothingly up and down her back. "You did what was necessary. Evil reaps its own reward."

Lindsey took a shuddering breath. "He . . . had Miss Valentine's stickpin. He was wearing it in his cravat. That's when I *knew*."

Thane's arms tightened. "If only I could have been here sooner, I could have spared you."

"He wanted you dead, too." She swallowed, her throat a little sore from the noose. "Oh, Thane, he committed the murders in order to gain fame by solving them. But when you offered to help, your rank overshadowed him. He would have stopped at nothing to implicate you."

Thane smoothed her hair. "Shh. It's all over now. You're safe; we're both safe—"

"What's all the hubbub down here?"

Lord Wrayford came shambling down the staircase. Barefoot, he wore the same yellow coat and dark breeches as he had on the picnic, although now the garments were muddied and wrinkled. With his sandy hair in wild disarray, he resembled a drowned rat.

"I heard caterwauling," he went on, glowering at Lindsey. "Why did you roust me out of bed, anyway? 'Tis *I* who should be demanding a word with *you*. Pushing me out of my own carriage indeed! Leaving me out in a rainstorm! Why, I had to take refuge under a tree until dawn, then ride a farmer's hayrack back into the city."

The ridiculous image lightened Lindsey's spirits. She bit her lip to keep from laughing. "I'm ever so sorry."

"I'm not," Thane said, staring at Wrayford. "You deserve my fist in your face for attempting to steal my woman."

Wrayford froze on the bottom step. "I meant her no harm, I swear it—"

"You wanted her dowry in order to pay back that IOU. Well, you may consider the debt forgiven, so long as you go back to bed this instant."

Slack-jawed, Wrayford gaped at him. "What? A thousand guineas . . . and you won't hold me to it?"

"One more word from you and I'll change my mind."

Wrayford instantly reversed course and scuttled back up the stairs. A moment later, the distant sound of a door slamming echoed through the entrance hall.

"That's an enormous sum to absolve," Lindsey marveled. "Why on earth did you do that?"

Thane shrugged. "If I didn't, the fool would prey on some other heiress. Besides, I never wanted the money. I played cards with him a few times merely to gain his confidence for the purpose of my investigation."

She reached up to stroke his cheek. "Then you aren't really an unprincipled rogue."

He flashed her a crooked grin. "You wouldn't say that if you knew the thoughts in my mind right now."

His hands roved down her body, lifting her to him so there was no mistaking his meaning. Her blood quickened in response. "Mmm," she said, undulating her hips. "That sounds enticing, my lord. I would vastly enjoy another night of sin."

"This time we'll be married," he said sternly. "I've a special license in my pocket. We could be wed by nightfall."

She caught her breath, her eyes searching his. "Truly?"

"Truly. So long as you think your family will forgive us."

The vulnerable look on his face proved he would willingly defer to her wishes. He knew the pain of being denied the close bonds of family. She felt a fierce longing to give him the happiness he had never known.

"They'll come around," she said. "Blythe will be excited, of course. Papa will be thrilled to see me happily settled. And Mama will be in a snit, but she'll recover, especially when she's allowed to throw a huge celebration for all of society."

"Then you'll soon be my wife." Thane leaned his brow to hers briefly before he drew back to look deep into her eyes. "I love you, Lindsey Crompton. You're my heart and soul. Forever."

Giddy with joy, she traced his lips with her fingertip. "So you really *were* destined to find your one true love, after all. To think you scoffed when Kasi read it in your palm."

"What a blind fool I was."

"I more so than you." Lindsey brushed a kiss across his smiling mouth. "Allow me to make one more prediction. You'll forever be my dearest Lord Mansfield."

Look for the first novel in this sensational
new series from

Olivia Drake

SEDUCING THE HEIRESS
ISBN: 978-0-312-94345-5

"Readers will adore."
—*Romantic Times BOOKreviews*

Available from St. Martin's Paperbacks

www.oliviadrake.com